JAMES H. PENCE

BLIND

TYNDALE HOUSE
PUBLISHERS, INC.
CAROL STREAM • ILLINOIS

Visit Tyndale's exciting Web site at www.tyndale.com

TYNDALE and Tyndale's quill logo are registered trademarks of Tyndale House Publishers, Inc.

Blind Sight

Designed by Dean H. Renninger

Edited by James H. Cain III and Curtis H. C. Lundgren

Published in association with the literary agency of WordServe Literary Group, Ltd., 10152 S. Knoll Circle, Highlands Ranch, CO 80130.

Library of Congress Cataloging-in-Publication

Pence, James H.
  Blind sight / James H. Pence.
    p. cm.
  ISBN 0-8423-6575-3
  1. Cults—Fiction. I. Title.
  PS3616.E53 B47 2003
  813'.6—dc21   2002156540

New repackage first published in 2009 under ISBN 978-1-4143-3479-0.

Printed in the United States of America

15	14	13	12	11	10	09
7	6	5	4	3	2	1

DEDICATION

To the Sovereign God.
He is Lord of my life and Lord of my circumstances.
"You are my God. My times are in your hands."

PSALM 31:14-15, NIV

ACKNOWLEDGMENTS

John Donne wrote, "No man is an island, entire of itself; every man is a piece of the continent, a part of the main." Never is that more evident than in a project such as this. Many people have had a part in the production of this novel, and I am deeply thankful for each one.

Laurel, my wife and my best friend. Thank you for believing in me.

Chris and Charlene, thanks for being patient during Daddy's many hours at the laptop.

Reg Grant and Sandi Glahn, thank you for guiding me in the art and craft of fiction writing, and for being a constant source of encouragement.

Michael and Barbara, thank you for representing me so well.

Jan Stob, thanks for taking a chance on a new author, and for being patient through all my rookie mistakes and seemingly endless rewrites. Likewise, thanks to Jamie Cain for doing a fantastic job of editing. You both took a good story and helped lift it to a higher level.

Joyce Camp, thanks for helping me check my facts about the Thousand Islands, and thanks to Julio Alongo for assisting me with the JFK Airport scenes.

Special thanks to those who have read (and often reread) the various drafts of this novel since its inception and offered their encouragement and support: Jack and Bernadette Pence, John and Henrietta Pence, John and Sherry Bryant, Don and Jean Lindholm,

Chris Pence, Donald "Ralph" Powell, Theda Gasway, Bernice Carr, Deanna Harris, DeLena Loughmiller, Cindy Cuny, Janice Cuny, Jeanna Cuny, Sharen Semerenko, Rita Reynolds, Pauline Jennings, Tracy Finch, Tiffany Finch, Kevin and Valorie Sutterfield, Becky Freeman, Ben Smith, Tom Hooten, Kathleen Crow, Susan Dennis, Angie Barrett, Donna Wilson, Wanda Johnson, Frank Simon, and Kelley Mathews. If I have forgotten anyone, please chalk it up to my increasingly gray "gray cells," not to intentional omission.

All of these folks have played a significant part in the development of *Blind Sight*. Any mistakes that remain are my own.

Sometimes the best place to hide is in plain sight.

Peter Bishop didn't know whether or not that particular adage was true, but for his children's sake, he hoped it was.

Their lives depended on it.

Standing in line at the EconoAir ticket counter, Peter muttered in frustration. Flight check-ins were always tedious. Yet every second that Micah and Michelle stood exposed, their danger increased.

Peter flicked his eyes back and forth, scanning the steady flow of pedestrian traffic. Four women in dark blue uniforms paraded along, pulling small suitcases behind them. A gray-bearded man trotted in the opposite direction. A suntanned young couple stood in front of him, gazing into each other's eyes. The woman carried a bright yellow bag with *Cancún* printed on it.

Honeymooners.

Maybe.

Peter looked them over and wondered if they were also killers.

Something bumped his heels. Peter inhaled sharply, balled his hands into fists, and swung around to face a middle-aged brunette pushing a baby stroller.

She drew back, a flash of fear reflected in her eyes. "I'm so sorry. Did I hurt you?"

Peter mumbled a reply and an apology. He let out a quiet sigh and turned around, rubbing his eyes.

Got to relax.

But Peter knew he'd never relax until Micah and Michelle were safely on board EconoAir Flight 298, bound for Dallas. He glanced toward the ceiling-mounted TV monitors.

Still on time.

Departure time: 5:55 p.m.

He glanced at his watch: 5:16 p.m.

Peter felt his right eyelid twitch. He raised a trembling hand and tried to rub away the annoying tic. He had been careful to the point of obsession in planning the children's escape. He had even ordered the children's tickets from a public-access Internet terminal rather than his own computer, and had them mailed to a postal box he'd rented just for the occasion. But Peter knew that Sawyer Wynne's people would catch even the tiniest slip. And if that happened, they would dispatch a conversion team.

The hit would be efficient, untraceable—and merciless.

Conversion. Nothing but a sanitary term for murder.

Peter would *not* let that happen. Thus, he had to proceed on the assumption that someone *had* uncovered his plan and that somewhere in JFK Airport a killer waited for them. Peter looked down at the two children standing beside him.

"Michelle," he whispered, "do you have the envelope?"

The ten-year-old rolled her eyes and tossed her curly blonde hair off her shoulder. "Daddy! For the fiftieth time, yes, I have the envelope." She reached into the front pocket of her faded denim jeans and pulled out a white business envelope, folded into thirds and already frayed along the edges. She held it up for her father. "See?"

Peter bit his lower lip and nodded. "Good girl. Put it back now and don't give it to anyone except—"

"Uncle Thomas?"

Peter ran his fingers through her hair. "Right."

"But, Daddy—"

"Shhhh." Peter put his index finger on his lips.

A ticket agent signaled that she was free, and the honeymooners ambled toward the counter.

Peter and the children would be next.

"It's almost time to go now. Micah, you still with us?"

Peter's son stared straight ahead. Stringy brown hair tumbled into his eyes. Grim faced, Micah nodded.

Peter Bishop managed a weak grin and smoothed his son's hair.

"Next, please," called a sharply dressed young man.

"Over there." Peter motioned toward the left.

"Come on, Micah," Michelle said.

The boy put his left arm on his sister's right shoulder and allowed her to lead him to the ticket counter.

Turning, Peter took a second to scan the crowd once more.

"Hurry up, Daddy!" Michelle called to him.

Peter strode over and handed the children's e-tickets to the ticket agent. The young man took the tickets without comment, looked them over for a second, and began typing on his keyboard.

"The children are traveling alone?" he asked without looking up at Peter.

Something in his tone made Peter nervous.

"Y-yes. I paid the fee for unaccompanied children when

I bought the tickets. Here are the forms." Peter handed the agent some papers. "Is there a problem?"

"No problem." The young man's voice sounded mechanical as his eyes scanned the paperwork. "Just need to make sure you've arranged for the children to be picked up." He glanced up at Peter. "Thomas Kent will be meeting the children?"

"Yes." Peter spoke through clenched teeth. *I don't think everybody heard you. Why don't you announce it over the PA system?*

The truth was, Peter hadn't called Thomas Kent yet. Any phone contact with Thomas before the children were on the plane was an unacceptable risk. He *had* sent a few e-mails, but even those had been cryptic. Once the children were safely airborne, Peter would make a call from one of the airport pay phones.

The agent began typing again. "Checking any luggage?"

"No." Peter's fingers drummed a staccato rhythm on his trouser legs.

Come on. Come on.

Finally the agent put the children's boarding passes into an envelope and handed them, along with a fluorescent green card, to Peter.

"Your flight will be boarding at Gate 9. These are the children's boarding passes, and this card will alert security that you are permitted to accompany the children to the gate. When you get to the gate, give the card to the gate agent. She'll tell you what to do."

Assuming we get that far.

"Come on." Peter herded the children off to the left toward the security checkpoint.

Ironically, going through security was the one thing Peter *wasn't* worried about. The Fellowship would never plant one of their people in such an obvious place. True to Peter's expectations, he and the children passed through the metal detector and under the security personnel's watchful eyes without incident.

Once they were through security, Peter took the children to a small newsstand near Gate 21. He didn't want to wait at the boarding area any longer than necessary. He preferred the confined space of a newsstand, as it allowed him to keep an eye on everyone entering and leaving. They would stay put until the very last minute, then dash for Gate 9.

Peter had chosen EconoAir Flight 298 because its boarding time coincided with several arriving flights. He hoped the volume of travelers in the concourse would conceal them and interfere with any attempt to stop them.

Across the concourse, a high-pitched whine signaled an arriving flight. Peter peered through the inky blackness outside the windows as a magnificent silver and gold 727 lumbered into view. The jet's lights illuminated an oddly serene swirl of snowflakes drifting toward earth.

Peter swore under his breath. The last thing he needed now was a delay for deicing. He'd counted on airport security to offer some small measure of protection. Any delay could allow that tenuous protection to evaporate.

Winding down like a toy with dying batteries, the engines' screaming dropped off. A moment later, Gate 21's Jetway rolled toward the plane, attaching itself to the airliner's side like a giant parasite.

Not long now.

His plan was simple. They'd walk against the flow of arriving passengers, using them as shields, and if he timed it right, they would arrive at Gate 9 just as the attendant called for pre-boarding. He'd have no trouble getting the kids VIP treatment.

Ten-year-old twins traveling alone, one of them blind.

Across the concourse, a troop of men in dark suits and white shirts marched up the Jetway, briefcases and cell phones in hand, looking like a Fortune 500 drill team.

Not yet. Wait for the families.

He didn't have to wait long. People of all ages and sizes followed one another off the plane. A young woman with frizzy, platinum blonde hair and five earrings in one ear appeared, carrying a curly-haired toddler. A group of what appeared to be college students trailed after her. Soon the trickle of arriving passengers became a flood, surging up the Jetway and out into the concourse.

"Now!" Peter whispered to the twins.

He stepped from the safety of the newsstand, tugging Michelle's left hand. Her movement pulled Micah into action. His hand resting on her right shoulder, Micah followed with cautious, halting steps.

"Daddy, slow down! Micah can't go that fast."

"He's got to."

"Straight ahead, Micah," Michelle told her twin brother.

Micah nodded, fixing the corridor with a vacant but determined stare. His legs strained as he tried to match his father's pace.

Peter glanced over his right shoulder and hissed through clenched teeth. "Come on! Speed up!"

The same moment he felt someone brush against him. Peter whipped around, panic in his eyes. But the offender, a young man wearing baggy denims and a black T-shirt, didn't even notice. He continued down the concourse in his own private world. Peter felt a bead of sweat trickle down his spine. His fingers twitched as his eyes fixed on a ceiling-mounted digital clock.

It was 5:45.

Peter saw the sign at his left. Gate 12. The timing was wrong. They needed to run.

They plodded.

Peter urged his children on. "Come on. We've got to hurry."

"But Micah can't go any faster."

"I'll take care of him."

Peter stooped down and threw his arm around Micah's thighs.

"Jump, kiddo."

Micah brought his arms around his father's neck, wrapping his legs around his waist.

Peter groaned as he hoisted the boy. He broke into a trot, Michelle keeping pace beside him. Overweight and out of shape, Peter winded quickly. His chest heaved. Sweat burned his eyes. He clamped his jaws tight and blew out hard through his teeth, moving as fast as he could while lugging ninety pounds of boy.

Peter heard an announcement break through the noise on the concourse. "We'll now begin boarding Flight 298 with service to Dallas/Fort Worth. Will all first class and passengers needing additional assistance please approach the gate?"

No. Can't wait in line.

Peter glanced at the sign to his left.

Gate 10.

Fierce pain shot through Peter's back and down his right leg. He stifled a cry, dropping to one knee. "Can't—carry—run!"

Michelle took Micah's right hand, Peter his left.

"Clear path ahead," Peter said between breaths. "Run straight. Now!"

Up ahead he saw the sign for Gate 9. A long line snaked its way from the gate out into the concourse.

Got to get them on board.

Peter bulldozed to the front of the line, pushing in front of a short, elderly woman. A heavy black purse dropped from her hand, spilling its contents as it hit the floor. A chorus of disapproving voices rose behind him.

"Wait your turn, jerk!" somebody shouted.

Leaning on her cane, the elderly woman fastened a glare on Peter that was so stern and wilting she must have

been a retired schoolteacher. "I believe I was here first, young man," she said.

Peter ignored her, shoving the tickets at the gate agent. "I've got to get these kids on the plane right away."

The gate agent, a middle-aged woman with arrow-straight black hair, pushed Peter's tickets back toward him. "You'll have to wait your turn, sir."

Michelle spoke up. "Please. We're traveling by ourselves. And my brother is blind."

The schoolteacher's expression softened. She smiled at Michelle and Micah, then said to the attendant, "It's all right. Let the children go first." Scowling at Peter, she said, "I have to pick up my things before I can get back in line anyway." Another passenger bent down and helped her gather the contents of her purse. She moved to a nearby seat and began to repack it.

The gate agent scanned the boarding passes, then handed them back to Peter coolly. "You'll have to escort the children to the plane," she said, "and turn them over to the senior flight attendant personally."

Peter nodded, shoved the ticket envelope in his hip pocket, and led the two children down the Jetway. As they rounded the corner, Peter stopped a few feet short of the airliner's door. He knelt down beside the boy and girl, tears welling in his eyes. "Michelle, you'll take care of Micah?"

"Yes, Daddy, but why can't you come too?"

Peter caressed her cheek with the back of his hand. "I love you, honey."

"But, Daddy—"

"Shhhhh," he said and put his finger on her lips.

Peter reached over to Micah and gently turned the boy's shoulders so that he faced him. "You won't forget what I told you, Micah?"

Micah shook his head as his hands traced their way up Peter's shoulders, to his ears, and felt their way around his face. When his fingers crossed the moist trails under his father's eyes, they stopped. He brought his fingers, wet with his father's tears, to his own face.

Peter pulled his two children toward him and embraced them. "Come on. Let's get you situated."

As they entered the jet, the senior flight attendant smiled cheerfully. She spoke to Michelle and Micah. "Well, hello. I hear you two are making this trip by yourselves."

Michelle nodded; Micah's empty gaze remained unchanged.

"Going to see your grandma for Christmas, maybe?"

Michelle shook her head. "Uncle Thomas."

The flight attendant smiled.

Peter broke in. "I'd better get going. Kiss your mother for me. I love you guys."

"Daddy?" Michelle's voice quavered. "Are we going to see you soon?"

Peter's lips pressed into a tight smile. "Go on, now."

The flight attendant took the boarding passes from Peter, then patted his shoulder. "Don't worry. We'll take good care of them." Turning to Micah and Michelle, she said, "Now, let's get you to your seats."

Michelle took Micah's hand and placed it on her shoulder. She stood there for a moment as other passengers squeezed by. Her eyes were red, but no tears came. Then she turned and led her brother down the aisle after the flight attendant.

Peter trudged back up the ramp and out onto the concourse. Tears blurred his vision as he stumbled through the milling crowd. He hated sending the children alone like this, hated staying behind. But it was the children's best chance of escape. If he could mislead the Fellowship long enough, they might have a chance.

Peter waited for what seemed like an eternity before the huge aircraft was pushed back from the gate. He gazed

through the windows, watching the jet until it receded from view.

"I love you, Justine." Peter spoke the words softly.

There was still one thing he had to do before he returned to the Center. Across the concourse stood a wall of pay phones. Peter swiped a credit card through one, punched in a PIN, and quickly keyed in Thomas Kent's number.

The phone rang once.

Twice.

Three times.

Someone brushed past him. Peter paid no attention.

Fourth ring.

He felt a sharp prick in his calf. A burning sensation followed instantly. Peter winced at the pain, then swung around. The old woman he'd pushed in front of stood beside him, smiling.

He heard the hiss of an answering machine picking up. "This is Thomas Kent. I'm not in. Leave a message if you feel like it."

The woman's face began to blur. Peter's head swam. He heard the beep of Thomas Kent's answering machine. Peter fought to stay conscious.

As his throat constricted, Peter choked out only a few words, "Save . . . my . . . children."

He dropped the receiver and put his face in his hands. Peter staggered, trying to shake off the dizziness. He sucked in hard, but no air came. He tried to speak, but only an anguished gurgle escaped.

He thought the old woman smiled; then all went black.

• • • • •

"Help! Somebody help! Over here!"

The gate agent rushed from her post at the elderly

woman's cry. When she saw the overweight, balding man on the floor, she pulled a walkie-talkie from her belt. "Man down at Gate 20. Get the EMTs over here. Now!"

The old woman stood by, wringing her hands. "He just collapsed."

A small crowd gathered as the EMTs arrived and began working on the still figure lying by the window.

"He's crashed," one called out. "Get the defibrillator!"

Another tore Peter's shirt open and began chest compressions.

As a crowd formed, the little white-haired woman edged to the rear. Finally, she eased around and shuffled down the concourse, leaning on her cane. Out of sight from Gate 9, she lifted her cane and removed the tip, taking care not to prick herself with the small needle that protruded from it. Then she opened her purse, pulled out a boarding pass, and tore it in two. She dropped the pass and the cane tip in a trash can. She was glad. She didn't want to make a round-trip to Dallas, particularly in December. Too far from home. Too cold for a senior citizen to be traveling. Now she could go back to the Center, make a nice cup of tea, and put her feet up.

It felt so good to be useful. She had served Father Antoine well. As she shuffled down the concourse, a middle-aged brunette pushed a baby stroller from the newsstand. She rolled over to the elderly woman and regarded her with upraised eyebrows.

The grandmotherly woman nodded, then patted the brunette's hand. "All done," she said.

"And the children?"

"On their way."

A grin crept across the younger woman's lips. She held out her arm. The elderly woman took it. Leaving the empty stroller behind, they walked arm in arm toward the exit.

S ave my children—9/20/42 PB"

Thomas Kent frowned at the subject line of the e-mail notice displayed on his computer screen. When he saw that the e-mail had a file attached, he punched Delete.

"Creeps," he muttered.

Across the room, a massive black German shepherd raised its head in response to his comment. The dog whined.

Thomas leaned back in his chair and stroked his sandy-colored beard.

"Can you believe it? You'd think that someone intelligent enough to develop a computer virus could manage to find a productive use for all that brainpower. Well, they're not going to crash my system. That's for sure."

The gargantuan animal pushed himself to his feet and lumbered over to Thomas, head low and tail wagging. He put his muzzle on Thomas's leg and whined again.

"What do *you* want?"

The dog's ears perked and

he pranced over to the back door. Looking back at Thomas, he let out a yip, his tail sweeping back and forth like a feather duster.

"No way. It's freezing out there."

The dog stretched and let out a sound that was a mixture of bark, growl, and yawn.

"Oh, all right."

Thomas stood up and grabbed his jacket from the back of his chair. He pulled it on as he reached down to unlock the door. The instant the door opened, the dog shot out like a racehorse at the Kentucky Derby. Thomas ambled around to the front porch and sat down on a weather-warped porch swing. The tired swing groaned in protest under Thomas's weight. A shiver ran through his body, and he tugged the collar of his jacket tighter around his neck.

Thomas gazed at the dead winter landscape. Frigid mist drifted from a uniformly gray sky, its chill penetrating everything. Birds, rabbits, and coyotes had all taken refuge from the life-draining cold that swept the north Texas landscape. Cows huddled together behind a shed in a nearby pasture. They sensed the coming storm. And instinctively they knew things would get worse.

Thomas wrapped his arms around himself. "Hurry up, dog," he growled through clenched teeth.

A muffled bark and a rustling in dry bushes off to his left revealed perhaps the only one who did not find the cold disturbing. Thomas could see a long tail swishing and powerful hind legs diving into the bushes, invading the domain of a rabbit that thought it had found a secure place.

"Gumbo!"

Black fur, erect ears, an intelligent look on his face, the German shepherd's head popped up from the bushes as he chuffed a reply. After years of living with the dog, Thomas could translate. *Please, just a few more minutes.*

A faint smile spread across Thomas Kent's worn face. "Okay, okay, but be quick about it."

Watching Gumbo reminded him of the winter fun he used to have when he was a boy, when winter meant sledding down hills crusted with mountains of white snow. Then his body had possessed a seemingly super-human resistance to chill, allowing him to ignore the cold's effects for hours while he delighted in the glories of snowball fights, homemade igloos, and sled races with his friends. The only thing better than playing in the snow was warming up afterward. After he finally succumbed to the cold and went inside, he'd sit by the fireplace, relish-ing the heat as it brought feeling back to his toes. He'd sip a mug of hot chocolate, three swollen marshmallows covering the top. Delicious warmth from the cup would trickle down his throat, making him feel as if he'd put the whole fireplace inside him.

But on this dreary Friday afternoon, Thomas felt worlds away from those warm memories. You didn't enjoy north Texas winters; you endured them. Their only redeeming quality was that they were short. Texas's alter-native to snow was freezing rain and sleet. Instead of the proverbial "wonderland," a winter storm usually turned Grant City, Texas, into a wasteland.

Beginning with a cold mist silently drifting to the ground, the temperature would slide and the mist would start freezing on everything. Tree limbs, fences, and road surfaces would soon bear layer upon layer of ice. Power lines, not designed to take such stress, would crash to the ground, the shattering ice shards mingled with a deadly shower of sparks. The simplest car trip could instantly become a life-threatening experience.

But the worst part of an ice storm was the silence of it all. At least a thunderstorm came with some dramatics thrown in. The ice storm would drag on for hours with only the rifle-shot sound of snapping tree limbs punctuating the stillness. The silence ruled until at last the wind lifted up a wail that sounded as if it came straight from the grave.

If the weather prognosticators predicted correctly, people would remember this coming storm for decades.

"Gumbo!"

The shepherd swung around and bounded toward his master like a little boy whose mom has called him in. Playtime's over, but that's okay. It's time for the hot chocolate.

Thomas swung open the front door and Gumbo, covered with droplets, swept past him into the house.

Thomas glowered at the drab gray sky above him. "I hate winter," he muttered as he walked through the door.

• • • • •

Closing the door behind him, Thomas stood still, allowing his gaze to roam around the living room. He stood with a hushed reverence usually reserved for museums. This time of year, the quiet room would normally be splashed with red and green. A seven-foot, freshly cut Christmas tree would stand in one corner, its twinkling lights silently marking anticipation of good things to come.

Thomas had thrown out the Christmas decorations the previous year.

Instead, a three-foot-tall stuffed giraffe stood in the Christmas-tree corner. An autographed junior football lay between the giraffe's front feet. A thirty-gallon aquarium bubbled in another part of the spacious room. But the aquarium was a ghost town. The last fish had died over a year earlier. Thomas just left it as it was, adding water but no more fish. Neat stacks of *Redbook* and *Woman's Day* magazines covered the coffee table in front of the sofa. In a basket beside the sofa an unfinished cross-stitch sampler was carefully laid out, with needle and thread still attached.

A short hallway to the left led from the living room to three bedrooms. Thomas had not opened the bedroom doors in nearly two years.

A leaded-crystal vase filled with twelve fresh, red roses

formed the centerpiece of the dining room table. Thomas replaced the flowers weekly. A Mickey Mouse place mat lay at one end of the table; a *Star Wars* place mat adorned the other.

A deep heaviness descended on Thomas whenever he entered this part of the house. That's why he almost never did. He closed his eyes for a moment, trying to ward off the feelings.

"Get a grip," Thomas muttered.

He wandered back toward the portion of the house where he and Gumbo lived, a small den off the kitchen. Thomas sat down on the open, queen-size sleeper sofa that gobbled up most of the floor space. Sheets lay in a pile at the bottom of the bed alongside a heap of dirty clothes. A thirty-five-inch television sat in front of the bed, blaring some inane talk show. Thomas always left the set on. He despised the tomblike silence that overshadowed the once-busy house.

On a desk across the room sat the computer where Thomas tried to write. Not that he needed to. An insurance settlement had left him independently wealthy. He wrote to escape. He wrote in a desperate attempt to forget what he never could.

Truth was, all Thomas Kent wanted was to die.

Thomas rested his head in his hands. The rhythmic clicking of Gumbo's toenails on the kitchen floor alerted him to his companion's approach. The dog whined and shoved his head into Thomas's lap.

His hand rambled over the dog's head. "You're right. We need to run to the store and stock up before the storm hits. And we'd better hustle. This is going to be a bad one."

* * * * *

An hour later, Thomas swung his black pickup truck back into his long rock driveway. As he drove the quarter mile from the road to his house, Thomas thought how silly it was for him to still be living here. A hundred acres seemed a bit much for just him and Gumbo. But he couldn't bear to sell it—not now, and probably not ever.

Thomas pressed a button clipped to the sun visor above the windshield. Up ahead, the garage door rumbled open like a giant mouth. Thomas guided the polished, black Dodge Ram 4x4 into the garage while Gumbo sat beside him, whining. Gumbo didn't mind riding in the cab, but the dog preferred the bed, where he could feel the wind and let his tongue flap in the breeze. But when the ride was over, Gumbo was ready to get out—immediately.

"Just a second. Don't get your nose out of joint. You could've stayed home, you know."

Thomas knew that while the big dog might have settled for that option, he never could. Thomas didn't go anywhere without Gumbo. Couldn't bear to let the hairy beast out of his sight for more than a few minutes. Yeah, it limited him. Couldn't eat at restaurants anymore. Only drive-ins. It didn't matter; he didn't have anyone to eat with anyway. Not particular about atmosphere, Gumbo was more than happy to devour his hamburger on the truck's vinyl seat.

As for shopping, well, most of the stores in town wouldn't allow the dog in. But Gumbo was content to sit in the back of the pickup and "people watch" while Thomas bought his groceries. In the smaller establishments, Thomas's friends would often let the big dog join his master. They understood the situation. They knew that Gumbo was Thomas's last desperate link to sanity. So they bent the rules.

Another push of the button, and the metal garage door squealed its way closed. Dismal gray daylight dissolved into dungeonlike murkiness. Thomas walked around the truck and pulled the passenger-side door open.

Gumbo hopped out onto the concrete and trotted toward the kitchen door. Thomas hauled out three plastic shopping bags and followed the dog.

As he entered the kitchen and plopped the bags on the counter, spilling out a pile of frozen dinners, Thomas noticed the red, blinking message light on his answering machine. He felt like ignoring it but pushed the Play button anyway. The old machine clicked and whirred as the tape rewound to the proper place. Thomas picked up a handful of frozen dinners and pulled open the freezer. As he tossed the boxes in, he heard a faint hiss, then what sounded like crowd noise.

"Sounds like it's coming from Grand Central Station," he muttered. He stopped short when he heard the voice on the answering machine.

Above the background noise, Thomas heard someone gasping for breath, then strangling out the words, "Save . . . my . . . children."

A preternatural chill swept over him. Thomas listened in horrified silence as his answering machine continued playing. Above a babel of voices Thomas heard a call for EMTs and what sounded like repeated attempts to defibrillate someone. Finally Thomas heard a click, then a dial tone.

His hands trembled as he pressed the Replay button. The machine clicked and whirred as the tape rewound. The strangled words chilled him once more. He was listening to a dying man's last words—words directed at him.

"Save . . . my . . . children."

Thomas Kent retrieved the e-mail from his deleted file, then stared at his computer screen in disbelief. When he deleted the e-mail earlier, he had given no thought to the subject line.

"Save my children—9/20/42 PB."

The second part of the subject wasn't a date; it was a code.

He tried to remember how many years had passed since he thought about that old code. Certainly enough years that he hadn't recognized it the first time he saw it. It was a silly thing, really. Just a game between stupid college kids. Juvenile. Thomas couldn't believe anyone had actually taken it seriously. He never had.

Thomas clicked the paper-clip icon to open the attachment, no longer afraid that it might contain a destructive virus. An hourglass flickered in front of his eyes, and then text filled the screen. The first page contained a brief note:

BLiND
SiGHT

Remember the promise.

Urgent package arriving DFW at 8:30 tonight,
Baggage Area 9. Please pick up and deliver, along
with this file. Address on package.

Must be picked up tonight.

MY CHILDREN'S LIVES ARE AT STAKE.

Please, don't let me down.

The message was signed "PB."

Thomas paged through the rest of the document.
Nothing made sense to him. The document contained
columns of data. Across the tops of the columns was a
bizarre series of names: "Zone, Phase, Osmosis Code,
Target Code, Conversion Date, Strategic Advantage,
Completion Code." The data in the columns consisted of
alphanumeric combinations, all meaningless to Thomas.

Thomas saved the file to a floppy disk. When the drive's
active light went out, he removed the floppy, labeled it
Stuff, and plopped it on top of a stack of twenty other disks.

He read the e-mail again.

"Remember the promise."

It was stupid, a kid thing.

"9/20/42."

Thomas reached over to his bookshelf and pulled
down a hardcover Bible. Pulling a pair of reading glasses
from his shirt pocket, he opened to the ninth book,
1 Samuel, then paged over to the twentieth chapter and
ran his finger down the page to verse forty-two: "The
Lord is witness between you and me, and between your
descendants and my descendants forever."

Thomas's mind raced back to his freshman year at the
University of Texas. He arrived on campus an inexperienced
and frightened kid, and it would be a few years before he
became the star of their men's gymnastics team. Thomas
found it tough, living as a Christian on a secular university
campus, and he wasn't sure if he could handle it. Fortunately
he wasn't alone. In the interest of surviving with their faith

intact, about thirty Christian freshmen formed a campus fellowship. They called their group Ecclesia under Fire.

While some of the people came to meetings to find dates or just to socialize, a small core held together tenaciously. When one of them came under attack in a class, the others rallied to encourage him. Over four years, the group become a virtual family. Occasionally new members would come and others would move on, but the core group held together the entire four years of school.

As graduation drew near, no one wanted it to end. They planned a weekend "going away" retreat at a camp not far from campus. On the last night of the retreat, after they'd sung some songs and prayed, someone opened the Bible to the book of 1 Samuel and read the story of David and Jonathan.

As they listened to the story of these two young men and their love for each other, someone got the bright idea that all of them should make a covenant like David and Jonathan's. They would promise that if any of them or their families were in danger or need, the other group members would help. It would be a lifetime commitment.

They even established their own code, based on 1 Samuel 20:42. Nobody else would understand the code because it would look and sound like a date: 9/20/42. But instead of referring to September 20, 1942, the number would serve as a personal 911.

> Jonathan said to David, "Go in peace, for we have sworn friendship with each other in the name of the Lord, saying, 'The Lord is witness between you and me, and between your descendants and my descendants forever.'"

They agreed the code would only be used in cases of desperate need.

"Remember the promise."

But it was just an emotional evening. Besides, I don't even remember anyone in the group with the initials PB.

BLINDSIGHT

Thomas dragged a dusty copy of *The Cactus* off another shelf. The year 1975 stood in raised numbers on the outside cover. He opened the index to the *Bs*— and groaned.

There must be fifty people with the initials PB.

He located each picture, each face, each name. Nothing. Finally, he flipped to the autographs in the back of the book. Among all the notes from friends, instructors, and acquaintances, one caught his eye.

"Best wishes for a bright future. Peter."

Peter.

Thomas paged back to the index. He found a listing for a Peter Bishop. When he turned to the page where Bishop should have been listed, all he found was a blank frame with the words *Photo Unavailable*. Under the frame was the name "Peter Bishop."

No wonder he didn't remember. Unlike the rest of the group, who had been together for four years, Bishop had transferred in during his senior year. He came into the group when he began dating one of the members. As far as Thomas knew, Peter Bishop hadn't even been a Christian when he started coming. A quiet sort who didn't stand out, Peter had stayed on the periphery and rarely interacted with other group members.

Thomas had completely forgotten him.

"Remember the promise."

How did he even find me?

A swell of anger surged up inside Thomas. His life was messed up enough already. He didn't need anyone complicating things. Thomas had no intention of being Peter Bishop's delivery boy. Bishop could use FedEx if he needed his package delivered quickly.

Then the words from his answering machine echoed through his mind like an insistent Klaxon. The strangled words, a dying man's plea.

"Save . . . my . . . children."

T he windshield wipers on Thomas Kent's truck
thumped back and forth like two giant metronomes
as they brushed away the mist that blurred his vision.
As he rolled along Interstate 30 west toward Dallas, an
onrushing river of headlights reminded him that it was
Friday night. When the weekends rolled around, it
seemed everyone in Dallas had somewhere else to go
and wanted to get there in a hurry.

Even now, at seven thirty, the traffic had not let up.
The line of cars escaping the city formed an unbroken
chain. Fortunately, Thomas was headed in the opposite
direction. On his side of the highway, traffic was unusually
sparse. Except for 18-wheelers rocketing past him with a
blast of wind and spray, comparatively few cars braved
the road.

Thomas glanced down at Gumbo. The big dog lay
sprawled on the seat, eyes closed and head nuzzled up
against Thomas's leg. Thomas
reached down and stroked the

BLIND SIGHT

shepherd's side. "What a life. Eating and sleeping," he said.

Gumbo didn't budge.

A mournful country-western song drifted from the radio speakers. Thomas didn't much like country music, or any other kind of music for that matter, but he needed to keep tabs on the weather, and this station was the least objectionable he could find. When the song finally stopped, Thomas heard the familiar music announcing the news and weather segment. He reached down and turned up the volume.

A cheerful female voice brought unwelcome news.

"That front we've been watching has pushed its way down into our area faster than expected. Current temperatures are just above freezing, and we're expecting the mercury to dip very soon. There's still a lot of freezing precip in the forecast, and road conditions will deteriorate quickly. If you don't absolutely have to go out, stay off the roads and stay warm."

"Nice advice if you can take it. Right?" Thomas glanced at Gumbo, who yawned.

"I can't believe I'm doing this," Thomas said.

Fleeting images of his own children flashed through his mind.

"My children's lives are at stake."

"Don't kid yourself, Kent. You know *exactly* why you're doing it."

* * * * *

Still dressed in his janitorial greens, Sonny Pritchard rolled his custodian's cart out of the restroom and onto the concourse. He'd been about to punch out for the day when his cell phone chirped. The Elders had an assignment for him: Watch for twin children coming off Flight 298 from JFK, and see who picks them up. Follow them and *do not* lose them. Once he tracked them to their destination, he was to use his cell phone to call the Center and report on their whereabouts.

Sonny pushed his cart to the edge of Gate 9's waiting area and began emptying trash cans. Overhead monitors told him that the JFK flight had touched down and would roll into the gate any minute now.

He wondered who these two children were. The Elders hadn't told him much, but they had made it clear that his assignment was of crucial importance. Sonny understood what that meant.

It meant that he'd best not screw this up.

Sonny tossed a half-empty coffee cup into a trash can. He tried to convince himself that he wasn't nervous about the assignment. His stomach churned as he waited for his quarry to arrive. Though it was warm in the terminal, Sonny's bony fingers felt like ice. He rubbed his hands, then cupped them together and blew into them. As feeling crept back into his fingers, Sonny found them involuntarily tracing their way along the needle tracks on his forearms.

Sonny's nerves were ragged, because for the first time he would have to carry his assignment out *alone*.

• • • • •

The truck's defroster blew furiously, struggling to maintain a clear field of vision for Thomas as he turned off Airport Freeway and headed north into DFW. Icy streaks under his windshield wipers showed the effect of the dropping mercury.

This had better be one quick claim at Baggage Area 9 or I'll be spending the next few days in the terminal.

Ahead, the sign for Terminal A glowed red in the mist. He signaled left and swung the big truck around the exit ramp. Thankfully, the ramp hadn't started to freeze over yet, or he'd never even make it as far as the terminal.

Thomas glanced down at Gumbo and grinned. The German shepherd was snoring.

• • • • •

Sonny Pritchard knelt on the carpet near the tall windows that looked out toward the taxiway. As he picked up the remnants of some brat's potato chips, Sonny searched the crowd, hoping, praying that his Mentor might somehow appear miraculously from nowhere.

"Ain't much chance of that happenin'," Sonny muttered to no one in particular.

Kevin, his Mentor, had phoned shortly after the Elders. Kevin was stuck in traffic on the northbound 35E corridor. Even if traffic cleared up immediately, he probably wouldn't get to the airport on time.

"Can't hurt to check one more time," Sonny said as he pulled a small cell phone from his trouser pocket. He pressed a speed-dial button and was instantly connected with Kevin.

"Antoine is lord," Kevin's voice came through clearly.

"My lord always," Sonny replied.

"What's up?" Kevin asked.

"Where *are* you, man?" Sonny said. "They'll be here any second."

"Sorry," Kevin said. "It's a parking lot here. Couple of tractor trailers got tangled up, and the interstate's virtually shut down. You're on your own tonight."

"I'm not s'posed to be on my own," Sonny protested.

"Nothing I can do about it," Kevin replied. "You'll be fine. If you need any help, you can call me. Trust me; with this traffic, I'm sure to be right here."

"But I don't wanna mess this up."

"You won't. All you have to do is follow the kids. If it'll make you feel better, once you're tailing them, you can talk to me the whole way. I'll guide you through it."

"I ain't ready for this, Kevin."

Kevin's voice became stern. "Whether you're ready or not doesn't matter anymore. You are the only person we have out at the airport right now. Father's will must be done, and you must rise above your own weakness to fulfill it."

"But if I screw up, I'm finished."

A quiet chill crept into Kevin's voice. "If you fail to obey instructions, you're finished already."

The line went dead.

Sonny slipped the phone back into his pocket. He slapped his hands against his trouser legs, trying to drive away the shakes.

Sonny had much to be thankful for. He had been out of a job, homeless, and on drugs when the Fellowship found him. They took him off the street, gave him a place to live, and got him off the junk. Now he'd gladly be a janitor for Father Antoine for the rest of his life, if that was what the Fellowship wanted.

But he had never expected this. He never expected to be abandoned. Sure, they could blame the weather, the traffic, anything they wanted to blame it on. The fact remained that Sonny was on his own.

Father Antoine and the Elders had changed his life. They were going to change the world.

But they weren't too big on forgiving.

On Chateau Antoine's thirty-second floor, Sawyer Wynne sat dwarfed behind a solid oak desk. At five-foot-one and 155 pounds, Wynne allowed no jokes about his stature. No one would dare joke about him, anyway. They all knew better. They knew his nickname.

Coral Snake.

It was a name he'd given himself, an image he fostered.

Wynne kept a living icon of his persona in a thirty-gallon terrarium in his office. The telltale red, yellow, and black stripes of the coral snake stood in bold contrast to the earth tones created by the rocks, sand, and dry tree branches that decorated its habitat. The snake lay motionless, curled around the base of a white limestone rock.

Unlike a cobra or rattlesnake, this creature would not spark instant fear into the hearts of those who confronted it. On the contrary, it appeared deceptively small, innocent, docile. Its striped bands made it almost a thing of

BLIND
SIGHT

beauty. The uninformed or unsuspecting tended to underestimate the danger they were in.

That was what made it so marvelous. How incredible that something so thoroughly *un*intimidating could nevertheless harbor such deadly poison.

Sawyer Wynne's unintimidating stature often caused people to underestimate him—to their great peril. Like the coral snake, Sawyer Wynne was small but deadly.

Members of the Fellowship loved Anthony MacAsland; they feared Sawyer Wynne. MacAsland was the public face, Wynne the private power. He made the ugly decisions with which MacAsland could not afford to be associated. Sawyer Wynne decided who would live and who would die, and he took great delight in doing so.

Wynne sat, fingering a magazine article he'd been staring at for over an hour. Turning to his computer, he typed in the name "Bishop, Peter." Instantly the screen filled with data regarding Peter Bishop, including his record as the coordinator of the Fellowship's computer department and the surveillance data they had collected on him over the last few weeks. Until a month ago, Bishop's loyalty was beyond question. In fact, he had been one of Wynne's key people.

Beside Bishop's name, Wynne clicked *Status*.

The monitor flashed back in pastel green letters. "Converted."

Wynne's lips formed a tight line.

What a colossal waste.

Bishop's resourcefulness in designing computer systems enabled Wynne to keep track of every member of the Fellowship, every satellite center, and every detail of the Project. And it was that same resourcefulness that nearly enabled Bishop to spirit his children away from the Fellowship's grasp before Wynne's orders could be put into effect. And along with them would have gone Wynne's best chance to silence the one person who still posed a threat.

Fortunately for Wynne, Peter's behavior had become somewhat erratic over the past few weeks. Suspicious, Wynne had placed him under constant surveillance. He guessed Peter was planning an escape when an operative reported that Bishop had visited a local shopping mall and used a public-access Internet terminal. Peter had cleared the Internet browser's history file when he had finished, and the person tailing him had not been able to trace the Web sites he'd visited. But a check of Peter's credit card records turned up a sizeable payment to an online travel site. Wynne assumed Bishop had purchased airline tickets for his children, so the watch on Bishop was doubled, and Wynne alerted his people at Syracuse Hancock International to be ready to intercept.

This morning, when Bishop didn't show up at the Center, Wynne was sure that the escape was under way. He touched base with the surveillance teams and was furious to discover that Peter Bishop and the twins had disappeared.

Peter had called 911, reporting a fire in his apartment building. In the ensuing panic and evacuation, he and the children had managed to dodge the surveillance. What was worse, it quickly became clear that Bishop and the children were not flying out of Syracuse. Frantically, Wynne ordered teams to cover every major airport within a day's drive of Syracuse. For a while, Wynne feared the worst. Not that he meant to prevent the escape. Indeed, Sawyer Wynne *wanted* the children to escape. In fact, he had planned something similar for the children. The only way to draw their mother, Justine, out of hiding was through her children. He had confided this to Peter Bishop only a month ago. Evidently, Peter hadn't liked the idea of his children being used as bait.

No matter. Things had been dicey for a while, but one of the teams picked up Bishop's trail as he and his children arrived at JFK.

Wynne now knew that the

children were headed for Dallas. Not long ago, the report had come in that the twins were on EconoAir 298 to DFW. The Dallas Center had a man in place, watching the gate. Now, all they had to do was wait until someone met Micah and Michelle at the airport. Unsuspecting, they would lead them straight to Justine.

The corners of Sawyer Wynne's mouth drew upward in a self-satisfied grin. Peter Bishop had played a valiant game, but in the end he had lost. In fact, he had played right into Sawyer's hands. The children were exactly where he wanted them to be.

Wynne heard a knock at the door and looked up to see a plump, fortyish woman with salt-and-pepper hair tied back in a neat bun enter. The grim expression on her face did not please him. "Spit it out, Jeanette."

"Sir," she said, "we examined Peter's e-mail records."

Sawyer sat up straight, leaning forward. "And?"

"Late last night," Jeanette continued, "he accessed our computer systems, copied some files, and e-mailed them to someone. We don't know to whom the files were sent, but the address is tkent@texweb.net. The server is based in Texas, and we're trying to narrow it down."

Sawyer glared at Jeanette. "I thought we were monitoring his computer use, locking him out of sensitive areas."

Jeanette nodded. "We were, but he must have found another way in."

Sawyer Wynne slammed his fist down on the desk and let out a string of expletives. He stood and walked over to the floor-to-ceiling window overlooking downtown Syracuse. He put his hands on his hips and breathed deeply. As he exhaled, he hung his head.

"What files?"

"I beg your pardon?" Jeanette said.

He ground out the words between clenched teeth. "What files did he steal?"

Jeanette didn't answer.

Wynne swung around, eyes narrow, black eyebrows pushed together. "Project files?"

She nodded.

"Which ones, Jeanette?"

"Osmosis."

The color drained from Wynne's face. He walked back to the plush chair behind his desk and flopped into it. Jeanette remained standing, clutching a legal pad in front of her as if it were a shield.

"Do you think he sent the files and the children to the same person?" he asked.

"It's possible. But we don't—"

"You don't know," he said, biting sarcasm in his voice.

"No." Jeanette's voice quavered slightly.

"Find out. Immediately."

"Yes, sir." Jeanette turned on her heel and hurried out.

Sawyer Wynne sat quietly at his desk, his jaw muscles working furiously. He turned his gaze toward a large bowl of unshelled nuts that sat near the front of the desk. He reached into the bowl and withdrew a walnut and a nutcracker. Wynne placed the nut between the nutcracker's pincers and began to squeeze.

Peter and Justine Bishop had betrayed the Fellowship.

Wynne's hand trembled as he slowly increased the pressure on the nutcracker.

Peter had paid for his disloyalty; Justine would pay soon enough. But now the situation hung in a delicate balance. It was reasonable to assume that the children and the files were being sent to Justine, who had committed herself to the Fellowship's destruction.

The walnut shattered with a crack like a rifle shot. Wynne released the nutcracker and let it drop, along with the broken shards of the walnut, on top of the magazine article that he had been reading.

Sawyer Wynne brushed the debris away from the article.

BLIND
SIGHT

The headline read "Anthony MacAsland: Hero or Fraud?" Wynne focused on the byline: "By Justine Bishop."

He ripped the article from the magazine and spoke to the small picture of Peter Bishop's ex-wife at the bottom of the page. "I'll find you. And when I do, you will die slowly and painfully."

The Coral Snake crumpled the article into a tiny ball and threw it into the trash can beside his desk.

"I promise you that."

Thomas Kent swung his pickup truck into the parking place closest to the terminal he could find.

"Hold down the fort," he said to Gumbo. The dog's ear twitched in reply. Thomas slammed the door, leaving it unlocked. Pity the poor car thief who dared put his hand inside the door.

Even in the relative shelter of the parking garage, a blast of frigid wind sliced through Thomas's jacket. He pulled the collar tighter around his neck. As he crossed from the garage to the terminal, Thomas noticed delicate icicles forming on the bottom of a No Parking sign. The concrete already felt slippery under his feet.

Thomas glanced at his watch.

Nine o'clock.

Good. Thirty minutes late. They would have unloaded the plane by now. The package was probably making the rounds of the baggage claim carousel. He had no idea how he would identify it. Bishop had given him no description.

Automatic doors slid apart at Thomas's approach. He glanced toward the ceiling signs to get his bearings. An arrow pointing right directed him to Baggage Area 9.

The baggage claim area was clear except for a couple of kids sitting in some chairs beside an exhausted-looking flight attendant. Almost all the passengers had claimed their luggage and moved on. The stainless-steel baggage carousel ahead of him still rotated, a few pieces of luggage still riding the merry-go-round. A janitor who looked like a rescue-mission reject mopped the floor in a distant corner of the room.

Strange there aren't more people here. Plane must have gotten in early.

Thomas walked over to the carousel and examined the unclaimed luggage. He didn't know which bags, if any, were the ones Peter Bishop had intended for him. None of the labels had either his or Bishop's name. This wasn't what he'd bargained for.

Well, I tried. I'm truly sorry, Peter. I wanted to help, but you didn't give me enough to go on.

"Excuse me." A voice spoke from behind him.

Thomas turned around. The flight attendant who had been sitting with the children now stood beside him.

"Would you by any chance be Thomas Kent?" Her voice carried a tinge of frustration, perhaps desperation.

"Yes," Thomas said. "Yes, I am."

"Oh, thank heavens," the flight attendant gushed. "I was afraid you weren't coming. The children are over here." She turned back toward them as she continued. "With the weather being as bad as it is, well, I was afraid that you might not be able to get here to pick them up. That would have caused some real problems. We can't just leave these little ones with *anyone*. We've got to see that they are safely delivered to the person specified by their par—"

Thomas caught her arm and turned her back to face him. "Children?"

"Yes, children." She hesitated, then said, "Aren't you Thomas Kent?"

"Well, yes, but—"

"And didn't their father—" she flipped open a folder holding some flight coupons and read from it—"Peter Bishop, ask you to pick them up?" She handed the folder to Thomas.

Thomas opened it. "Peter asked me to come to the airport to pick up a . . ."

Thomas paused. On the flight coupon, he could see that his name and address had been hurriedly scrawled. But what caught his attention was what Peter had written below the address: "9/20/42 PB."

Thomas's heart froze. *Save my children.*

"Peter phoned me earlier today."

"Wonderful," the flight attendant said. "Now, one last thing."

Thomas looked back at her.

"I need to see a photo ID before I release the children to you."

Thomas reached into his back pocket and took out his wallet. He fished out his driver's license and handed it to the woman.

As she checked his license, Thomas looked at both children. He wiped his palms on his trousers. He shivered as a cold chill coursed through his body. Thomas knew that this chill had nothing to do with the weather.

Oh, Peter. Don't ask me to do this. Please.

Thomas could feel his throat constricting.

"Sir?" The flight attendant's voice jarred him back to reality.

Thomas simply stared at her, his face blank.

She handed him a clipboard with a form attached. "This certifies that we delivered the children to you safely. Just sign here by the *X*, and we can all be on our way." Her words were short, clipped, as if she were in a hurry.

Thomas returned his gaze to the children and, because he couldn't think of what else to do, he signed the form.

"Thank you. If you don't mind, I'm going to scoot. They say it's getting pretty bad out there. Have a nice Christmas." As the attendant turned away, she waved at the children. "Merry Christmas, kids."

The girl waved back; the boy didn't react at all.

A sudden wave of nausea swept over Thomas. He fought for control. He forced himself to walk over to where the girl and boy sat. The little girl looked up at him, her bright green eyes partly covered by ringlets of thick blonde hair.

"Are you Uncle Thomas?"

Thomas's eyes blurred. His throat tightened as he stared into the little girl's eyes. Thomas knew he was losing control. "I gotta get out of here," he said.

"What?" the girl said.

Thomas swung around and saw that the janitor was now mopping only a few feet away. The man's long, dirty blond dreadlocks nearly covered his gaunt face. He seemed painfully thin, half-starved. But at the moment, Thomas couldn't care less *what* the man looked like. He was an airport employee.

Thomas's voice was thick and halting as he grabbed the man's arm. "These kids don't have a ride. Maybe their parents are having problems with traffic or something. Could you find someone to help them? Thanks, buddy."

Thomas patted the custodian's shoulder and walked backward toward the door.

"W-w-well," the custodian stammered.

"Thanks. Thanks a lot," Thomas said, waving his arm and turning toward the exit. Shivers racked his body as if he'd spent the last few hours outside without a coat. He had to get out of there. Get away from the kids.

He broke into a run, heading for the automatic doors, but stopped dead when he heard the girl's voice call out.

"You *are* Uncle Thomas, aren't you?"

Thomas turned around slowly.

The girl held a tiny picture in her hands.

Thomas willed his feet to move, but he remained stock-still.

She came toward him, holding the picture at arm's length in the palm of her petite hand. The picture, cut from a college annual, was Thomas's senior portrait. If any doubt remained, the numbers written under the photo eliminated it.

In red ink someone had written "9/20/42—PB." Thomas took the picture from her hand. He looked at the little girl, her ears reddening, a plaintive expression on her face. He glanced over to the brown-haired boy sitting on the chair, staring blankly into space.

Deep within Thomas's mind, he began to hear the sounds of tires squealing, of children screaming. Saw the terror in his wife's eyes. Felt the car explode through the guardrail. And then a numbing, deadly chill.

Thomas dropped the picture, brought his fists to his temples, trying to pound the images from his mind. With an anguished cry, he whirled around and stumbled from the terminal into the night.

The elevator doors opened into the lush penthouse suite reserved for Anthony "Father Antoine" MacAsland. Sawyer Wynne marched into Anthony MacAsland's outer office.

"Is he in?" he asked MacAsland's secretary as he breezed past her desk.

"He's in the middle of a conference call right now, Mr. Wynne," the secretary, an attractive blonde young enough to be MacAsland's daughter, called out. She spoke the words rapidly, trying to complete her sentence before Wynne burst into MacAsland's office. "Mr. Wynne, you can't go in there!"

Wynne snorted, dismissed her protest with a wave of his hand, and opened MacAsland's door.

Sawyer Wynne hated going into Anthony MacAsland's office and avoided the distasteful experience whenever he could. Unfortunately, the events of the day mandated that Father Antoine be informed.

Since Father would never deign

to come down and visit lesser individuals such as him, Wynne had no choice but to go up to the penthouse.

MacAsland sat in a tall, black leather executive's chair, facing toward the window and the Syracuse skyline. A cloud of ash gray smoke ascended from the front of the chair, giving MacAsland a dusky halo.

"Anthony," Wynne said.

A hand, holding a lit Cuban cigar, popped up from behind the chair, signaling for Wynne to be patient—and silent. MacAsland didn't even turn around.

Wynne's jaw muscles worked furiously. He felt his ears grow hot as he listened to the voice coming from behind the chair.

"Yes, Senator, I'm delighted to learn of the president's confidence in me. Yes, of course. I'll be flying down tonight. Good-bye."

A quiet beep told Wynne that Anthony MacAsland had broken the connection. There was a brief pause, followed by a fresh cloud of cigar smoke, and the chair slowly rotated around to face Sawyer Wynne.

MacAsland took another drag on his cigar, tilted his head back, and blew out a new column of smoke. He looked Wynne in the eye, grinned, and said, "That was Senator Lewis. The nomination is set to be announced next Tuesday. The word for public consumption is that I'm on the president's short list, but the senator says— off the record, of course—that the nomination is mine. He says I should be confirmed with votes to spare."

"How nice for you," Wynne replied in a monotone.

"I'm flying down to Washington tonight to do some schmoozing. I'll be back in time to initiate the novices on Sunday. Then I'm heading back down there for some preliminary staff meetings, and—of course—to be on hand for the big announcement." MacAsland raised his coal black eyebrows and flashed a toothy grin in Sawyer Wynne's direction. "I'm almost there, Sawyer.

Can you believe it? I'm within striking distance of the White House."

Anthony MacAsland giggled like a delighted boy who has just discovered a litter of puppies in his backyard. He stood to his feet, his six-foot-four frame instantly dwarfing Sawyer Wynne. "Sawyer, do you realize what this means? What I'll be able to do?" He walked around the desk and clapped Wynne on the back.

Wynne started to speak, but MacAsland had already turned away and was walking toward his "gallery," a wall of photos picturing him with celebrities, political figures, and power brokers. He stopped at every one of the framed pictures, surveying each as if seeing it for the first time. He pointed to one of himself shaking hands with the president.

"Did you ever imagine I'd make it this far, Sawyer?"

Wynne glared at MacAsland. "Just don't forget who got you there, Anthony."

MacAsland whipped around and pointed his cigar at Wynne. "Antoine!" he scolded. "My name is Father Antoine. I am not to be called Anthony—at least not around here. Do you understand?"

Wynne raised an eyebrow. "I will call you whatever I *choose* to call you." He sauntered behind the giant desk and sat down in MacAsland's chair. "Now put out that filthy cigar before you suffocate both of us."

The cigar drooped in MacAsland's hand, and he extinguished it before sitting down in one of the small chairs in front of his desk.

"Peter tried to escape with the children today," Wynne said.

"What happened?" MacAsland asked.

"He's dead, of course."

"And the children?"

"They should be arriving in Dallas as we speak."

MacAsland's face blanched. "Dallas? I thought your people were better than that."

"You needn't worry about

my people," Wynne said, his eyes flashing. "They did exactly as they were instructed."

"You let them go?"

Wynne nodded. "We're following them. As long as Justine Bishop is free, the Project remains in jeopardy. She's managed to evade us for three years. The twins are the only way to draw her out of whatever hole she's crawled into."

MacAsland sat silently, as if processing Wynne's words.

Wynne reached across the expansive desk and took a gold pen from its holder. He scrutinized it briefly, then began twirling it like a baton with his fingers. All the time he stared at Anthony MacAsland.

"Is there something else?" MacAsland asked.

Wynne nodded, his eyes never leaving MacAsland. "Peter e-mailed Project files to someone in Texas shortly before he escaped. We don't know anything at this point, but it would seem logical that the files and the children are headed to the same person."

"Justine?"

Wynne nodded again. "Of course."

MacAsland's face reddened. He cursed and stalked back toward his photo gallery. Running his fingers through his jet-black hair, he turned back to face Sawyer Wynne. "If she gets hold of those files—"

"I am well aware of the consequences."

MacAsland stormed back over to his desk and leaned on it, facing Wynne down. "So what are you doing about it?"

Wynne closed his eyes and drew a deep breath. He released it with a quiet sigh, then stood and walked toward the exit.

MacAsland called after him. "Sawyer, what are you *doing* about it? I've spent years positioning myself for this. I *deserve* to be where I am. Find her, Sawyer. Find her and get rid of her."

Wynne paused at the door and spoke without looking back. "You worry about your part of the Project. I'll take care of mine."

Wynne walked through the door and closed it behind him.

D ana Shipp tried to look at her watch, but there was nothing there. A man who looked like he should be moonlighting as a bouncer had taken it from her almost two weeks ago. At five-foot-one and 105 pounds dripping wet, Dana had cooperated. Nevertheless, force of habit kept her glancing at an empty wrist.

Dana combed her fingers through her short auburn hair. She wasn't even sure what day it was anymore. *Maybe Friday.* On the twentieth floor of Syracuse's Chateau Antoine, it was easy to lose track of time. The windows on this floor were completely blacked out. All Dana could remember was that she had arrived on a Monday. As for the current session, judging by the ache in her back and her growling stomach, she'd been sitting on a hard metal chair in a small classroom for too long. This was hardly what she'd expected when she was invited to attend a two-week, Christmas-break conference of the Fellowship for World Renewal.

Dana took off her glasses

and rubbed her eyes. She didn't dare fall asleep. The last person to do that had been publicly humiliated before the whole group. But if she didn't get the chance to move around soon, she'd nod off for sure.

"Is there a problem, sister?" a lordly voice called out.

Dana's head jerked up. Startled, she fumbled as she tried to put her glasses back on. They slipped out of her hand and clattered to the floor.

Dana felt as if every eye in the room was focused on her. She crouched down and felt around on the floor until her hands passed over the fallen glasses. She picked them up and put them back on.

A muscular man with wispy blond hair came into focus. His intense blue, almost navy, eyes glowered at Dana.

"No," Dana said. "Uh, my eyes were just itchy and I rubbed them and—"

"Do you mind if I continue?"

"No, uh, Master Llewelen. Go ahead." Dana pushed her bangs out of her eyes and managed a weak grin. Llewelen's dark gaze made her want to crawl under her chair.

She cast a sidelong glance at her best friend, Coventina Wilcox. Coventina refused to look at her. She just sat there like a statue, her arrow-straight blonde hair framing her delicate face.

Dana felt her face flush. "Sorry," she whispered.

Coventina ignored her.

Dana bit her lip, trying to hold back the tears that threatened to fill her eyes. She wondered how much more of this she could take. Oblivious to her needs or wants, Llewelen droned on.

Sonny Pritchard leaned on his mop, watching the tall bearded man run away. Sonny's assignment was to follow the children and whoever met them. Now the man who was supposed to pick the children up had apparently abandoned them. Sonny had to think of something quickly, but he had no idea what to do.

Sonny looked down at the little girl standing beside him. Her gaze was still fixed at the sliding doors through which "Uncle Thomas" had stumbled. Tears welled up in her eyes.

Sonny crouched down beside her. "Don't cry, honey. I'll help you."

"You can't," she said, shaking her head.

Sonny looked into her eyes. "I bet you're hungry, ain't you? Sure. They don't give you nothin' to eat on them planes anymore 'cept a few peanuts. C'mon," he said, stretching out his hand.

The little girl turned away and walked back to where her

brother was sitting. She put her hand on his shoulder and looked up at Sonny.

"No," she said. "We'll wait here."

"You can't stay here forever, sweetie."

When the girl replied, her voice was weak and tentative. "We don't have anywhere else to go."

"Right. You think that dude's gonna come back? He took off the minute he saw you. He don't want to be bothered with kids."

The boy's hand traced its way along his sister's arm until he found her hand. He grasped it and said, "Michelle, what if he doesn't come back? We can't stay here."

She pressed her lips together. "Micah, we're not leaving."

Micah sighed. "We'll never find Mom."

Sonny knelt and put his hand on Micah's knee. "So, you're tryin' to find your mama. Well, why didn't you say so? I'll take you right to her. My shift's over anyway. What's her name, boy?"

Micah didn't answer.

Michelle looked at Sonny. "Her name is Justine Bishop. And we don't *know* where she lives."

At the mention of Justine's name, Sonny stood silently, gazing in wonder at the two children. Justine Bishop's name was burned into the mind of every member of the Fellowship. Her rebellion against Father was well known. If Antoine was good, Justine Bishop was evil. If Antoine was god, Justine Bishop was Satan. Every member of the Fellowship had standing orders to listen for news of her.

Sonny instantly understood why his assignment had been described as "crucial." Father Antoine hated Justine. He wanted her dead. If the children could lead Sonny to her . . .

Sonny needed a plan, but the Fellowship hadn't given him any. He needed to call Kevin. This was too big a decision for him to make on his own.

Sonny's voice was hushed but urgent. "Jus' wait here for a couple of minutes. I'm gonna punch out. Then I'll take you to your mama."

Michelle started to protest.

"I ain't gonna listen to any more," Sonny said. "Y'all are comin' with me." He knelt down and took the boy's hand. "Micah—that's your name, right? Well, you jus' sit tight. I'll be right back."

Sonny knew he was taking a risk in leaving the children alone, but he had to call Kevin, find out what to do.

This was his moment.

* * * * *

Michelle watched the janitor hurry away.

"Come on, Micah. We're getting out of here." Michelle zipped up her winter coat and pulled the hood over her head.

"Why?" Micah said.

"I don't like that man."

"Michelle, we've got to trust somebody."

"Not him. I don't like how he looked at us. He makes me feel like we're mice and he's a cat." Michelle reached down and began zipping up Micah's coat. She handed him a toboggan hat. "Here, put this on quick. It's cold outside."

"Outside? Are you crazy? All we'll do is freeze out there."

"We'll get a taxi or something. I don't know. I just don't want to be here when he comes back."

"But, Michelle—"

"Micah!" Michelle grabbed her brother's shoulders. "Daddy put me in charge. You've got to listen to me. Let's get out of here now!"

Micah shook his head and pulled on the toboggan cap. "This is really stupid."

Micah held out his hands,

BLIND
SIGHT

allowing Michelle to pull him to his feet. Then she turned around and waited for him to take hold of her shoulder. "Let's go," she said.

Step by careful step, she escorted him to the automatic doors that led outside. A blast of cold wind gushed in through the doors. The children leaned against it, heads down, pressing their way into the frigid night.

●　●　●　●　●

Thomas Kent hunched his shoulders over the edge of his truck's bed. His forearms rested on the side panel, and he hung his head between his arms, trying to recover his senses. His breathing came in rapid gasps, taking bitter freezing air into his lungs and expelling it almost as quickly as it came in. He balled his hands into tight fists as he fought for control. Thomas tasted blood seeping from where he'd bitten his bottom lip.

He wanted desperately to help Bishop's kids.

But not this way. Not this close.

His own pain was still too fresh, his wounds too raw. Every little boy he saw looked like Steven, every girl like Sarah.

They'll have to understand. It just hurts too much to be around them.

Thomas stood up. His ears and face stinging from the savage bite of the night air, he turned to face the terminal. He noticed two small figures creeping along the sidewalk. The figure in back had his hand on the elbow of the one in front of him.

●　●　●　●　●

Sonny Pritchard's heart hammered as he pulled open his locker. He knew he had a big problem. The guy that met the kids certainly wouldn't come back. Sonny had seen his face, the haunted look of the man as he ran from the terminal. No, he wouldn't come back. But without him, there was no way to find Justine.

Sonny yanked his coat from his locker with one hand while the other hit the speed-dial button on his cell phone. He heard the phone ring once, twice, three times.

"Come on, Kevin, where are you?"

There was a muffled click; then a soft, cold voice came on the line. "Antoine is lord."

Sonny hesitated. This wasn't Kevin. He paused a second longer, then gave the reply expected of an indoctrinate. "My lord always."

"Where is your Mentor?"

Sonny's panicked mind could only generate thought fragments. "Bad weather. Accidents. He's—he's stuck in traffic."

"Calm down," the voice commanded. "What do you need?"

"The children got here, but the man who came to pick them up just ran away and left them."

Sonny waited. There was no response.

"Did you hear me? The children—"

"I heard you. Where are the children now?" The soft voice had sharpened considerably.

"They're in the baggage claim area, waiting for—"

"And you left them alone?" the voice demanded.

"I–I didn't know what to do. I had to get my coat, had to call—"

"Listen carefully. If the man has abandoned them, then he is already aware of our little game. We must not risk losing the children. Do whatever is necessary to bring them in at once."

"But I don't think—"

"You are not expected to think. Bring them in." A click told Sonny that the connection had been terminated.

Sawyer Wynne laid the receiver of his desk phone back in its cradle. He had ordered that all calls from DFW Airport be routed directly to him. Wynne had no idea what Justine and her minions were up to, but he knew that the Fellowship's destiny hung precariously between success and disaster, and he was taking no chances.

They could survive the loss of the computer files, provided Justine had no assurance of her children's safety. They could even survive the loss of the children, provided they recovered the files. But if they lost the children *and* the files, events would most likely spiral out of his control—and disaster would be the certain outcome.

Wynne had reviewed Sonny Pritchard's personnel file when he'd learned the twins were headed to DFW. Pritchard's digital dossier still occupied the flat-screen monitor on Wynne's desk. As he paged through it, Wynne noted that Pritchard's loyalty was unquestioned, but his abilities and IQ were less than stellar. He wasn't a screwup, just not very bright. He had been assigned to work as a janitor at DFW, mostly to monitor travelers who were under the Fellowship's watchful eye. But Pritchard was still supposed to be under a Mentor's watchful eye. Unfortunately, that person was sitting in a car somewhere on a Dallas freeway.

Sawyer Wynne rested his head in his hands. Thanks to bad weather, the future of his brainchild was in serious jeopardy. And everything depended on one novice of below-average ability.

●　●　●　●　●

Sonny hurried back toward baggage claim. He didn't reckon the children would be a problem, particularly since he'd won the boy over. Sonny was pleased to find the baggage claim area still free of travelers, but he spat out a curse as he approached the empty chairs where the twins had sat only moments before.

This was indeed Sonny's moment. But he could tell from the tone of the voice on the phone that if somehow he lost the children, he'd have no more moments—ever.

• • • • •

Michelle led Micah along the sidewalk leading to the next section of Terminal A. She had no idea where to go but instinctively knew she wanted to get as far away from the overly friendly custodian as possible.

Micah gripped his sister's elbow as he walked behind her. The thin layer of ice covering the sidewalk made their path treacherous. Micah struggled to keep his feet from slipping out from under him. "What do you see?" he asked.

"Nothing but more sidewalk and a parking garage," Michelle said. "It goes on forever."

"Aren't there any taxis or anything?"

"No. They must all be gone."

"I'm cold. I want to go back inside."

"No. Not yet. Not till he's gone."

Michelle suddenly pulled Micah off to the right and began crossing the road to the parking garage.

"Where are we going?"

"Maybe someone left their car unlocked. At least we can get out of this wind."

• • • • •

Thomas watched Bishop's children cross over into the parking garage.

What happened to the custodian? Why didn't he help them?

As Thomas stood by the

driver-side door of his truck, he noticed a man running out of the terminal and across the street, straight toward the children.

● ● ● ● ●

Holding Micah's hand, Michelle walked along a row of cars looking for one that was unlocked. She came to an old Ford station wagon. "Stay here while I try the doors," she whispered.

The station wagon's owner had locked it tight.

Next to the wagon was a BMW sports car. She turned around and pulled on the door handle. The car's security system began whooping like a police car in hot pursuit.

Michelle jumped back from the car and hurried back to her brother. "Let's get out of here," she shouted above the siren.

The two moved as quickly as they could into the center of the parking lot, away from the cars.

"Hey! You kids. Stop!" a man's voice commanded.

Michelle and Micah slowed to a stop and turned to face a man in a dark blue, hooded parka walking toward them. As he stepped closer to the twins, a sodium-vapor streetlamp cast a pale orange glow across the man's face. His hood shielded most of his face from the light, but enough showed for Michelle to recognize him.

"You're the janitor."

"Right. And you're comin' with me."

"I said we didn't want your help."

The man gripped Michelle's arm, squeezing tightly.

"Ow! You're hurting me."

"I'll hurt you worse if you don't come," he said.

"Leave my sister alone!" Micah screamed, his fists flailing. He caught the man across the face. The man let go of Michelle, then whipped around and shoved Micah, sending him sprawling on the pavement.

"Micah!" Michelle screamed.

Michelle jumped backward just as a flash of black fur struck the custodian and knocked him to the ground. Time seemed to stop for her as she heard fierce growls intermingle with her would-be kidnapper's screams. She couldn't believe it; a huge dog had knocked the man down and was standing over him, baring its teeth.

A pickup truck rolled to a stop beside her. The door opened and a man hopped out. "Get in, quick," he said. "I'll get your brother."

"But . . ."

"No time to argue," the man said. "Just listen to Uncle Thomas." He ran to the front of the truck and picked up Micah. "Come on, young fella; we've got to make tracks."

Uncle Thomas plopped Micah into the passenger seat as Michelle scooted in from the driver's side.

The janitor lay on his back paralyzed with fear while the big dog stood over him, teeth still bared and ready to pounce. Uncle Thomas closed the door beside Micah and ran around to the driver's side.

"Gumbo. Come."

The big dog broke off its attack and trotted back to its master, hopping into the truck.

"Good thing this truck's got a big cab," Thomas muttered. "Buckle up, everybody. This is going to be one nasty drive home."

Sonny Pritchard clambered to his feet, then broke into a run. His head was swimming with conflicting choices. Uncle Thomas had taken the kids. Maybe things were looking up. Sonny could follow them to Justine now. No, that wouldn't work. They were onto him. Besides, the voice on the phone made it clear that he was to bring the children in.

But how?

Sonny's Ford Festiva sat in a parking space not far from where he now stood. He jerked open the driver-side door and slid behind the wheel. He spat out a curse when he realized that his keys were still in his pocket. Sonny straightened his legs, shoved his hand into the front pocket of his trousers, and pulled out his key ring. Even though the car was freezing, a cold sweat formed on Sonny's brow as he fumbled through keys till he found the right one.

The cold engine complained, turning over and over as it resisted Sonny's attempts to bring it to life. He punched the accelerator, and the engine rumbled and coughed, spewing a cloud of blue exhaust behind the little car.

He glanced at a tiny digital clock glowing pale blue on the dashboard. Uncle Thomas had a two-minute head start already. Sonny knew the icy roads would slow them down, but he had to move quickly or lose them at the fork for the north and south exits.

Sonny had one advantage over his targets. He was fully prepared for the storm. The Fellowship drilled into its people that they must be ready for anything. With an ice storm in the forecast, Sonny had made sure his little car was outfitted for the worst. He'd filled the back of the car with six fifty-pound bags of sand. Three hundred extra pounds of ballast would improve his traction, and if he should get stuck, he could dump some of the sand under the tires to get moving again.

Sonny smiled. He knew he would soon catch up with Uncle Thomas and the kids. The children would go to Father Antoine. Sonny might even be a hero.

He quickly put the car into reverse and backed out of his space.

But first he had to catch them.

* * * * *

Thomas Kent drove his oversize pickup away from the terminal, his foot barely touching the accelerator. The roads had deteriorated badly. Within the next hour only someone with a mighty strong death wish would be driving the Dallas freeways.

He considered stopping to find a motel where they could wait out the storm, but there was no telling how long they'd be stranded. It could be days before the roads became passable again. Crazy as it sounded, the only reasonable option was to try to drive all the way home.

Thomas kept the truck in low as it crept down the exit

ramp. He prayed nobody would be coming as he turned left onto the access road that would lead him to the main exits. When he felt the rear of the truck losing traction, sliding to the right, Thomas gently turned the wheel in the direction of the skid, being careful not to hit the brakes. As the truck came back under his control, he applied easy pressure to the accelerator. The truck sped up slightly as Thomas approached his first obstacle—the ramp up to the south exit. Even though it had already been sanded, new layers of ice had formed over the sand. He would have to take the uphill curve fast enough to keep from sliding backward but slowly enough to keep from skidding off the side of the road.

As Thomas increased his speed, he heard a whimper to his right. He peeked at the children out of the corners of his eyes. The boy sat pressed up against the door. The girl had placed herself between Thomas and her brother, like a mother protecting her baby.

Gumbo sat on his haunches, facing forward, then glancing between the children and Thomas, as if trying to figure out the new seating arrangements. A whine from Gumbo made the girl scoot backward, pressing her brother even tighter against the door. Her wide-eyed gaze expressed sheer terror.

"It's okay. He won't hurt you. He's a big baby." Thomas smiled at her.

Gumbo chuffed, as if in agreement.

The approaching ramp drew Thomas's attention from the children and he said, "Hold on tight. Here we go."

He pressed down harder on the gas, making the truck's powerful engine give off a deep rumble. "The key here," Thomas said, talking to himself as much as to the kids, "is steady and careful movement. Nothing sudden. A nice easy roll up the ramp without stopping."

Just as he finished his sentence, the truck began to fishtail and slide downward and to the right. He heard the unmistakable whine of wheels spinning on ice. Thomas pressed his lips together and gripped the wheel with white-knuckled determination. Lifting his foot off the gas, he waited till the wheels caught again. But as soon as he pressed the accelerator, the pickup started back into its slide.

Thomas lost his cool and gunned the engine. The powerful motor roared and the wheels spun furiously. But the truck skated backward down to the bottom of the ramp and off onto the right shoulder.

Thomas slammed his palms on the steering wheel. "Kids," he said, shaking his head, "it's gonna be a long night."

• • • • •

As soon as Sonny wheeled his Festiva onto the access road, he grinned at the scene before him. Not far ahead, bathed in the amber glow of sodium-vapor lights, sat Uncle Thomas's big black pickup truck.

This is going to be easier than I thought.

Sonny slowed his car to a crawl and pulled a dark blue ski mask from the seat beside him. He slipped the mask over his head, then pulled on a pair of gloves. Pulling up the hood of his coat, he tugged at the drawstrings until the cloth was wrapped snugly around his face.

Since they'd never seen his car, they wouldn't know who was coming to help them. Just a friendly neighbor reaching out to someone in trouble. They would welcome his assistance.

But how would he get the children away from Uncle Thomas?

• • • • •

Thomas stepped out of the truck and slammed the door. Arctic blasts, peppered with sleet and freezing rain, stung his cheeks and ears with the fury of a sandblaster. He walked behind the truck to see how badly he was stuck.

He noticed a small car about fifty yards behind him. He wouldn't have paid much attention to it, but it was the only other car on the road at the moment. And it had stopped dead in the middle of the road.

Probably looking for directions to the nearest motel.

Thomas turned his attention to more important matters. The right rear wheel rested about three inches deep in mud. The left was still on the road's concrete shoulder. The front wheels were in better shape, both still on the road. By taking it nice and slow in four-wheel drive, they might just get out of this without having to call a wrecker. Thomas reached into the back of the truck and pulled out a scrap of plywood, sliding it under the front part of the right rear wheel. That should do the trick.

He stood up and brushed grit off his hands.

●　●　●　●　●

Sonny couldn't believe it. Uncle Thomas had gotten out of his truck and was standing behind it. The man on the phone had told him to do whatever was necessary to bring the children in. Sonny knew what that meant. His grip on the wheel tightened as he made his decision. It was time to take Uncle Thomas out of the game permanently.

Sonny aimed the car straight at Thomas and punched the accelerator.

The sound of polite applause startled Dana Shipp from an almost hypnotized lethargy. She looked around through glazed eyes. People stood to their feet and shuffled around her, but Dana could hardly will her body to move. Sensing movement out of the corner of her right eye, she turned and saw Coventina standing there.

Coventina offered her arm. "Come. We have a ten-minute break for restroom visits and refreshments."

Ten minutes? Is she kidding? I've been sitting for hours. I've got to take a walk. Go outside, get some cold night air to wake me up.

Dana didn't voice her objections. She knew better than to express *any* dissatisfaction with the program.

"Come *on*, Dana! There isn't time to waste."

Dana stood up. Her legs felt heavy. Her empty stomach screamed for food. Too tired to protest, she allowed herself to be led like a child toward the ladies' restroom. As she walked, Dana glanced at the refreshment area, a long

BLIND SIGHT

table stocked with ice water, bowls of carrots, and individual containers of plain yogurt. Dana closed her eyes and groaned silently. For two weeks now, Dana's diet had consisted of yogurt, carrots, and rice. She felt like she was living at a fat farm.

Dana waited in line, not because the demand on the restroom facilities was too great but because Llewelen and the Mentors controlled access. She had learned early on that the Mentors made every decision for her. At first it seemed kind of cute; now Dana felt like a second grader again. She forced a smile as Coventina rejoined her.

Coventina's expression telegraphed her disapproval. "You need to maintain focus, Dana, or you'll never enter the Sphere."

"I'm sorry, Coventina. It's just that after two weeks of this, I'm *so* tired."

Coventina raised her eyebrows. "The rest of us have been here as long as you have. You don't see any of us falling asleep in Llewelen's teaching sessions."

"I know. I guess I just wasn't expecting things to be so long and drawn out."

"What *did* you expect, Dana? After all, the FWR flew you up here at its own expense. They're putting you up for two whole weeks at Chateau Antoine—one of the most exclusive new hotels in Syracuse. They're giving you the chance to meet Father Antoine himself. And you complain because you have to sit through some long sessions?"

Dana looked at the floor.

Coventina took Dana's hands in her own. "Dana, you were invited up here because you are special. Do you think you were selected from all the other students at the University of Pittsburgh at random? As Father says, 'Many are called, but few are chosen.'"

Dana looked up at her friend and college roommate. Coventina Wilcox was perhaps the first real friend Dana ever had. From the moment Dana had first walked into her dormitory room at Pitt, Coventina had become like an older sister. After a lifetime with an abusive father, Dana was ready for someone—anyone—who would treat her kindly.

After a few weeks, Coventina had invited her to attend a meeting of Anthony MacAsland's campus environmental group, the Fellowship for World Renewal. Even though she'd never been very interested in environmentalism, Dana was impressed by the group's commitment to reclaiming the environment and preventing its further destruction by greedy capitalistic interests. In fact, the FWR had grown so powerful under Anthony MacAsland's direction that it now rivaled Greenpeace as one of the most influential environmental organizations in the world.

After only a few months, the FWR had become Dana's passion. Of course, it didn't hurt that the group's founder, Anthony MacAsland, was drop-dead gorgeous. The man had looks that could shame Hollywood's most handsome leading man. Not that Dana had ever actually met him. MacAsland was too important. Too big. Too awesome. But even being a small part of this great man's work gave Dana a feeling of significance she had never experienced before.

She had begun attending FWR meetings regularly, going out on protest rallies with the other group members, and participating in letter-writing and e-mail campaigns. She volunteered her considerable computer skills to help the group design a new information-management system.

Then Coventina had suggested she attend the Mentors' Retreat over Christmas break. To be invited to a Mentors' Retreat—a two-week seminar held at Anthony MacAsland's exclusive hotel—was a rare privilege. At this retreat, Dana would be invited to enter the Sphere, Father Antoine's inner circle. She would be assigned a Mentor. She would even get to meet MacAsland himself. She *was* a little disappointed that her invitation had not come during the summer. In the summer months, these conferences were usually held at Anthony MacAsland's private castle in the Thousand Islands. From what Dana had heard, Shelby Castle on Diamond Island made Chateau Antoine look like a dump.

Still, Dana wasn't kicking about it. It was an invitation reserved only for a special few. Even though she hardly ever got to go back to her room to rest and even though the food was less—a lot less—than she'd expected, Dana remembered that this was sort of a "boot camp" for those who wanted to follow the Master more closely. Dana supposed that she could endure anything for two weeks. It was a small price to pay for significance.

W hen Thomas heard the car's engine roar, he
assumed the driver had become impatient with
the icy roads and gunned the engine in frustration.
But as his eyes caught the headlights rushing toward
him, he realized the driver of the car intended to run
him down. Thomas had only seconds to react before
the car crushed him. Wanting to protect the children,
Thomas stepped away from the truck and stood on a
dry patch of concrete that had been sheltered by the
overpass.

The headlights raced toward him and the car's engine
screamed.

It's been a long time. Hope I can still do this.

Thomas held his ground till the last possible instant,
then launched himself toward the pickup, vaulting over
the side and into the cold metal bed. He landed hard and
hit his head against one of the wheel wells. Sharp pains
shot outward and down his
neck. Thomas felt a blast of air

as the car rushed by, then heard a loud crash and the tinkling of glass.

He rolled over onto his stomach and pushed himself onto his knees. The little car had slammed into a concrete pillar, virtually disintegrating on impact. The pillar now rested in the front seat alongside the driver.

Thomas climbed out of the pickup's bed and made his way across the icy ramp. The car's side windows had blown out on impact, scattering tiny chunks of safety glass in a semicircle around its shattered front. The driver lay back in his seat, his face covered by a dark ski mask. Rattling sounds escaped from his lips as he tried to breathe.

"Hold on a second," Thomas said. "Let me cut this off you. You'll breathe easier." He took out a pocketknife and sliced through the bloody material, then peeled it away from the man's face.

"There you go," Thomas said. "That's bet— " Thomas stopped short when he recognized the custodian. The compassion left Thomas's voice. He spoke firmly. "Who are you? What did you want with those kids?"

The man focused his eyes on Thomas, the corners of his lips curling upward slightly. He coughed, then whispered, struggling with every word. "You . . . can't . . . hide."

"What?"

"They'll . . . find . . . you."

"Who? Who'll find me?"

"Run . . . while . . . you . . . can." The man's eyes glazed over and his jaw went slack.

"What do you mean? Run from what? Answer me!" Thomas shouted.

Looking toward his truck, Thomas could see the little girl's face framed in the driver-side window. Her petite features stood in contrast to the fear reflected in her eyes. Thomas didn't know who was after these children, but whoever they were, they meant business.

The tortured voice from his answering machine replayed in his mind. *"Save my children."*

Thomas walked to his truck, pulled open the door, and slid behind the wheel. The girl retreated to the far side of the cab, leaning against her brother to protect him.

Thomas's lips pulled into a tight smile. "Don't worry. I'm not going to hurt you."

He turned the key and the engine roared to life. Putting the large, four-wheel-drive vehicle into gear, he gently eased down on the gas pedal. Thomas felt the front tires grip the road and the right rear wheel bite the plywood scrap. In a few seconds, his truck slowly rolled up the ramp.

Thomas glanced over toward the children. "You two get some sleep. First, we've got to get to my place. Then I need some answers."

Dana figured it must be the middle of the night. Her ten-minute "break" had been hours ago. After he allowed a snack of carrots and unflavored nonfat yogurt, chased down by a cup of water, Llewelen's interminably long sessions had resumed. But Dana noticed a shift in Llewelen's emphasis.

Now he solicited testimonies from those assembled. "Who among us is ready to share what Father Antoine has done for them? Don't be shy. Stand up and share with us."

After a few seconds of expectant silence, across the room a young redheaded woman stood up. Her spindly arms and legs gave her a fragile appearance, and her short hair looked like straw. The dark circles under her eyes gave her the look of a "heroin-chic" fashion model. Dana suspected that this woman's look came not from makeup but from the real thing.

"My name is DiDi."

Her voice was so soft, Dana could barely hear her.

"I was in a methadone clinic in Los Angeles when one of Father's angels found me," she said. "I was brought to their drug-rehab center, and they got me cleaned up. I haven't used in a year and a half. They put me in their job-training program, and now I'm a maid in one of the biggest hotels in LA." The woman hesitated; then tears began to spill unchecked down her face. "If it hadn't been for Father Antoine, I'm sure I'd be dead by now."

The room broke into spontaneous applause as the woman sat down.

As the applause died down, a tall black woman who looked like she was in her thirties stood up. Dana observed that this woman appeared as strong and healthy as DiDi had appeared weak.

"My name's Tameka, and I just want you all to know that this is reality! I'm from Chicago. My husband left me to take care of four children by myself. We were about to be evicted from our apartment and thrown onto the street. But the FWR came to our rescue. They took us into their emergency shelter and let us stay there until I could find a job. They even provided day care when I went to work. These people care, and I'm proud to be one of Father Antoine's children."

The rest of the people in the room clapped as Tameka sat down. Dana scanned the room, wondering who would be the next to sing Father Antoine's praises.

Coventina nudged her.

Dana shook her head.

Coventina nodded toward the front of the room.

Llewelen was looking straight at Dana. "Do you have something to share with us, sister? Don't be shy."

Dana looked around. Everyone was looking at her and smiling. Tameka nodded and encouraged her. "Go on, sweet thing. We're all family here."

Dana swallowed. Her throat and mouth felt like they

had gone instantly dry. She stood. "I—I'm not very good at this sort of thing."

Everyone looked at her expectantly.

Dana took a deep breath, brushed her auburn bangs out of her eyes, and began. "I was really lonely when I first came to the University of Pittsburgh. I've never had a lot of friends." There was a slight catch in her voice, but she continued.

"My father was an alcoholic. He used to beat my mother and me whenever he would get drunk. Since he got drunk four or five times a week, we got beaten a lot. Mom put up with it. If I knew he was drunk, I'd hide in the basement and barricade the door. I can still hear him hammering on the door with his fist and screaming at me."

"Is that why he threw you out, honey?" Tameka asked.

Dana shook her head. "No." She took a deep breath and let it out with a shudder. "I came home one afternoon and found my mother in the bathtub. She'd cut her wrists." Dana paused, blinking back the tears that filled her eyes.

Tameka handed her a tissue.

"I guess she just couldn't take it anymore. I don't know what happened to me, but I freaked. I didn't call 911 or the police or anything. I just got a baseball bat and waited for my father to come home." A faraway look came into Dana's eyes. "I wanted to kill him for what he'd done to me and my mother." Dana dabbed at her eyes with the tissue. "He was such a hateful man."

"You poor thing," Tameka said.

"I waited in a closet until I heard him come into the house. I was going to sneak up behind him and hit him, but I came out too soon. He was bigger and stronger than I was. Funny thing was, he didn't even hit me. Just took the bat away from me. But I'll never forget the way he looked at me, the hate in his eyes.

"After my mother's funeral, he told me to pack my bags

and never come back. I haven't seen or spoken to him since that day.

"I'd already graduated from high school and been awarded a full scholarship in computer studies at Pitt. I just went on to school a little early. That's when I met Coventina." Dana motioned toward her friend and noticed for the first time that Coventina was no longer sitting beside her. She had evidently slipped out of the room while Dana was talking.

"Anyway," Dana continued, "Coventina led me to Father. Ever since I've been part of the FWR, I've had a purpose and joy in my life. But more than that, I've found a family."

When Dana sat down, Llewelen jumped in, almost as if on cue. "You have all been touched in one way or another by Father Antoine's vision to save Mother Earth. You've all received great things from Father. Are you now ready to go to the next level? Will you become one with Father, enter the Sphere, and journey to true spiritual reality? If you are, then stand up. You heard me," he shouted. "I said stand!"

Dana sat frozen where she was. More than anything, she wanted to stand to her feet, to be the first in the room to commit to Antoine's vision for the world. But her legs felt like jelly. She heard a sound on her left. A young man rose to his feet. Then across the room two women stood, hand in hand. The sound of chairs scraping the floor began to fill the room as one after another stood up to surrender to Father Antoine.

Forcing her legs to respond, Dana rose.

She felt a presence at her right side. Coventina had returned. Dana opened her mouth to speak to her friend. But Dana was speechless when she saw how Coventina had changed.

Coventina now wore a floor-length white robe. Long sleeves, made of an iridescent material, made her look more like an apparition than a person. Her flaxen hair flowed down her back like a golden river. Her cat green eyes held Dana in a piercing gaze, and she wore an enigmatic Mona Lisa grin that Dana couldn't quite read.

"I'm glad you stood up," Coventina said. "Come with me. It's time to enter the Sphere."

"Oh, I don't know if I'm ready for that."

"You're ready. Come." Coventina turned and walked toward the door.

Like an obedient puppy, Dana followed.

Coventina led Dana out of the small meeting room and down the long hallway toward the elevators. Walking slightly behind her, Dana noticed for the first time that her friend was barefoot. Since the moment they left the room, Coventina had remained silent, almost trancelike. Dana felt like she was following a ghost. The elevator doors opened, and Coventina floated aboard with Dana in tow. Something about the new Coventina unsettled her. Nevertheless, Dana followed.

"Where are the others?" Dana asked, noticing for the first time that only she had left the room.

"Their Mentors will bring them at the proper time," Coventina responded.

The numbered buttons on the console inside the elevator went up to thirty. Coventina pressed the button for the thirtieth floor. Instantly the elevator surged upward, making Dana's stomach lurch.

Dana's eyes wandered up and down Coventina's body as the numbers on the elevator ticked up toward their destination. She still couldn't believe the change that had come over her friend in just a few minutes. Her white robe hung on her loosely.

The only jewelry adorning her was a single ring, worn on a finger of her left hand. Dana had known Coventina for months but never remembered seeing that ring. It was a smooth band of white gold, with no decoration, no markings. In the center, a plain setting held a small pink stone.

"That's a lovely ring you're wearing," Dana said, breaking the silence. "I've never seen you wear it before. Did it belong to your mother?"

Coventina looked at her with her Mona Lisa grin. "It marks my journey."

"Pardon me?"

An electronic tone announced their arrival at the thirtieth floor. Dana's stomach returned to its place as the elevator stopped.

"You'll understand," Coventina said, turning toward Dana. "You will journey."

Coventina produced a key from her right hand and inserted it into the elevator's console. She turned it to the right. The elevator surged up again, then stopped. The number over the doors was thirty-two.

Coventina turned back toward Dana. She smiled and said, "To achieve true oneness, you must journey to the center of the Sphere."

Before Dana could respond, the elevator doors opened.

"Come, child," Coventina said, walking through the doors.

Wordlessly, Dana followed.

They entered a massive ballroom. Recessed ceiling lights cast a dim amber glow. It took Dana's eyes a few minutes to adjust to the room's dimness after the brilliance of the elevator.

A large assembly gathered in the far end of the ballroom. Most wore white, like Coventina. The men sported white slacks and white turtleneck shirts. The women dressed in the same iridescent gown that Coventina wore. Dana felt as if she had been invited to a formal dinner party and had arrived dressed for a costume party. She rubbed her hands up and down her floral-print dress, as if to wipe out the colors and make it as white as the others' clothing. Suddenly Dana felt very out of place.

Dana followed Coventina to one corner of the room, where she saw rows of shoes laid out neatly. Coventina turned back toward her and said with a whisper, "You may leave your shoes here."

Without a word of dissent, Dana removed her shoes and laid them beside the others.

"Come now," Coventina said. "Let's join the group."

"But," Dana whispered, "what are we going to do?"

"Shhhh," Coventina warned, a frown darkening her face. "The Master won't like it if you talk during meditation. We must enter the Sphere."

Dana noticed a handful of other people dressed in street clothes among the group. Coventina pointed to a spot on the floor and nodded toward Dana. Dana knelt down. Coventina knelt beside her.

Dana realized the entire group was breathing in unison.

Inhaling. Exhaling.

Dana listened.

Inhaling. Exhaling.

The rhythm of the breathing quieted her. She closed her eyes.

Inhaling. Dana matched her breathing to theirs.

Exhaling. She breathed out through her mouth.

As Dana's breathing matched that of the rest of the group, the room's silence became tangible. Yet a tranquility filled the air like nothing Dana had ever experienced. She relaxed. Tension flowed from her body as a river toward the ocean. She wished she could kneel forever.

But soon, Dana's body began to remember what time of night it was and how long ago she had last eaten. Her feet started to tingle as if tiny needles were pricking them. Soon they lost all feeling entirely. Sharp pains began to shoot from her back to her hips. Dana looked around to see if anyone else felt as uncomfortable as she did. A disapproving glance from Coventina caused her to turn her head forward and close her eyes again. But the pains continued, spreading to her knees.

Just when she thought she couldn't take any more, a young woman with long black hair said, "Stand."

Along with the rest of the group, Dana stood up. Her feet felt as if they'd been set on fire. Every muscle in her body screamed in pain. She twisted around, trying to shake off the painful aftereffects of the kneeling meditation, but noticed that no one else was moving. Everyone stood at attention, with their arms stretched out, palms upward. Dana looked at Coventina, who nodded at her as if to say, "Do this too."

With a sigh, Dana raised her arms and stretched them out in front of her. She turned her palms upward and closed her eyes again.

The leader called out again, "Enter."

The rest of the group responded in perfect unison, "Enter."

"Enter," the woman repeated.

"Enter," they chanted.

"Enter."

"You must enter the Sphere," a young man near Dana called out.

"Enter," the group responded.

Dana heard Coventina's voice call out, "Begin your journey."

"Journey," they answered.

Across the crowd, another woman chanted, "Journey to Father."

"Father," the crowd murmured with hushed reverence.

"Become one with Father," the leader shouted in cadence.

"One with Father," they said in chorus.

"Become one with Mother," a woman cried out from behind Dana.

"One with Mother."

The chanting continued. Dana's arms felt like lead. The crowd now swayed back and forth, arms waving overhead.

Dana looked over at Coventina.

Coventina smiled at her and gave her a look of acceptance that filled Dana with a warmth she had never felt before.

Dana raised her hands over her head and began to sway with the crowd.

"Enter the Sphere," someone said.

"Enter the Sphere," Dana responded with the rest.

The chants became more rapid, the cadence more intense. The group leader encouraged the others to step up the pace. "Enter," she said. "Enter now. Say it fast."

"Enter now. Enter now. Enter now. Enter now."

"Shout it louder. Shout it harder. Like you believe it," she commanded.

"Enter NOW. Enter NOW. Enter NOW."

Dana felt herself being carried along like a boat in rapids. She waved her arms and cried with the group, "Enter NOW. Enter NOW. Enter NOW."

A wave of light-headedness swept over Dana. She felt as if she had been filled with helium. Dana was floating.

"ENTER NOW! ENTER NOW! ENTER NOW!" Dana could hear her voice rising above the others. An exquisite tingling sensation spread through her fingers and toes.

"Enter now enter now enter now enter now." Dana machine-gunned the words breathlessly and uncontrollably.

The tingling spread up her arms and legs and exploded like fireworks inside her head. Her whole body felt as if it had left the ground. White spots appeared and danced before her eyes. Her vision blurred. Waves of dizziness surged over her. She closed her eyes, surrendering to the glorious experience.

She was falling backward.

She didn't care.

She was floating on a cloud.

"En . . . ter en . . . ter," she gasped softly.

Finally, unable to speak any longer, Dana just panted, eyes closed, exhilarated.

She wanted to float.

Never stop.

Float forever.

As Dana opened her eyes, she found herself lying on the floor, surrounded by about twenty men and women, all dressed in white.

Tameka was there. And DiDi. And Coventina.

They were smiling at her.

They loved her.

She felt someone touching her left hand.

Dana raised her head and looked at the person who was touching her. It was Coventina.

Coventina stretched out her hand and helped Dana to her feet. Dana's muscles were limp rags.

Coventina embraced Dana. One by one, the other members hugged her.

"Congratulations, daughter." Coventina said, her hand cupping Dana's cheek. "You have entered. You are chosen."

"What?"

Coventina lifted Dana's left hand and pointed to her ring finger. "You've begun your journey."

Dana held up her hand.

She was wearing a ring identical to Coventina's in every respect except one.

The stone in Dana's ring was black.

Saturday, December 7

T homas Kent awoke like someone fighting his way out of a coma. A dull ache spread from his neck into his shoulders. He stretched, trying to find a more comfortable position on his recliner, but no matter which way he turned, he just hurt more.

What was worse, he was freezing. He could hardly feel his nose. His ears stung in the cold air. As he forced his eyes open, the first thing he noticed was the mist created by his breath. He might as well have slept on the front porch.

Got to get some heat on.

He pulled himself to a sitting position, then looked around him. Gray morning light leaked through the blinds, promising another dreary winter day. Silence enveloped the house like a fog. He stepped out of the recliner, pulling his blanket around his shoulders, and stumbled toward the den.

Under the down comforter

on his sleeper sofa lay a cozy trio: the girl on one side, her brother on the other, and Gumbo in between. The boy lay with his left arm thrown over Gumbo. The big shepherd's muzzle rested against the boy's face. Gumbo's ears perked at the sound of Thomas's approach, but the dog made no attempt to leave the bed's warmth.

Thomas walked back through the dining room. He couldn't read the thermostat in the dark hallway. He switched on the light. Nothing happened. He flipped the switch up and down several times. Thomas reached around the corner and tried the switch for the dining room lights.

Nothing.

Great. Ice must've snapped the power lines.

If the storm had downed a lot of power lines and the ice kept coming, he and the kids were in deep trouble. Moving quickly to the living room's front window, he raised the blinds.

The scene before him took on an almost surrealistic air. It was as if someone had removed most of the color from the surrounding landscape, repainting it in shades of gray, black, and white. The sky was a drab gray blanket, allowing minimal sunlight to force its way through. The ground had turned white. Everything else bore the appearance of fine crystal, which in turn reflected the somber sky.

The world had transformed from color to monochrome overnight.

Thomas looked toward the sky to see if any mist still drifted down. Nothing. The precipitation had stopped. It had still been going strong when Thomas and the kids had finally arrived home at three in the morning.

The painfully slow drive from DFW Airport had taken almost six hours. Thomas stopped every few miles to clean his windshield. By one thirty, the temperature had dropped enough to turn the icy rain to snow, allowing Thomas to drive without the deicing stops. But by that time the roads were ice rinks.

Exhausted, Thomas had fought hard to stay alert while he drove. Rarely could he get his speed above twenty miles an hour. Sharp wind gusts threatened to push his truck off the highway. Every inch of the trip home was a battle to maintain control. By the time he rolled into his own driveway, he felt as if he'd gone twenty or thirty rounds with Muhammad Ali in his prime.

The kids were sleeping when they'd pulled into the garage and too tired to protest when he tucked them into his own bed. Gumbo had already adopted the children, escorting Thomas like a fussy, overprotective mother as he carried the boy, then his sister, and put them under the covers. Then the dog found a place at the foot of the bed where the blankets were not tucked in. He burrowed under the covers until his nose poked out between the children at the other end.

As far as Thomas could tell, Gumbo hadn't moved all night.

Thomas released the blinds at the living room window and walked back to the kitchen. On the wall by the kitchen window sat a digital, indoor-outdoor thermometer. The temperature outside registered three degrees above zero. What concerned him more was the temperature inside: thirteen degrees. The house had gone below the freezing point.

He reached for the kitchen faucet and turned it. Not a drop. He jogged down the hall toward the bathroom and turned on the bathtub faucets, hot and cold. Nothing. Everything had frozen solid.

No power. No water.

No heat either. Jenny and he had discussed whether or not to put in a fireplace or a wood-burning stove when they built the house. But since the children were small at the time, Jenny felt it would be safer to have neither. She was always looking out for the children's safety. Always concerned. Always caring.

Thomas rubbed his fingers

against his temples. Making his way to the dining room, he pulled out a heavy wooden chair and flopped down at the dining room table. His eyes came to rest on a number-ten business envelope. Battered and folded into thirds, the envelope had been in the girl's hand when he'd carried her in. She'd kept shoving it toward him as if she wanted him to take it. To settle her down, he'd taken the envelope, then tossed it on the table without looking at it.

Now he noticed the numbered code that he'd seen too many times in the past twenty-four hours—a code he'd come to wish he'd never heard of. In red ink on the front of the envelope, someone had written in large numbers *9-20-42*. The return address listed Peter Bishop's name and a Syracuse, New York, address. Thomas's hand trembled as he reached for the envelope. The numbness that clung to Thomas's thick fingers made the envelope difficult to open. Finally he tore off one of the short ends. He pulled out a single sheet of yellow legal paper on which someone, presumably Peter Bishop, had scrawled a message.

> My children are in danger. I remembered that you are from south Louisiana. Please help. Take the children to their mother, Justine. She escaped three years ago and is hiding down there.
>
> Take the files I e-mailed you and give them to her. She'll know what to do with them. I can't give you any more details. Any explanation would only put you all in greater danger.
>
> Move quickly. And trust no one. If they haven't found you yet, they soon will.
>
> Please—save my children.
> Peter Bishop—43/9/21

Thomas read and reread the letter. It sounded more like the ravings of a paranoid schizophrenic than the plea of a caring father. And the code by Bishop's signature made no sense at all. The numbers were wrong *and* in the wrong order. Thomas surmised that Peter must have scrawled the note in such a hurry that he didn't get the code right.

On a whim, he pulled out his Bible and opened to the forty-third book, The Gospel According to John. Quickly flipping through pages, he came to chapter nine. With his finger, he located the twenty-first verse: "But how he can see now, or who opened his eyes, we don't know. Ask him. He is of age; he will speak for himself."

"What's that got to do with anything?" Thomas said to himself. He closed the Bible and read the letter again. Nothing made sense.

For all Thomas knew, the children's mother could still be in New York somewhere, panic-stricken about her two babies who had disappeared. Thomas just might have become an unwitting accomplice in a kidnapping last night. It was all too crazy.

Before he did anything, he'd have to try calling Peter's home and make sure there wasn't a grieving mother left behind, wondering where her children were. But if Thomas was going to do any investigating, he'd better do it soon. Once the children woke up, he'd have to tend to more basic matters such as food, heat, and survival.

Thomas pushed back his chair and walked into the kitchen. He crossed his fingers as he picked up the receiver and breathed a relieved sigh when he heard the dial tone.

At least the phone's still working.

He flipped through the pages of the phone directory and located the area code for Syracuse, New York. As he dialed directory assistance, the thought occurred to him that the kids weren't necessarily from Syracuse. But they had flown out of JFK. He knew that much from their tickets. Oh, well, it was his best lead and he'd follow it until it played out.

Thomas heard a beep on the line, and then a young woman's

voice, heavy with a Brooklyn accent answered, "New York Bell, what city?"

"Syracuse."

"Go ahead, sir."

"I need the number for a Peter Bishop." Thomas gave her the address on the envelope.

"Just a moment."

Thomas noticed that his palms had become sweaty despite the cold. He rubbed his free hand on his trouser leg.

"Hold for the number, sir."

"Thank you," Thomas said.

A recorded voice cheerily relayed the information. "The number is 555-4217. If you would like us to dial the number for you, please hold."

Thomas hesitated a moment, trying to decide whether or not to allow the call to go through.

"You can't hide," a strangled, dying voice whispered in his mind.

His hand trembled as he held the receiver.

"They'll find you," the raspy voice continued.

He heard the tones firing off in rapid succession, dialing the number.

"Run while you can."

He heard the dying janitor choking the words out again, grinning while he said them.

"You can't hide. They'll find you."

One ring.

"Run while you can."

Thomas looked at the note. Scrawled carelessly. Written hurriedly.

"If they haven't found you yet, they soon will."

Two rings.

"Trust no one."

Three rings.

"Move quickly."

Someone picked up on the other end. "Hello?" It was a woman's voice. "Hello?"

"Yes, hello. I—uh—I'm trying to reach Peter Bishop's wife."

There was a brief pause. "She's not available right now. Could I take a message?"

"Who am I speaking to?"

Another pause.

Why does she have to think about her answers?

"Run . . . while . . . you . . . can."

The dying janitor's grotesque, grinning face flashed before his eyes.

Thomas quickly broke the connection.

Thomas walked back to the kitchen window and looked at the thermometer. The temperature outside and inside was still dropping. And it had started to snow again.

I never thought I'd be happy about a crippling ice storm. But one thing's for sure. No one's crazy enough to be out in weather like this. If someone is after these kids, at least the storm will buy us some time.

Thomas heard the creak of the sleeper sofa's springs, then the click of Gumbo's claws along the tile floor. The big dog yawned and padded over to Thomas, putting his head underneath his master's hand.

Thomas took the dog's front paws and put them on his chest. He gave the back of Gumbo's neck a vigorous rub with both hands. "Good morning, King Tut. Are we quite rested?" As he looked over the animal's shoulder toward the den, he saw the girl and her brother standing in the doorway.

• • • • •

Jeanette Marshall surveyed the chaos that used to be Peter Bishop's apartment. At Sawyer Wynne's insistence, she and two others had spent the entire night tearing the small flat apart, looking for some clue that would lead them to the stolen files. An entire night of searching turned up nothing.

Jeanette dreaded going back to her boss with bad news.

Hungry and tired, Jeanette was ready to lead her team home when the phone rang. A young woman went over to answer it.

"Hello? . . . Hello?"

She waved to Jeanette. "She's not available right now. Could I take a message?"

The young woman motioned for Jeanette to bring her something to write on. She covered the phone with her hand. "Someone's trying to reach Justine."

"Hello? . . . Hello?" She shook her head. "He hung up."

Beside the phone, a small caller ID box displayed the words "Thomas Kent, 903-555-6985."

Jeanette looked at her notes. The e-mail address Peter had used was tkent@texweb.net.

Tkent.

Thomas Kent.

Relieved, Jeanette pulled out her cell phone and pushed the auto-dial button.

"Mr. Wynne? We've found him."

15

"Y ou ain't never gonna amount to nothin', boy. Why, you
  ain't even worth the powder it'd take to blow you away."
Even thirty-five years later, the words still tormented.

For three-quarters of his life Sawyer Wynne had struggled to erase those words. Now, thanks to Justine Bishop,
it was all slipping away. And he didn't know if he could
prevent it.

Sawyer Wynne's treadmill sat in his spacious living
room, facing huge windows that took in a picturesque
view of the lake and the Syracuse skyline. The machine's
belt kept the little man going at a brisk walk while strains
of Mozart drifted from speakers built into the ceiling.
Sweat trickled down his face. Dark spots had formed on
the back of his shirt and under his arms. He glanced down
at the timer. Forty minutes gone, ten to go.

Wynne had retreated to his lakeside home late Friday
evening to wait for news from Jeanette. He found it impossible to concentrate at Chateau
Antoine. He desperately needed JAMES H. PENCE 93

to think, and he did that best when he was exercising. He had already put in forty laps in his indoor pool. Now, on his treadmill, his heart raced, pumping oxygenated blood to his brain. Sawyer Wynne's mind raced as well.

Jeanette's call had come in about dawn. They had traced the stolen files to the recipient. So far they only had a name, phone number, and general location. But Wynne knew it would be only a short time before they knew precisely where Thomas Kent lived. The question was, what to do then? Once Kent had the files, he could reproduce them and forward them on in a hundred different directions before Wynne would have a chance to recover them. Once that was done, it would all be over.

The other nagging problem was that Wynne had heard nothing from Sonny Pritchard since he had instructed him to follow the children. He presumed—hoped—that Pritchard was following the children to Justine. But based on Sonny's record, that was far from a sure thing.

He had only two choices, both risky. The first was to just keep the children under surveillance in hopes that this Thomas Kent, whoever he was, would try to pass the files on to Justine Bishop. The problem with that approach was that the information Peter Bishop sent this man was volatile. It would bring the Fellowship down, sending most of the members to prison. It could send Sawyer Wynne and Anthony MacAsland to death row.

Wynne's other option: forget about the children and send someone to recover the files and kill Thomas Kent. But the children were the last hold he had over Justine. Once they were safely with her, she would be free to go to the authorities and expose the Fellowship. On top of that, this was probably the last chance Wynne had to punish Justine for all the damage she'd done.

And he *would* punish her.

"Punish her? Ain't never gonna happen, boy. It's like I said. You ain't worth nothin'."

The owner of the voice was long dead, but it screamed in Sawyer's head like the relentless whistles of the freight trains that rushed past the tiny farm where he grew up.

Wynne ground his teeth together and turned the treadmill on high. He was jogging now. Rivulets of sweat streamed down his face.

He had been only eight when those words first ripped through his soul. His grandmother had sent him out to help his grandfather butcher chickens.

"I–I d-d-don't want to," Sawyer said.

His grandmother pointed at him with a wooden spoon. "You stop that stuttering, and don't give me none of your back talk. Now get out there and help Silas."

It was never "Paw-Paw" or "Grandpa" or even "Grandfather." His grandmother always called her husband "Silas." Sawyer always called him "Sir."

Silas Wynne stood in the chicken yard, clad in a red flannel shirt and dirty overalls. Beside him was an open fire with a large pot of boiling water. The steam blew in Silas's face. He wiped his balding head with a red bandanna.

"Get over here, boy," Silas growled. On his best days Silas Wynne sounded like he had a throat full of gravel. He had smoked three packs of cigarettes a day for too many years. "You're old enough to help out round here. Now, kill one o' them chickens and bring it to me."

Sawyer just looked at him, wide-eyed.

Silas Wynne scowled and got right down in the boy's face. Silas's body odor made Sawyer's eyes water, and his breath reeked of stale tobacco and whiskey. A two-day stubble of dirty gray whiskers covered his face. He grabbed Sawyer by the shoulders. "Now look here, boy. I don't have time to waste. These chickens gotta be butchered and you're gonna help."

Silas turned and grabbed a chicken that had wandered nearby. He took Sawyer's hand and put it around the chicken's neck. "You've seen me do it before. Now kill it," he growled.

Sawyer's eyes widened. He couldn't move. The best he could manage was a weak "N-n-no."

Silas cursed. Then he grinned at Sawyer—a scornful, mocking grin. "You afraid? Don't want to get messy?"

Silas's strong hands covered Sawyer's and forced him to wring the chicken's neck.

The deed done, Sawyer dropped the still-flopping bird at his grandfather's feet—and vomited on his grandfather's shoes. Sawyer never saw the hand coming. He just felt his grandfather's brutal backhand as it knocked him to the ground.

Sawyer licked away the blood that came from his swollen lip. He read the disgust on his grandfather's face. "You ain't never gonna amount to nothin', boy. Why, you ain't even worth the powder it'd take to blow you away. Get up."

Tears welled in Sawyer's eyes, and with a dirty hand he brushed his hair away from his forehead.

Silas Wynne grabbed him by the hair and pulled him to his feet. "I said get up!"

He let go of Sawyer's hair and grabbed him by his upper arms. He gripped the boy's arms tightly and shook him. Sharp pain shot down to Sawyer's fingers. "Now look here. Bertha and I took you in when your pa died and your ma ran off. She was never worth nothin' either. But I don't have the time to coddle you. You're goin' to pull your weight around here. Understand?"

Sawyer nodded.

"Now grab another chicken and kill it."

Tears streaming silently down his face, Sawyer obeyed.

"Now kill another one."

Sawyer obeyed. But it didn't do any good.

Sawyer learned to butcher chickens that day. He also learned that nothing he did was ever good enough for

Silas Wynne. No matter how Sawyer tried to prove himself, he was always "worthless." He grew to loathe that gravelly voice.

And he grew to hate the man who possessed it.

And when he had a chance, he silenced it.

Sawyer was sixteen when his grandmother sent him to carry lunch to Silas in one of the remote fields he was plowing. Sawyer took Silas's '57 Ford pickup, loaded a basket of fried chicken and biscuits, and drove out to the field. When he arrived, he found Silas pinned underneath the tractor. Somehow, the old man had managed to roll it.

"Thank God you're here, boy," Silas said. "Get some help fast. I'm bleedin' bad."

He was bleeding, indeed. The old man's face was nearly white. Sawyer was surprised he was still conscious.

Sawyer just stood there.

"Come on, boy," Silas said, his voice weakening. "What're you waitin' for?"

Sawyer walked around to the front of the truck, picnic basket in hand. He sat down on the front bumper, reached into the basket, and took out a chicken leg. A look of horror came across Silas's face as Sawyer bit into the piece of chicken.

"You gotta help me, Sawyer," Silas pleaded. "Please, son, don't do this."

Sawyer sat, watched, and waited. He was no doctor, but he knew that he wouldn't need to wait long.

Silas Wynne did not speak again.

About fifteen minutes later, when he was convinced that Silas Wynne was dead, Sawyer went for help.

He had silenced the voice—or so he thought. But Sawyer discovered that his grandfather's scorn was not so easily quieted. At every uncertain moment, Sawyer could hear Silas Wynne's disapproving comments haranguing him like an omnipresent heckler.

Sawyer convinced himself that the only way to rid himself

of the voice was to do something nobody else could do, attain something no one else could attain. He'd spent thirty-five years doing exactly that. And now it all hung in the balance because of a treacherous woman named Justine Bishop.

Sawyer Wynne had not forgotten her. For three years now she had successfully eluded the Fellowship's grasp. They knew she was somewhere in south Louisiana, but she had concealed herself so well they had no clue where. A sharp electronic beep pierced the air, signaling the end of Sawyer Wynne's fifty-minute workout. He switched off the treadmill and it rolled to a stop. Stepping off the machine, he grabbed a towel and began to rub his face. When his cell phone chirped, Wynne dropped the towel and answered immediately. He knew it would be Jeanette.

"Jeanette, what do you have for me?"

"The report just came in," she said. "We checked with the airline. A man named Thomas Kent picked up the children. He lives on a hundred-acre ranch about fifty miles northeast of Dallas. I e-mailed you his address information." Jeanette hesitated. "And, sir?"

"Go on."

"The recruit that was supposed to follow them?"

"Sonny Pritchard."

"Yes, sir."

"Well, what about him?"

"He's dead, Mr. Wynne."

"What happened?"

"His car crashed into a concrete pylon. When he didn't report as scheduled, his Mentor went to check on him. They finally found the hospital where he'd been taken, but it was too late."

"The fool probably deserved it," Sawyer Wynne said as he broke the connection.

Wynne smiled. Peter Bishop had made a fatal mistake in sending the files *and* the children to the same person.

Now Sawyer could wrap this all up without breaking a sweat.

He sat down at his dining room table and opened a laptop computer. Wynne pulled up and read Jeanette's e-mail, then opened another program and briskly typed in a complex ten-character password. Soon, a screen came up with a list of options. Wynne clicked on the fourth: *Conversion*.

Another screen instantly flashed up three more selections: "Regional," "Personal," "Osmosis." Sawyer Wynne clicked on *Personal*, then entered another equally complex password.

A data-entry screen came up. Wynne carefully typed in the data, reading from Jeanette's report.

Name: Thomas Kent
Address: 1229 County Rd. 8543
City: Grant City
State: Texas
Center Responsible: Dallas
Orders: Convert
Timetable: Immediate
Special Instructions: Retrieve Micah and Michelle Bishop.
Seize all computers and disks in the house. Hold for
instructions.

Then the Coral Snake moved the mouse pointer to a set of two buttons. One read *Submit*; the other, *Cancel*.

Wynne clicked on *Submit*.

The computer prompted, "Enter Password to Confirm."

Sawyer Wynne typed his password and pressed Enter.

The screen flashed the message: "Order confirmed. Estimated time to completion: 12 hours. Will notify upon conversion."

Sawyer Wynne leaned back in his chair. Within thirty

minutes, a conversion team would be dispatched. Inside of twelve hours, Thomas Kent would be dead, the information recovered, and the children in the care of the Fellowship.

Think you got the better of me, Peter Bishop? Think again. I'll find another way to get to Justine if I have to. Your children are mine.

Sawyer Wynne stood up and walked to the master bathroom. Time for a shower.

"M y brother needs to use the bathroom." The girl stood there, her hair frizzy and messy from the night's sleep. Her droopy eyelids revealed how sleepy she still was. But the fear that had been so evident in her eyes last night was gone now.

On the other hand, the boy showed no expression at all.

"Yeah," Thomas said, "it's just down the hall to your right." Thomas turned and pulled a flashlight out of one of the kitchen drawers. He handed it to her. "Here. He'll need this. There aren't any windows in the bathroom and the power's out."

The girl took the flashlight, a puzzled expression on her face. "He'll be okay, but I'll need it."

Thomas felt like kicking himself.

Sharp move, Kent. Offering a blind kid a flashlight. What'll it be next? Ask him if he wants to look at picture books?

Thomas looked around the

kitchen. He hadn't thought about it before, but the children would be hungry, and aside from frozen dinners, there was precious little to eat around his house. He pulled open his refrigerator door. The interior was dark, but even had the light been working, there wouldn't be anything to see except a few cans of Coke.

At least he had enough junk food in the pantry to take care of the immediate problem—hunger. Thomas pulled out two large bags of barbecue-flavored potato chips. He plopped the bags onto the table just as the boy and his sister made their way into the kitchen.

Thomas pulled out a chair for the boy. His sister took his hand and led him over to the chair and put his hand on the back of it. The boy felt his way along the back and side of the chair, easing himself onto it. His sister ambled toward the far end of the table and gingerly sat down on another chair.

For a moment the three stared at each other. Conversation hadn't been an issue last night. The children were too frightened and things were happening too fast. Thomas had been able to push aside painful memories and concentrate on surviving. Now, back in the quietness of his home, Thomas began to realize how difficult it was going to be having two children around. His heart ached every time he looked at these two helpless faces.

Feeling tears welling up in his eyes, Thomas began to fumble with a bag of chips, looking down at it rather than at the children. "Not much food in the house," he said, shaking his head. "No power. Can't cook anything." His voice thickened with emotion as the bag finally tore open. "We'll have to get by on junk food." He handed the open bag to the girl.

She took some chips from the bag and dumped them on the table in front of her brother. "Here, Micah, something to eat."

Thomas watched in amazement as the children

handled the chips. He'd expected them to dive in and gobble them by the handful. Delicately, the girl picked up a single chip. The boy felt the texture of his chip with his fingers, touched it with his tongue; all the while a puzzled look framed his face. The girl nibbled the end of one chip before looking over at Thomas.

"What are these?" Michelle asked.

"You're kidding, right?" Thomas said.

She looked expectantly back at him, her head cocked slightly to one side.

"Haven't you ever had potato chips?"

She just raised her eyebrows and shook her head.

"Ever eat potatoes?"

"Sometimes."

"Just think of these as potatoes with an attitude. Try some."

She put one in her mouth and scrunched her face.

Thomas laughed. "You look like you just ate a sour lemon. What's wrong?"

"It's salty. And hot! Do you have any water?"

Her question reminded him of the seriousness of their situation. "No, I don't. And we're going to have to figure out what to do about *that* problem pretty quick."

The sound of crunching brought Thomas's attention back to the table. The boy, at least, had developed a taste for barbecued potato chips. He began to eat them one at a time, as if he were savoring some expensive exotic food.

Thomas chuckled. "Look's like your brother likes them, anyway. What did you say his name was?"

"His name is Micah. And I'm Michelle." With a bit of pride, she added, "We're twins."

"Pleased to meet you, Micah and Michelle. You already seem to know my name. And this," he said, pointing to the German shepherd asleep on the floor, "this lazy bag of bones is Gumbo."

The dog's massive tail thumped the floor at the sound

BLIND SIGHT

of his name, but he kept his head down and eyes closed.

Thomas noticed Michelle was shivering. "What have I been thinking about? You two need to warm up. Come on. Let's get some coats on you. Then we'll figure out what to do."

Thomas went through the kitchen to where he'd dropped the children's coats the previous night. He carried them back to them. Michelle put her own on. Thomas helped Micah with his. "Here we go," Thomas said as he zipped the front of the coat up and pulled the hood over the boy's head, tightening its strings. "How's that feel?"

Micah's brown eyes just stared straight ahead. He said nothing.

Thomas looked at Michelle, a puzzled expression on his face.

"He's afraid," she said.

Thomas looked at Micah. "Micah. I won't hurt you. You may not believe that now. But I promise. I'm going to do everything I can to help you."

Thomas walked quickly toward a closet near the front door. He pulled out a heavy coat and put his arm in one of the sleeves. "First things first," he said, pulling the coat the rest of the way on. "We need food and we need to get warm. And we won't be able to do either here."

"Where are we going?" Michelle asked.

A dark expression crossed Thomas's face for a moment, then passed. "A place no one has ever seen but me." Thomas looked down at the sleeping dog. "Gumbo!" The shepherd clambered to its feet immediately. "Let's go to the cabin."

In far north Dallas, sprawled over two hundred fifty acres of prime real estate, lay a community of quiet, religious people. When they first began to build, the neighboring homeowners opposed it. Visions of temples and saffron-robed people dancing in the streets flooded many people's minds. But the members of the Fellowship for World Renewal quickly overcame the prejudice against them.

This was no shantytown they built. The group had money to work with, and they used it well. They built high-quality houses that rivaled anything around them. Their development functioned as a self-contained, gated community with its own community center, an Olympic-size swimming pool, its own grocery store, and its own church. The singular oddity of the group was that most of the members chose not to live in single-family dwell-ings. Each of the spacious houses harbored at least four families.

Unlike other groups, which

seemed extremist and isolationist, these folks enjoyed the company of their neighbors. Their landscaping and flower gardens were the envy of the Dallas Arboretum. They even adopted two miles of highway for litter cleanup. Not only did they clean up trash, they planted flowers and trees along the roadside as well.

Everyone around agreed the Fellowship for World Renewal was different. But in an atmosphere of religious tolerance, people also saw them as good citizens, not as fanatics. They certainly did their part in caring for the environment and making their small corner of the world more attractive. Five years passed, and the local neighborhood came to accept these people as equals, to trust them, and ultimately, to ignore them.

The followers of Antoine would have it no other way.

They were chosen to rule.

But before they could rule, they must infiltrate.

As a stone causes ripples on the still water of a pond, they would spread out from a central location. As a drop of red food coloring, left to itself, will eventually turn a gallon of water bloodred, they would slowly, imperceptibly seize power.

As the natural process of osmosis allows a plant to take in nourishment by slowly bringing in nutrients through a cell wall, so the Fellowship would osmose into society.

Not everywhere at first.

Not quickly.

Carefully, methodically, they would come to power.

And eventually, the rest of the world would obey them.

For that reason, the residents of the Dallas FWR Center worked hard to achieve anonymity. Their goal was to blend in, to be as inconspicuous as possible. Only then could they properly function. Only then could they do their part in helping Father Antoine achieve Osmosis.

The different members of the Dallas Center functioned much like members of an ant colony. New recruits lived exclusively at the Center, under the supervision of the Elders and Mentors. Elders directed the Center's affairs; Mentors supervised the novices. A novice was not permitted to pass the front gates unless accompanied by a Mentor. Spread among the various homes, novices functioned in more mundane areas such as food preparation, landscaping, and maintenance.

Their rank was identified by the color of the stone in the rings they all wore. A black, blue, or green stone indicated a novice. One who had to be taught. And watched.

Novices, when sufficiently indoctrinated, could be safely released into the world. Still under a Mentor's supervision but with more freedom, indoctrinates were given a ring with a lighter-colored stone. Pink or aqua indicated that they were ready for partial Osmosis. But instead of sending these members to raise funds in airports or sell flowers on streets, the FWR placed them in strategic jobs out in the world. Taught to blend in, those who achieved partial Osmosis appeared perfectly normal. Yet at the end of the day they would return to the colony and report on what they had accomplished for the Master.

A clear, diamondlike stone indicated the last level of the journey. This minority had achieved full Osmosis. They were the only ones who were permitted to live away from the Center. Their goal was to blend in, to become part of society. They were to be so inconspicuous, so normal, so perfectly camouflaged that not even the best investigators could detect anything unusual in them.

Ones who had achieved full Osmosis were so yielded to the will of Antoine, they would do anything they were told to do.

No questions asked.

Told to lie, they would lie.

BLIND SIGHT

Told to steal, they would steal.

Told to kill, they would kill.

All that mattered was Father's will.

Of this group, only the most elite were chosen for conversion teams. This select group of people had committed themselves to removing any obstacles from Antoine's path to power. They could be trusted to do the job carefully, properly, and discreetly. They didn't look at their actions as murder. Those given the honor of converting others viewed their responsibility as holy, as righteous. They were the representatives of Antoine. His personal angels of death.

In ten years, the teams had converted over one thousand people around the country. Not a single conversion had ever been traced back to the Fellowship.

They were helping Father achieve Osmosis.

On an icebound Saturday morning in Dallas, a team assembled in the FWR regional center to receive its instructions.

Three people stood before a computer terminal in the community center's office. Dressed in dark green goose-down parkas with fur-lined hoods tied tight around their heads, two men and a woman waited for the instructions to flash across the screen. The first man, average height, with coarse black hair peeking out from under his hood, typed in a password. The second man confirmed it. The woman typed in a third separate code.

A few seconds later, a ten-digit random sequence of numerals and letters flashed on the screen. To the casual observer, the alphanumeric sequence was unintelligible. To the three team members, it represented a code that informed the leadership in New York that the conversion attempt had begun. A laptop computer taken along with them was the means by which they would inform the Fellowship the moment conversion was complete. The black-haired man, the team leader, was the only one of the three who knew anything about the target.

The three walked silently outside to a waiting Range Rover. They were on their way to Grant City, Texas. The blue vehicle pulled out slowly, navigating the icy streets with care. The trip to Grant City would be tedious, but ultimately satisfying.

They would do Father's will.

T homas pulled the emergency release and raised the garage door. The pitch-black garage instantly flooded with daylight, revealing Thomas's pickup truck, and beside it a Yamaha four-wheeler. Climbing onto the four-wheeler, Thomas turned the key. The cold engine groaned and complained, but finally started with the noise of a thousand lawn mowers. Micah and Michelle covered their ears. Leaving the motor idling, Thomas hopped off and attached a small trailer.

He gestured toward the trailer. "Hop in."

Michelle led her brother to the trailer and tried to helphim climb into it. But Micah, unsettled by the noise and unaware of what he was climbing into, resisted her attempts at helping him. Gently, Thomas came alongside. "Come on, son. Put your arms around my neck." The boy quietly obeyed, and Thomas lifted him into the little trailer.

Michelle shouted over the four-wheeler's roar. "Why aren't we taking your truck?"

"Where we're going, the truck won't fit. Hop in."

As Michelle climbed into the trailer, Thomas pulled open a chest freezer and removed several large sacks. He handed them one by one to her. "Here. Put these beside you." Then he opened a storage room off one of the garage's walls and pulled out two cases of soda. "Not very nutritional, but that ought to tide us over for a bit," he said. "Let's go."

"What about Gumbo?" Michelle asked, her hands still covering her ears.

"He doesn't like the four-wheeler," Thomas shouted back. "Too noisy. He knows where we're going."

Gumbo already had made his way around the house, heading south toward a large wooded area.

Thomas hopped on the four-wheeler, gunned the engine once more, and gently rolled out of the garage. He swung the vehicle around to the front of the house. Stopping for a moment, he climbed off and walked back to the garage. Ice crunched like shards of glass underneath his boots. Thomas could feel the wind slicing through his coat like a thousand razor blades. He pulled the door down, then returned to the vehicle. Putting it into gear, he eased the throttle upward, and the huge wheels began to roll.

Thomas called over his shoulder, "You okay?"

Michelle nodded, giving Thomas a "please hurry" look.

About fifty yards ahead, Gumbo turned around and barked as if to say, "What are we waiting for?"

Snow blew across their path like a pure white sandstorm as they moved away from Thomas's house and down a gentle incline. A line of trees stood about two hundred feet away, apparently barring their path.

Up ahead, Gumbo ran with his nose to the ground, as if looking for a rabbit to chase. As the dog drew near the tree line, he darted off and disappeared into the woods. Thomas guided the four-wheeler, carefully follow-ing the dog's tracks. A small gap in the trees, invisible from a straight-on view, opened up before Thomas. He throttled the four-wheeler to a crawl. Slowly, the trio passed inside the tree line.

Gloom reached out from the trees to envelop them. To the left lay an immense pond. The water surface, frozen solid, was sprinkled with dry brown leaves. Dead branches jutted through the ice at various angles, looking like the bones of long-deceased creatures whose misfortune had been to stumble into an unforgiving, deadly pit. A tiny one-man boat, encrusted with ice, lay moored along the pond's edge.

Around the shore to Thomas's right, a small path circled counterclockwise behind the pond. Partially covered with crusty snow, the path was nearly obscured. Thomas knew the path well; so did Gumbo. Although the dog was nowhere in sight, Thomas could see his tracks.

Moving at a speed barely faster than a walk, Thomas urged the little four-wheeler around the pond's back edge.

As they reached the far end of the pond, the path moved into the trees. Thomas called this part of his woods "a claustrophobic's nightmare." Standing like dead gray pillars adorning both sides of the road, so thick were the trees that only a little light filtered through. The mass of cedars and intertwined branches of the willows and bois d'arcs isolated all who followed this path from the rest of the world. That's why Thomas had chosen to build out here.

Overhead the wind whistled through the branches, rustling and groaning a weary welcome as Thomas and the twins moved carefully along. Twigs snapped under the wheels as they rolled through the tight passageway.

Finally, the trees opened into a small clearing, barely fifty feet in diameter. A tiny shack stood at the back. Constructed like a box, the little building was not built for

BLIND SIGHT

aesthetic value. Unpainted siding, made of full sheets of four-by-eight plywood, had turned a mottled grayish black from exposure to the weather. Even the door was only a piece of plywood nailed to a two-by-four frame. A padlock sealed the building from intruders, although Thomas couldn't imagine intruders worse than coyotes or raccoons.

In front of the building sat a single plastic lawn chair covered with mildew and fallen leaves. A Little Smokey barbecue grill stood near the chair. In front of the chair were the remnants of a campfire, encased in a thick layer of ice.

Gumbo sat by the shack's front door. Ears erect, tongue hanging out, billows of vapor accompanying each breath. He gave his master a what-took-you-so-long look.

"Here we are," Thomas called behind him. He throttled all the way back and turned the key, allowing the engine to die. It coughed once or twice in protest, then fell silent. He looked over his shoulder at the children, who had huddled down into as tight a ball as they could possibly make. Micah's head was down, with Michelle's arms around him, covering him with her head and upper body. Slowly she lifted her head and looked around.

A strong gust of wind rattled the tree branches above them, sending down a dusting of snowflakes. "It's not much, but it will keep us alive," Thomas said, helping Michelle, then Micah, out of the tiny trailer. "Spend most of my time here, actually." Thomas looked around him, his beard flaked with snow. "Except in this kind of weather. Come on. Let's get inside and get warmed up."

Thomas unlocked the padlock. He had to tug on the door, but it finally gave way with a groan and opened. Michelle walked carefully over the fallen twigs and debris scattered around the outside of the cabin. Micah kept his left hand on her right shoulder as she led him inside.

Gumbo followed the two while Thomas grabbed the frozen sacks from the trailer and brought them in.

The shack was as spartan on the inside as on the outside. An army surplus cot and sleeping bag lined the back wall. Gracing the center of the plywood floor was a small woodstove, its chimney pipe running through the ceiling. On the far side of the room, Thomas had built a tiny plywood table and placed a metal folding chair beside it. A large plastic ice chest served as a refrigerator. In another corner, an Ozarka Natural Spring Water dispenser stood, a new bottle waiting beside it. And on the center of the table, a Coleman lantern would provide the light.

Thomas set the sacks inside the ice chest and walked back outside, leaving the children standing by the old cot. Soon he returned, carrying an armload of wood. Pulling open the front of the black-iron stove, he quickly began building a fire.

"What we need more than anything is heat. Then we'll talk about getting some food."

He tossed in some smaller scraps of wood and then tucked some paper underneath the rest. Striking a match on the side of the stove, he lit the paper, and the fire quickly engulfed the wood.

"There," he said, closing the door. "That'll get us nice and warm." Gumbo ambled up to the stove and plopped down in front of it. "See," Thomas said, "the fur ball knows where to sit. In short order we'll be as warm as toast fresh from the oven." Thomas had barely finished speaking when he heard his stomach growl.

"Uh, I guess I shouldn't talk about short orders and hot toast right now. Not till I fix us some grub. Now you two just pull the cot up by the fire and get warm. The only way I can cook around here is on Little Smokey outside." Thomas grinned. "Great day for a cookout, isn't it?"

Micah and Michelle, standing huddled together by the

cot, didn't respond. They just stared at Thomas. A hint of fear had returned to Michelle's eyes. "I'll be right back," Thomas murmured quickly and went back outside to the trailer.

"Stupid," Thomas chided himself as he reached into the trailer and pulled out a bag of charcoal. "You're rattling on and scaring the poor kids to death. They probably think you're crazy, bringing them out here to this dump." He ripped open the bag and dumped some charcoal into the pan. Grabbing a can of lighter fluid from the trailer, he doused the charcoal, then tossed in a match. Soon hot flames shot up from the canister-shaped smoker. The surge of warmth felt good against the backdrop of frigid air. Thomas put the lid back on. Steam rose and mingled with silvery smoke, drifting toward the flat gray of the sky above.

Thomas took a deep breath, silently telling himself to settle down. He had been keeping as busy and active as possible to avoid having to talk to the children. But he knew he couldn't put it off much longer. If there really was someone after these kids, he had to figure out what to do—and soon. And the only way to do it was to find out what he was up against. Unfortunately, neither Peter nor the janitor had given him anything more than dark hints.

Thomas looked through the trees back toward his house. During the spring and summer, the trees around the cabin completely blocked any view of the house. But this time of year he could see the outline of the roof. For a moment he thought he could hear the porch swing squeaking.

It didn't seem possible, but it had been almost twenty years since he and Jenny had built that house. She had inherited 150 acres from her father and couldn't bear to sell it.

Jenny had grown up in Grant City, an only child with a widower for a father. She didn't remember her mother, only that she'd died when Jenny was four and that her father chose never to remarry.

Instead, Jenny's father had devoted himself to raising her. He'd bought the acreage at a sheriff's auction several years before Jenny was born and had run Texas longhorns on it ever since. When Jenny's mother died, members of their church had taken turns caring for her while her father tended his herd. Eventually, when she wasn't in school, she'd accompanied him wherever he went. It wasn't long before she had her own horse and spent the bulk of her time helping her father.

She had grown up on this land, knew every rolling hill, every pond, every tree.

Her father died when Jenny was twenty. He didn't have much of an estate, but he left her the land. He wanted her to sell it all and use the money to take care of herself. Jenny chose to sell fifty acres and keep the rest of the land.

She used the money to send herself to North Texas Bible College, where she and Thomas met. Because he felt called to be a pastor, Thomas had enrolled there after graduating from the University of Texas.

To say that their romance was a "whirlwind" would be a gross understatement. It was more like a hurricane, with Jenny sweeping *him* off his feet. Thomas met her on the first day of class and knew that day that he wanted to marry her.

When he finally proposed, Thomas gave her a small pewter cross pendant along with the engagement ring. As he fastened the pendant around her neck, he said, "The ring represents my promise to marry you; the cross is my promise to always be there for you."

They were married in her home church, Grant City Bible Church, during Christmas break. Some of the people there joked that Jenny must have gone to a "bridal" college rather than a Bible college.

Thomas chuckled as he thought of it now.

By the time he graduated from the pastoral program at North Texas Bible College, Jenny's home church was without a pastor. It seemed only natural that they should call him. So Thomas became the pastor of Grant City Bible Church.

Instead of giving them a parsonage, the church members pitched in to help build them a home on Jenny's land. They moved in.

And life was wonderful.

They chose not to have children right away, but when Steven came along, followed by Sarah, Thomas knew he had been deeply blessed by God.

Pastoring a small but loving church.

A lovely wife.

Two beautiful children.

Their dream house on a hundred acres of north Texas woods and rolling hills.

Life couldn't have been better.

On lazy summer evenings Thomas and Jenny would relax on their porch swing as Steven and Sarah darted back and forth in front of sprinklers, squealing and laughing. Gumbo, just a puppy then, would join in the fray, barking and leaping after the children. Thomas could almost hear their voices again.

"Daddy, watch this," Sarah called.

"Look at me, Daddy." Steven's voice came through.

"No. Watch me." Giggles of sheer delight.

"Daddy, watch."

"DADDY, WATCH OUT!" The delighted giggles morphed into screams of terror.

"Daaaaadddy, helllp."

Thomas shut his eyes and whirled away from the scene, pounding his temples with his fists. "No! Stop it! Stop it!"

He collapsed to his knees, falling forward and catching himself with his hands. Tears streamed down his face as every muscle in his body trembled. For a few minutes, he remained on all fours, like a statue frozen in the snow. He scarcely felt the biting cold of the snow and ice on his fingers. His breath came in short gasps and he felt like his body had turned to gelatin.

I can't do it, Peter. I just can't do it. You've got to understand. I couldn't save my own children. How can I possibly save yours? I'll take them into town tomorrow and drop them off at Child Protective Services. They'll know what to do.

Thomas came up to his knees, wiping his eyes with the backs of his hands. The cold had penetrated his coat and he began to shiver. Looking back through the trees toward the house, Thomas said to himself, "I'll take them in tomorrow. It's the right thing to do."

Thomas pushed himself the rest of the way to his feet and stumbled back inside.

The Rover rolled at a slow but steady pace across the Lake Ray Hubbard Bridge toward Rockwall, Texas. While the lake itself hadn't frozen—it rarely got cold enough in Texas for that to happen—everything around it had been layered with multiple sheets of ice.

The residents stayed at home; almost nobody ventured out on this bleak day. The result was that the long bridge spanned a gap between two apparently dead cities. From Dallas to Rockwall, only a brave few could be found on the roads: truckers, people who had to go to work, and a blue Range Rover plodding east along Interstate 30.

In the backseat, forty-two-year-old Derek Rainart scraped his fingernails clean with a pocketknife. He studied the two members he'd chosen for his conversion team. Frank Torrance and Lupe Saldivar were loyal, albeit gullible, servants of Anthony MacAsland. Rainart himself had never been able to acquiesce to MacAsland's ego trip and call him "Father Antoine." But then, Rainart came to the Fellowship via a different path than they did.

His introduction to the Fellowship came when he answered a classified ad in a magazine that catered to mercenaries and survivalists. As he perused the ad section, Rainart noticed an enigmatic listing that read "Assembling an elite security force to protect a wealthy and powerful American. Need skilled and dedicated men and women willing to risk their lives for good pay."

Intrigued, Derek had phoned the number listed in the advertisement. A message on an answering machine told him to leave his name, address, and phone number. So he took a chance and submitted his vital information. Then he waited and hoped to have his lifelong dream fulfilled.

Guns and combat had fascinated Derek from the time he could point his finger and say, "Bang, you're dead." But unlike most boys, who as they matured either lost interest in guns or directed their interest into hunting or target shooting, Derek preferred darker activities.

Derek killed his first dog when he was nine. He moved on from there, mostly taking strays unfortunate enough to cross his path. Tempting them with food and treats, he would take them home and torture them mercilessly before he finally killed them. He found an adrenaline rush in shooting a dog or cat that he never experienced on a hunting trip with the guys.

But for years Derek nursed a desire to cross the ultimate line—to kill a human. He'd come close on a number of occasions, hanging around playgrounds and watching the kids. But he always stopped short. He didn't think it was a problem of conscience. As far as Derek could tell, he'd never had one. But despite the desire, the craving to kill a person, he hadn't gone through with it.

He convinced himself he was waiting for the right

opportunity. Perhaps he just wanted to be careful so he wouldn't get caught and wouldn't have to stop with only one person.

Then he saw the ad. He responded to it on a lark, not really expecting much. But he did think it would be neat to be in a position where he might have to kill someone and get paid to do it.

Within forty-eight hours of the time he'd responded to the classified, two men knocked at his door. At first he thought they were cops or the FBI. He almost ran out the back door. But before he could, they told him they represented the billionaire Anthony MacAsland and asked if they could come in. Never in his wildest dreams could Derek have imagined that he might be working for Anthony MacAsland.

That afternoon the two men personally escorted him to a training center where he underwent a physical, a battery of psychological tests, and countless interviews. When they told him he'd been accepted for the force, Derek couldn't believe his luck. He told them that he'd return for training as soon as he could get his affairs in order. They told him that wouldn't be acceptable. If he was to be a member of MacAsland's security, he had to disappear completely. It was the only way he'd be allowed to join the team, with total secrecy and anonymity.

It wasn't much of a decision for Derek. His family had disowned him years earlier, and he didn't much care for his minimum-wage job. So he agreed and began his indoctrination immediately. That was twenty years ago.

Ironically, in those twenty years he had never even met MacAsland, the man he'd been hired to protect. At first he thought it strange, but he quickly learned that he was to provide a different type of protection than he had expected.

He learned early on that he would report only to Sawyer Wynne, one of the two men who had come to his house, and that his job would be to "protect" MacAsland by taking out his enemies.

Derek admired Wynne deeply. Wynne was pragmatic enough to realize the necessity of having professionals direct his conversion teams. In the business of killing people, amateurs get caught too easily. The Fellowship could not afford to let that happen. But Wynne also was smart enough to know that he'd have better control over his hit men if he had personally recruited and trained them. Thus, Sawyer Wynne had created his own elite team—a group of young men without conscience, and loyal only to him.

Derek didn't know how many other men were on Wynne's "security force." In fact, he didn't *know* any of the other men. Secrecy was priority one. Derek was just proud to be one of the elite.

Wynne gave him his orders and he carried them out dutifully, although he didn't conduct each conversion personally. Often, he merely had the task of planning the perfect murder and assigning someone else to carry it out. He was always careful and always creative. And to this day, no one had ever even come close to catching him.

On special occasions, however, Derek took no chances and directed the conversion teams himself. Over the last twenty years, he'd personally directed fifty successful conversions. This would make fifty-one. Despite the lousy weather, he'd caught a red-eye flight out of Syracuse and connected into DFW. Even though he rarely saw Wynne face-to-face anymore, the instructions forwarded to him through the Fellowship's network were very clear: "No foul-ups accepted on this mission. Get it done right." Derek understood the message.

He didn't understand what Wynne was so worried about, though. This job looked to be a piece of cake. One man and two kids in an isolated location. Even the weather was working to his advantage. He knew his targets wouldn't be going anywhere. And if they were tipped off somehow, they couldn't run. With the roads the way they were, Thomas Kent and the Bishop twins would be snuggled up together, trying to stay warm.

Derek folded his pocketknife and put it in his pocket. It was the perfect setup. The perfect hit. He was confident his team members would perform well. He made it a point to know everything he could about the people who were assisting him.

Lupe Saldivar, the lone female of the team, grew up in the barrio. Although raised by devout Catholic parents, she had been recruited into a Hispanic gang before her twelfth birthday. She'd had two abortions before she was fourteen and had already spent time in a center for delinquents on an assault conviction. Written off as incorrigible by everyone who knew her, Lupe ran away one evening and wound up on the streets of Dallas. She was a hopeless sixteen-year-old heroin addict, working as a prostitute when the Fellowship found her.

Before she knew what was happening, they whisked her into a van and took her to their center in north Dallas. They cleaned her up and fed her, then took her through their own drug-rehab program. Inside six months Lupe had a new lease on life and a lifelong debt to Father Antoine. She committed herself to the Fellowship with the express intent of giving them the rest of her life.

Derek Rainart had chosen Lupe for this mission because of her background in the gangs. Once Thomas Kent had been dispatched and the children recovered, they would ransack his house and spray it with gang graffiti. When the sheriff finally discovered his body, there would be little doubt in the minds of the investigators that gang activity had migrated from the city to invade the once tranquil countryside.

Lupe sat in the front passenger's side of the Rover. Her long black hair framed a composed face with a dark complexion and eyes that looked like drops of India ink on white parchment. Rainart saw no hint of nervousness or troubled conscience in her demeanor. Good. Conscience was a fatal flaw.

Sitting next to her, driving the Rover, was a huge man with a pockmarked face and white hair cut into a flattop. Frank Torrance, a career truck driver, had been driving an 18-wheeler on a run from California to New York. In North Carolina he'd picked up an attractive young hitch-hiker who said she was on her way to Syracuse. Bored with radio and CDs and longing for someone to talk to, Torrance had picked up the hitchhiker, figuring he could always dump her if she was too much trouble.

By the time they reached Syracuse, she invited Frank to a special weekend meeting the Fellowship was having. She even promised to attend it with him. With a few days to kill before his next load, Frank agreed. Besides, how could he pass on such a gorgeous date?

When the weekend was over, Frank phoned his boss and quit his job, committing his life to the Fellowship. They assigned him to the Dallas Center, where he'd lived for the last five years. Now he drove for Father Antoine. His life was a ministry, helping to bring about the salvation of the world.

Derek had selected him for the team because of his driving skills. Frank Torrance would get the job done.

Derek recognized a fundamental difference between Torrance and Saldivar and himself. *They* were loyal servants of Father Antoine. *Derek* was a trusted employee of Sawyer Wynne. Together, they would eliminate the threat posed by Thomas Kent.

And they would return the children to Sawyer Wynne for his disposal.

The blue Range Rover methodically pressed its way toward Grant City.

Thomas felt as if he'd aged twenty years in five minutes. As he stepped back into the cabin and closed the door behind him, he struggled to find the right words to tell the children he planned to dump them.

"Look, kids, I'd really like to help, but I just—"

Thomas stopped when his gaze fell upon the children. They sat huddled together on the floor by the woodstove. Michelle had pulled the sleeping bag from the cot and thrown it around herself and her brother. In between them, ears erect and tongue lolling over the side of his mouth, sat Gumbo. Micah had his arm around the dog and was resting his head against the huge animal's furry shoulder.

A wave of guilt washed over Thomas. He couldn't tell them. Not just yet. These two kids had been ripped away from everything they knew and dumped into a ten-by-twenty ramshackle, plywood hut in the middle of a north

Texas ice storm. He'd have to break the news eventually. But not right now.

Thomas flopped down on the floor beside them. "Well, the fire's roaring away outside. Won't be long and I'll be able to throw some chicken and potatoes on the old smoker and we'll have a grand dinner. Till then, we'll have to make do on chips and candy bars."

He reached behind him and pulled one of the sacks toward him. Taking out a box of Snickers bars, he offered it to the children. Gumbo shoved his nose into the box, sniffing at its contents.

"Uh-uh. Not for you. You get these." Thomas pulled a rawhide chew bone from the sack and tossed it toward Gumbo, who made a perfect catch. The shepherd lay down between the children, propped the stick of rolled rawhide between his paws, and began gnawing contentedly.

When the children finished their candy bars, Thomas knew he had to break the silence.

"I guess it's time we had a little talk," Thomas said, his eyes looking at the floor. "We've been running so much since we first met last night. I guess it would really help me to know what's going on if I'm to try and help you. Your daddy sent me a little note."

"He's dead, isn't he?" A quiet voice spoke up.

It was the first time Thomas had heard Micah speak. The little boy stared straight at him. The mournful expression in Micah's sightless brown eyes pierced Thomas.

"We don't know that for sure," Thomas said.

Micah nodded. "He's dead. I know it. They killed him." Micah's chin quivered a bit, but he showed no other sign of emotion.

Thomas leaned toward the boy. "Who, Micah? Who are 'they'?"

Micah dropped his head. He said nothing more.

Thomas looked at Michelle and raised his eyebrows as if to ask her to continue for her brother.

"The Fellowship," she said. "We belong to Father Antoine."

"What do you mean? I thought you were Peter Bishop's children."

"Peter Bishop was our earthly father. But our true father is Antoine." Michelle reached into the box for another candy bar as she continued. "We belong to him."

The little girl was matter-of-fact about her revelation. But what struck Thomas was the difference in their reactions. She brushed back her curly blonde hair with her left hand, picking up another candy bar with her right, all the while explaining to Thomas that she and her brother belonged to someone called Father Antoine. But the whole time she was speaking, Micah kept his head down, shaking it back and forth as if he wanted to shout, "No. No. No."

"If you belong to this Father Antoine, why did your daddy send you to me?"

"He's sending us to Justine." Michelle spat out the name as if it left a bad taste in her mouth.

Thomas's eyes flicked over to Micah. The boy with the ratty brown hair silently formed a word. Thomas, though not a lip reader, had no problem figuring out what Micah was saying. He had mouthed the word *Mom*.

●　●　●　●　●

The digital clock on the dashboard of the Range Rover registered 12:32. Even with the help of the Texas Department of Transportation's sand trucks, it had taken them a little over two hours to make the drive to Grant City. A quick check of directions via a handheld GPS system, and the team quickly found themselves rolling along County Road 8543.

By the look of the tracks, only a few had ventured along

the rural road since the ice storm had set in. Derek Rainart scanned up and down the road as far as he could see. Not a vehicle in sight. The right side of the road was pastureland. The black and brown shapes of cattle standing by massive cylindrical bales of hay were the only living things in sight. On the left, a thick stand of trees limited Derek's view.

Frank Torrance rolled the Rover along at five miles per hour, carefully negotiating the gentle sequence of turns and rolling hills covered by the slick road. Lupe Saldivar had fallen asleep, her head resting against the passenger-side window.

But Derek was alert, assessing the situation, formulating a plan for an assault on Thomas Kent's house. According to the mapping program, they were within a mile of Kent's property. According to the intelligence e-mailed to Derek by the Fellowship's research teams, Kent's driveway would be off on the left, leading a half mile into the place before coming to the house. Because the driveway wound through wooded areas lined with cedar trees, they could actually drive in fairly close to the house before he'd be able to see them coming.

About a hundred yards ahead, Derek saw the black form that was almost certainly Thomas Kent's mailbox.

"Turn left up there." Derek's voice was cool and measured, as if he were merely directing Torrance to the house of an old friend.

Fresh snow crunched as Frank Torrance expertly wheeled the Rover into the driveway. When they neared the last bend in the road before Kent's house, Derek Rainart directed Torrance to pull over. Frank allowed the big vehicle to rumble to a stop. He killed the engine, then turned back to Derek. "What now?"

Derek pulled the fur-lined hood over his head and grabbed a pair of binoculars lying on the seat beside him. "You stay here. I'll cut through the woods and see what we've got to deal with." He pulled the handle and the door popped open, flooding the warm vehicle with cold air. "Leave the engine off. We can't risk them hearing it." Derek stepped out of the Rover and moved quickly into the trees.

Snow fell like fine dust in the air as Derek forged his own path through the tightly packed evergreens. Pine needles scratched his face, and scrawny blackberry thorns tugged at his trousers in the surprisingly dense undergrowth. Even though he'd been out of the car only a few minutes, his fingertips felt the sting of the cold. But he hated wearing gloves and wouldn't do it even in weather like this.

As he drew closer to the edge of the wooded area, he could see Thomas Kent's house standing about seventy yards away. Derek found a tight gap between two twenty-foot cedars. He lay down on his stomach and crawled underneath and between the two trees until he could get a clear view of the house while maintaining his own invisibility.

Putting the binoculars up to his eyes, he scanned the house for any sign of activity. The blinds were closed on all the windows. As he swept the house with the binoculars, something caught his eye in front. An irregularity in the snow. Zooming in tight, he saw the tire tracks of Kent's truck, something he'd expected to see. But he also observed another set of tracks. Wider tires on a narrower base. He followed the tracks as they curved from the garage doors in front of the house, down an incline toward a stand of trees off to his right.

The tracks appeared fresh. For some insane reason, Kent had left the house. Derek had no way of knowing why or if they had come back. So now he had to have two plans. One if the house was empty. Another if it was occupied. A broad grin spread across his face.
Derek loved a challenge.

• • • • •

"I don't understand," Thomas said. "Why wasn't your mother, Justine, with you?"

Michelle reached for the open bag of potato chips in front of her, pulled out a handful, and began to munch. She sipped an open can of soda that Thomas had given her.

"Father Antoine sent Justine away when we were—" she looked at the ceiling as if that would help her remember—"I guess about eight. She was a traitor and wouldn't obey Father anymore. So he said she had to leave." Michelle shoved another handful of chips into her mouth and washed them down with more soda.

Micah shook his head. Thomas noticed but chose not to pursue it.

"And your dad, Peter. Didn't he have to leave too?"

"Oh no. He was important to Father. Father would never send him away."

Thomas looked over at Micah. His head faced downward and his eyes were closed. He appeared to have withdrawn into his shell again, reacting neither positively nor negatively to what his sister was saying.

"So why did your father send you to me and ask me to take you to Justine?"

The little girl's face darkened. Her bottom lip pooched out in a pout. "I didn't want to leave."

Thomas took a deep breath, trying to summon the courage to break the news to these children that the only person they trusted was about to send them away. He closed his eyes, almost as if he were breathing a silent prayer. "Michelle, Micah, we've got to talk about something. I just don't think I'm the right person to . . ."

Thomas heard Micah whisper something. It was almost inaudible. The little boy's lips moved but scarcely a sound came out. All Thomas could make out was "He wants to."

"Micah? Did you say something?"

This time the boy spoke a little louder. In an almost robotlike monotone, Micah said, "He wants to kill her."

"Your father? Peter wants to kill her?"

"Mr. Wynne wants to kill her," Micah said.

Michelle's face reddened. "Micah, that's not true."

"Yes it is, Michelle."

"Who's Mr. Wynne?" Thomas asked.

Micah kept his empty gaze fixed on the floor in front of him. "Mom wants to stop him. He's been trying to find her, but she's hiding."

Thomas said, "Is Peter part of the plan? Did he agree to try to trap your mom?"

Micah shook his head.

"Why did he ask me to take you to her, then? Isn't that playing right into their hands?"

Micah looked in the direction of Thomas's voice. "He wanted to get us away from there. He hoped we'd be safe with you."

"B-but I don't understand," Thomas stammered.

"He wanted you to take us and the files he sent you. Get us to Mom. He wanted you to help her stop Mr. Wynne before it's too late."

"Stop him from doing what?"

Micah again turned his vacant gaze toward Thomas. He was about to answer when a low rumbling sound stopped him. Unnoticed during the conversation, Gumbo had stood and moved silently to the cabin's door.

Thomas looked toward the shepherd. Gumbo's head was down and the hair along his spine stood erect. The muscles of his body were tensed and his ears alert. A low, throaty growl escaped from the dog's mouth.

Micah reached over toward his sister and grabbed her hand. "They found us," he said quietly.

• • • • •

Tick. Tick. Tick.

The brass door knocker resonated through the metal door, sounding like a woodpecker trying to work its way into a tin can.

Lupe Saldivar waited a few seconds for a response. When no one answered, she tried the knocker again, this time harder.

Tack! Tack! Tack! Tack!

Acid-cold air stung Lupe's cheeks as it rushed around the front porch of Thomas Kent's house. The porch swing careened wildly back and forth as if a troop of ghostly children rode it, trying to see how high they could go.

After waiting for what seemed like an eternity, Lupe tried the door one final time—this time with her fist.

Bam! Bam! Bam!

She called out in her best helpless-female voice, "Hello? Is anyone there? I need help. My car slid into a ditch down the road, and I need to use the phone. Please. I have small children in the car. We need help bad."

She waited again.

Then she stepped to a window and peered through cracks in the blinds into Thomas Kent's large living room. She could see only the living room and dining room from this vantage point. And not very well at that. But from what little she could see, she didn't detect any movement or activity. She walked to the end of the porch and stepped off the concrete into the encrusted snow. Her feet broke through the top layer of snow to the ground beneath as she walked around the north corner of the house.

"Nobody home," she said to the two figures huddled against the garage door.

"Why would they leave?" Frank Torrance asked.

Derek Rainart shrugged. "Don't know. But they'll get a huge surprise when they get home. Let's find a way inside."

Frank observed the tracks leading off toward the

woods. "Probably won't do any good, but we shouldn't ignore the obvious." He grabbed the frigid, steel garage-door handle and tugged. With groans and squeals of protest, the door rolled upward.

The team stepped inside. Frank was about to pull the door closed when Derek held out his hand to stop him.

"Wait. Lupe, find a light switch."

Lupe ran toward the garage's inside wall and flipped a switch by the door. Nothing happened. She switched it on and off several times, as if for emphasis. "No power," she said, looking back toward Derek and Frank.

Derek nodded toward Frank Torrance. "Leave it up. Let's roll."

The three moved wordlessly into action. Lupe reached into the deep pockets of her jacket and pulled out two cans of black spray paint. Frank unzipped his parka and took out a 9mm pistol equipped with a silencer. From underneath his coat, Derek withdrew a double-barreled, sawed-off shotgun.

Derek stood facing the door that led into the house, both barrels directed toward it. Lupe stood to the side. Frank grabbed the doorknob, twisting it gently. He pushed the door open and stepped back out of the way. Derek took the lead, stepping into a tiny mudroom. He pointed toward the large dog bowls sitting on the floor. Frank and Lupe nodded. They didn't need a translation. Watch out for a dog.

Derek stopped, listening for any sound of movement. Frank and Lupe held back behind him, waiting in the garage. The mudroom door stood open so Derek had a clear view of the empty kitchen. He stepped quickly into the large room and swung the barrel of the shotgun around. A small den, with an open sleeper sofa, was off to the right. Derek checked the room quickly, making sure nobody was hiding there. Then he signaled the other two to follow him.

They moved through the kitchen and into the dining room. Both rooms were immaculate—almost as if nobody lived there. Down a short windowless hallway stood four doors, two on the left and two on the right. Through the nearest door, Derek could see a bathroom sink.

Derek decided to tackle the darkened bathroom first. He held out his hand toward Frank, signaling for a flashlight. Frank pulled one from his parka and came up beside Derek. At Derek's signal, Frank turned the light on and shone it into the room. Derek quickly swung around, ready to fire off two blasts into the tiny bathroom as soon as he saw movement. There was none. The bathroom was empty.

Three doors were left. Derek pointed to the two on the left side of the hallway. Frank and Lupe took their positions at each door. "On three," Derek whispered, taking his position at the lone door on the right side of the hall. "One. Two. Three."

Simultaneously, the three kicked the doors. Wood splintered as the hollow-core doors easily gave way.

"Look at this," Frank called.

The other two joined him in the first small bedroom.

It was a little girl's room. Pink lace curtains. A fluffy pink comforter with bunnies stitched into the fabric and a large pile of stuffed animals covered the bed. A massive stuffed panda sat in a rocking chair. At the head of the perfectly made bed lay an eight-by-ten gold picture frame holding the portrait of a little girl who looked about five years old. Black hair, deep brown eyes, and a vivacious smile radiated from the face in the photograph. At the bottom of the portrait, someone had inserted a note under the glass: "Sarah. My sweetheart. Love, Daddy."

Silently, the trio moved to the next bedroom. It, too, was perfectly preserved. Soccer trophies covered the top of a dresser. Several team portraits stood behind the trophies. Beside the photos, an oval opening in the cardboard frame held the picture of a ten-year-old boy with sky blue eyes, golden hair, and an I-can-lick-the-world grin on his face. Beneath the frame was the name "Steven Kent."

An NFL bedspread covered the bed, and on the pillow lay a gold-framed portrait of Steven Kent. The note at the bottom of the picture frame read, "Steve. My champion. I'm proud of you. Dad."

The team moved to the master bedroom. This room smelled faintly of perfume. It, like the others, appeared to be frozen in time. Memorabilia from a marriage decorated the room. Scrapbooks lay neatly arranged on the dresser, displaying pages filled with theater-ticket stubs, souvenir restaurant menus, photographs from a vacation to the Bahamas. On the queen-size bed, in a sixteen-by-twenty gold-leaf frame, lay a glamour portrait of a beautiful woman. In front of the picture lay a small cross on a silver chain. Below the cross was a note. It read, "I wasn't there for you. I'm sorry. Thomas."

The three examined the room, shocked into silence by the surreal nature of the scene before them.

Frank Torrance finally broke the silence. "Place feels like a mausoleum."

Derek looked around him, a sneer curling his upper lip. "Yeah." He turned to Lupe and Frank. "Trash it." He turned toward the door and walked out of the bedroom. Behind him he heard the sound of shattering glass and the crash of overturned furniture. Soon he caught the caustic smell of spray paint.

Derek ambled to the living room window and pulled the blinds apart a crack. He looked out at the tracks that went off toward the woods.

Where did you go, Thomas Kent?

* * * * *

Thomas Kent edged his way around the frozen pond. He had reassured the children that Gumbo was probably growling at a raccoon or coyote, but he knew better. The shepherd had as many different barks and growls as most people had facial expressions. A coyote or raccoon would draw urgent barking and tail swishing, followed by a mad dash through the door as soon as Thomas opened it.

Gumbo reserved the low, throaty growl for times when unknown or unwelcome visitors were making their way toward the Kent house. Gumbo had positioned himself away from the door between the intruders and the children, apparently ready to defend Michelle and Micah if necessary.

Thomas left the kids with the dog, telling them that he would check around just to make sure it was safe. Now he had made his way all around the pond and to the tree line facing his house. The house appeared quiet. He saw nothing out of order.

Maybe the old dog's losin' his touch.

Thomas was about to turn around and head back to the cabin when movement caught his eye. He waited, not sure if he'd actually seen anything. The movement had come from the master bedroom window.

There it was again. The blinds moved against the window, almost as if something had been thrown up against them.

He watched for another full minute; he saw nothing else.

But Thomas Kent was certain.

Someone was in his house.

• • • • •

"So. What do we do now?" Frank Torrance asked.

Lupe Saldivar sprayed the last of her black paint on the living room wall, adding some artistic flourishes to the shape of a shark with sharp teeth and a vast gaping mouth.

"For now," Derek said, "we wait."

"What about the computers and disks?" Frank asked.

"They're not going anywhere. We'll get them *after* Kent and the children are taken care of," Derek replied.

"What if they ran?" Lupe asked.

"They haven't," Derek said. "Kent must have a cabin back in those woods somewhere. Power's out. No heat. No food. He's trying to get the kids warmed up and fed."

"How do you know he didn't leave for a motel? Or go stay with a neighbor?" Frank asked.

"Truck's still in the garage. And the tracks around the front of the house are too small to be anything but a small ATV." Derek fixed a cool glance on the front door. "No. Our friend Thomas hasn't gone far. He'll be back. Maybe to get more supplies. Or he'll come back with the children when the power's back on. Sooner or later he'll come waltzing through the door."

"But we can't wait forever," Lupe protested. "Father's will must be done as soon as possible."

"It will be," Derek said. "The sun will be going down in about four hours. If he hasn't come back by nightfall, we'll get the night vision goggles and go after them." Derek ran his hand up and down the barrel of the shotgun, anticipating the fun to come. "Don't worry. Thomas Kent isn't going anywhere."

● ● ● ● ●

Thomas trudged back around the pond toward his cabin. He couldn't believe what was happening to him. All in the world he wanted was to be left to wither and die in his own way. He wanted to hide from the world. Now the world was flooding in around him. Two kids he didn't want had been dumped in his lap. Somebody had broken into his house.

Into the bedrooms.

Into *their* bedrooms.

A flash of anger warmed his face in spite of the cold. They had no right. No right at all to go there. No right to violate the sanctity of those rooms.

But the hot anger that flowed through Thomas quickly chilled as the dying janitor's words echoed again in his mind: *"You can't hide. They'll find you. Run while you can."*

As he neared the cabin, Thomas broke into a jog. He passed the little smoker, smelling the mesquite-smoked chicken as it cooked. He pulled open the door and stepped inside.

Micah and Michelle sat together on the army surplus cot, the sleeping bag wrapped around their shoulders. Gumbo stood guard in front of them. The big shepherd ambled over to his master, wagging his enormous tail.

Thomas patted the dog's head, then went over and knelt down in front of the twins. "Micah, Michelle, somebody is in my house. We've got to get out of here."

"How?" Michelle asked.

"I can bundle you two up with Gumbo in the trailer. We can use the four-wheeler to cut through the woods. I'll take some wire cutters with us so we can get through the neighbors' barbed-wire fences. Then we'll go overland into Grant City. We'll call the sheriff from there. If y'all stay huddled together, you'll be plenty warm."

"That won't help," Micah said. "You've got to take us to Mom."

"Justine," Michelle corrected.

Thomas dropped his head. "Micah, look. I'm not the man to help you. This is too big for me. The best thing I can do is to turn you over to the authorities. They'll protect you. And they can—"

"NO!" Micah shouted, his eyes staring at a blank wall. "*You* have to help us. You're the only one who can. Daddy chose *you*."

"Your daddy was wrong!" Thomas shouted back. He heard the anger in his voice, but he was helpless to control it. "I'm not a hero. I'm a coward. I run away from trouble." He walked to the far end of the cabin and leaned with his palms against the wall. He continued as if nobody else was in the room.

"Reverend Thomas J. Kent. Pastor. Civic Leader. Example to one and all." Bitterness and self-reproach tinged his voice. Tears streamed down his face, trickling into his beard. He continued speaking into the bare wall, his voice trembling with emotion. "Reverend T-Thomas J. Kent. The man who couldn't save his own family. Sentence by the state: two years, suspended. Sentence by God: unspeakable guilt for the rest of his life." He turned back toward Michelle and Micah. He looked at the floor and shoved his hands into his pockets. "I can't help you."

For a long time, the only noise in the room was the steady ticking of a battery-operated quartz clock on the wall.

Then Micah spoke, looking in Thomas's direction. His voice was weak, timid, barely audible. "But we need you. The only place we'll be safe is with our mom. No matter where else you take us, they'll find us, just like they found us here."

Thomas flopped down to the floor and leaned his back against the wall, his arms around his legs, resting his head against his knees. Gumbo whined and walked to his master. He shoved his muzzle underneath Thomas's arms and tried to lick his face.

"They won't leave you alone either," Micah whispered. "Not now."

Thomas felt a hand on his arm. He looked up and found himself face-to-face with Micah.

"Uncle Thomas. They'll kill you."

Thomas looked Micah in the eye, even though he knew the boy couldn't see him. "Son, I died two years ago. My body just hasn't caught up yet."

Still grasping Thomas's arm, Micah said, "They'll kill us too. When they're done. When they have what they want. They'll kill us."

Thomas looked toward the

BLIND SIGHT

cot. Michelle sat with her hands clasped together in her lap. Thomas turned his gaze back to the little boy who held his arm. Stringy brown hair spilled down into Micah's dark eyes.

These kids deserved better than what life had handed them. And, for better or for worse, they had now been handed over to him.

Shaking his head, Thomas said, "Your dad made a lousy choice of heroes, kid. I can't make any promises. We'll just have to take it a day at a time. For starters, how are we even going to find your mother? Peter didn't give me a clue about where to look, except that she's somewhere in Louisiana," Thomas said.

"I can help," Micah said calmly.

"What? You know her address?" Thomas said, half mockingly.

"No, but I know where to start looking," Micah replied.

"Oh, great," Thomas said, "I have a ten-year-old guide."

Still holding Thomas's arm, Micah felt his way up Thomas's arm until he found his ear. Micah whispered, "John 9:21."

"What did you say to him, Micah?" Michelle demanded. Micah didn't respond, and Michelle flashed an angry glare at her brother.

Thomas recalled the verse Peter had led him to. In context, the "meaningless" verse now made sense to Thomas. Two simple words originally spoken about a man born blind: "Ask him."

Good thinking, Peter.

Thomas nodded. "Okay, even if we know where to start looking, we still have two other problems. One, my truck is still in the garage. And two, those files your dad sent me are on a floppy disk inside my house."

"And three," Micah added, "*they're* up there!"

"Yeah," Thomas said. "*They're* up there!"

The antique china place settings on Sawyer Wynne's polished mahogany dinner table were worth more than some people's houses. Wynne sat alone at the head of the table, sipping springwater from a crystal goblet while he waited for his dinner to be brought to him.

He had come a long way since Silas's untimely death, trying to silence his grandfather's scornful words, trying to prove that Sawyer Wynne could, indeed, amount to something. Ironically, the old man had provided Sawyer with the perfect means.

Silas Wynne had held everyone and everything in contempt, but he had reserved special animosity for religious folks. He used to mock people when he saw them going to church. In those rare moments when his grandfather was in a pleasant mood, he would nudge Sawyer with his elbow and say, "Those idiots'll believe anything. In fact, if you want people to follow you, tell 'em a lie. And the bigger the lie is, the more dedicated they'll be."

BLIND
SIGHT

When Sawyer entered Syracuse University as a freshman, he'd already decided on his life's work.

He was going to start his own religion. But Sawyer planned to do more than gather a ragtag group of followers and head off to some desert retreat. He was going to create a religion that would wield power at the highest levels of society.

He would show the world that Sawyer Wynne did indeed amount to something.

True, he wasn't able to do it on his own. He was wise enough to know that he didn't have the charisma to develop a following. He needed a front man, and he found one in fellow student Anthony MacAsland. A spoiled rich kid just dying to rebel against Daddy, MacAsland fit the bill perfectly. He fairly dripped with charisma, and as an added benefit he also dripped with money. Wynne had his messiah, not to mention unlimited financing. And as long as he allowed MacAsland to feed his own ego, MacAsland was happy. No matter how frustrating it was to deal with Anthony at times, Wynne knew that MacAsland was the perfect choice for a front man. Very few men could inspire blind loyalty on the part of his followers yet function seamlessly with the outside world. Much as Wynne hated to admit it, he needed MacAsland.

Wynne was also aware that he couldn't be everywhere at the same time. With a growing organization, it was essential that new recruits be properly brainwashed. It didn't take him long to recruit Jerry Braddock, a confidence man with an eye for a good scam, who had run almost every con game known to man. Given Braddock's checkered past, Wynne agreed that a name change was in order. From the day he joined Wynne's inner circle, Braddock was known only as Llewelen. He kept the recruits in line.

But the prize player in Wynne's bull pen was Derek Rainart. Rainart had taken longer to find. In fact, Wynne and Llewelen had screened scores of "applicants" for the job. They needed someone with no scruples, someone who loved to kill, yet someone stable enough not to be counterproductive. After wading through every conceivable type of sociopath, they had found Derek Rainart. Rainart cleaned up the messes. He kept people from revealing what Wynne and the others were up to. Rainart's planning and execution were flawless.

Which is why Wynne could relax and eat his dinner in peace. Even now, Rainart was cleaning up the mess created by Peter and Justine Bishop. Soon, all would be under control again. Soon, Wynne's project would be back on track.

"Here's your salad, Mr. Wynne," said a young man dressed in a white robe. He set a large vegetarian salad before Sawyer Wynne. "Dressing on the side, as you requested."

Wynne nodded, dismissing the young man.

Wynne held up his glass in a mock toast. "Here's to you, Silas."

* * * * *

The winter night air was still bitter cold, but at least the wind had died down. Thomas was thankful for that. As he skirted the tree line around the back of his property on foot, he glanced toward the sky. The clouds had finally moved east, leaving a dazzling array of stars on display. It was the kind of sight that used to capture Thomas's imagination for hours. Undiminished by city lights or even security lights, thanks to the power outage, and with only a quarter moon gracing the blackness, tonight's sky had become a wonderland.

Filled with more stars than a person could possibly imagine, the splendor of the heavens used to offer Thomas a quiet reminder that God was still in control. Grim faced, Thomas now turned his attention back to the task at hand. He wasn't sure God was in control anymore. If God was in control—and He was good—how could He let anything happen to three such beautiful people as Jenny, Steven, and Sarah? And how could He allow the countless tragedies that happen all over the world every day? And how could He allow evil people to exist and prosper?

Thomas still didn't know what to think about the Fellowship and all the fanciful stories the kids had told him as they devoured smoked chicken and washed it down with diet soda. It all sounded too far-fetched to believe.

Still, he couldn't deny what happened at the airport. But there *were* other possible explanations for that. The world was full of crazies who wanted to kidnap defenseless kids for their own warped purposes. Maybe the janitor last night was one of those sickos.

He also couldn't deny that someone had broken into his house. Fellowship or no Fellowship, he was being careful. He didn't know who was in his house, or if they were even still there, but Thomas was taking no chances.

Assuming the intruders were still in the house, the power outage gave him a distinct advantage. His computer was in the den, near the back door. He knew the layout well enough to find his way in the dark, snatch the computer disk, and rejoin the kids. That is, if the intruders were watching the front and not the back.

But even if he did get the disk, he'd never get to the truck without them hearing him. So, when he returned to the cabin, they'd take the four-wheeler and trailer overland into Grant City. He had some friends who would loan him a truck without asking questions. And, hard as it would be, he could leave Gumbo with them. Too hard making this kind of trip with the big dog.

Thomas was thankful he had taken so many nocturnal walks. Many nights, when sleep fled from him, he aimlessly strolled Jenny's hundred acres. In two years he had become as familiar with this land at night as during the day. Now he completed the circuit of the trees behind his house and stood about a hundred yards from his back door. This was the most dangerous part of his approach. Except for a couple of large junipers, he would have no cover as he crept toward the door.

Thomas crept toward the door, pulling his keys from his pocket. He had taken off his bulky winter gloves so as not to accidentally drop the keys. In this darkness and snow, he might not find them again. A thick layer of ice covered the brass doorknob. Thomas gently inserted the key into the lock, then turned it as slowly as he possibly could. He felt the dead bolt draw back into the door and heard a muffled *click*.

The knob felt slippery and stung his already stiff fingers. Thomas eased it to the right until he felt the door latch give way. Gently pushing forward, Thomas entered the pitch-black house.

Unaided now by moonlight, Thomas relied totally on his memory. He knew he was standing in the mudroom. Thomas stretched out his left hand until he could feel the washing machine's cold surface. Three or four steps straight ahead would take him into the kitchen. Inching his way forward, keeping his hands out in front to guard against bumping into things, Thomas wondered if this was what it was like for Micah. Never able to see what was around him. Always unsure of where to step. Relying on touch and his memory to allow him to navigate.

Thomas's fingers felt the door's sharp edge, and he carefully moved it out of his way. He sensed the doorframe off his left shoulder. Taking another step, he could feel he had entered the kitchen. Thomas stood still for a moment, straining to hear any movement.

Total silence.

Whoever they were, they must be sitting quietly in the

house, like deer hunters waiting in a blind. Not moving. Not making the slightest sound. Waiting for their unsuspecting quarry to wander by. And in the next instant, blasting them into eternity.

Thomas was the quarry.

But where are the hunters?

The darkness felt like a cavern to Thomas, and for a moment he felt paralysis gripping him. He hardly dared to breathe, waiting and listening for an eternity.

No good staying here, Kent. If you don't move, they'll get you for sure. So go for it. Thomas took two sideways steps to the right, aligning himself with the entrance to his den and makeshift bedroom.

He was about to step forward when he heard a sound. A surge of acid rushed through his stomach. The electric hum of the refrigerator's compressor signaled the last thing on earth he wanted right now. The power had come back on!

Delayed for a few seconds by the frigid temperatures, the fluorescent lights in the kitchen and dining room flickered. Then in an unwelcome burst of brilliance they came to life.

Thomas stood for a second as if hypnotized; then the spell was broken by a beeping sound coming from the den. His computer was booting up. Noting that the den was empty, Thomas crouched down and moved in, staying close to the wall and trying to remain silent. Thomas waited in the still-darkened room.

No sound. No movement.

Surely they would have turned the lights back off by now. Either they were never here, or they left, or . . .

"They're on their way to the cabin," Thomas said out loud. He grabbed the black computer disk where he had saved Peter's files and thrust it into his shirt pocket, then whirled around and dashed toward the front door. He had to get to the cabin before it was too late.

As he entered the dining room, he stopped dead. "No," he said, shaking his head. No other words could escape his mouth. He stood, dumbstruck by the devastation before him. The walls were covered with black paint. Graffiti of some kind. The dining room table had been overturned, the crystal vase and its roses smashed.

Thomas forced his feet to follow the path of destruction. The bedroom doors stood open. He walked into the master bedroom and turned on the light. Someone had overturned the dresser. Graffiti marred the walls and the furniture. But Thomas's eyes were drawn to the floor.

The gold-leaf frame lay broken into several pieces, its glass smashed. As if instinctively knowing they could inflict no greater pain on him, they had ripped Jenny's photograph into tiny pieces. Jenny's cross lay in the midst of the shattered glass, its chain ripped off.

Thomas knelt by the broken photo, sifting bits of glass and torn photo in his hands, not caring that the glass pricked his fingers in several places, drawing blood. He took Jenny's cross in his bleeding fingers.

The cross is my promise to always be there for you.

His head dropped. He squeezed back the tears, bit his lip. Had to keep control. He didn't want to, but he had to check the other bedrooms. See what else they did. Thomas slipped Jenny's cross into his pocket and walked across the hallway to Steven's room.

Someone had snapped all of Steven's trophies in two, like dry twigs. His portrait, like Jenny's, lay shredded into tiny pieces. Sarah's room was a nightmare. Her stuffed animals were ripped open and strewn about the room. Someone had slashed her picture. Deep knife marks across her beautiful little face. Scars that would never heal.

Thomas felt like a zombie. The intruders had ripped his soul from his body as adroitly as a seasoned fisherman guts a fish. He wished they had just killed him outright. That way he'd be beyond hurting. He slumped against the doorframe, almost catatonic. Staring. Gazing at the devastation.

Then a voice rang out in the inner recesses of his mind. A voice he'd heard too many times in the last two days. Peter Bishop's voice.

"Save my children!"

With the resolve of a man with nothing left to lose, Thomas returned to his study and pulled open the bottom drawer of his filing cabinet. Tucked back behind the files was a Smith & Wesson .32 caliber revolver. Thomas had bought it a year earlier, intending to kill himself, but had never mustered the courage—if that's what you call it— to take his own life. He pulled the gun from the drawer, made sure it was loaded, and headed back toward the cabin.

● ● ● ● ●

Lupe Saldivar despised the night vision goggles. They gave everything a sickly green color, like a painting done by a preadolescent boy who has seen too many monster movies. They also felt bulky and unnatural, and she found it difficult navigating in them. She felt particularly nervous as she trudged the precarious route around the pond.

Walking single file behind Frank Torrance and Derek Rainart, Lupe didn't like how this conversion was proceeding. There had been too long a delay and too many unexpected turns. It wasn't supposed to be this difficult.

She was committed to doing Father Antoine's will. But if it wasn't done properly and they were caught, she knew the Fellowship would abandon them. A convenient explanation for her actions would be found, and any connection with Anthony MacAsland would be carefully covered up. She understood that this was how it had to be. She knew she was but one small part of Father's overall plan. If she had to be sacrificed to advance or protect the Project, so be it. But she quailed at the possibility of losing her place of service to the Master.

Lupe accepted the fact that she had to make whatever sacrifice was necessary for Father, whether it be giving her own life, taking someone else's, or remaining silent and taking the blame for what the evil world system called a "crime." She was psychologically prepared for that possibility, but she didn't want to experience it as reality.

Nevertheless, as the trio came around to the back side of the frozen pond, Lupe followed dutifully, clutching her pistol and giving her full attention to her team leader. She watched him as a dog watches its master.

Her attention was focused solely on Derek Rainart.

And she was caught totally off guard when a gloved hand covered her mouth and she felt what she guessed was a gun barrel pressing into her back.

A man's voice whispered in her ear. "Not a sound. Understand?"

She nodded.

"Give me the gun."

She raised her right hand, and the person behind her took the 9mm from her.

"Now the goggles."

Lupe pulled the night vision goggles from her face and was instantly plunged into blackness so deep she felt as if she were swimming in ink.

A hand reached from behind her and took the goggles.

"Let's go quietly."

Lupe walked forward, urged on by the man behind her and by the gun in her back.

●　●　●　●　●

Micah and his sister lay huddled together, completely covered by the sleeping bag, with Gumbo in between them.

The big dog kept shuffling back and forth, clearly not appreciating the cramped accommodations. Micah didn't much care for them either. He felt the cold seeping in through the old sleeping bag. He had no idea how long they had been hiding. Uncle Thomas told them to "stay put" no matter what happened. They weren't to move until he came to get them.

Uncle Thomas also said to keep a tight hold on Gumbo. So Micah lay at the dog's side with a hand clamped tightly around Gumbo's leather collar.

Gumbo stopped shuffling. His muscles tensed, and Micah could feel the beginnings of a low rumble in the dog's throat.

"Easy, boy." Micah used his free hand to rub the dog's ears. "Shhhhhhhh." A few seconds later, Micah heard muffled voices not far away.

• • • • •

Derek Rainart detected the aroma of barbecued chicken drifting from the outdoor smoker as they neared the cabin. A single curtain obscured the cabin's front window. Derek could see a dim light shining through, and he guessed Kent was making use of a kerosene lamp. He saw white smoke drifting heavenward from a small pipe in the roof of the little structure.

All the comforts of home. What a quaint little family. Sorry we're going to have to disturb your picnic.

Standing ten feet from the door, Derek glanced over his shoulder and motioned to Frank Torrance with his shotgun. Frank moved toward a corner of the cabin.

"Drop your guns," a voice from behind him said.

Derek swung around, pointing the shotgun toward the sound. Lupe Saldivar stood about twenty feet away. A man slightly shorter than she stood behind her, holding her gun and using her as a shield.

"Drop them, now!"

"Please," Lupe said. "Do what he says."

Derek pointed the shotgun at Lupe and Thomas. "Kent, you can't kill all three of us."

"I don't intend to kill any of you," Thomas said. "Now drop your guns."

Frank Torrance wavered, then tossed his gun to the snow-covered ground.

"You next," Thomas said, pointing at Derek.

Derek raised his eyebrows and shrugged.

Then he fired the shotgun.

● ● ● ● ●

The world exploded in a flash of light, searing pain, and a thunderous roar. Thomas felt the thud of the buckshot as it struck his prisoner, throwing them both backward. He landed hard, the wind knocked out of him, the woman's lifeless body weighing him down. A burning sensation pulsed through his right hand. It felt wet and warm. Blood trickled down his scalp. Scorching pain coursed through his right cheek and ear.

The large man at the corner of the cabin yelled, "Rainart, are you crazy?" He lunged toward the man with the shotgun. Rainart swung around and fired a blast at his companion, sending him flying backward and to the ground.

Thomas rolled the body off him. His hand felt like it had been dipped in acid. He swept the frozen surface with his left hand, frantically searching for the revolver he'd dropped. Then he remembered the 9mm he had taken from the woman. He fumbled in his coat pocket, trying to retrieve the pistol with his good hand. Just as he pulled it from his pocket, he froze. The click of the shotgun barrel told him that the man had reloaded.

With both barrels leveled at Thomas, the man—Rainart—said, "Throw that over here."

Still on his hands and knees, Thomas tossed Lupe's 9mm at Rainart's feet. "He was right," Thomas said, nodding toward the man's fallen companions. "You *are* crazy."

The man kept the shotgun focused on Thomas and shrugged again. "Sociopath, actually. At least that's what all the psychiatrists said. Get up," he said, motioning with the barrel.

Thomas stood, cradling his injured hand.

The man with the shotgun stood with the gun still trained on Thomas. "You screwed everything up when you came here. My first scenario won't work anymore. So I've got to go with Plan B. Drug deal gone sour. Just have to plant some drugs on these two." Rainart gestured toward the two bodies. "You went crazy and it ended up a murder-suicide. I just happen to have the drugs in the Rover. Always come prepared, you know. After I've dealt with you, I'll set up the scene. Then I'll take the kids and be on my way."

Disgust and utter disbelief clouded Thomas's face. "You killed your own companions."

"What, them?" the man replied. "There's a big difference between them and me. They worshiped Antoine. I just work for him. Now, move away from her." The man waved the gun barrel at Thomas, then walked over to the woman's body and crouched down to pick up Thomas's gun.

● ● ● ● ●

At the first blast, Gumbo began straining, pulling, trying his hardest to escape Micah's grasp. The boy held on but his hands tired quickly. Micah pulled back hard on the shepherd's collar. But the second blast startled him into relaxing his grip slightly. In a flash, Gumbo broke free, leaped out of the little trailer, and tore off down the trail toward the cabin.

Micah wanted to call out after the dog but knew that he didn't dare. Michelle was crying. Micah put his arm around her, felt around for the sleeping bag, and pulled it over them.

●　●　●　●　●

Derek Rainart felt more than saw a black form rushing toward him with lightning speed. He dropped the pistol and grabbed the shotgun with both hands, trying to point it at whatever was hurtling toward him. Swinging to his right, Rainart fired off a wild blast that illuminated for an instant the horrific image flying toward his throat. For a split second, Derek Rainart saw what he thought had to be a wolf. Bared teeth. Red eyes. Chilling snarl. He brought his forearm up to protect his throat, then screamed in pain as sharp teeth clamped down on his arm like a nail-studded vise.

Derek dropped the gun and fell backward, screaming.

As he fell, he felt his head strike something hard. And for Derek Rainart, all went black.

●　●　●　●　●

Thomas Kent's four-wheeler chugged along the trail leading behind his cabin. He wore the night vision goggles he had taken from the woman. Back in a circular stand of cedar trees sat the little metal trailer, covered with a sleeping bag.

"It's okay, kids. You can come out now."

The sleeping bag drew back, and out popped Michelle's and Micah's heads.

"What happened?" Michelle asked.

"Nothing good," Thomas answered as he pulled the trailer out and attached it to the four-wheeler. "We've got to get out of here, and now."

"Where's Gumbo?" Micah asked. "I tried to hold on to him but he got away."

"Don't worry about it. He saved my life. Saved all of our lives."

"Where is he?" Micah asked.

For a second, Thomas didn't answer. Then he said thickly, "I'll take you to him."

The little four-wheeler chugged its way back to the cabin, pulling the trailer behind it. Thomas stopped at the front door and shut down the engine. He hopped off and turned back to Micah and Michelle. "Wait here. I've got to do something inside the cabin. Then we'll be on our way."

Thomas pulled open the cabin door. Inside, he had carefully laid out and covered the bodies of Derek Rainart's two victims. Rainart himself, woozy and just returning to consciousness, Thomas had tied securely to the cot.

Thomas slapped Rainart to wake him up. He put his face close to Rainart's. "You're lucky I have to take care of those kids. 'Cause I'd like nothing better than to kill you right now."

"Get outta my face," Rainart mumbled.

Thomas held up Rainart's key ring. "Hope you don't mind me borrowing these, Rainart. Fire'll keep you warm," Thomas said. "It's more than you'd have done for us. I'll be placing a 911 call before we leave. Sheriff's deputies will be here to untie you soon." Thomas patted Rainart's cheek. "Have a nice day."

Thomas left the cabin, putting the padlock in the door but not locking it. He walked back to the children. "That oughta hold him for a while, anyway."

Micah and Michelle were shivering in the cold. Micah, teeth chattering, said, "Wh-what about Gumbo?"

Thomas paused for a second before responding. "Come with me."

He helped the children out of the trailer and took

them around to the back of the cabin. In the darkness lay the still form of the big dog. Thomas had covered all but his head with an extra blanket. He led Micah and Michelle by the hand over to Gumbo.

Michelle just stood, looking at the shepherd. Tears streamed down her face.

Thomas helped Micah kneel down beside the dog's body, then took the boy's hand and put it on Gumbo's head.

"What happened?" Micah asked.

Thomas stroked Gumbo's fur. "The man who was trying to hurt us fired a wild shot when Gumbo attacked him. Missed him for the most part, but I guess a few pellets hit in just the right place. He went quickly."

Micah stroked the dog's head. "I'm sorry," he said. "I'm sorry, Gumbo."

Micah's chin quivered; then great sobs racked his body. Thomas put his arm around Micah, drawing the boy's head into his chest. Thomas knew these tears ran much deeper than the death of a dog. These were the tears of a boy who had lost his father.

"It's okay. Hush, now." Thomas turned around and gathered Michelle toward him. She offered no resistance. "Listen. Your daddy gave his life to save you; Gumbo just did the same for all of us. Now we'd better get moving or the sacrifices they made will be wasted. Are you with me?"

The two children nodded in unison.

Michelle put her hand to Thomas's cheek, touching his wounds. She reached down and took his right hand. "You're hurt."

"It's nothing. Only some flesh wounds. I've got some stuff up at the house that will help. Come on. We have to hurry."

Thomas and the children rode back to his vandalized home. He told them to sit in his truck while he went inside and treated his wounds.

He then took the night vision

BLIND SIGHT

goggles, jogged down the driveway, and found Rainart's vehicle about halfway out to the road. In the back of the Rover he found a small suitcase. One of the smaller keys on Rainart's key ring opened it. Inside were several small bags of crack cocaine, the drugs Rainart planned to use to set up his fake murder scene.

Thomas hopped into the driver's seat and started the engine. He drove the Range Rover to the house, put it in park, and left the engine running.

He ran up to his own truck and called to the children. "Come on. We haven't got much time." He helped Michelle down, then Micah. He carried the boy out to the Range Rover. "Hope you don't mind, Micah, but it's faster this way." Putting them both in the backseat, Thomas said, "Michelle, help your brother get buckled. I have two more quick errands to run."

Thomas ran back into the garage. He pulled from his coat pocket the pistol he had taken back from Rainart. Methodically walking around his shiny black pickup truck, he fired a bullet into each tire.

If he does get loose, at least he won't be using this.

He thrust the pistol back into his pocket, grabbed the suitcase, and hopped on the four-wheeler once more. Thomas gunned the engine and raced back to the cabin, where he found the shotgun and the other pistol. Thomas flung the weapons toward the frozen pond. He took his revolver and threw it in with the others. The ice cracked like glass, and the water bubbled as the guns sank to the bottom. He tossed the suitcase in after the guns. Then he stood beside the four-wheeler and kicked the engine into gear. When he let out the clutch and gave it throttle, the little vehicle lurched forward and rolled into the pond.

Thomas looked over to where the body of his dog lay. "I'm sorry I can't take care of you right now. You deserve better. But I'll be back. I promise."

Returning to his garage, Thomas dialed 911 on an

extension phone by the garage door. "We need help out here," he said, dropping the phone.

A man's voice came through the receiver. "Hello? Sir? Are you there? What is the nature of your emergency? Sir?"

Thomas climbed into the Rover and buckled himself in. Looking over his shoulder, he said, "Everybody ready?"

Michelle spoke up. "Why are we taking their truck and not yours?"

"If we took mine, every state trooper in Texas would be looking for it before long. On the other hand, I don't think the Fellowship's going to report one of their vehicles stolen, particularly one that was used by their hit squad. So for a while, this one's clean. At least clean enough to get us where we're going."

He turned back to Micah, who was seated directly behind him. "And where, exactly, are we going, Micah?"

The little boy looked toward the sound of Thomas's voice. "Lake Charles, Louisiana."

"Let's go, then. We'll be there before the sun comes up." Thomas threw the Rover into gear and drove off into the night.

Sunday, December 8

Dana Shipp floated, drifting along in a dreamy world of constantly changing images. Crazy, distorted pictures of rings and people in white clothing and someone named Father flashed before her. People shouted at her, telling her to give all to Father, to surrender.

The images fled as shooting pains in her neck and shoulder brought her back to reality. Sharp spasms radiated down to her lower back. She twisted her hips and arched her back, trying to find a comfortable position. But the pillowless foam mat on which she slept was unforgiving. No matter which way she turned, every bone in her body cried out in agony.

As she fought the pain, Dana slowly became aware of her empty stomach's demands for attention. She felt as if an animal were gnawing her insides. Her right hand rubbed her midsection, trying to drive away the hunger.

Lower, she felt like an over-filled water balloon. Discomfort from a full bladder soon drowned out all the other pain Dana felt. She rolled onto her side and curled into a fetal position, trying to hold on to her fitful sleep. But it was no use. Dana propped herself on one elbow and surveyed her surroundings. Around her, Dana could see about thirty quiet lumps in the dim ceiling lights.

So far, entering the Sphere and becoming part of Antoine's inner circle were not all they were cracked up to be. Granted, her room on the twentieth floor wasn't exactly a luxury suite, particularly with its windows painted black, but it was considerably more comfortable than the current accommodations.

She hadn't known what to think Friday night when Coventina told her she wouldn't be going back to her room.

"What about my things?" Dana asked.

"They're being brought up here," Coventina reassured her.

"But why can't I go back there?"

Coventina smiled. "Daughter, now that you've entered the Sphere, you must learn that such things are mere illusions. By staying here with us, you will discover the true path to understanding is in denying the body and feeding the soul."

"But—"

"No more questions, now. We must worship."

Dana didn't see how a good night's sleep in a soft bed would corrupt her spirit, but she didn't have a chance to ask. Before she could protest further, Coventina whisked her off to another marathon "worship" session. More chanting, more swaying and calling out to "Father." More lectures by Llewelen. Almost no food.

Friday had dissolved into Saturday. And as Saturday wore on, Dana's senses grew duller with every passing hour. Strangely, she began to feel euphoric. Llewelen actually began to make sense.

Dana didn't fully understand it. But perhaps they were right.

Perhaps she had "entered the Sphere," whatever that meant.

Dana lifted her left hand and held it in front of her face. In the dim light, she could barely see the ring that Coventina had put on her finger. She twisted the cheap metal band around, feeling more than seeing the black stone mounted in the center. Looking at the ring, she felt at first a sense of accomplishment. For a moment she felt special. Then an inexplicable fear seeped through, chilling her.

Dana began to feel as if a river's strong current were sweeping her along. So far, this retreat had been the most exciting experience of her life. There was something winsome and attractive about these people, the first people who had ever truly accepted her for who she was. But Dana wasn't sure if she was ready to spend her life with them.

I need time to think. Got to put this all in perspective. If I could sneak out, just for a little while, I could process some of this.

Her fingers traced their way down the white robe she wore, and her heart sank. When they had given her the robe, they took away her other clothes "for safekeeping." Even if she could get away, it would be barefoot and with the equivalent of a bedsheet for clothing. She couldn't see herself running through the snow-covered streets of Syracuse like this. Besides, the Fellowship had flown her up here. Without them she had no way home.

Like it or not, Dana had to see this through to the end. She'd figure it all out when the retreat was over. At least there was a light at the end of the tunnel. This was the last day of the retreat.

"Everybody up," a man's voice called out, just as brilliant fluorescent lights blinked on overhead.

BLIND SIGHT

Dana squinted at the bright, intrusive light, throwing her forearm over her face to cover her eyes. Rustling sounds around her told her that the other bodies on the floor were moving, putting away their mats, obediently preparing for the day's activities.

Dana just lay there.

Soon she heard muffled chants coming from other parts of the room. Then she sensed someone standing by her. Opening her eyes, she saw Llewelen. His arms were folded, and the frown on his face telegraphed his disapproval.

Dana glanced around the room. The others had arranged themselves in formation around something that looked like a huge plastic globe. The Sphere, made of clear plastic, appeared to have a number of smaller globes inside it, all rotating within each other and faintly lit with different colors. The group, kneeling around the globe, had begun to chant in unison.

"I said everyone up!"

"I really need to go to the bathroom," Dana whispered. "Is there one around here?"

A look of disgust darkened Llewelen's face, and he nodded in the direction of the others. "Over with the group."

"But really, I need to go."

His expression hardened, and a sneer curled his lip. "Wait a minute, everybody," he called.

The others stopped chanting and turned to face him.

"This one says she *really* needs to go to the bathroom," he said, mocking her tone.

Muffled snickers and chuckles came from the group. Dana felt her face flush.

"Anyone else here need to go *really bad*?"

They all held up their hands.

"What comes first?"

In unison they replied, "Communion with Father."

He turned his hard gaze back to Dana. "We do what is *important* first. Physical needs are *not* important."

Glaring at her, he stretched his arm out and pointed to the group.

Dana understood the order. Her lower lip trembled as she stood and shuffled to where the others had assembled. She knelt down at the rear of the group and blinked back the tears that threatened to force their way into her eyes.

Now, like a drill sergeant calling cadence, Llewelen cried out, "Journey to Father."

The others echoed his chant. Dana falteringly joined in. And like the first night, the chants rose and fell with a rhythm all their own.

This time, though, Dana experienced no euphoria, no ecstatic relief. She repeated the chants, digging her fingernails into her palms to distract her from the increasing pain in her distended bladder, praying that she wouldn't lose control before they stopped.

The chanting continued while tears streamed down Dana's face. And when she'd just about given up, all fell silent.

"Everybody up," Llewelen said.

They all stood to their feet.

He walked to the front of the group and stood with his eyes fixed on Dana. Her ears felt hot as she remembered how he had embarrassed her only a short while before. His gaze made her uncomfortable. She wanted to look away, hide her eyes. But she knew she didn't dare.

"It's time for a short break," he said, "but first I have something to say about our new member."

Dana gritted her teeth together, waiting for the next onslaught.

"I have never—" he paused for emphasis and began to walk toward her—"I have never seen any novice who has grown as quickly as this one," he said, pointing at Dana. "Even when your flesh complained and fought you,

you drew near to Father. You have truly entered the Sphere."

He reached into the pocket of his robe and pulled out another ring, its stone a deep, rich blue. Taking Dana's hand, he removed the black-stoned ring and replaced it with the new one.

"I'm proud of you, sister. Today will be a great day for you. Today you will receive your new name. And you will meet Father."

Llewelen embraced Dana. Stunned, she accepted the embrace, not knowing what else to do. Soon she felt herself surrounded by the others, all praising her, encouraging her.

Surrounded by a sea of warm, smiling faces, Dana's carefully constructed wall of defenses began to crumble. Her tears flowed freely—tears of joy, grief, frustration, and confusion all mixed together. She would see the two weeks through willingly now.

Fifteen minutes later, after having had time for a quick trip to the bathroom, Dana sat on the floor with a bowl of unflavored yogurt in front of her. She scooped out every drop she could with the small plastic spoon they had given her, then tried to lick the bowl clean. Where her tongue wouldn't reach, Dana used her fingers to clean out the last of the yogurt. Two weeks earlier, she wouldn't have touched the stuff, comparing it to white glue. Now she relished it, licking her fingers as if it were the finest French vanilla ice cream she had ever tasted.

Dana smiled and waved when she saw Coventina enter the room.

Coventina sat beside her. "I see you've journeyed," she said, pointing to Dana's blue-stoned ring.

"Yes," Dana said, fingering the white gold band. "Coventina?"

"Yes, daughter?"

"Llewelen said I was going to get a new name. What did he mean?"

"When you've entered the Sphere, you must leave your past behind. Father Antoine has given us all new names. Each one has a special meaning."

"What does *Coventina* mean?" Dana asked.

"Water goddess."

Dana looked over toward Llewelen. "What about him?"

"His name means 'ruler,'" Coventina replied in a hushed voice. "Master Llewelen is one of the great ones. He's in charge of the novices."

Dana nodded, leaned back against the wall, and closed her eyes. She felt herself drifting off to sleep when Coventina's voice broke through the fog.

"Come, child. We must go."

"Won't Master Llewelen be upset if we skip worship session?"

"He understands." She held out her hand and helped Dana to her feet. "Come with me."

As they walked into the hallway, Dana could hear a new round of chanting beginning. Secretly, she was glad she didn't have to stay.

"This is your special day," Coventina said.

Dana's head jerked up. "What do you mean?"

A broad smile crossed Coventina's face. She spoke in a whisper, as if she were sharing a secret. "Today's graduation day."

"Do I get to go home after graduation?"

"After you meet Father, you will *be* home."

Coventina led Dana to a small conference room. A polished-oak table surrounded by several plush chairs sat in the center of the room. On the table lay a single manila folder. Coventina motioned Dana to one of the chairs. Then she sat down on the opposite side of the table.

Coventina opened the folder and pulled out what looked to Dana like some kind of legal document. A small white envelope tumbled out of the folder. Coventina handed it to Dana. "Open it," she said.

Dana tore the end of the envelope and peered inside. She dumped the contents of the envelope onto the table. Out fell a ring, this time with a green stone.

Dana held up the ring. "Is this for me?"

"Not yet," Coventina said, smiling. "First, you must complete your journey into the Sphere." She motioned toward the document.

"I thought I'd already entered the Sphere. What is this?"

"Your journey to the next level."

"Huh?"

"Everyone out there in the world—" Coventina made a broad circular motion with her hand—"is outside the true Sphere of reality. Only we share genuine existence. Now the rest of our lives we grow by delving deeper and deeper into Father's reality, losing ourselves along the way.

"To draw near to Father and his power, you must abandon everything that holds you to the false world, keeps you out of the Sphere."

Dana studied the document before her. Despite the legalese, she understood the document well enough to know that it would sign away all her earthly possessions. Once her name was on that paper, her bank account, car, and anything else she had would belong to the Fellowship. Evidently, that was the price for delving deeper into the Sphere.

It was the price of salvation.

Dana didn't have many possessions anyway, so there wasn't much to lose, but nevertheless her hand hesitated over the pen, fingering it but not picking it up.

"What's wrong?" Coventina asked.

"I don't know," Dana said. "I'm not sure about this."

Dana heard a door open behind her, and she turned around to see who was coming into the room. She saw Llewelen standing behind her.

Llewelen put his hands on his hips. "Is there a problem here?" he said.

"Not really," Coventina replied. "She's just having second thoughts."

Llewelen raised an eyebrow. "Is that so?" he said.

Dana turned and fixed her eyes on the document. Llewelen's presence so intimidated her that she could barely speak. In a whisper, barely audible, she said, "I'm just not sure about this."

She turned to face Llewelen. She was startled to find that he had crouched down and was now face-to-face with her. Dana inched back in her seat, not comfortable with Llewelen's face right in hers. His deep blue eyes were so intense she felt they could burn a hole right through her.

"Not sure about it? Not sure about power? Don't you realize what you'd be turning your back on? We're changing the world, sister. The Fellowship is bringing in a new order. Father's at the head, and we're up there with him. Sister, you're going to rule over people! And you're worried about signing a little piece of paper?" Llewelen stood and whirled away, shaking his head in disgust.

Dana ran her fingers through her hair. It felt matted and dirty. What she wouldn't give for the opportunity to take a shower. "It's just that this is such a big step. I need time to think."

Coventina walked over to Dana's side. She put her arm around Dana's shoulder and said, "Dana, there's nothing to think about. When you find the truth, you hold on. You don't stop to think about it."

Dana turned and put her elbows on the table, resting her head in her hands. "I just don't know. I'm so tired. I need more time."

Llewelen slammed his fist on the table so hard that Dana

brought her hands up to her face in self-defense. For an instant her father's angry, unshaven face flashed before her eyes.

"I thought you would be a great one," he shouted. "I was sure you'd see the power of Father and enter the Sphere. And now you're willing to throw it all away because of a few possessions." Llewelen walked to the door, then looked back at Dana. "You want time to think? You have it. But only a few minutes. This is your point of no return, sister." He opened the door and stormed out, slamming it behind him.

"Why is he so angry?" Dana asked.

"He cares," Coventina said. "He wants you to be a part of the greatest thing that's ever happened to this world. And he knows that if you turn away now, you'll be lost. We'll be back in a few minutes. And then you've got to decide, daughter."

Dana watched the door close behind Coventina.

She looked at the document before her on the table. Why had they suddenly let off the pressure, left her alone? Dana looked at the large mirrors on one wall. No. She wasn't alone. They were watching her. She knew it instinctively.

She thought of Llewelen's burning blue eyes right in her face. His fist slamming on the table. He was trying to browbeat her, intimidate her into signing. She thought he was going to hit her like her father used to.

Dana's mind floated unwillingly back to images she had long ago buried. Images of her drunken father. He was thin and blond, much like Llewelen, only he didn't shave when he'd been drinking. She remembered lying in her bed at night, being awakened by her mother's screams as she pleaded for him to stop beating her. Ironically, Dana didn't want her mother to stop screaming, because she knew that when the house became silent, her father would be coming for her. But he wouldn't be coming to beat her. What he would do to Dana would be worse, far worse.

More times than she could remember, Dana had rushed to her feet, pulled on a tattered pink bathrobe, and crept from her bedroom down the back steps and into the basement. She would pull an old two-by-four from a special hiding place and prop it under the doorknob so he couldn't get to her. Then, cowering in a corner behind the old oil furnace, shivering in the cold basement, she waited for her father's angry bellows to dissolve into growls and mutters and, finally, snores.

In the morning, when the old man finally regained consciousness, she would see hatred smoldering in his eyes, knowing she'd defeated him this time.

It was his eyes she remembered.

His eyes she couldn't get out of her mind.

She saw the same look in Llewelen's eyes.

And it frightened her.

For the first time since Friday, she knew what she must do. She had to get away somehow. To buy time, she would sign the contract. She could have it voided later, anyway. She picked up the pen and signed the document turning over all her possessions to the Fellowship.

Within seconds, Coventina and Llewelen came back into the room.

Both were smiling.

Dana paid no attention to Llewelen's smile. She focused on his eyes.

They were the eyes of a predator.

She had to get out.

It wouldn't be easy.

But Dana would find a way.

Dana Shipp was a survivor.

● ● ● ● ● ●

"Jeanette, what have you got?" Sawyer Wynne's voice reflected the tension growing within him.

"Nothing, Mr. Wynne. No news at all."

Wynne cursed and broke the connection.

The early morning sun broke over the horizon as Wynne sat in a lounge chair beside his indoor pool. Wynne had planned to swim his morning laps after he checked in with Jeanette and gotten Rainart's report. Now he simply sat, holding a printout of the e-mail Jeanette had sent him the previous day.

He didn't feel like swimming anymore.

Rainart should have reported by now. He had never failed to keep Wynne in the loop before. This was not a case of "no news is good news," either. If Rainart failed to report, something had gone wrong. Seriously wrong.

Wynne rubbed the white stubble on his face. He hated the dirty feeling of being unshaven, and normally shaved twice a day.

He didn't feel like shaving.

He gazed blankly at the paper in his hands.

It held all the information necessary to bring everything back under control. Thomas Kent had the children and the files. Wynne began tearing small pieces from the sheet and flicking them into the swimming pool, where they drifted away.

The children and files had to be recovered before they fell into the wrong hands. Into *her* hands.

Wynne flicked another piece of paper into the pool. The gentle motion of the water drew the paper out of his reach. Sawyer Wynne had often joked privately that he could write a book titled *The Making of a Messiah*. He had chosen the perfect messiah in MacAsland, a brainwasher in Llewelen, and an enforcer in Rainart.

Three more scraps of paper went into the pool.

The last two pieces of the puzzle had been equally easy to find.

He'd found an organizer in Peter Bishop.

But before he found Bishop, he'd found an essential cog for his machinery. He'd found a recruiter. Someone as devoid of conscience as he was. Someone who would convincingly lie through her teeth to get people to follow Anthony "Antoine" MacAsland.

Wynne's lips curled into a sneer as he ripped the rest of the printout into tiny pieces, then stood up and hurled them into the water.

He'd found Justine.

"Screwed up again, didn't you?" The hoarse, gravelly voice of Silas Wynne echoed in his mind with hysterical laughter.

Wynne swept from the room as the tiny pieces of paper on the water's surface floated away like pieces of a puzzle that was inevitably coming apart at the seams.

The odor of cigarette smoke and musty carpet awakened Thomas Sunday morning. He tried to go back to sleep, but it was no use. There was no escaping the smell in this dump of a motel. Thomas glanced at the digital clock by the bed. Nine thirty. He'd only been asleep for three hours.

The sun was just beginning to peek over the horizon when he and the children had arrived in Lake Charles. His prediction of their travel time had not been far off the mark. Needing rest and a safe place to lay low for a while, Thomas rented a room in a cheap motel and moved the sleeping children inside.

Mercifully, the trip had been uneventful. The roads had begun to clear as they drove south, and soon traveling became easy. Thomas felt that he'd had enough excitement to last him for the rest of his life.

After leaving his place in Grant City, Thomas had cruised to several local ATMs. Exhausting his daily limit on all his cards, he scraped together about three thousand dollars in cash. He knew that whoever had tried to kill him might be able to trace him through credit card usage. He didn't want to give them any edge, any idea where he'd gone.

Besides, the authorities were probably looking for him now. He didn't want to do anything to draw attention to himself until he had safely delivered the children to their mother.

If they ever found her.

The one thing Thomas couldn't figure out was how Peter had been so confident he'd be able to locate this woman. Micah seemed assured of that fact, too, although he'd been somewhat enigmatic about the whole thing.

Early in the trip, Thomas asked him, "Do you know where your mother is?"

"No."

"Then how are we supposed to find her? Louisiana isn't the biggest state in the Union, but there are still a lot of places she could be hiding."

"We'll find her," Micah said. "Don't worry."

Thomas just drove on.

Now, as the dingy room began to brighten with the morning sun, Thomas sincerely hoped the boy knew what he was talking about. But he found it hard to believe that they would succeed where a ruthlessly efficient organization had failed repeatedly.

Thomas put his hands behind his head and watched a cockroach skitter across the ceiling toward the grimy bathroom door. He couldn't go back to sleep, but he didn't want to disturb the children by getting up. After what they'd been through, they needed as much rest as they could get.

A rustling from the next bed drew Thomas's attention away from the cockroach. Micah was awake and sitting up. Thomas didn't move, hoping the boy might go back to sleep. Still in the rumpled clothes he had been wearing at the airport, the little boy stretched his arms and yawned.

"Uncle Thomas?" Micah whispered.

"I'm right over here, Micah," Thomas called back softly.

"What time is it?"

"A little past nine thirty. Why?"

Micah pulled back the covers and swung his legs over the side of the bed. "We need to go."

"It's okay, Micah. They're not going to find us here. We don't have to hurry. In fact, it'd probably be a good idea to stay here for a while and let our trail get cold."

Gazing in the direction of Thomas's voice, Micah spoke urgently. "No. We have to go to church this morning."

Thomas raised an eyebrow. "Church?"

Micah nodded. "It's Sunday morning, isn't it?"

"Well, yes, but—"

The boy stood up and held out his hand. "We have to go." He called louder, "Michelle. Get up. Hurry."

Michelle bolted upright, her eyes widened in fear.

"It's all right, Michelle. Micah just wants us to go to church this morning."

The little girl visibly relaxed. Her tense body drooped, and now she, too, stretched and muffled a yawn with her hand.

"Micah," Thomas said, now sitting up in bed, "we don't even know any churches here in Lake Charles. Besides, God and I haven't exactly been on speaking terms lately."

Micah had begun to feel his way to the foot of the bed. "Which way's the bathroom?"

Michelle called over to him, "To your left, Micah."

The boy used his hand to guide himself along the bottom of Thomas's bed. He hesitated when he reached the end of the mattress.

"Straight ahead, Micah,"

Thomas said. "About three steps. Then turn left."

Micah felt his way along into the bathroom and closed the door behind him.

Thomas looked over at Michelle. She still sat on her side of the bed, looking like she would rather go back to sleep. "Did you guys go to church every Sunday with your father?"

Michelle shook her head. "We worshiped Father Antoine every day. And we weren't allowed to go to churches."

"So why does Micah want to go now?"

Michelle shrugged her shoulders.

They heard the sound of the toilet flushing as Micah emerged from the bathroom. "Michelle? Are you up? We have to hurry. We don't want to be late."

Thomas let out a sigh. "Micah, you've got to understand. It's just not smart for us to go out right now. I don't think we were followed. But if those people know where we are, it could be dangerous to go to a church. We could be endangering other people's lives."

Micah shook his head so violently that his scruffy hair flew in all directions. "No!" He felt for the bottom of Thomas's bed, then using his hands, traced his way along the sheets until he found Thomas's arm. Micah climbed up on the bed and knelt in front of Thomas. He reached out and put his hands on the older man's shoulders. His voice became shrill and whiny as he faced Thomas. "We—have—to—go!"

Thomas felt the tension in the boy's body, his arms shaking as they rested on Thomas's shoulders. He looked into the sightless eyes that confronted him and noticed tears welling in them.

"Okay, Micah," he said softly, cupping the boy's cheek in the palm of his hand. "Okay. We'll go."

Michelle came over and sat beside Micah on the bed. She put her arm around her brother and rested her head on his shoulder.

Thomas chuckled. "You know, if we're going to go

to church, we'd better look into getting some different clothes. The three of us look like rejects from the bargain basement. By the way, Micah, do you have any idea which church we should attend? Or should we just check out the yellow pages?"

Micah nodded. "Prien Lake Bible Church."

Thomas reached over to the bedside table and pulled open the drawer. He took a tattered copy of the Lake Charles phone book and turned to the yellow pages' church section. "Here it is," he said. "Morning worship is at eleven o'clock. That gives us about an hour to get some breakfast, new clothes, and find the church. Let's hustle."

A quick trip to Wal-Mart outfitted the children in clean clothing. Michelle chose a short-sleeved pink dress with tiny flowers embroidered around the top and lace around the sleeves and hem. Micah wore a crisp pair of blue jeans with a blue flannel button-down shirt. Thomas bought khaki slacks and a dark green pullover.

"Well, at least we don't look quite so seedy now," Thomas said as they rolled through a McDonald's drive-through. He glanced at his watch. "Ten forty-five. Just enough time to get to the church."

"Do you know how to find it?" Michelle asked.

"No problem. I lived down here a long time ago. Don't remember this church, but that's no surprise. Lots of churches in this city."

Micah sat beside Thomas in the Range Rover's front seat. Thomas glanced sideways at the boy. He kept his hands folded in his lap, but Thomas could tell by the way he was wringing them that Micah was ready to explode.

Thomas patted him on the knee. "We'll get there on time. Don't worry."

● ● ● ● ●

Prien Lake Bible Church, a
small, white building covered

with old asbestos shingles, was not exactly what Thomas had expected. In various places along the bottom, the shingles had broken, exposing black felt underneath. Apart from the broken shingles, though, the building looked neat. The exterior appeared freshly painted, as did a simple cross made of one-by-twos attached to a small steeple. A lush green Christmas wreath hung on the front door.

A parking lot paved with crushed seashells sat to the right of the building. Tufts of grass grew between the shells in various places. As Thomas parked on the roadside, he saw a few other latecomers making their way up the crumbling sidewalk and into the plain building.

Thomas felt a quiver in his stomach as he opened the Rover's door for Michelle and Micah. He stared at the building as if it were a house of horrors, not a house of worship. This would be the first time he'd darkened the door of a church since the funerals. Thomas didn't know if he'd be able to hold it together. However, for the moment at least, Michelle provided a distraction. For once, she did not lead the way. Her reticence to enter the church forced Thomas to lead them both by the hand—guiding Micah, pulling Michelle. When they neared the door, Michelle put on the brakes as effectively as a mule.

"What's wrong?" Micah asked.

"Just a minute," Thomas replied, kneeling in front of Michelle.

"We've got to go in, Michelle," Thomas said.

Fear and distrust clouded her expression. Michelle shook her head and said, "No."

Thomas ran his hand through her curly hair. "Nobody's going to hurt you in there, sweetheart. I promise." He took her hand and could feel her quivering.

"Besides," he said, "I'm probably more scared to go in there than you are. Tell you what. I'll hold your hand and you hold mine. And if anything bad happens, we'll both leave. Deal?"

She nodded, and Thomas led her and her brother inside.

Inside, twelve solid-oak pews with ornate, carved ends sat on each side of a center aisle. A mammoth pulpit, painted white like the exterior of the church, dominated the platform. Behind the pulpit sat two carved oak chairs. Three choir pews stood at the back of the platform. And behind them a small window opened into a baptistry. The lighted back wall revealed a tranquil painting of a lazy river, presumably the Jordan. Thomas smiled at the primitive style of the artwork. It was probably done by one of the little old grandmothers in the church and presented as a gift.

In front of the pulpit a Communion table was decorated with two large poinsettia plants, their scarlet blooms contrasting beautifully with the green leaves. Polished pine floorboards squeaked underneath Thomas's feet.

A short, pudgy man with coal black hair and wearing a gray suit that looked twenty years old greeted them. "G'mornin'," he said. "Good to have you today." A slight Cajun accent colored his speech. He smiled and offered Thomas a church bulletin. Since neither Michelle nor Micah would release his hand, Thomas politely refused.

Thomas nodded to the man and looked for the nearest empty pew. About sixty people sat scattered around the room. Thomas had hoped to sit in back in case he needed to make a quick exit. But the early arrivers had already filled the back rows. The only pew with room for all three of them stood toward the front of the sanctuary. Thomas led Micah and Michelle to the pew, and they sat down near the aisle. Micah relaxed immediately; Michelle sat on the pew's edge, her back straight.

As they waited for the service to start, hushed conversations mingled with the sound of a baby crying. An elderly woman with curly silver hair played "Away in a Manger" softly on the organ. Thomas fidgeted with a church bulletin he'd found in the pew. He looked at Michelle and Micah. Michelle's eyes, alert and watchful, scanned the crowd; perhaps she was wondering where the "enemies" were that Father Antoine had warned her about. Micah was alert, too, but his face displayed a different expression. He appeared eager, expectant, as if he knew something good was about to happen.

An organ crescendo drew Thomas's attention away from the children. As the organist played the processional, the choir—all seven of them—entered the platform from a side door. Two men in brown suits climbed the double steps up to the platform. The younger of the two, a handsome kid with a peach-fuzz clean face stood behind the pulpit to begin the service.

That one's got to be fresh out of Bible college.

"Good morning. And a Prien Lake Bible Church welcome to all of you. Let's open our hymnbooks to number 232 and sing that song Ruth has just been playing, 'Away in a Manger.' Stand with me and let's sing all four verses."

All around him, Thomas heard the shuffling noise of people rising to their feet.

He remained seated.

As the strains of the song echoed through the church, Thomas's eyes focused straight ahead. The rest of the building became a blur, but in front of the platform he saw three platinum gray coffins. One large. Two smaller. Flowers surrounded them. The strong congregational singing wilted into the faint, torturous, maddeningly anemic strains of a funeral-home organ. Sitting on each of the coffins was an eight-by-ten photograph in a gold frame. Jenny—beloved Jenny. Steven. Sarah.

He heard Jenny's voice. "Thomas."

No. Not here.

"Thomas?"

Thomas felt his hands trembling. Ice-cold sweat trickled down his face. The walls were closing in on him. His throat constricted. He couldn't breathe.

"Thomas?"

"Jenny. I'm sorry. I'm sor—"

"Uncle Thomas?"

Thomas felt someone pulling on his right arm.

"Uncle Thomas, are you okay?"

The coffins disappeared, and he found himself in the little church again. Still shaking, he turned and saw Michelle's worried expression. As he looked around, he noticed some of the people in the church were looking at him. Others, too polite to stare, kept their faces forward. But Thomas knew what they were probably thinking. *The poor guy has had too much to drink, and he's coming here to cleanse his conscience.*

Thomas mumbled a quiet apology and fixed his gaze on the floor. He didn't look up again until the pastor approached the pulpit for the morning message. This man was somewhat shorter than the young song leader. Thomas noticed a weary expression on his face.

Battle scarred.

Thomas carried a few of those scars himself. Scars derived from caring for people, often more than they cared for themselves. Scars that came from pulling people from the fires of self-destruction, only to watch them cast themselves back in again. Scars of a shepherd who has discovered that some of his sheep have claws. Scars of one who has suffered for the sheep, sacrificed himself for the sheep, given himself for the sheep, only to have the sheep turn on him.

Thomas bore those scars. Most of them he did not begrudge; they came with the territory. But he deeply resented the ones inflicted after Jenny and the children died. When he was left alone, abandoned by his congregation just at the time he needed them to care for him. Perhaps he could have borne their rejection better if he hadn't also felt abandoned by God.

Thomas tried to shake off the anger.

He looked at the pastor of Prien Lake Bible Church. As the pastor opened his Bible and prepared to speak, his eyes surveyed the congregation. His gaze passed to the children and remained there momentarily. Thomas saw a brief flicker of recognition, quickly muffled.

And for the first time in two days, Thomas felt a glimmer of hope.

F ather is here!"
A massive wave of excitement surged through the crowd. This was the highlight of any recruitment retreat. Antoine would make a personal appearance. To novice and veteran members alike, a personal encounter with Antoine provided a thrill beyond description. And even though Dana Shipp had already decided she had to escape, she still felt the tingle of excitement at the prospect of seeing Anthony MacAsland in person.

The strange irony of the Fellowship, Dana noticed, was that while they all worshiped Antoine, they rarely ever saw him face-to-face. However, though his followers only saw him rarely, the rest of the world knew MacAsland's face well. They saw him on the cover of *Newsweek* and *Time*. He made appearances on *Nightline, Good Morning America, Oprah*, and other talk shows. Newspapers and magazines printed interviews with him regularly, allowing him to share his opinions on solving the problems of the environment and world hunger.

The world loved Anthony MacAsland. His looks alone could practically earn him a spot as a Hollywood leading man.

But MacAsland wasn't just a prominent leader. From the beginning, Dana had been especially impressed with his background. The only child of oil and gas billionaire Robert MacAsland, Anthony used his family's fortune to help others. After his father died, Anthony had seized control of the company. He stunned the board of directors by immediately issuing a public apology for the damage his father's drilling interests had done to the environment. Then he put feet to his apology by establishing the Fellowship for World Renewal, a nonprofit organization whose mission was to reverse environmental damage done by corporate profiteers.

Not long after this, MacAsland attended a state dinner at the White House, pledging to assist the government in cleaning up the environment. He offered matching funds to any organization willing to invest money for preserving endangered species. Most important in the eyes of many, he cared for the poor. Scattered across the United States were FWR-sponsored clinics, offering quality medical treatment for those who couldn't afford to pay. Several large cities boasted of MacAsland's housing projects for low-income families.

Dana remembered reading an article where a grateful resident of MacAsland's projects told a *Newsweek* reporter, "If I didn't know better, I'd think Jesus was walking the earth again. This man is so kind and good, I just can't believe it."

Dana Shipp sat toward the back of the white-robed throng. Their group leaders had ordered them to assemble and wait quietly for the Master's appearance. And so for the last sixty minutes they had knelt in the large auditorium Dana remembered from Friday evening. A stage stood at the front of the room, a dark maroon velvet curtain shielding whatever—or whoever—was behind it from the large crowd assembled out front.

From the moment she had decided to escape from the Fellowship, Dana's mind raced with possibilities. She knew she'd have only one chance to get out. If she blew it, the opportunity would never come again.

She knew she mustn't panic and try anything prematurely. But she also understood that lack of time limited her options. Coventina had told her it was "graduation day," but deliberately evaded her queries about going back home after graduation. Dana had no idea what plans the Fellowship had for her, but she was fairly certain that Father's appearance meant decision time had arrived. Instinctively, Dana understood she would not be permitted to leave after graduation. Time was slipping away.

While the soft hum of meditation filled the room with an eerie sound, Dana flashed quick glances in different directions around the auditorium.

Four exits.

All of them covered.

Dana's heart sank. Trying to make a break for any exit would be futile. They would catch her before she got within ten feet of the door. Eyeing the exits to her right, she knew she would definitely not go that way. Coventina stood at one door. Llewelen glowered at her from the other. He thrust a finger toward the stage. Dana obeyed the silent command and turned her attention back toward the front of the room.

There would be no slipping out unnoticed—at least not that way.

Ethereal music began to waft through the room as the houselights dimmed. Dana noticed a mist drifting underneath the curtain and around its edges. Stringy wisps of

BLIND
SIGHT

vapor trailed like airborne spiderwebs off
the edge of the stage and into the crowd.
Anticipation pulsed through the room as
the believers focused hushed attention
toward the curtain. The curtain pulled away to the sides,
revealing an empty stage, backlit with intense blue light.

A baritone voice erupted from speakers surrounding
the room, sounding like an all-powerful messenger from
heaven. The resonant sound had a peaceful, melodic quality that could quickly lull the receptive into a restful,
acquiescent state.

"Silence, children. I have come."

An expectant murmur surged through the white-
robed throng. Dana noticed the music was building in
volume and intensity as the voice boomed through the
speakers.

"Are you my children?" the voice asked.

"Yes, Father," the crowd responded.

Drums. The music grew toward a climax.

"Are you my followers?"

"Yes, Father," they chorused.

"Would you die for me?"

The music approached an earsplitting amplification.
Dana's head throbbed with each beat.

"Yes, Father, yes." As one voice, the crowd answered
urgently.

The voice cried out, "Then worship, my little ones,
worship."

The music continued its seemingly unstoppable accel-
eration, and instantly the stage and houselights went out,
leaving the ballroom in complete blackness. For seconds
that seemed an eternity to Dana, absolute darkness
flooded the auditorium. She could only feel the unbear-
able throbbing of the music, the pounding of the drums.
Then, with an explosive crescendo, a blaze of blinding
blue-white light radiated from the back of the stage, high-
lighting the silhouette of a man. Thickening mist appeared

as a cloud of glory around him. An automated laser danced through the cloud, creating an ethereal, other-worldly effect. Strobe lights flashed as the dark figure stood stock-still, arms outstretched on the stage.

When a single spotlight revealed MacAsland's face, the crowd exploded in sheer ecstasy. This was the emotional-ism of Friday evening multiplied to the hundredth power.

And Dana instantly recognized it as her one chance to escape.

People stood to their feet, waving their arms, jumping up and down, dancing. Some rolled on the floor. Everyone was screaming, shouting, swept along in the emotional tsunami that threatened to blow the walls out of the place.

Dana sprang into action. She stood, threw her arms straight above her head, and began swaying back and forth like a palm tree in a hurricane. "Father, Father!" she cried in a high-pitched tremolo that sounded like a birdcall. Swaying her arms and dancing in little circles, Dana capered about, always moving toward the exit on her far left.

Dana targeted the exit at the side of the room farthest from Llewelen and Coventina. She wished she could see if they were watching her but didn't dare risk stopping to take a peek. As she spun around, she caught a glimpse of the person who was guarding her door. Evidently the guards were under strict orders not to leave their posts. The young man standing by the door had not moved an inch. In fact, he didn't seem to be caught up in the frenzy at all.

Here goes.

Dana spun around in tighter circles, heading right for the short, red-haired guard standing in front of the door. She wanted to be dizzy when she got there. Spinning like a ballerina, Dana collapsed, breathless, into his arms. "Father, Father," she trilled between gasps.

When the redheaded watchman shoved her away,

Dana fell backward to the floor. "Get back to your group," he growled.

Dizzy and wobbly from her spinning, Dana clambered to her feet and staggered back to the guard. "Isn't this wonderful?" she said, a stupid grin spread across her face.

"Yeah, yeah, wonderful. Now go back."

Dana allowed the silly smile to fade from her face and replaced it with the woozy look of one who's had too much to drink. She brought one hand to her forehead and the other to her stomach. Starting to waver back and forth like a tree about to topple, she looked at the door watcher and muttered something.

"What did you say? I can't hear you."

Dana motioned for him to bend over so she could speak into his ear. "I said, I think I'm going to throw up." With that, she threw both arms around his neck and began to make guttural, burping sounds. She gritted her teeth and knotted her jaw muscles as if she were trying to hold back the inevitable.

A look of disgust came over the guard's face. He pushed the door open a crack, motioning Dana through. "Restroom's down the hall. Get yourself together and get back here, fast!"

Covering her mouth with her hands and ballooning out her cheeks for effect, Dana ran through the door and dashed down the corridor toward the restroom. When she heard the auditorium door click shut, she slowed her pace. She held her breath as she stopped and risked a glance behind her.

The corridor was empty.

For the first time in several days, Dana was alone.

But if she didn't act quickly, she wouldn't be alone for long. She had no doubt that the guard would come looking for her in just a few minutes.

If she was going to escape, she had better do it now.

Jeanette Marshall stifled a gasp when Sawyer Wynne entered her office. Mr. Wynne, who normally presented a flawless appearance, looked like an alcoholic who had fallen off the wagon. His suit, normally pressed and crisp, couldn't have been more rumpled if he'd slept in it. His hair was uncombed. Jeanette couldn't ever remember seeing a stubble of beard on his face, but there was one there now.

"Anything?" he demanded.

Jeanette shook her head.

Wynne grimaced, walked past her, and slammed his office door behind him.

Jeanette followed him with her eyes, an expression of disbelief clouding her face.

The Coral Snake was losing it.

25

As the organist played the final bars of the closing song, Thomas and the children filed into the center aisle of Prien Lake Bible Church. They made their way slowly to the back, where the pastor greeted the members of his congregation as they exited.

An inexplicable uneasiness came over Thomas. Throughout the service, the pastor's eyes had alighted on them frequently. But his fleeting glances reflected puzzlement, as if while preaching his sermon the pastor was pondering their presence and what it might mean. There was also a wariness in his expression that disturbed Thomas. Even now Thomas noticed the pastor's eyes periodically flicking back toward them. Something was not right.

Micah and Michelle stood in front of Thomas. Michelle led the way, as always, with Micah's hand on her shoulder, but Thomas noticed that she was still tense, wary, glancing all around her as if she expected an assault to begin any second.

Ahead of them, a frail-looking dowager with wispy, silver-blue hair leaned on a bamboo cane and began to lecture the pastor on one of the finer points of his message. Refusing to release the man's handshake, she appeared to have settled in for an extensive critique of the morning's message.

Thomas tried to suppress a grin. More than once he'd been on the receiving end of a similar post-sermon evaluation. Thomas also noticed the pastor's patience and graciousness never wore thin with the little lady.

Finally she released his hand and turned, shuffling down the steps toward the road. The pastor's eyes followed her protectively for a moment, then turned back to Thomas. His stiff, formal expression took Thomas aback. The pastor didn't offer the broad grin or smile he had reserved for the rest of the congregation. Instead, his eyes passed briefly over the children, then focused on Thomas. He held Thomas in his gaze for several seconds, not speaking a word.

Thomas broke the silence, offering his hand. "I'm Thomas Kent."

The pastor took Thomas's hand and gripped it like a vise. He held on for several seconds, saying nothing. But as he glared into Thomas Kent's eyes, Thomas felt hostility radiating from the man in waves.

Finally the pastor spoke. "Michael Guidry. You'll be having lunch with us today. Light blue house next door. My wife's already there. Make yourselves at home." The pastor dropped Thomas's hand and turned his attention to the young mother and baby standing behind them.

Thomas just stood there for a moment, dumbstruck at the pastor's curtness. Then he felt Michelle tugging at his hand. "Uncle Thomas. Come on. We're holding up the line." Her words jolted him into action and he stepped forward, following her down the steps and toward the little blue house.

They entered the house and found themselves in a small but neat living room. "Hello?" Thomas called. He detected a tantalizing aroma he hadn't encountered in years.

Michelle curled up her nose. Micah inhaled deeply. "What's that?" he asked.

Before Thomas could reply, a woman's voice called out, "Dat's crawfish étouffée, young man." Thomas turned toward the large opening that led into the dining room. In it stood a short, plump woman, wiping her hands on a towel. Her round face and broad smile provided a welcome contrast to the sternness of the pastor. "I'm Mary Guidry," she said in a thick Cajun accent, her eyes never leaving the children. "Please, sit down." She motioned toward a large sofa. "My husband will be over in a few minutes."

"We're sorry to barge in on you like this," Thomas said as he guided Micah toward the sofa. "We didn't mean to invite ourselves to lunch. I hope it's no inconvenience."

"No trouble at all," Mary said. "I always plan for guests on Sunday. Michael usually ends up inviting somebody or other home."

Heavy footsteps on the front porch signaled the arrival of the pastor, Michael Guidry. Thomas turned to see the short, stocky man with the drill-sergeant haircut walk through the front door and into the living room. He closed the door behind him and walked directly to the sofa.

Looking at the children, warmth and kindness flooded his voice. "Hello, Michelle. Hello, Micah. It's so good to see you again."

"Who are you?" Michelle asked.

"I'm your uncle. Your mama's brother."

"Can you help us find her?" Micah blurted out.

The man flashed a glance toward Thomas. "We'll talk about that later. Right now, we got to eat some dinner."

"Right," Micah said. "We're having étou . . . étou . . ." He turned in the general direction of Mary's voice. "What are we having?"

Mary Guidry sat down on the sofa next to Micah and put her ample arms around him in a bear hug. The boy relaxed and fairly melted into her arms. "Eh—too—fay," she said. "Crawfish étouffée. Now say it with me."

"Crawfish étouffée," they said together. As the words came out, they both broke into laughter. And for the first time since he'd met Micah at the airport, Thomas heard him laugh. But Michelle's old fears seemed to have returned. Her eyes rarely left Mary and Michael Guidry. But her cautious expression revealed that she didn't trust them.

Thomas wasn't sure he trusted them either.

"Come on," Mary said, helping Micah to his feet. "It's time to eat."

She took Micah by the hand and led him into the next room, where a long oak dining table awaited. Mary had already set the table, and she seated Micah at the corner near the head. She pointed to a place across the table and said, "Michelle, dat's your seat."

Michelle turned her nose up and walked deliberately to the chair beside Micah. "I'll sit here," she said.

Mary nodded. "Whatever you want, sweetheart."

Thomas stood across the table from Michelle. Michael Guidry took the chair at the head, with his wife at the corner to his left.

"Let's ask the Lord to bless our dinner," Michael said. Then his hard gaze fell on Thomas. "Would you care to ask the blessing, Mr. Kent?"

Thomas felt as if someone had just punched him in the stomach, knocking the wind out of him. Thomas hadn't prayed for God's blessing on anything in a long time. He wasn't even sure he could bring himself to do it anymore.

"I . . . well, I . . . uh."

Thomas locked eyes with Michael Guidry. For a moment each searched the other's face, grasping for a hint of the private man behind the public persona.

Thomas instinctively understood that for this meal, a quick "ThankyouGodforthisfoodAmen" would not suffice. Thomas knew that if his prayer was found lacking, any information or guidance that Michael or Mary Guidry could provide would be sealed away as tightly as if locked in a bank vault. And he would leave with nothing. In many respects, this simple blessing would have to be the prayer of his life. A tall order for a man who was hardly on speaking terms with God.

"Sure," Thomas said, clearing his throat. "Let's pray," he said as he bowed his head and stretched out his hands.

The little group joined hands around the table as Thomas began with faltering words.

"God . . ." Thomas paused, searching for words. "You said, 'in everything give thanks.' In the good times and the bad times; when we're happy and when we're sad; when we have everything and when we have nothing." Thomas suppressed a catch in his throat as he continued. "Things are pretty rough right now. We've lost a lot, and we don't know what's going to happen in the future. But we thank You for this home, we thank You for Michael and Mary's hospitality, and we thank You for providing this food, because we know that if it weren't for You, we'd have nothing. And we pray this in the name of Your Son, Jesus. Amen."

Thomas opened his eyes and looked at Michael. The man had visibly relaxed. While all the questioning and distrust had not evaporated from Guidry's face, his expression was appreciably softer.

Tears welled in Mary Guidry's eyes. She dabbed her eyes with her hand towel. Sniffling, she headed toward the kitchen and said, "I'll bring the food right out."

Thomas was relieved at the change in Guidry's demeanor.

But Thomas couldn't miss an even more significant change in himself. The only prayers he had prayed in the last two years had been voiced in anger. He had railed at God, accused God, grumbled at God. He had not thanked God. For anything.

Thomas had felt as if the doors of heaven had been slammed shut, and his prayers fired back at him with a deafening cacophony.

But for the first time in two years, Thomas wondered if it had been heaven's doors that were shut—or the door of his own heart.

●　●　●　●　●

After dinner, Michael Guidry stood to his feet. "Would you like some coffee?" he asked Thomas.

"Love some. I take it black," he added, anticipating Guidry's next question.

The stocky man walked into the kitchen. His heavy footsteps echoed throughout the house. In a few moments he returned with two steaming mugs and handed one to Thomas.

Thomas breathed in the aroma of the dark-roasted Seaport coffee. He rolled his eyes and said wistfully, "Haven't had a cup of this in ages." He sipped the deep black coffee as if it were fine wine. "Thanks."

Guidry tossed his head toward the back door. "Why don't we take a little walk?"

Thomas nodded and pushed back his chair. "Thank you, Mary. That was a wonderful meal."

"It was my pleasure," Mary replied, beaming.

As Thomas stood up and followed Guidry toward the door, Michelle's anxious voice broke the silence. "Uncle Thomas? Where are you going?"

Thomas returned to Michelle. "I'm just going to take a little stroll with your uncle. I'll be right back."

Her chin quivered and tears began to well in her eyes. "Don't leave us."

Thomas knelt down and looked Michelle in the eye. "I'm not going to leave you. I promise. Not till you're with your mother. You can count on that."

"Besides," Mary's voice broke in, "you can watch dem the whole time, if you want to. Dey're just going into the backyard to talk. Come wit' me and stand by the window. Dey'll never leave your sight." Mary reached a pudgy hand down to Michelle.

Michelle shook her head, keeping her eyes cast down toward the wood floor.

Thomas patted her head. "I'll be right back. I promise." He turned and followed Michael Guidry outside.

In the crisp December air, Thomas couldn't help contrasting Louisiana's sunlit brightness with the dingy ice-covered wasteland he'd left behind the day before. Harsh winter weather hit down here occasionally, but not very often.

Michael Guidry leaned at the back fence as Thomas walked up behind him. Guidry's arms rested on the wooden top rail, cradling his coffee mug in both hands. He gazed into the pasture that ran behind his house. A beautiful brown mare and her colt grazed peacefully in the thick rye grass.

Guidry spoke quietly, keeping his gaze fixed on the mare and colt. "I suppose you want me to help you find Justine."

"If it's not too much trouble," Thomas replied.

"It *is* too much trouble, young man. Too much trouble, too much risk, too much danger. For *all* of us. Leave the children here. Everybody'll be safer."

"I promised to take them to their mother."

"We'll see that they get to her—eventually."

Thomas took another sip of coffee. "Are you trying to tell me you don't *know* where she is?"

Staring into his mug as if he were trying to read a crystal ball, Guidry replied, "Ever hear of the witness-protection program?"

Thomas stood up straight, disbelief masking his face. "Come on. She's not in the witness-protection program, is she?"

"Not the government's. Just our version of it."

"I don't understand."

"When Justine left the Fellowship—"

"Why did she leave?" Thomas interrupted.

"Say again?" Michael replied.

"I've been struggling with this ever since those two kids showed up," Thomas said. "Why would a loving mother leave two beautiful children like Micah and Michelle in the hands of a cult? If she really loved them, why didn't she take them with her?"

Guidry bristled at the question. "She left because she finally realized that she was part of a lie, that MacAsland and the whole crew were false prophets."

"You mean she became a Christian?"

Guidry studied Thomas for a few seconds, then looked back out into the pasture—and nodded.

"But why did she leave the children behind?"

"They threw so many legal roadblocks in her way that she didn't have a chance."

"And why didn't Peter leave with her? Couldn't they all have escaped in the night or something?"

Guidry's dark eyes flashed as he glared at Thomas. "Peter Bishop is as big a liar as the rest of them. He's the reason Justine had to leave the children behind. When Justine left the Fellowship, they put out a contract on her life. She never knew where they were going to show up— or when. She stayed here for a while, but it wasn't long before someone tried to kill her."

"How?" Thomas asked.

"Mary had taken her to the mall to shop for some

clothes—she had nothing but the clothes on her back when she came to us. Anyway, they'd just stepped off the sidewalk into the parking lot when someone in a red Camaro tried to run her down. Justine never saw it coming. Mary pulled her back just in time."

"How do you know it wasn't just a drunk or a reckless driver?"

"Mary got a good look at him. Said she'd never seen a face like it before in her life. Full of anger and hate, all of it focused right on Justine."

"Okay, a homicidal maniac or a random act of violence. There are any number of possibilities other than a planned hit."

"Maybe," Michael said. "But Mary insisted on reporting it. The Camaro had been reported stolen by its owner the day before. They found it ditched a few days later down near Cameron. That was when we knew Justine couldn't stay here. So she went into hiding."

"You mean you don't ever see her?" Thomas asked. "You don't know where she is? You don't even write?"

"As long as they're looking for her, she's got to stay very well hidden. That means those of us who love her have to pay a price. We don't dare try to make any kind of contact. We keep hoping that one of these days it will be safe to contact her again."

Guidry drained his cup, then said, "Leave the children with us. We'll take good care of them. Even if we could take you to Justine, leaving the children with her would only put their lives in danger. Let us keep them."

"I don't know if I can do that."

Guidry rested his elbow on the fence rail and studied Thomas again. His expression hardened. "Why not?"

"I promised them I'd take them to their mother." Thomas glanced back at the house and saw Michelle's face pressed against the dining room window. Gesturing toward her, he said, "Look at her. You saw how Michelle was

BLIND
SIGHT

in there. After what they've been through, I can't leave them."

Doubt clouded Guidry's expression.

"Suit yourself," he said. He straightened and began to amble back to the house. "But take a few minutes to think about it anyway. I'll be right back."

Thomas studied the pasture and sipped his coffee. It had grown cold during his talk with Michael Guidry. With a flick of his wrist, he tossed the contents of the cup over the fence.

Thomas gazed at the tranquility of the pasture, hardly believing this turn of events. Not twenty-four hours ago he had convinced himself that he wasn't the hero type and the best course of action was to hand the kids over to someone else. Now the chance to dump them had dropped in his lap like an early Christmas gift. This was his golden opportunity. He could leave the children with the Guidrys, knowing they'd be loved, cared for, and as safe with them as they would be anywhere. He'd have fulfilled his commitment to Peter. He could return to his hermitage and quietly resume the process of withering.

He reached into his trouser pocket. His fingers absent-mindedly traced their way around Jenny's cross.

He remembered the house.

What they'd done to it.

He thought about the ruthless man Rainart and how he had killed his own companions without remorse. Rainart was out of the way, but Thomas knew instinctively that this group wouldn't give up so easily.

He thought about Jenny and Steven and Sarah. He hadn't been there when they had needed him, hadn't been able to protect them.

He could at least be there for Micah and Michelle. It wouldn't bring his own children back, but maybe in some small way it would help him cope with his own loss.

Thomas's finger traced the outline of the disk in his

shirt pocket. There was also the matter of this disk that Peter had sent him. Thomas Kent knew virtually nothing about this killer group called the Fellowship. But from the little he'd seen, Thomas knew that someone needed to stop them. And if Justine Bishop was trying to bring them down, then Thomas had every intention of making sure she had the ammunition with which to do it.

It wouldn't be fair to ask the Guidrys to become further involved. He couldn't leave the disk with them and ask them to forward it. He believed Michael when he said he hadn't communicated with his sister in nearly three years. To get the disk to Justine, the Guidrys would have to break their silence and risk their own lives. Thomas would not ask them to do that.

Thomas had nothing left to lose. He had to take the children and the disk to Justine Bishop. And he would do it, whatever it took.

The sound of footsteps behind him startled Thomas. He swung around quickly to see Michael Guidry's bulk approaching. "Change your mind?" Michael asked.

"Thanks for the offer, but I've got to see this through."

"Okay," Guidry said. He held out a small scrap of paper.

"What's this?" Thomas took the paper from him.

"Drive east to Henderson this afternoon. Go to this place with the children. You'll find the information you need there." Guidry turned and walked back toward the house.

"I thought you said you didn't know where she is."

Guidry didn't answer as he sauntered back to the house again.

Thomas looked at the paper. Scrawled in black ink were the words *Richard's Landing*.

"You better head out soon," Guidry called over his

shoulder. "It's already two o'clock. Sun'll be down not long after five. You'll need to get there before sunset."

"Why?" Thomas asked.

But Michael Guidry didn't answer.

"I said why?" Thomas called out after him.

"Kids're waitin' for you out front. You'd better go."

Walking around to the front of the house, Thomas found Michelle and Micah standing on the small porch.

Mary Guidry stood by them, dabbing her eyes with a handkerchief. "You be careful now," she said to the children. She hugged Michelle, then Micah, then nodded at Thomas and went inside the house, closing the door behind her.

As Thomas took the children by the hand and led them to the blue Range Rover, Micah spoke up. "Did he tell you where my mom is?"

"No. But I guess he's sending us to someone who does know, and that's where we're going right now. With any luck, you'll be with your mom before you go to bed tonight."

Thomas pulled open the Range Rover's passenger-side door and helped Micah climb up. Micah's foot kicked a small rectangular object under the front seat. "What's that?" he asked.

Thomas picked it up. "Looks like a notebook computer. Probably belonged to one of the welcoming committee that visited us last night." He chuckled and set it on the floor behind the passenger's seat. "Know what we call that in Louisiana?" Thomas continued speaking in a mock Cajun accent, "We call dat *lagniappe*. It means 'a little something extra.' All I was bringing your mom was a floppy disk full of information. Depending upon what's on that computer, we might be bringing her the key to their whole operation." Thomas reached out for Michelle. "In you go." Michelle climbed into the backseat, behind her brother.

Thomas closed the door and walked around to get in the driver's side. "We're off to Henderson," he said, turning the ignition key.

"To find Mom," Micah echoed.

Using her foot, Michelle gently nudged the notebook computer under the seat in front of her.

Dana Shipp strolled down the corridor, trying to appear inconspicuous. She figured the easiest way to do that was to act like she belonged. She resisted the urge to run, moving instead at a relaxed pace toward the elevators. As she had hoped, the floor was deserted. Everyone in the auditorium was so excited about Father's appearance.

Dana's heart sank as she reached the elevators. There were no buttons. Only a key controlled the elevators at this level. She couldn't even call it up.

Stairs. There have to be emergency stairs. Now where would they be?

Dana turned and strode to the end of the hallway. A red Exit sign stood over a metal, windowless door.

Yes!

She picked up her pace as she neared the door, but found no escape there either. A digitally keyed lock controlled the door. Without the code, Dana knew she was sunk. She turned the knob, just in case. But as she expected, it was no use. Dana and all the rest of the recruits were prisoners on the thirty-first floor of Chateau Antoine.

Dana's options, not to mention time, were quickly running out. She could try finding a place to hide, but they would know she had no way of getting off the floor. Llewelen and his cronies would start a thorough search and eventually find her. When they did, she'd have to explain why she left the meeting, why she was hiding. She might be able to bluff her way out of trouble. Then again, she might not.

Hiding was not an option.

The only other possibility was to find either an elevator key or the stairwell code. All she could think to do was to try and find another stairwell. Dana walked around the corner to her right. She froze when she heard a door opening halfway down the hall. She wanted to turn and run in the opposite direction, but instead, she slowed her pace and kept moving toward the open door.

A matronly looking woman emerged, wearing an attractive blue dress and carrying a clipboard with some papers. Dana was momentarily stunned to see someone dressed like a normal human being again. Her stomach seized as the woman looked her way.

Dana gritted her teeth and smiled, continuing to walk slowly toward the woman. But the woman appeared to have no interest in Dana. She merely nodded and walked toward a door at the far end of the corridor. Dana could see that the door was also controlled by a numeric keypad.

Thankful for once that she was barefoot, Dana broke into a trot, hoping to get near enough to the woman to read the code but not near enough to be noticed.

The woman stopped at the door and shifted her clipboard into her right hand. She reached down with her left hand to punch in the numbers.

Dana grimaced. The woman's body totally blocked the

keypad. Hearing the click of the electronic lock disengaging, Dana watched in despair as her last hope went down the tubes.

Immersed in her own thoughts, the woman flung the heavy door open and walked through, allowing the closing mechanism to slowly shut it behind her.

Dana's eyes widened as she realized her good fortune.

She lunged for the door and caught it an instant before the lock clicked back into place. Keeping the lock from engaging, Dana stood still for a few seconds, trying to catch her breath. Then, holding her breath, she stepped through.

As the door clicked shut behind her, Dana surveyed her surroundings, surprised to find herself in a corridor rather than a stairwell. The soft, cool feel of heavily padded, plush carpeting under her bare feet was a delicious contrast to the tile floors she'd endured over the last few days. Dim overhead lights cast an amber glow, illuminating exquisite cherry paneling on the walls. The place looked like a law office.

Walking in virtual silence on the mattresslike carpet, Dana became acutely aware that her white robe made her stand out against the paneled corridor like a white moth on gray tree bark. Even though Llewelen and his crew would be unlikely to look for her here first, Dana needed to keep moving or find a secure place to hide while she figured out the next part of her escape plan.

The first door on her left bore a picture of the globe and the initials FWR. On her right, several doors were spread evenly along the corridor walls. None bore labels or markings.

Dana quietly crossed the hall and tried the first knob. It was unlocked. She opened it a crack and, peering inside, saw walls filled with filing cabinets. She opened the door a little wider, scanning the room to make sure it was vacant. Then she stepped inside and closed the door behind her gently.

BLiND
SIGHT

The room reminded Dana of a library research room. White filing cabinets lined three of four walls. Against one wall sat a long table with two computer terminals. A table with four padded metal chairs stood in the center of the room.

Dana realized she had only a few minutes before a search for her would begin in earnest; however, the fact that she had found her way through a locked door into the administrative wing bought her some time. Hopefully, they would assume that she couldn't have gotten out of the secure area, and would cover it thoroughly before they expanded their search.

In spite of the extra time she had, Dana also understood that she was still trapped in the Chateau Antoine. She couldn't go roaming about the Fellowship's offices aimlessly. They'd find her eventually. And even if she could find an elevator or staircase, a key or numeric code would probably control it.

Her best chance of escape would be to use the computers to find the door or elevator codes, a map of the building—anything that would help her find a way out. It was a long shot at best, but it was her only chance for survival.

Dana swept quickly across the room to the computer terminals. She pulled out a chair and sat down in front of one of the screens. The flat-screen monitor displayed the same logo she had seen on one of the doors—a globe with the letters FWR. On the computer, though, the globe was spinning and the letters orbited it like a satellite.

She hit the Enter key, and the globe disappeared, replaced by a green log-on screen. The computer prompted her for a user name.

Dana thought a moment; then her fingers quickly spelled out "Coventina."

The computer responded, "Password?"

What I wouldn't give for a password-cracking program

right now. Dana was practically a professional programmer, but she was no hacker. She didn't have time to figure out Coventina's password, even if she *did* have password-cracking software.

She reflexively looked at her watch, then remembered she had no watch to look at. She estimated she'd been on the run about ten minutes. Hopefully, Father Antoine's presence and his message to his followers would grab everyone's attention for a little while longer. She shuddered to think of the possibility of Llewelen pursuing her and what he might do if he found her.

Okay. Take a deep breath and relax, Dana. Most people use passwords that are easy to remember. Maybe Coventina is more predictable than she thinks.

Dana decided to take a few stabs at guessing Coventina's password. It was risky and probably useless, but she had no other options.

Dana had known Coventina for over a year, and they spent a great deal of time together. She knew enough personal details about Coventina to make some reasonable guesses.

Let's try the obvious: her birthday. She typed in Coventina's birthday: "031168."

"Invalid password. Access denied."

Dana pressed her lips together.

Okay. Let's try European style.

Dana could feel her heart pounding. Her fingers trembled as she clicked the numbers on the keyboard in a different sequence.

"110368."

"Invalid password. Access denied."

Dana pounded her fists on the desk.

"Come on! I don't have all day here." Her voice echoed off the bare walls.

Even in the cold room, rivulets of perspiration trickled down her cheeks. Her face flushed, and she could feel a droplet of sweat tracing its way down her spinal column. She wiped her clammy hands on her robe and took a third try at the keyboard.

Tentatively, as if she feared the terminal might explode with the wrong keystroke, Dana keyed the date in, starting with the year. As an afterthought, she added Coventina's last name.

"680311wilcox."

She pressed Enter.

The screen cleared.

Dana held her breath, unaware that she was crossing her fingers.

Then "Welcome in the Name of Father Antoine" splashed across the screen. A menu screen with several options followed quickly.

Dana raised her fists over her head in a victory salute. "Yes!"

Then she began to examine the menu options.

"Now, where do I go from here?"

● ● ● ● ●

Down the hallway, in a room lit only by closed-circuit video monitors, an electronic alarm sounded. Simultaneously, a dual-monitor system clicked on. The monitor on the left showed the display of a computer terminal. The monitor on the right displayed a surveillance video feed.

A short, young man with flowing chocolate brown hair and wearing a communications headset, turned his attention away from the video feed of Antoine's appearance. Sitting in a wheeled secretary's chair, he rolled across the narrow room to the monitors. Touching a button on the keyboard, he silenced the alarm.

The video screen revealed a petite young woman, clad in the white robe of a novice, sitting at a research room terminal. At the moment, she was merely staring at a list of menu items. It didn't matter what she chose at this point. Every choice, every mouse click, would be duplicated on his monitor in the security office. As she attempted to surf through the Fellowship's computers, he would be able to observe her every move.

Triggered by three incorrect log-in attempts, the automated security system was designed to give an intruder access to the Fellowship's systems after the third attempt, thus keeping her busy until security could apprehend her. The system had been conceived by the Coral Snake and designed by the late Peter Bishop.

The security monitor pressed a button on the console before him. "Jeanette? This is Bryce."

"Yes?"

"Someone's trying to hack into the computer system. I think Mr. Wynne should see this."

"He'll be right there."

⬤ ⬤ ⬤ ⬤ ⬤

Dana examined the three options before her. Option one simply was listed as "Phase Information." A second choice was "Projects." Third on the list was "Conversions."

None of the three choices gave her a clue as to how to find a way out of the building. She decided to eliminate "Phase Information" and "Conversions," because they didn't sound like they would have what she needed.

That left only "Projects."

Dana clicked on it.

The screen cleared and brought up another series of choices.

This time Dana faced three more possibilities: "Environmental," "Social," and "Osmosis."

Dana ran her fingers through her hair in frustration. Beyond any hope, she had gotten into the Fellowship's computer systems. But now she felt like a rat in a maze. She

BLIND
SIGHT

had no idea which way to turn, and the choices seemed to make no sense.

Trembling, knowing that her time was surely running out, Dana stopped to take a few calming breaths and get her wits about her. She was losing control and thus losing her opportunity for escape. She closed her eyes and rested her head in her hands.

Just for a moment.

Just to think.

• • • • •

The door to the security room opened and Sawyer Wynne swept through. "Show me what you've got."

"The alarm went off—" Bryce stopped short, taken aback by his boss's appearance.

"Go on," Wynne growled.

"Uh, the alarm went off about five minutes ago," Bryce said.

"Do you know who she is?"

Bryce looked up at Wynne. "Not yet," Bryce said. "But I've sent word to the recruiters to check their lists. It's a sure bet she came from across the hall. Should I send someone down to take her?"

"No. Not yet," Wynne said. "Give her a little room and see where she goes."

"Yes, sir."

As the two men watched the monitor, the mouse pointer wavered indecisively among the three options. It finally moved toward option three: "Osmosis."

A cold grin spread across Sawyer Wynne's face as the pointer turned into a small hourglass. She had clicked on *Osmosis*. He spoke softly, "So, she finally found a way to penetrate us. I never thought she'd be that bold."

Bryce gave Sawyer Wynne a puzzled look. "Who are you talking about?"

Wynne sneered at the man as if he'd just asked a stupid, childish question. "Who do you think?"

Bryce's jaw dropped. "You mean that's Justine Bishop?"

"Does that look like Justine?" Wynne snapped. "I don't think so. Not unless she's really let herself go in the last three years." Wynne moved closer to the screen. "But whoever that is, Justine sent her. I'm sure of it."

At that moment, the security room door opened and Wynne's assistant, Jeanette, walked in. "Llewelen reports a Dana Shipp missing from the novices. They've searched the entire floor but can't find any trace of her. Should I get him over here to give us an ID?"

Wynne nodded. "Before you go, come take a look at Justine's spy."

Jeanette's sharp intake of breath at the sight of the monitor caught Sawyer Wynne's attention. "What? What do you see?" he asked.

"Mr. Wynne, I'm sorry! I saw her in the hallway outside the auditorium not more than a half hour ago. I should have reported her then, but nothing seemed unusual. I'm so sorry."

Bryce noticed Jeanette's hands shaking. He understood. Displeasing Sawyer Wynne could have fatal consequences, particularly when it involved allowing someone to enter as deeply into the Fellowship's systems as this young woman had. He was glad he wasn't the one who'd messed up.

Wynne dismissed her apology with a wave of his hand. "No. No. This is perfect. Justine overplayed her hand this time. We've lost track of Thomas Kent and the brats. But we can make *this* one talk."

Wynne turned to face Jeanette and Bryce. The sadistic expression on Wynne's face made Bryce shudder. Wynne's voice lowered to a thin whisper. "She'll lead us to Justine." The little man leaned over and spoke directly to the monitor. "You'll tell us where she is before you die. Won't you, Dana?"

The electronic alarm

BLIND SIGHT

beeped again, startling Jeanette. "I'll go get Llewelen," she said.

Wynne nodded, then looked at Bryce expectantly as Jeanette hurried out of the room.

"She's trying to access the Osmosis Project with the same failed password that set off the alarm in the first place," Bryce said. "The system wants to know whether or not to authorize. Shall I refuse her access?"

"Oh no," Wynne said, pulling up a chair. "Let her through." He raised his eyebrows, grinning at Bryce. "A cat likes to play a while before killing its prey. Let her see what she came to see. She'll never live to tell anyone."

Wynne leaned back in the chair and crossed his legs. "This will be fun," he said.

●　●　●　●　●

Dana wasn't exactly sure why she had chosen the "Osmosis" option, other than that "Social" and "Environmental" didn't appear to present any possibilities for escape. For all she knew, "Osmosis" wouldn't help either. But she had to try something.

Once she typed in the password, she waited for clearance again, hoping that a different password wasn't required. As the seconds ticked by, Dana began to worry. It was taking too long. Something could be wrong. On the other hand, the system could just be overloaded and taking a little longer than normal to respond to her access request.

Finally, a new menu screen appeared with another list of choices.

Dana groaned. *Too many doors to go through. I'm never going to find a way out of this place.*

The menu before her gave four choices: "Current Status," "Project Progression," "Codes," and "Phase Analysis." Her eyes fixed immediately on the "Codes" option. "Oh, please," she muttered under her breath as she selected that one.

Almost instantly, a spreadsheet-like database form came up on the screen. Across the top of the screen, the database categories were listed: "Zone; Phase; Osmosis Code; Target Code; Conversion Code; Conversion Date; Strategic Advantage; Completion Code."

Below the categories, a list of records filled the screen. At the bottom, the words "Record 1 of 2145" told Dana the size of the database. The records themselves were numeric. The first record read like a jumble of meaningless statistical data: "Zone: 23; Phase: 1; Osmosis Code: 03481; Target Code: 29167; Conversion Date: 082192; Strategic Advantage: 93208; Completion Code: 10243."

Great! First I couldn't find any codes at all. Now I have more than I know what to do with.

A cursor blinked in a search window at the bottom of the screen. Dana typed in the number from the first Osmosis Code. "03481."

The screen went blank for a moment. Then it prompted for a password.

Dana mouthed an expletive.

This is taking too much time. I've got to get out of here. I'll try this once; then I've got to try and find another way out.

She typed in the password that had worked twice before.

The database disappeared. A profile screen, complete with pictures, replaced it. The name at the top was "Thomas Lorenz." A color photo displayed a middle-aged man with thinning black hair and a pencil mustache. Below the name, the man's position was listed: "CEO Environ-Clean, Inc."

The other code numbers from the database now appeared as hypertext links. Dana clicked on the blue number beside "Target Code."

A new window opened. It read "Hunting Accident/Shotgun."

Dana felt her throat constrict. A chill overcame her and she suppressed a shudder. Her hand visibly shaking, she maneuvered the mouse to another link and clicked on "Conversion Date."

Another window opened with a date and a scanned news item. The date was November 5, 1992. The lead read "George Halpern, CEO of Environ-Clean, Inc., Atlanta, Georgia, was killed in an apparent hunting accident on Saturday."

George Halpern? But the name by the picture said Thomas Lorenz. What's going on here?

Dana clicked on the code marked *Strategic Advantage*. A third window opened, displaying a United States map that highlighted the Atlanta area.

Dana clicked on the highlighted area, and it expanded to a larger map of Atlanta and the surrounding areas. Red and green pushpin-like buttons were scattered at various places over the map. Each pushpin bore the name of a bank or corporation. Some of the names Dana was familiar with. Others, like Environ-Clean, she'd never heard of.

Finding the Environ-Clean button and noticing that it was green, Dana clicked on it. A window with a picture of the Environ-Clean corporate offices popped up. A commentary beside the picture described the "strategic advantage":

"Environ-Clean has become a major player in recent years in the disposal of toxic waste. They are under consideration for a major government contract for the disposal of nuclear waste. It is important that the Fellowship gain control of this corporation. The resources it provides could be useful in the long term."

Below the commentary, Dana clicked on another hypertext link, marked *Update*. "Update status: current. CEO converted. Lorenz placed. Phase 2 Complete."

Dana closed the extra windows and looked again at the picture of the balding, mustached man. Her eyes flickered to the words *hunting accident*. A wave of nausea swept over her as she suddenly understood what was before her.

She selected another Osmosis Code. This time the picture of a young woman appeared on the screen. "Cherise Scranton" was the name. She managed a mortgage company. Beside her name was the caption: "E. coli food poisoning."

Dana's hand trembled almost uncontrollably as she clicked on a third Osmosis Code. The name: "Philip Norcross." His picture revealed a distinguished-looking man, probably in his late fifties. He was the president of Mercantile Bank in New York City. Beside his name, under "Conversion," was "auto accident."

A wave of nausea swept over Dana as she realized what "conversion" really meant.

She clicked on another Osmosis Code.

"Password?" the computer prompted.

Dana heaved a sigh and typed the password in again.

"Invalid Password. Access Denied."

Dana's brow furrowed. She typed it again.

"Invalid Password. Access Denied."

Practically hyperventilating, Dana tried a third time.

"System Breach Attempted. Security Notified."

Dana jumped to her feet, the chair clattering to the floor behind her. She looked around for a place to hide. Nothing but bare walls and filing cabinets.

She rushed to the door and jerked it open, then drew back in fear.

Standing in the doorframe, leering, with an almost maniacal expression on his face, was the imposing figure of Llewelen.

The sun had already begun to set by the time Thomas drove the Range Rover along the levee near Henderson, Louisiana. Thomas had driven in silence almost the whole way from Lake Charles. The children, weary from their ordeal, fell asleep soon after they were on the road. Micah's head leaned against the window, cushioned by a pillow borrowed from Mary Guidry. Michelle lay sprawled across the entire backseat, with another of Mary's pillows.

Thomas surveyed the landscape, savoring its unique beauty. He loved Louisiana, even though he wasn't a native. Thomas had lived most of his childhood in western Pennsylvania. It was a good place to grow up, a good place to be a boy. But his life had changed drastically when he was twelve years old. One cold evening, the police knocked on the door of their house. He remembered seeing the cruiser parked out front, the sad expression on the officer's face, his mother collapsing into the officer's arms when he told her about Dad. Thomas's entire life had changed because a drunk driver ran a stop sign.

A few months later, his mother decided to move the family—three daughters and one son—to Louisiana to be near her sister. Thomas didn't like the idea of moving, and he gave his mother quite a bit of grief about it. But finally he resigned himself to the inevitable, and they moved to Lake Charles.

Thomas missed having his father around as he was growing up. His mother did the best she could to compensate, trying to be both Mom and Dad to a family of four children. Thomas grinned now as he remembered how she had bought herself a baseball glove so she could play catch with him in the backyard. And how she'd camped out with him one summer night when his sisters were away at camp. Mosquitoes had practically eaten them alive that night.

And she had never let them miss church. Some of his earliest memories were of Mom getting the family up and dressed on Sunday mornings. A quick breakfast of cereal and milk got them going. Then off they would drive to a tiny Baptist church down the road.

Pastor Robin delivered his sermons in a folksy style through a thick Cajun accent. Thomas remembered how difficult it had been for him to learn to pronounce the pastor's name. "*Row-ban*, Tommie," his mother had chided. "Not *robin*." How Thomas loved to listen to his stories! Stories of fishing and hunting and all the things a boy loved to do, somehow woven into the fabric of messages that ultimately led Thomas to place his faith in the Great Fisherman.

From the time Thomas believed in Jesus, the entire focus of his life changed. Almost from the beginning Thomas knew that he would enter the ministry and become a preacher like Pastor Robin. Even through the normally turbulent years of adolescence, he never wavered. Thomas figured it was a fair trade. Out of love, Jesus had given His life for Thomas; out of gratitude Thomas would give his life for Jesus.

But a growing gloom had settled over his mother. It was as if his father's death had ripped open a hole in her heart that refused to heal. Often in the evenings, Thomas would sit down on the couch by his mother as she lay with a cold cloth on her forehead, and he would read her passages from Psalms.

"It's going to be okay, Mom," he'd say, patting her hand and watching as the tears leaked out of her eyes and down her cheeks. "We can trust God. He's good."

He'd spoken those words often since those days. In the long years when he'd gone to the University of Texas, then Bible college. When he'd met and fallen in love with Jenny. When he'd entered the ministry and accepted the pastorate of Grant City Bible Church. He'd spoken the words at the graves of friends, congregation members, sometimes people he'd never met.

"We can trust God. He's good."

He'd spoken them to grieving families, to people who had just been diagnosed with terminal cancer, to tearful young parents who'd lost their babies to SIDS. He'd spoken them to his congregation when their building had burned to the ground.

"We can trust God. He's good."

He'd spoken those words so often they flowed from his lips almost automatically. The affirmation of God's goodness had become a cliché to Thomas. So much so, he had long since ceased to contemplate its meaning.

"We can trust God. He's good."

But on the day Thomas drove their little sedan off the side of the Lake Ray Hubbard Bridge, on the day his wife and children plunged into the icy waters, on the day he came up out of the waters in shock, the words died on his lips.

He had not uttered them since.

We can trust God. He's good.

Yeah, right.

• • • • •

Ahead, a plywood sign that read, "Richard's Landing," in peeling, fading red paint, hung from a metal signpost, squeaking as it gently swayed in the breeze. The sign stood next to a steep driveway curling down from the levee to the boat landing. Thomas slowed the Rover to a crawl and read the rest of the sign. "Tour the Bayou by Boat or Helicopter." And in smaller letters, "Closed Sundays and Christmas."

"Closed Sundays!" Thomas said. "Great. There's no phone number. How am I supposed to find them?"

Shaking his head, Thomas drove down the driveway and parked. He stepped out and closed the door quietly, trying not to wake the children. The chill breeze sent a shudder through his body. Even though it was not nearly as cold as where they had come from in Texas, the high humidity added a penetrating quality to the cold, making it sink right to the joints. Thomas flexed his fingers and rubbed his hands together.

On his left stood a small wooden dock. A flat-bottomed boat on huge aluminum floats gently bobbed in the water. Thomas assumed the boat was for the bayou tours.

He chuckled as he looked at its "accommodations." About thirty white plastic lawn chairs sat neatly arranged on the deck. *Hopefully those chairs are bolted down.* A green- and white-striped canopy stood over the boat, presumably to protect the tourists from the scorching Louisiana sun in the summer season.

A homemade helipad was off to the right, crudely painted but apparently effective. A small helicopter, capable of seating four people, rested dead center on the circle. A fluorescent orange windsock whipped in the breeze.

Straight ahead, a small building with a gift shop and restrooms stood dark and silent. Thomas went up to the window and peeked in. No signs of life. The wind blew his hair into his eyes.

"Wind's pickin' up. Storm might be brewin'." A voice spoke from behind Thomas.

Thomas's heart leaped into his throat. He caught his breath and turned around. A tall, thin man, wearing faded denim overalls and a heavy jacket over a long-sleeved, red flannel shirt, stood looking at Thomas. The man had parted his inky black hair low on one side, pulling it up over top of his head to conceal an obvious bald spot. He had a sizeable bulge in his right cheek.

The man brought a soda can to his lips and spit into it. "Like a chew?" he said, offering Thomas a packet of Red Man tobacco.

"No. Thanks."

"Good thing I saw you. Was about to go home. Still time to give you a tour before da sun goes down."

"I don't want a tour. I'm trying to find—"

"Shaw you want a tour of da bayou. Nothin' prettier than the Atchafalaya Basin at sunset."

"You don't understand. I'm not a tourist. I have got to find—"

The man's tone sharpened. "I said, you *got* to see the bayou! Now you wanna go? Or am I gonna go home?"

"I've got a couple of children with me."

"I know. Bring 'em along." The man spit into his can again and raised his eyebrows expectantly at Thomas.

"But how could you kn—" Thomas stopped in midsentence. He nodded at the man and walked back to the Rover. "Michelle. Micah. Wake up. We're here."

"Mom?" Micah said, bolting upright.

"Not yet, but soon," Thomas said. He looked back toward the boat. The man had moved on board and was firing up the engines. "Very soon, I think."

Michelle sat up, quietly rubbing the sleep from her eyes. "First we have to take a little boat ride."

Thomas helped Michelle, then Micah, out of the Rover, then led them toward the dock. Thomas held Micah's hand and guided him along the narrow wooden pier.

Michelle read the crudely painted sign. "Richard's Landing?"

"Dat's pronounced Ree-shard's Landing, young lady," the man called out from the boat. "I'm Charles Richard."

"Just hold my hand and move straight ahead," Thomas said to Micah. "Now, here's the edge of the boat. Step down and in."

Micah reached out his left foot, then pulled it back.

"It's okay, Micah. I won't let you fall. Just hold tight onto my arm and step down with your left foot. Then give your hand to Mr. Richard."

Micah stepped down, his small body trembling with fear. As his left foot touched inside the boat, Charles Richard put his hands around the boy's waist and carried him the rest of the way in.

"Dere you go, young man. Now, let's get you a good seat."

"Not close to the edge," Micah said.

"All right. We'll put you right on the center aisle. How's dat?"

"Thank you," Micah said, his gaze fixed straight ahead.

"Got another one for you," Thomas called out.

Richard helped Michelle in and gave her a seat beside her brother.

Thomas stepped into the boat and replaced the gate behind him.

"Ready to go?" Richard asked.

"Ready," Thomas said. He looked toward the sky. The pink had turned scarlet. Dark thunderheads billowed in the west. Thomas had already seen some flashes of lightning. "Are you sure we've got time for this?"

"We got all the time we need. Have a seat."

Thomas sat next to Michelle, on the seat nearest the side of the boat.

Richard hopped onto the dock, untied the bow and stern ropes, then stepped back into the flat-bottomed boat. He sat at the pilot wheel, about halfway back, and started the engine.

Slowly the boat drifted from the dock as Richard gave it some gas. The chugging sound developed into a throaty roar as he turned the boat into the waters of the bayou.

"It's a nice day to see the bayou, *cher*!" Richard laughed as the landing disappeared behind them.

In less than two minutes the little boat left all traces of civilization behind as Richard navigated it through the maze of the bayou. Tall cypress trees, draped with an apparently endless supply of Spanish moss, stood on either side of the narrow waterways. Thomas was grateful he didn't have to pilot the boat.

But Charles Richard obviously knew where he was going. He selected various channels through the swampy land as if street signs stood at each intersection. Occasionally, on either side of the boat, Thomas would spot a tiny island. As a blue heron flew parallel to the boat for a few seconds, Thomas reflected on the almost primeval quality of this place. The Atchafalaya Basin made you feel as if you were the only person on earth.

As a larger island drew near on the boat's port side, Richard slowed the motor to an idle. He stomped on the deck several times. As he walked to the front of the boat, Thomas said, "What are you doing?"

"Got to introduce you to Arthur. Wouldn't be polite not to." He stomped his foot again. Then he pulled a half-empty bag of marshmallows from his coat pocket. "Arthur! Where are you?"

Growing impatient with the delay, Thomas was about to say something when his eye caught a movement near the shoreline of the island. Although the sunlight was fading quickly and the shadows of the trees made visibility even more difficult, Thomas noticed a rippling in the water, moving directly toward the boat. The ripple spread out in a V pattern. As the ripple drew nearer, Thomas saw two dark shadowy lumps just above the surface. Within seconds, a large alligator swam up to the side of the boat.

Richard's eyes gleamed. "Hey, Arthur. Good boy." He took a marshmallow and tossed it into the water. With lightning swiftness, the gator's massive jaws swung sideways, snatching the floating white mass. A splash of water, and it was gone. Richard tossed in another marshmallow. The gator devoured it almost as soon as it hit the water. Richard turned and grinned at Thomas. "Just think what that could do to a man's hand."

"Look, Mr. Richard—"

"Charles."

"Charles. Hadn't we better be going? The sun's practically down now. The children are going to get cold if we don't get them out of this night air soon."

"You're right. We got to move on. I just can't bring people out here without introducing them to Arthur first."

"Well, thanks for the tour. But if it's all the same to you, we'd like to be on our way."

"Needn't worry," Richard said as he returned to his seat. "We're almost there now."

Thomas couldn't believe that they were anywhere near where they needed to be. All he had seen were herons, an alligator, and an occasional nutria swimming along. "I'll have to take your word for it," he said as he looked at the rapidly darkening sky.

Richard turned the boat back out into the bayou, cranking the engine up to full throttle. The boat darted quickly through the various waterways and within a few minutes was drawing near a large island. Thomas scanned the land as it became clear to him that this was where Richard intended to stop.

Couldn't be. There's no sign of life anywhere. The trees are so thick, you can't see twenty feet into the place. This has got to be another side trip.

"Here we are," Charles said, swinging the boat so it drew parallel to the shoreline.

"You've got to be kidding," Thomas said. "We're in the middle of nowhere."

"Trust me. This is where you need to be."

Thomas locked eyes with the man.

"I don't have all night," Richard said.

Shaking his head, Thomas said, "What do you want me to do?"

"Hop onto the shore and I'll throw you the rope. You can tie us to one of those trees."

Thomas stepped over the side of the boat, sinking almost waist deep. He sucked in a deep breath at the shock of the frigid water, then clambered onto the island. As he turned around, he could hear the boat's engines moving up from an idle. He held out his hand. "Throw me the rope."

Richard just laughed. He had already reversed the engines and was slowly backing away from the island.

"What are you doing?" Thomas yelled. He could see a worried expression coming over Micah's face. The boy grabbed his sister's hand.

"What's happening?" Michelle cried.

Thomas was about to jump into the water and swim toward the boat, when Charles Richard produced a small

BLIND SIGHT

pistol from his coat pocket. "I wouldn't do that," Richard warned.

The boat backed farther out into the channel, then swung around to head back down the waterway. "Have a nice night," Richard said, laughing. "And watch out for Arthur."

Thomas watched the boat—and the children—disappear into the night.

D ana Shipp lay on a cold floor in a pitch-black room,
her ribs aching. Running her tongue along the outside corner of her lips, she tasted crusty, dried blood. The
throbbing in her head and around her left eye came in
relentless waves, as if some sadistic blacksmith had used
her head for his anvil. Dana brushed her fingers over her
eye. The skin around it felt like a soft marshmallow, but
the instant her fingers touched the tender area, it felt more
like a pincushion. She winced and dropped her hand.

After resting for a few minutes, Dana pushed up to a
sitting position. Her elbow bumped into something on
her left side. The unmistakable metallic clatter told her
she was sitting next to a mop bucket. She detected a faint
odor of ammonia and cleaning solutions. Dim light trickled underneath the door. Dana's right hand traced its way
up the doorframe till she felt the knob. She wasn't particularly surprised to find it locked.

Woozy, she rested her head
against the corner of the wall

near the door. The moments after her capture replayed in her mind.

When Llewelen had entered the research room and locked the door behind him, Dana feared he intended to rape her. Llewelen had no such designs. He beat her savagely, even kicking her when she'd curled into a fetal position on the floor. Dana thought she was going to die right there. But another man's voice had broken off Llewelen's attack. "That's enough. I don't want her seriously damaged."

Llewelen had pulled her to her feet and thrown her into one of the chairs around the table. Barely conscious and able to see clearly through only one eye, Dana noticed a short man standing beside Llewelen. He tried to question her, asking repeatedly, "Who sent you?" and "Was it Justine?" Dana could scarcely sit up, let alone answer questions. She had gazed through blurred eyes at the man as he pressed her about this person named Justine.

Dana's silence infuriated him. He scowled at Llewelen. "You idiot! How can I question her when you've beaten her within an inch of her life? Possibly our only link to Justine and you've nearly killed her. Get her out of here. I'll deal with her later."

That was the last thing Dana remembered, until she woke up on the cold floor of a janitor's closet.

Whoever this Justine is, I feel sorry for her when they find her.

Dana braced herself as she heard footsteps approaching. She groped around desperately for anything that might serve as a weapon against another assault from Llewelen. Biting her lower lip to distract her from the pain of movement, Dana swept her hands back and forth on the floor until she felt the cold metal of a toolbox. She flipped it open and fingered the contents. When she found a small hammer, Dana jerked it out of the box. As she heard the sound of a key being inserted into the door, she scooted back to where she'd been sitting against the wall and, holding the hammer in her left hand, hid it behind her.

Just one good swing. Just let me get one good swing at him. He'll never hit anyone else again. I may never survive this, but neither will he.

The door opened and the flood of light temporarily blinded Dana. She squinted her good eye closed for a second and tightened her grip on the hammer, waiting for the sound of Llewelen's voice.

Instead she heard a woman's voice. "Come on, Miss Shipp. Mr. Wynne wants you."

Dana opened her eye and looked toward the sound of the unexpectedly kind voice. The woman who stood before her was the same one she'd seen in the hall earlier, the one who had inadvertently allowed Dana to sneak into the Fellowship's office complex.

Dana sat where she was. She looked at the woman's face, her body language, her eyes. She was one of them; Dana knew it. But she wasn't like Llewelen or the other man. Dana reached out her hand for the woman to pull her up. She released her grip on the hammer, laying it gently on the floor behind her.

Dana stood slowly, holding the woman's hand and bracing herself against the door. Patiently, the woman led the way out of the closet and into what looked like a small dining room/kitchen suite.

"Would you like something to drink?" the woman asked.

Dana nodded.

"Sit over here," she said, leading Dana to a small dining table.

Dana eased herself down into a chair, resting most of her weight against the table. Her ribs screamed with every breath she took. Standing made her head throb with renewed vigor.

"Could I have an aspirin?" Dana called out toward the small kitchen.

"Certainly," the woman's voice came back.

In a few minutes, she came out of the kitchen with a large glass of orange juice and two aspirin. Dana tossed the pills into her mouth and chased them down with juice.

"Don't drink too quickly, now. You'll make yourself sick."

"Thank you," Dana said, looking at her questioningly.

"Jeanette."

Sipping a little more juice, Dana asked, "Why are they doing this to me, Jeanette?"

"I think you know the answer to that."

"No I don't."

"Give Mr. Wynne what he wants. It will go easier with you later."

"What do you mean?"

Closing her eyes and shaking her head, Jeanette said, "Just tell him what he wants to know. Come on. We'd better get to his office. Mr. Wynne doesn't like to be kept waiting."

Dana finished her juice and, holding a hand across her abdomen, pushed herself up from the chair.

Jeanette led her into a darkened hallway. They turned to the right and made their way toward a door that bore the name "Sawyer Wynne" printed in gold letters.

She opened the door and, with her hand on Dana's right elbow, brought her through a spacious waiting room with a secretary's desk. Dana noticed the nameplate on the desk: "Jeanette Marshall, Executive Secretary." She led Dana toward an inner door and opened it, bringing her into a large office with several huge windows facing the Syracuse skyline.

"Sit over here," Jeanette said, motioning toward a plush chair upholstered in burgundy leather.

The soft chair eased Dana's pain as she sank into it.

For the moment, Dana didn't mind being questioned as long as she could stay in this chair.

"Mr. Wynne will be in shortly," Jeanette said as she left the room.

Dana looked at her surroundings carefully. At first glance there wasn't much to distinguish this office from any other executive suite. Expensive furniture. Huge oak desk. Beautiful skyline view.

But what struck Dana was the room's utter sterility. The room was immaculate. Not a thing out of place. In the office of the most fastidious executive, some evidence of the person would be detectable. Mementos, family pictures, artwork, awards—something to reflect the person who sat behind the desk. Here, absolutely nothing presented itself. The place looked like a model room you might find in an office furniture store. Sterile. Cold. Dead. Ironically, not even a photo of Anthony MacAsland, the patron saint of the place, adorned the walls of this office.

In the middle of Sawyer Wynne's desk sat a brass bowl. Filled to nearly overflowing with unshelled walnuts, pecans, Brazil nuts, almonds, the bowl appeared unused. A nutcracker and one pick had been carefully arranged on top. No shells or fragments were anywhere in evidence.

The only thing in the room offering any sign of life was a large terrarium of some kind. A bright light shone into the glass encasement, where a small but brightly colored snake lay coiled on a rock. As a rule, Dana hated snakes, but the beautiful red, yellow, and black striping held her attention. There was something fetching, something almost enigmatic, about a snake that looked so quietly beautiful. For several minutes Dana stared at the snake, almost forgetting her situation and her surroundings.

"It's a coral snake, Miss Shipp," came a voice from behind her.

Startled, Dana swung around toward the voice. The

sharp pain in her ribs reminded her that sudden movement was not a good idea.

The man who stood in the doorway of a small bathroom adjoining the office was the same man who had watched Llewelen beat her. He appeared to have just finished cleaning up. Dana could tell that his graying hair was freshly washed and combed, and he was wiping shaving cream from his face with a towel. Short and slightly built, the man seemed almost spindly to Dana.

His expression chilled her. Stone cold, he reflected no emotion. His face appeared as though frozen by the sight of some dark Medusa. His eyes showed no expression, yet they pierced Dana like ice picks.

He walked over toward the terrarium. "Coral snakes are amazing creatures," he said, looking down into the terrarium. "Hard to believe that such a quiet, gentle animal can be so deadly, isn't it?"

Dana didn't answer.

Wynne lifted the cover and reached in. He expertly handled the snake, grasping it behind its head. "Funny thing about coral snakes. Even their bite can be deceiving. If one should bite you, you might be tempted to ignore the bite. There would be very little pain."

Wynne walked over toward Dana, still carrying the snake.

Dana felt herself beginning to tremble; cold shivers racked her body.

"You see, a coral snake doesn't strike like a rattler. Its head and fangs are too small."

Wynne moved closer.

"It has to chew on its victim." He held the snake close to Dana's face.

A cold bead of perspiration trickled down the back of Dana's neck.

"Even then, the wound would appear minor. Very little pain or necrosis." His voice chilled to a whisper. "But if you are sufficiently envenomed, about ten hours later you'll start to have difficulty breathing. Then muscle spasms and paralysis will set in."

The coral snake was now only inches from Dana's cheek. She was shaking so hard, the chair trembled with her.

Wynne's voice burned like dry ice. "Finally your heart will shut down."

Wynne held the snake's head less than a finger's width from Dana's face.

"It's not a pleasant death, Miss Shipp. Not pleasant at all."

Dana was drenched in cold sweat. Her breath came in ragged gasps.

Wynne pulled the snake back and turned toward the terrarium. A fleeting smile crossed his face as he returned the snake to its glass home. Then he sat down in the executive chair. His eyes never left Dana.

For several minutes he said nothing. Yet Dana would have almost preferred his screams rather than the acidic glare in which he held her. The quiet became palpable. And Sawyer Wynne's gaze continued to hold her captive.

As the minutes ticked by, Wynne's silence became maddening, but Dana didn't dare break it for fear of what she might unleash. It was as if the spider sat contemplating how it would devour its prey. Black eyes, like drops of India ink, focused their coldness on her. Heavy eyelids, like thick velvet curtains, drooped over the man's emotionless eyes.

He sat there, the fingertips of his hands pressed against one another, resting against his chin.

When Dana felt like screaming, just to hear the sound of her own voice, Sawyer Wynne reached toward the bowl of nuts. Selecting a particularly large walnut, he fitted it between the nutcracker's ornate metal prongs. He held it, still fixing his eyes on Dana, and slowly began to squeeze. As if he were in no hurry to actually open the nut, Wynne compressed the two prongs together with slowly increasing tension. The muscles of his hand quivered with the pressure.

A sharp crack echoed through the room as the nut exploded in Wynne's hand, crumbling in a shower of shell fragments, dust, and nut particles. They dropped into Sawyer Wynne's lap and fell on the floor.

Wynne sat, oblivious to the shattered pieces of walnut now soiling the once immaculate office. Still holding Dana in his caustic scrutiny, he reached into the bowl and selected another nut, a Brazil nut this time. Placing it between the nutcracker's pincers, he closed his eyes, squeezing until a riflelike crack echoed off the walls.

Dana shuddered.

Sawyer Wynne spoke. His eyes remained closed. His voice barely rose above a whisper. But its calmness and quietness did not deceive Dana. His was a voice that embodied more evil than Dana had ever experienced.

"Have you ever had a vision, Miss Shipp?" he said. "A dream so powerful, so all-encompassing, so over-whelming, that it literally consumes you? It eats away at your thoughts, gnawing into the depths of your mind until you either have to pursue the dream or go insane."

His eyes still closed, Wynne grasped a pecan, enclosing it in the pincers. "And then someone betrays your dream. Threatens it. Seeks to destroy it."

Dana could hear the tension mounting in his voice as he spoke.

"You can't just sit back and let them destroy it, can you? You have to do something." Tremors rippled through his arm and wrist as he gripped the nutcracker, tighter and tighter. "Stop them any way you can."

The nut shattered.

Sawyer Wynne opened his eyes and fixed a cold stare on her. He lowered his voice. "Do whatever you have to do."

Dana felt as if the temperature in the room dropped thirty degrees instantly. She wanted to draw her knees up into the chair and wrap her arms around herself to fight off the waves of cold horror threatening to overwhelm her.

Her body tensed as Sawyer Wynne dropped the nutcracker and rose from his seat. She didn't know what he intended, but she wasn't giving up without a fight. She would scratch the little man's eyes out if she had to.

Wynne turned away from her and walked toward the expansive windows behind his desk. He clasped his hands behind him and gazed out into the snow-covered canyon of downtown Syracuse.

Shaking his head, Sawyer Wynne said, "Justine Bishop really should have changed her name when she left us. 'Judas' would have been much more appropriate, considering the damage she's tried to inflict on us."

He turned from the window and walked to the front of his desk. He sat down on the desktop, his face not three feet from Dana's. "I want her, Miss Shipp. And you're going to help me find her."

Dana knew nothing of Justine Bishop or of this man's hatred for her. But she was smart enough to understand that Justine was her only link to survival. As long as Sawyer Wynne thought she could lead him to this woman, he would keep Dana alive. Her only chance was to play along.

"What if I can't find her? She moves around a lot, you know."

A grin crossed his face. "Would you like to know what we do to traitors, Miss Shipp?"

Before Dana could respond, he continued. "Coventina Wilcox had an unfortunate accident today. Killed by a hit-and-run driver while she was out on a little errand for me."

The words exploded from Dana's mouth before she could restrain herself. "Coventina knew nothing about this."

Wynne leaned forward,

BLIND SIGHT

bringing his face within inches of Dana's. "That may be. But she was responsible for bringing you into the Fellowship."

A sneer curled his lips. "You see, we're not a very forgiving lot."

Dana dropped her head. Tears fell unchecked into her lap.

"Are you going to tell me where Justine is?"

Dana didn't answer.

"Very well." Sawyer Wynne stood up and walked behind his desk. "You obviously need some help in jogging your memory." He pushed a button on his telephone console. In seconds the door opened. Llewelen and a man she didn't recognize entered, both wearing street clothes and heavy coats.

Dana's mouth went dry.

Sawyer Wynne sat down in his executive chair. "We can't deal with you properly here. Too great a risk of discovery. So we're going to take you to a nice quiet place where you'll have some time to think." His lips curled back and his eyes gleamed with a sadistic twinkle.

Before she could respond, a strong hand pressed a wet handkerchief over her mouth and nose. As noxious fumes invaded her nostrils, Dana felt nauseating waves of dizziness washing over her.

And all went black.

29

Thomas watched in stunned disbelief as the flat-bottomed boat chugged out of sight, its rumbling engine dissolving into the restless sounds of bayou twilight. He stood on the shore, gazing into the channel's rippling water, hoping that it all might be some crazy nightmare from which he would soon wake up. He half expected to see Charles Richard's portly figure pilot the boat around the other side of the island, laughing and calling in a singsong voice, "April fool!"

But April was still nearly four months away.

Thomas turned away from the water and stalked back toward a massive cypress tree, his hands closing and opening as if he were a madman looking for someone to throttle. He grabbed a large piece of driftwood and swung at the giant tree, slamming the partially rotted wood against it. The driftwood exploded, showering slivers and fragments into the air. Thomas stood there, holding only a stub of

wood in his hand. With a cry, he whirled
around and flung it into the water.

He stood where he was and glared
up toward the storm clouds building
in the twilight sky. "Is this some kind of sick joke?" he
screamed, grabbing handfuls of his hair. "Do You get
Your jollies by making people squirm?"

A low rumble of thunder was the only answer Thomas
received.

"Wasn't it enough for YOU to take my wife and kids?
What kind of God are You?"

Chill wind swirled through the Spanish moss that
hung from the towering cypress trees, swishing them back
and forth. For the first time Thomas felt the coldness of
the air on his wet trousers. He hung his head. His voice
dropped to a tortured whisper.

"God, why do You hate me?"

A strong gust roared through the bayou, nearly
knocking him off-balance. Behind him came the shattering sound of a tree branch splitting, wood crackling, then
crashing into the water with a huge splash.

Still facing the shoreline, Thomas could barely see
it now that the sun had nearly set. All he could make
out were the faint outline of the shore and the water's
empty blackness. Lightning struck the cypress tree behind
him. The blinding flash and deafening explosion knocked
Thomas to the ground. He lay there dazed.

He could hear children singing.

"Jesus loves me, this I know."

Sarah. Steven.

"For the Bible tells me so."

Rain pelted the windshield. The wipers beat like
metronomes.

"Little ones to Him belong."

An 18-wheeler blasted past their little car, almost over-
whelming it with its spray. Thomas felt the little station
wagon shudder in the truck's wake.

"Idiot," he muttered.

He felt Jenny's hand pat his knee, reminding him not to use such language in front of the children.

"They are weak but He is strong."

Sheets of water assaulted the car as it followed Interstate 30 from Rockwall toward Dallas. The cold front and its accompanying torrent had caught them by surprise. There had been plenty of warning for anyone who had listened to the weather reports for that day. They hadn't. And traveling after dark, they couldn't see the black, swirling clouds rolling toward them. So they were totally unprepared for the fifty-mile-per-hour winds that buffeted their little car.

"Yes, Jesus loves me."

Jenny had suggested they sing to keep the children's minds off the storm.

"Yes, Jesus loves me."

Two cars shot past, one on either side of them. Thomas bit his lip as he gripped the steering wheel.

"Yes, Jesus loves me."

Thomas could see almost nothing as he and his family rolled down the hill toward Lake Ray Hubbard. He wondered if he should have taken the last exit to wait out the storm.

"The Bible tells me so."

"That was great, kids," Jenny's voice echoed, straining to be heard over the pelting rain. "What song can we sing next?"

"'This Little Light'!" Sarah squealed.

"This little light of mine," all three voices rang out.

Normally Thomas loved to hear his children sing. At this moment, he couldn't stand it. The pelting rain now peppered with hail, the relentless wash of other cars and trucks rushing by, his inability to see ten feet in front of the car had all worn his nerves to a frazzle. The children's singing now seemed to Thomas as the screeching of fingernails on a blackboard. It may have been settling them, but it was driving him crazy.

"*I'm gonna—*"

"Could you stop, please?"

Sarah giggled, then sang louder.

"*I'm gonna let it—*"

Thomas raised his voice. "No more."

Steven joined in the game, now bellowing.

"*I'M GONNA LET IT SHINE.*"

Thomas swung around, glaring at the kids. "I said quiet down! Can't you see I'm trying to drive here?"

"Thomas," Jenny said, "calm down and drive."

"How can I drive with all this noise?" He glared at Steven and Sarah again. "Now you kids keep quiet. Do you hear me?"

He saw the terror first in Steven's eyes.

"Daddy, watch out!"

He glanced at Jenny. Her gaze was fixed on a scene ahead of the car. A speechless expression of horror strained her beautiful features.

Thomas swung his focus back toward the windshield. In the next few seconds, rapid-fire images surged through his mind. The speedometer. He was going ninety. When had he lost track of his speed? Next a blurred mass of tail-lights. Traffic had stopped ahead.

Thomas slammed on the brakes and swung the car to the right. The tires found no traction on the drenched pavement. Thomas lost control.

The car slammed head-on into the concrete guardrail, then flipped over and into the darkness of the lake. He heard Sarah's screams as they fell, felt the jarring impact as the roof of the car hit the water.

Thomas was instantly disoriented. Upside-down. Icy cold water gushed into the car, churning with unimaginable force. The only light he could see was the greenish brown haze of the car's headlights shining through the murkiness of the lake.

Thomas gasped for air, breathing as deeply as he could as the inky blackness swallowed him.

All that was left was silence.

And the water's icy death grip.

Thomas was colder than he had ever been in his life.

Thomas blinked. He felt raindrops pelting, stinging him. He raised his arm to cover his face. He lay on the wet ground, soaked to the bone. Thunder roared overhead. Lightning streaked across the night sky, revealing the cypress trees of the Atchafalaya Basin.

He wasn't on Lake Ray Hubbard. He was in Louisiana, abandoned on an island by Mr. Charles Richard.

No. Not abandoned by Richard.

Abandoned by God.

Thomas lay there on the shore, feeling the rain beating his face. Not moving. Not caring. He felt life slipping away as the chill penetrated deeper and deeper into his joints and muscles. He managed a weak smile as images of Sarah and Steven flowed through his mind. He would see them soon. He'd simply go to sleep and wake up with them.

It was okay. He was tired of living.

As Thomas lay in a haze, slipping in and out of consciousness, he found himself experiencing the strangest sensations. Snippets of happy memories flashed before him: a trip to the State Fair of Texas; Christmas with the kids; a Fourth of July football game in the front yard. The delighted squeals of the children flowed through his mind. But the aromas were the best part. Thomas reexperienced glorious smells that reminded him of good times: cotton candy, pumpkin pie, seafood gumbo.

And coffee.

Not Jenny's. She didn't drink coffee, couldn't make it to save her life.

The aroma of dark-roasted Seaport coffee filled Thomas's mind. Coffee so strong it could make you cry

for mercy, then beg for another cup.
Thomas savored the aroma.
What a way to die.

. . . . . .

When Thomas felt shivers racking his body and warmth
creeping into his toes, he realized he wasn't going to die.
Barely conscious, he understood that someone had found
him on that desolate island and had saved his life. He
didn't know who it was. And when he met that person,
he didn't know whether he'd thank him or belt him in
the mouth.

Fighting off the desire to go back to sleep, he forced
his eyes open and raised his head to survey his surroundings. He was in a rustic cabin. The bed on which he lay
had been built into the wall with two-by-fours. Thick rope
had been woven through holes in the wood in a cross-
hatch pattern to create some semblance of a mattress. A
couple of ratty blankets lay beneath him and another on
top of him. They smelled musty, but not musty enough
to cover the bouquet of the coffee. At least that much he
hadn't dreamed. Across the room a woodstove generated
the heat. Someone had spread out his clothing near the
stove.

Wrinkling his forehead, Thomas looked underneath
the covers. Whoever had rescued him had also changed his
clothes. He now wore a blue plaid flannel shirt and a pair
of blue jeans at least two sizes too large by the feel of
them. On top of the woodstove Thomas saw the source
of the aroma: a beat-up tin coffeepot, the kind designed
to use on a campfire.

An old wooden table with three rickety-looking chairs
sat in the middle of the tiny room. Off to his left were two
doors. The dark window across the room told him it was
still night. The only light was coming from a couple of
kerosene lamps attached to the walls.

Thomas wanted to get up, to investigate, to discover what was on the other side of those doors. But as soon as he tried to move, his body informed him it wasn't ready to go anywhere. Thomas allowed his head to fall back onto the damp, musty pillow. He soon drifted off into a fitful sleep.

Monday, December 9

Rain pelted the cabin's tin roof, sounding like a steel-drum band gone sour. Thomas tried to ignore the racket, but it was no use. He opened his eyes and glanced toward the window on the opposite wall. Pale gray light filtered through tacky, checkered curtains.

Thomas sat up, allowing the blanket to fall away from him. He shivered. "Fire must've gone out," Thomas said, standing.

Waves of dizziness and nausea washed over him, almost making him sit back down. He steadied himself, then took several tentative steps across the room and put his hand near the top of the woodstove. It was cold. Thomas knelt down and opened the metal door on the front of the stove. Not a single glowing ember stood out. He grasped a poker from the floor and stirred the ashes around.

Nothing.

Using the poker as a cane,

BLIND
SIGHT

Thomas pushed himself back to a standing position. He picked up the tin coffeepot that had been the source of his only good dream last night. He lifted the top and put his finger inside.

"Wonderful. Iced coffee."

Setting the coffeepot back on the stove, Thomas turned toward two doors on the far side of the cabin. The one with the window obviously led outside. He pushed aside homemade red-checkered curtains and looked through a small window beside the doorframe. Rain dripped from the massive cypress trees surrounding the cabin. The trees told him that he was still in the bayou, but he had no desire to go out and explore—at least not until the rain stopped.

Thomas walked to the other door and pulled it open, revealing a small pantry with shelves loaded with canned and dry goods. Against the back wall of the cabin a cord of firewood lay neatly stacked, plus everything he needed to get a fire going. Several large bottles of water and a dispenser provided all the water he would need.

Within fifteen minutes Thomas had a healthy fire roaring in the woodstove and an extra-strong pot of coffee brewing.

Later, as he sat drinking coffee at the little table, Thomas noticed that the sound of the rain had lessened. The sky was still as gray as it had been when he'd awakened, and a quick glance through the window told him it was sprinkling. But at least he could step outside and have a quick look around without getting soaked. He considered the idea a moment, then quickly dismissed it. Instead he poured himself another cup of coffee. Soothing warmth seeped into his fingers as he cradled the mug with both hands.

As Thomas sat at the table listening to the rain on the cabin's tin roof, he thought about how close he'd come to death last night. A surge of anger swept through him.

Death had been tantalizingly near. He could practically feel it.

And he *wanted* to die. That's why he hated his rescuer. He didn't even know who had saved him. But he hated him. Hated him for making him continue a tortured existence, for forcing him to go on living when all he wanted was to curl into a fetal position and drift away.

Death wasn't an enemy to Thomas. It would bring peaceful release from all his pain. Reunion with Jenny, with Steven, with Sarah.

Of course he didn't have to wait for death to come to him. He could have ended his own life many times; indeed, on several occasions he'd given the idea of suicide serious thought. But something always stopped him.

It wasn't that he hesitated to kill himself out of some lingering fear of punishment. In fact, he was punishing himself—by living. And so Thomas suffered every day, yet he hoped daily that death would deliver him from his prison.

But after the last few days, Thomas felt as if a category-five tornado had leveled his life to the ground.

Gumbo was gone.

His carefully preserved memories of his wife and children had been brutally destroyed.

And he probably couldn't go home without facing charges for murders he didn't commit. Not that prison held any terror for him. Thomas had been in prison from the moment rescuers pulled him from Lake Ray Hubbard.

Ironically, the government did not hold him responsible for his family's deaths—not directly at least. He had faced charges of reckless driving in the accident, charges to which he pleaded "no contest" and received a suspended sentence. But the authorities did not consider Thomas liable in his failure to rescue Jenny, Steven, and Sarah. In their collective wisdom, it was a miracle that anyone survived the accident in the first place.

BLIND
SIGHT

No it wasn't. It was a curse. I should have died with them.

Thomas was about to pour another cup of coffee when he heard a familiar chugging sound in the distance. He hurried to the front door and looked out the window. He could see nothing.

He pulled open the door and stepped out into the cold drizzle. Taking the three steps down to the muddy ground, he looked around but saw only cypress trees and Spanish moss. Thomas ran around to the back of the cabin, where he saw a small dock on the shoreline about twenty feet away.

At the far corner of the island, a flat-bottomed boat with a green-striped canopy skimmed the surface of the water, heading in Thomas's direction. The pilot was wearing a hooded green poncho that reached halfway down his legs. The hood prevented Thomas from seeing his face, but he had no doubts about who it was.

"Charles Richard," he muttered, "if you've hurt those kids, you won't leave this island alive."

Thomas stormed toward the dock as the boat drew near and pulled alongside. The pilot motioned for Thomas to secure the bow. Thomas ran along the dock and secured the bowline, while the pilot brought the stern in. Then he waved Thomas back and tossed him the stern line.

Hastily securing it, Thomas shouted, "Get off that boat now!"

The man waved his hand and powered down the engine. But he moved slowly and deliberately, as if in no great hurry.

Unable to wait, Thomas hopped over the rail and into the boat. Racing through the plastic lawn chairs, he came around to the pilot wheel and grabbed Richard by the poncho. Whirling him around, he screamed, "Where are the children? Tell me now or I swear I'll take this boat to the middle of the swamp and feed you to Arthur! Where are they?"

As the man pulled back his hood, flowing ash-blonde hair tumbled out. Thomas stopped short as he gazed down into the soft, apple green eyes of a woman who could almost pass as Michelle's twin sister.

"The children?" she said. "They're okay. Thanks to you."

Thomas just stood there, speechless, gaping at her.

The woman looked him up and down, then glanced toward the sky. "Would you maybe like to get out of the rain?" she said. "Or would you prefer to stay out here until you're as soaked as you were last night?"

Thomas's mouth had gone dry. "I–I'm sorry. I just wasn't expecting . . . I mean, you kind of caught me off guard." Thomas extended his hand, feeling like a nerdy kid trying to introduce himself to a girl for the first time. "I'm Thomas Kent."

The woman smiled grimly as she took his hand. "Justine Bishop."

● ● ● ● ●

Inside the cabin, Thomas poured himself another cup of coffee. "Coffee?" he called out toward the storage room, where Justine Bishop was hanging up her poncho.

The woman nodded.

Thomas took a plastic mug, filled it with coffee, and handed it to her. He watched her as she sipped from the mug.

"Why are you looking at me like that?" she said.

Thomas chuckled and said, "I had planned on punching you in the mouth when you showed up. I think I changed my mind."

She raised an eyebrow and grinned. "I appreciate that."

He turned and sat down on one of the folding chairs. "I would like an explanation, though. Why the charade with

Charles Richard? Why leave me here in the middle of nowhere?" He tossed his head toward the window. "With Arthur and his pals out there just itching for a taste of me."

Justine smiled at the mention of Arthur. "Charles introduced you to his buddy, did he?" She sat on the edge of the bed, still holding the plastic mug. "It was the prudent thing to do. For all we knew, you were sent by the Fellowship, using the children as bait. We've expected for some time that they might try to make a play like that. So we decided if anybody ever showed up with Micah and Michelle, we'd separate them first, then isolate the person who brought them. That way we could buy enough time to find out if you were on the level."

A hint of irritation crept into Thomas's voice. "You had to make sure I was on the level?"

Justine sipped her coffee and nodded.

Thomas stood up and walked over toward the window. He looked out into the steady drizzle. His jaws clenched. The words came softly from his lips. "Do you have any idea what I've been through in the last few days?" He turned and fixed a hard gaze at Justine.

Her eyes met his.

"My life—what's left of it—has been destroyed. I sacrificed everything I had to get your kids to you. And now you tell me you had to leave me in this godforsaken place to make sure I was on the level?"

"Mr. Kent . . ."

Thomas pointed out the window. "If it wasn't for me, those two kids would have been in the hands of your Fellowship before they ever got out of the airport. And you had to make sure you can *trust* me?"

"We didn't have a choice," Justine said.

Thomas swung around and walked toward the door. "Oh, don't give me that. You had plenty of choices. There were other ways you could have checked me out.

You didn't have to risk my life. I could have died out there."

"But you didn't, did you?" Justine's voice remained calm. "Besides, what would *you* have done?" she asked.

"What?"

"If Micah and Michelle were yours and there was the slightest chance someone evil had them—someone so evil that they wouldn't think twice about killing them if it served their purpose—what would you have done?"

Thomas stood silently for a moment, then heaved a sigh and nodded. "I'd get the children away from them any way I could." He refilled his mug and sat down at the table. "I'm sorry. It's been rough."

"I understand," she said.

Thomas studied Justine's face. She seemed to have aged before Thomas's eyes. Creases and worry lines appeared where he hadn't noticed them before.

She cradled her coffee cup in her hands. "Join the club. I've been living with this for three years."

"Why did you leave the Fellowship?" Thomas asked.

"I couldn't support what they do anymore. I certainly couldn't worship Anthony MacAsland any longer."

"Why not?"

Justine shrugged. "It's a long story. Suffice it to say that I just couldn't be a part of them any longer."

"Why did you leave the children behind?" Thomas asked.

Justine shook her head. "I didn't know what else to do. I knew the Fellowship would come after me. And to tell you the truth, I didn't have much hope of escaping on my own, let alone with the twins. They were only seven at the time. With Micah's blindness slowing us down, I knew there was no way we'd be able to escape together. The Fellowship would have caught up with us before we'd gone ten miles."

BLIND
SIGHT

"But weren't you afraid they might hold the children hostage or something?"

Justine shook her head. "I knew Peter wouldn't let anything happen to them."

"So you just left them?"

She got up, slammed her empty coffee mug down on the table, and walked over to the window. Hot anger flashed in her eyes as she glared back at Thomas. "I didn't have a lot of choices, all right? I suppose you could have done better?"

"Well, I wouldn't have abandoned them."

"Oh, really? I suppose you would have rushed in there like a knight on a white horse, swept Micah and Michelle up in your arms, ridden off into the sunset, and lived happily ever after."

"I don't know. But the point is—"

"The point *is*," Justine said, whirling around to face Thomas, "that you don't know *anything*. I left those children there, not because I didn't love them but because I did. I never intended to abandon them to the Fellowship. But I knew I had a better chance of rescuing them once I was safely on the outside."

"And just how did you plan to do that?"

Justine was incredulous. "I don't have to explain myself to you."

Thomas stood his ground. "Look, I just risked my neck getting your kids back to you. On top of that, thanks to the Fellowship, I'm probably wanted for questioning in a double murder committed on my property. Even if I manage to survive this mess, I could spend the rest of my life in prison. So I think I'm entitled to know why I had to go through it all."

Justine ground out the words through clenched teeth. "I was going to expose Anthony MacAsland and the Fellowship to the world."

She sat down on the corner of the bed. Thomas could see her wilting before his eyes.

"I thought I could bring the Fellowship down. Once I was safe, I planned to enlist whatever help I could: newspapers, TV, Congress."

"What went wrong?"

She shook her head. "The Fellowship was always a step ahead of me. Since I had left my husband and family without any warning, they accused me of abandonment. The Fellowship's lawyers arranged a quick divorce for Peter, and the courts awarded him custody. Not long after that, Peter and the Fellowship sued to have my parental rights terminated. I couldn't oppose it without risking my life, so they won."

"What about the information you had that would bring the cult down?" Thomas asked.

Justine rested her head in her hands. "Stupid on my part. I assumed because I had been an insider, people would listen to me. I thought I could just go to the police, newspapers, somebody with authority, and tell them what was going on. I forgot about MacAsland's PR team.

"They beat me to the punch. Before I ever had a chance to tell my story, they leaked word to the press that a disgruntled member of MacAsland's organization had left with the intention of trying to destroy his reputation. They portrayed me as an abusive mother who deserted my own kids. By the time they were finished, the tabloids wouldn't even talk to me. Everybody figured I was a kook with an ax to grind.

"Ever since, I've done the best I can to alert people to what MacAsland is doing. I write articles and have a four-hundred-page exposé ready if I can ever find a publisher." She shook her head. "Nobody listens anymore."

Thunder rumbled in the distance. Justine cocked her head, as if trying to hear it better.

Thomas asked, "So, what was this earth-shattering information you had that was going to bring the whole Fellowship crashing down around MacAsland?"

Justine didn't answer. She walked into the storage room, and a second later she came out with her poncho and tossed a small plastic package to Thomas.

"What's this?" he asked.

"Another poncho. Sounds like the weather's getting worse. We need to get back to the landing. Put the poncho on. I'll tell you the rest on the way."

Thomas tore the plastic package open and removed the navy blue poncho. He pulled it over his head as he followed Justine out the cabin door and into the rain. The light drizzle had increased to a steady rain by the time they had untied the boat and pushed off. Justine stood behind the pilot's wheel and guided the boat through the maze of channels as skillfully as Charles Richard had the previous night.

Thomas sat on one of the white plastic chairs near Justine. "So, what's MacAsland's Achilles' heel?"

Justine's lips pressed tightly together. "I don't know if I'd call it an Achilles' heel."

"Okay. So what is it, then?"

"Most cults," Justine continued, "turn inward, retreat into their little groups. They regard the outside world with distrust and isolate themselves. Remember Jonestown? Waco? Heaven's Gate?"

Thomas nodded.

"Even when groups actively recruit new members, they maintain an isolationist mentality, passing it on to the novices. The cult leaders are content to lord it over little flocks of their own creation, at the same time claiming to be modern messiahs for the whole world."

Justine looked toward Thomas as the boat cruised between the massive concrete pylons of the Interstate 10 bridge. Thomas could feel the bridge vibrate as an 18-wheeler rumbled directly overhead. As they left the bridge behind them, Justine fixed her eyes on Thomas and said, "Anthony MacAsland isn't content to rule his little group off in some desert retreat. He wants real power."

"Small chance of that happening," Thomas said.

Looking forward, Justine steered the boat into another channel. "Don't be so sure. If the Project is on schedule— and I have no reason to believe it isn't—he could be well along the way to getting the political power he craves."

"The Project?"

Justine nodded. "They code-named it the Osmosis Project. It's a carefully choreographed attempt to insert loyal cult members into key positions in society. Not to take over everything, mind you, just to place people strategically so that they are able to create an environment where the cult can thrive—and influence society."

Thomas looked ahead toward the bow as they broke into a broad channel. Ahead in the distance he could see Richard's Landing, silent and deserted in the gray drizzle.

"Well, it's a free country. I guess they've got as much right as anyone else to try to influence things."

Justine smiled and shook her head. "Not the way they're doing it. They're idealistic, but not very patient. It would take at least a generation for the Fellowship to gain that kind of influence. MacAsland would be too old to enjoy the power."

"So how does he plan to speed things up?"

"The Project was designed with three phases. Phase one is ongoing and is called Molding. They recruit carefully selected men and women from all parts of society. Then they isolate them in a retreat center and break down their resistance until they are brainwashed to total loyalty to MacAsland.

"As soon as the recruits are molded into the Fellowship's way of thinking, they release them into phase two, Reentry. The novices are sent to one of the Fellowship's five community centers across the country. They stay there for a year or two and are slowly reentered into society, this time

BLiND
SIGHT

to act as the Fellowship's invisible representatives. They don't make waves, don't
try to make converts. They just do their
jobs well and wait for the Fellowship to call
on them. Some stay where they are from then on. Others
are moved on to phase three, Osmosis.

"What's Osmosis?"

"It's the power play. Depending on the members'
potential for placement in a powerful position, the Fellowship will use any resources at its disposal to move them
where MacAsland wants them."

"I take it the 'resources' are sometimes less than
legal," Thomas said.

"That's putting it mildly. Sometimes all it takes is a
little pressure on the right person, a little money in the
right pocket, or support for the right issue. Other times,
people in the way have been known to have 'accidents.'"

Thomas raised his eyebrows. "I'd have a hard time
believing that if I hadn't almost had one of those 'accidents' myself."

As Richard's Landing drew nearer, Thomas moved to
the bow as Justine guided the boat toward the dock. He
stepped over the rail, taking the bow line and securing it
as Justine gently brought the stern to the dock. Thomas
caught the stern line and tied the boat securely.

The two of them walked up from the landing toward
the souvenir shop.

"How did you learn so much about MacAsland's
plans?" Thomas asked. "I'd think he'd keep as few people
as possible in the loop."

"You're right," Justine said. "Actually, only a handful of people other than Anthony himself know the
details. There's Sawyer Wynne. He's the real power
in the organization. In fact, even the great Anthony
MacAsland answers to Wynne where the Osmosis Project is concerned.

"I probably wouldn't have known as much as I do

if it weren't for my ex-husband, Peter. He was gifted at designing computer systems. I recruited him when he was working on his master's degree in Syracuse. Later, with Anthony's blessing, Peter and I got married.

"Peter designed all the Fellowship's computer systems. He also designed the security systems." Justine shook her head and smiled. "He made sure that he was always able to access whatever information he wanted. And he never was much for keeping secrets. Everything he found out, he passed on to me. That's how I know so much."

"What made you decide to leave?" Thomas asked.

"What can I say? Someone led me to Christ. You can't have two messiahs in your life. Anthony had to go. And I had to leave."

"Why didn't Peter leave too?" Thomas asked. "Didn't he agree with you?"

"Deep down, yes, I think he did. But he was afraid of Anthony—and Sawyer Wynne particularly. So he remained loyal to the group."

Justine shook her head. "Something pretty drastic must have happened for him to have sent the children away like he did."

Thomas's mind flashed back to the message that played from his answering machine. A message from a man who was clearly about to die.

Thomas stopped on the sidewalk outside Richard's Bayou Tours and Souvenirs. The rain had stopped, and pale beams of sunlight sliced through the clouds above. He put a hand on her shoulder and turned her toward him. He gazed into her gentle green eyes, not wanting to tell her about Peter, yet knowing that he had no choice.

"Justine," he said, "I need to tell you something about Peter."

"I'd rather not talk about Peter," she said.

"But, Justine—"

"I said no!" Justine pulled away.

Surprised by the hostility in her voice, Thomas changed the subject. "What do you plan to do now that you have the children back?"

"I don't know," she said. "I've been consumed over the last three years with bringing down Wynne and MacAsland. Sometimes I wonder if there's much use in my trying to go on with that. The allegations are so crazy. Nobody believes me anyway. And I can't prove a thing."

"Peter e-mailed me some files," Thomas said. "I think they might be about the Project. And we have one of the Fellowship's laptops, courtesy of their latest hit squad. That should give you the ammunition you need."

Justine nodded. "Charles and I checked both of them out last night."

"Anything interesting?"

"The computer is useless. It only contains a communications program so the conversion team can report on their activities. About all we could do with it is contact the Fellowship, and I don't plan on doing that."

"What about the files?" Thomas asked. "Don't they give you the ammunition you need?"

"Yes, but . . ."

"But what?" Thomas asked.

"The information on the disk is exactly the proof I have needed, but now that I have the children back, I have to think of them. What if something happens to me?"

"You're giving up? Just like that?"

Justine's voice became defensive. "I didn't have anything to lose before. Now I do."

"So none of the rest of it matters now that you have your kids?"

Justine glared at him. "Do you enjoy heaping guilt on people? Or have you reserved this especially for me? If you're so concerned, maybe *you* should take up the fight," she said. "In fact, it might not be a bad idea for you to take charge of the evidence." Justine reached under her poncho and pulled out the disk. Thomas began to protest, but she stopped him. "Just for now," she said. "If anything *does* happen, the information is probably safer with you." She handed him the disk.

Thomas slipped it back into his shirt pocket.

Justine opened the door into Richard's Souvenirs. "Besides, it sounds like you have a score of your own to settle with them now." She motioned toward the door. "After you."

A buzzer sounded as Justine opened the door to Richard's Souvenirs, announcing their presence to an empty store. The little building, barely larger than a double-wide house trailer, was part souvenir shop, part restaurant, and part ticket booth. A small sign hung on the front wall, listing the prices for boat and helicopter tours. Several round tables stood near the back, with a counter and grill along the back wall. Thomas detected a trace of onion in the air.

Another part of the shop housed several display tables and racks filled with Cajun and bayou souvenirs. Racks containing spices and recipe books offered tourists a chance to take a little Cajun cuisine home with them. A giant inflatable crawfish hung from the ceiling, its red claws and black eyes facing off with a less-than-intimidating plush green alligator.

"Quaint place," Thomas said, pulling his hood off his head. "Where are the kids?"

"They were supposed to be

waiting here when I got back with you.
Charles?" Justine called out, walking
briskly to the back of the small building.
She pushed open the door to the back
room. "Nobody here," she said.

Thomas knocked on the restroom doors. "Hello?
Anyone home?"

Justine shrugged. "Maybe Charles took the kids out
for lunch."

"Why?" Thomas asked, gesturing toward the grill.

"Guess he figured there wouldn't be any tours on a
rainy day like today," Justine said, her face tightening into
a frown.

"Does he usually leave the place unlocked?"

Justine shook her head. Her brow furrowed. "Not
since someone ran off with most of a summer day's
income," she said.

Thomas called out, "Michelle? Micah?"

"I don't like this," Justine said.

"Neither do I," Thomas replied, heading back toward
the door. As he jerked the door open, a figure leaped at
him.

"Boo!" Michelle squealed, then began giggling hyster-
ically.

Thomas took a step backward, then drew a deep
breath, letting it out with a pronounced sigh, rolling his
eyes toward the ceiling. "Michelle! You're trying to give
me a coronary, aren't you? Where's your brother?"

Michelle lowered her voice. "He and Charles are
hiding in the truck. Micah wants you to come find them."

He looked over toward Justine. "Did you have a good
time, seeing your mom again after all these years?"

Michelle tossed her hair off her shoulders, turning her
nose up slightly. "It was okay, I guess."

Thomas raised an eyebrow. "Okay? Is that all you can
say? Why, you haven't seen your mom in three—" Thomas
cut his comment short when Justine shook her head. He

smoothed Michelle's long blonde curls and said softly, "Come on, then; let's go let your brother surprise us."

The three of them went out to the Range Rover. Thomas couldn't see clearly through the heavily tinted side windows into the front seat, but it appeared to be empty.

Michelle giggled and covered her mouth with her hands as Thomas approached the passenger-side rear door. He put his hand on the door handle and gently pulled upward until he felt the latch release. "Gotcha!" he yelled, pulling the door open wide.

The backseat was empty.

Thomas glanced over the backseat of the Rover. He could see something covered by a blanket. He looked at Michelle and Justine and nodded, pointing toward the back.

Thomas placed his hand on the latch at the rear of the vehicle and pulled upward. He put his finger on his lips. "Prepare to be scared," he whispered, winking at Justine and Michelle. "Surprise!" Thomas yelled.

The figure under the blanket didn't move.

"Come on, Micah," Thomas said, "game's over."

"Give up, Micah," Michelle chimed in. "I already told them."

Thomas noticed a small pool of blood near one end of the light blue blanket that had turned the cloth a deep purple.

Michelle reached out to pull away the blanket.

Thomas held her back. "No. Stay back."

"What's wrong?" Justine asked.

Thomas nodded toward the bloodstain.

Justine gasped, pulling Michelle to her.

"Just stay back a minute," Thomas said. He shielded the still figure from view with his own body as he reached down and with two fingers carefully lifted a corner of the blanket. Charles Richard's glazed eyes stared back at him.

BLIND SIGHT

Blood had nearly dried around a small bullet hole in his forehead.

Thomas's face blanched. He dropped the blanket and slammed down the hatch. Turning around, he leaned against it, gasping for air and trembling.

Justine brought her hands to her face to muffle the cry that escaped her lips.

"Where's my brother?" Michelle asked.

Thomas took her hand and started pulling her toward the boat.

Justine stood frozen in horror, facing the back of the Range Rover.

Thomas came back and caught Justine by the elbow. "We've got to get out of here right now."

"Not without Micah," Justine protested.

Michelle was screaming now. "Where's my brother? Where's my brother?"

Thomas grabbed Justine by the shoulders. "We're not going to leave him," he said. "But first I've got to get you two somewhere safe."

"The cabin?" Justine said.

Thomas agreed.

"Help my brother. Help Micah!" Michelle squealed, now beating on Thomas's back with her fists.

Thomas turned and pinned her arms to her side. "Michelle! Quiet!" he barked the command, stunning her into tearful silence. "I'm going to find your brother. But you've got to trust me. Okay?"

She consented.

He nodded to Justine. "Let's go."

The boat seemed slower than ever, even though Justine cranked the engine to full throttle. Thomas took the pilot's wheel as Justine navigated them back to the island.

"If I drive somewhere in a car one time, I can usually remember it from then on," he said. "I hope it works with a boat too."

He stopped at the island only long enough to make certain no one was waiting for them in the cabin or thick brush.

Thomas hopped back onto the boat and was about to fire up the engines. With his hand on the ignition, he stopped and looked at Justine and Michelle standing on the shore. He called out. "What if something happens to me? You'll be stranded here."

The sadness in Justine's eyes was palpable. "If something happens to you, there's nowhere else we can hide anyway."

Thomas nodded. "I'll make sure something doesn't happen."

He guided the boat out into the channel and back toward Richard's Landing.

● ● ● ● ●

Justine and Michelle stood silently as the sound of Charles Richard's boat faded away. Justine put her hand on Michelle's shoulder. "Come on. We'd better wait in the cabin."

Michelle pulled away from her mother's touch. "I can get there myself," she said, swinging around and marching off toward the cabin.

"Michelle," she called out, but her daughter went on as if she hadn't heard her. Justine blinked tears away as she watched Michelle. "Be careful," she called out as she saw Michelle walk past the cabin and into the woods.

"This isn't how it was supposed to be, Peter," she said quietly. "This isn't how it was supposed to be." Justine ambled toward the cabin's small front porch and sat down. Michelle was nowhere to be seen. "How could everything be planned so carefully yet turn out so badly?" Justine said to no one in particular.

From the moment she'd first recruited Peter Bishop

into the Fellowship, Justine knew there was something different about him, something that attracted her deeply. The attraction had been mutual from the very beginning. In fact, Justine wondered if Peter's attraction to her had become a set of blinders for him, obscuring what was really going on in the Fellowship.

She had learned early on about Peter's involvement with the Christian group at the University of Texas, the group where he had met Thomas Kent. But Peter had dismissed his encounters with Christianity as superficial. He evidenced no commitment to Christian beliefs and was clearly eager to become involved in the work of the Fellowship. He was also clearly eager to stay close to her.

As a rule, Sawyer Wynne discouraged romantic relationships in the Fellowship. He felt they tended to distract people from the mission. But in the case of Peter and Justine, a relationship was allowed to develop. Even then, Peter's exceptional talent for computer programming was seen as a valuable asset.

Justine knew Wynne well enough to realize that he saw in Peter Bishop a useful tool, and he was willing to do whatever was necessary to keep him. Eventually Wynne permitted Peter and Justine to marry, although the marriage was kept quiet so as not to cause jealousy among the other members.

Justine remembered that she and Peter had to ask Wynne's permission to get married, as if he were her father. Wynne had been so patronizing.

"Of course, my dear," he'd said to Justine when Peter was out of earshot. "What better way to keep Peter close to home and under my thumb. As long as you two are married, Peter will always be around."

Wynne smirked and patted Justine on the cheek. "Because if there's anything I know for a certainty, sweetie, it's that *you* will never abandon the Fellowship."

Once Thomas docked and tied up the aluminum tour boat, he headed for the souvenir shop.

This is a joke. I have no weapon and no idea of where to look. For all I know, Micah could be miles away by now.

Thomas stopped by the door, soaking in the eerie, rain-dampened silence. It didn't make any sense. Whoever had taken Micah wouldn't just stop with him. They wanted Justine. If they were this close, they wouldn't pull out now. Somewhere around here, the man who shot Charles Richard was hiding, waiting for the right opportunity.

Dark clouds now obscured the hint of sun Thomas had seen earlier. The dullness of the sky increased as a light mist began to wet his face.

Thomas returned to the Range Rover. On the front seat he saw a cell phone with a piece of yellow paper under it. Had it been there before? Holding the note by the edges, he unfolded it and read the contents:

> If you want to see the boy alive, take the cell phone, then go into the store and wait. I'll be in touch.
> P.S. Too bad about your dog.

The last line hit Thomas like a pitcher of ice water.

Rainart! It couldn't be. There's no way he could have gotten away. And even if he had, he could never have followed us.

Visions of the cold-eyed man flashed before him. The deafening shotgun blast. The blinding flash. A swell of anger tinged with fear swept over Thomas. His left hand traced the outline of the bandage on his right hand.

Back in the store, Thomas sat down at one of the round tables and waited. Barely a minute had passed when the little phone chirped.

Thomas picked it up and growled, "When I get the

chance, I'm going to wrap my fingers around your throat and squeeze until I can't squeeze anymore."

"Not a very nice greeting for an old friend." The voice belonged to Derek Rainart. "Besides," he continued, "I got somethin' you want."

"Let the boy go," Thomas said. He knew the words were impotent.

The caller ignored Thomas's command. "Go down to the boat and wait. Don't think about calling anybody."

"How do I know you won't hurt him?"

"You don't."

Thomas heard a click and the phone went dead. He slammed the phone down on the table. He knew he couldn't take much time, but he had to find a weapon. He checked underneath the front counter for a gun, but there was none.

Thomas's gaze fell on the grill at the back. He ran over and began jerking drawers open. In the midst of a pile of metal spatulas and spoons, Thomas found a small paring knife. He ran his thumb along the edge. Not razor sharp, but honed well enough to do the job if he got the chance. He slipped the knife into his trouser pocket, pulled his poncho hood over his head, and walked out into the rain. Before he shut the door to Richard's shop, he glanced toward the Range Rover, then flipped the sign from Open to Closed.

· · · · ·

Justine hated the feeling of powerlessness that held her in its grip. Although she had told Thomas that there would be no hope for them if he were killed, she had no intentions of giving up without a fight.

She owed her daughter that much.

She owed *Peter* that much.

Justine stood up and entered the empty cabin. Charles

Richard had built it for her as an emergency hideout when she had come to stay with him.

Charles.

In the flurry of activity and the rush to get Michelle to safety, she had forgotten all about Charles Richard. He was dead, most likely at the hands of a killer sent by the Fellowship.

She collapsed into a chair, stunned by the realization. A flood of grief threatened to overwhelm her, but she held it back, patching an emotional dike that must soon burst from sheer pressure.

But not now.

This is a war, and in a war grieving must be postponed. The best way to deal with my loss is to turn it into anger. To be prepared to avenge his death if I have to.

Justine forced herself to stand and walk into the small storage room. Against the back wall stood a cradle full of firewood. She tugged the handle on one side, pulling it away from the wall. Brushing away the dirt and sawdust behind it, she exposed a small trapdoor cut into the floor.

Grabbing a large flat-head screwdriver from a nearby toolbox, she pried the door open, revealing a scuttle hole. She pulled a flashlight from the toolbox and shined it into the hole—just to make sure there were no unwelcome guests waiting down there. The flashlight revealed a metal tackle box covered with dirt and debris.

Lying on her stomach, Justine reached into the scuttle hole and pulled out the tackle box. She opened it and pulled out a Glock 17 automatic pistol, an extra magazine, and a box of 9mm rounds.

They may get past Thomas. But if they come for me, I'm going to be ready for them.

Justine had just loaded a magazine and slapped it into the handle when the sound of Michelle's screaming ripped through the cabin.

BLIND
SIGHT

• • • • •

Thomas barely had time to start the boat's motor before he saw a teal green Taurus pull into the landing's parking lot. At first, he couldn't tell whether the occupants were Micah and his captor or just some tourists with an unbelievably poor sense of timing.

A thin man with greasy black hair climbed out of the driver's side, then walked around to the passenger rear door and pulled a boy out by the collar. It was Rainart.

By all appearances, Micah was unhurt. Rainart grabbed him by the elbow with his left hand, holding a pistol to his side with his right. Micah's wrists were bound in front with duct tape. He wore no coat, only the blue flannel shirt that Thomas had bought him in Lake Charles. As they drew nearer, Thomas could see that Micah's hair was soaked. His face appeared hollow and sunken, his eyes red from crying.

Thomas left the engine idling and went to meet them at the dock. Rainart's smugness was almost more than Thomas could bear.

"You okay, Micah?" Thomas called to the boy.

Micah nodded, his chin quivering.

"Surprise, surprise," the man said, smirking.

"How did you ever get loose?"

"Used to play Houdini when I was a kid. Not many people can keep me tied up for long. Have to admit, though, I'd have had a hard time finding you if it hadn't been for the tip."

"What tip?"

Rainart raised an eyebrow. "Now I can't reveal my sources, can I?" He waved the gun in the direction of the boat. "Let's get going."

"Where?" Thomas asked.

"You aren't *that* stupid," Rainart sneered. "Get this junk heap movin'."

"Why didn't you take us all when you had the chance?"

"I could have. But I wanted some quality time with you."

"Quality time?"

"Yeah. Right after you show me where Justine is, I'm going to have the pleasure of putting a bullet between your eyes and watching you float down the river. Now we don't want the ladies to see that, do we? Get the boat moving."

"What if I don't?"

"If you don't, I'll blow you away right now."

"You'll never find Justine that way."

"She can't stay out there forever. It'd only be a matter of time."

Thomas didn't move.

The man rolled his eyes, then pointed the gun at Micah's head. He raised his eyebrows and looked at Thomas.

Thomas stepped aside and allowed them to board the boat. As Micah walked by, Thomas took his elbow and guided him along the aisle to a seat near the pilot's wheel.

Rainart pointed the pistol at Thomas's head. "Put your hands on the counter."

He placed his hands on the counter in front of the wheel.

"Spread your legs."

Thomas spread his legs apart.

Rainart kicked his feet backward and farther apart until Thomas stood at nearly a forty-five-degree angle. He patted Thomas down, pausing when his hand felt Thomas's right front pocket. Reaching in, he pulled out the paring knife.

Rainart clucked his tongue. "Not smart." He tossed the knife overboard. Rainart continued the pat-down, and a few seconds later pulled the evidence disk from Thomas's shirt pocket.

"I saw her hand this to

you," he said, grinning. "Thanks for saving me the trouble of looking for it."

Standing a safe distance from Thomas and Micah, Rainart broke the disk's fragile casing and removed the floppy. He pulled a cigarette lighter from his pocket and held the disk over its flame. Thomas watched in despair as the evidence disk fell in molten drips to the aluminum deck.

After the disk was destroyed, Rainart nodded toward the wheel. "Get us moving."

"You'll have to untie the lines," Thomas said.

"Don't get any ideas," Rainart answered. "I've seen how slow this tub moves. I'd have plenty of time to nail you both." Rainart got out, untied the boat, and hopped back on, taking a seat in the back.

Thomas directed the vessel into the bayou. He glanced at Micah. The boy squirmed in his seat. His face was twisted in pain. "What's wrong, Micah?"

"My hands hurt. He taped 'em too tight."

"The boy's wrists are sore," Thomas called. "Okay if I take the tape off?"

"I guess he ain't goin' nowhere. Go ahead."

Thomas throttled the engine back and knelt before Micah. He tugged at the duct tape, which gave way grudgingly. Micah winced at the pain.

"Sorry, pal," Thomas said. He lowered his voice to a whisper. "You really okay?"

"I guess," Micah said. Then his voice quavered. "But he shot Charles."

"I know, son. I know. Just sit tight. It's going to be okay." The last of the tape came off, pulling hair with it.

Micah rubbed the reddened skin on his wrists. "I'm scared," he said. "Don't make me sit alone."

"I've got to pilot the boat, Micah."

"Please."

Thomas patted the boy's hands. "I'll see." He called back to Rainart, "He's afraid. Can he stand beside me?"

"No."

"Look, you've got a terrified ten-year-old kid here, not to mention the fact that he's blind. Like you said, he ain't goin' nowhere."

"Whatever," Rainart said. "Just get us movin'."

Thomas nodded. "Come on, Micah. You can stand beside me, if you can keep your balance, that is."

"I'll be okay if I can hold on to something."

"Here," Thomas said, helping the boy to stand. "There's one of the poles for the canopy right beside the wheel. You can hang on to that."

Micah grasped the aluminum pole as Thomas pushed the engine to full throttle and guided the boat into the channels that would lead them to Justine.

As the boat snaked along, Rainart became restless. He moved from the rear of the boat up to Thomas and Micah. "You wouldn't just be goin' in circles, would you? I wouldn't like that."

"I know where I'm going," Thomas said.

Rainart walked toward the front and stood at the bow. "Freakin' swamp all looks the same to me."

While Rainart's attention was focused off the bow, Thomas whispered to Micah, "Come here. Take the wheel for a minute."

"I can't steer it," Micah whispered back.

"Just hold it steady. We're in a broad straightaway. I just need a few seconds to look for some kind of weapon."

Micah stepped sideways and took hold of the wheel. He held it as if it were a piece of china.

Thomas bent down to the left of the wheel. He eased open the small door of a homemade storage cabinet. Glancing toward Rainart, he rifled through the contents of the cabinet. He muttered an oath when all he found were Charles Richard's spare bags of marshmallows.

"Blasted marshmallows," he muttered. "I need a knife, a gun, something."

He stood back up a second

before Rainart turned around to see Micah at the wheel. "What's he doin'?" Rainart asked.

"Just thought I'd let the boy have a little fun."

Rainart pointed the pistol and motioned toward the seat. "Sit him down."

"Okay. Come on, Micah."

"Did you find anything?" Micah whispered.

"Nothing but a bunch of marshmallows." Thomas's head jerked up. He looked ahead, then back at Micah as he took the wheel. "Listen," he whispered, "when I nudge you, stomp your foot on the deck and pretend to be sick."

"What?"

"Just follow my lead. And keep stomping until I tell you to stop."

Thomas surveyed the landscape. The cypress trees that seemed to stand as tall as skyscrapers lined the channel. Everything looked alike. But unless he missed his guess they were getting close. The timing had to be just right.

Rainart still stood at the front of the boat. He had put the gun in his jacket pocket.

Thomas lifted his foot and reached behind him, tapping Micah on the calf.

The boy stomped his foot on the floor.

Rainart looked back. "What's goin' on?"

Micah's feet slapped the floor repeatedly.

"What's wrong with him?"

Thomas raised his eyebrows. "I don't know. Micah? You okay?"

Micah groaned and grabbed his stomach.

The stomping continued.

"Stop it, boy!" Rainart yelled.

Thomas's brow furrowed. "Wait a minute. Have you fed him anything recently?"

"No," Rainart said.

"Fool!" Thomas frowned and jerked the throttle back to idle. "We've got to act fast."

"What? What do you mean?"

"Don't you know anything? This boy's diabetic. How do you think he went blind? His sugar's low. He'll go into a coma if we don't get some sugar into him."

Micah started jerking his arms and flopping both legs, kicking the deck with his heels.

Rainart's face went white. "If I don't bring that boy back, I'm dead! Do something!"

"I'm trying!" Thomas laid Micah on the deck and started unbuttoning his shirt. "Look in that cabinet. Maybe there's something in there."

Rainart jerked it open and quickly pulled out a bag of marshmallows. "How about this?"

"Perfect," Thomas said, jerking the bag open with his teeth and spilling half its contents into the water.

Micah slapped the deck with his arms and feet, making gurgling sounds and drooling.

Thomas took a marshmallow and put it in Micah's mouth. As he did, he glanced toward the water and saw the same V patterns he'd seen the previous night.

With one swift movement, Thomas swung around and tackled Rainart, shoving him overboard. He ran back to the wheel and pushed the engine to full throttle.

Rainart broke the water screaming, "You're dead!" He pulled the pistol from his pocket and pointed it at Thomas.

"Stay down, Micah," Thomas yelled as he directed the boat away from Rainart.

He heard a shot whiz by. Another ricocheted off the boat's aluminum hull.

Then he heard Rainart scream.

"No. Get away from me. No!"

Several more shots fired off in quick succession.

"Get aaawwwayy!"

Splashing.

Then silence.

Thomas slowed the engine down and looked back. All he could see was turbulence. "It's okay, Micah. You can get up now. We're safe." He took the boy's hands and helped him to his feet.

"What was *that*?" Micah said as Thomas helped him button his shirt.

"That," Thomas said, "was Arthur. And a few of his friends, I'd guess."

"Uncle Thomas?"

"Yeah?"

"I don't have diabetes. I was born blind."

Thomas grinned. "Yeah, but *he* didn't know that. Come on; let's go get your mom and sister."

⬤ ⬤ ⬤ ⬤ ⬤

Justine burst out the front door and tore across the island in the direction of Michelle's screams, chambering a round in the 9mm as she ran.

They couldn't have gotten here this quickly. They couldn't have!

She could hear Michelle screeching, "Help! Help me!"

"I'm coming, baby!" Justine shouted as she ran through the overgrown brush.

She could see Michelle through some trees just up ahead. The Spanish moss obscured most of her view, but she could see that Michelle had a large branch in her hand and was swatting at something with it.

Envisioning an alligator attack, Justine prayed, "Lord, please no," as she raced toward her daughter.

Reaching Michelle, Justine pushed in front of her and leveled the gun, ready to shoot whatever was threatening her. "Behind me!" she ordered Michelle, waving behind her with her left hand.

Michelle dropped her branch and stood in back of her mother.

Justine hesitated for a moment, released a long slow breath, and lowered the gun.

The water snake had been poised to strike. It remained in a defensive posture, hissing at its attacker.

"Aren't you going to shoot it?" Michelle asked.

"It's just a water snake," Justine replied. "It's not poisonous. Just back away slowly and let him go on his way."

Justine felt rather than heard Michelle turn around and storm away. She also felt the words that erupted like volcanic lava from her daughter's mouth.

"I hate you!"

• • • • •

Thomas gently turned the large boat around, directing it back toward the island. Micah stood beside him, holding on to one of the canopy poles for support.

Thomas heard Micah sniffling and turned to see him wiping his eyes on his sleeve. "You okay?"

Micah shook his head.

"I guess none of us are okay," Thomas said. "Not really."

"Charles was a nice man," Micah said. "Why'd he have to die?"

"I don't know, Micah. I don't have any good answers to that question."

"They're never going to leave us alone."

Thomas agreed. "I don't think so."

"My dad said they wouldn't."

Thomas directed the boat into another channel. He heard several muffled splashes as turtles left their logs for the safety of the water. "What else did your dad tell you, Micah?"

"That Antoine was a liar. That he was a false . . ."

Thomas finished the sentence for him, ". . . prophet?"

"Yeah. Dad knew we had

to get away from him and from Mr. Wynne."

"Micah," Thomas said, "last night, did you talk with your mom about Peter?"

"I tried, but she didn't want to listen."

"What did she say?"

"She said that Daddy's too smart to let them get him. He'd have gotten away somehow."

"She thinks he's still alive?" Thomas asked.

Micah nodded.

"Micah, why didn't your dad escape *with* you?"

"He wanted to . . ." Micah's voice faltered and he buried his face in his fists.

Thomas put his hand on the boy's shoulder. "It's going to be okay, Micah. It's going to be okay."

Thomas sincerely wished he could believe that.

● ● ● ● ●

Justine found Michelle sitting on a wicker chair on the cabin's front porch, glaring at her with a look of unvarnished hatred.

If her eyes were daggers, I'd be dead by now.

Before Justine could speak, Michelle spat out an accusation. "This is all your fault."

Justine bristled. "Now wait a minute."

"You killed my father!" Michelle shouted back, tears streaming down her face.

Justine felt as though she had been slapped. "How could you say that?" she demanded.

"It's true. If you hadn't left and he hadn't had to send us to you, he'd never have died."

"He's not dead, young lady!"

"Yes he is," Michelle screamed back at her. "Everybody knows he is—except you!"

Justine shouted her down. "Did you see him die?"

Michelle shook her head.

"I didn't think so." Justine turned away. "Your father escaped. This has been planned for years. There's no way they could possibly have gotten to him."

Michelle stood to her feet and pointed at Justine. "He's dead. And he died because you made him betray Father Antoine. He'd never have done it if you hadn't made him."

Justine wanted, on one hand, to spare Michelle's feelings; on the other hand, she wanted to slap her face. She mounted the porch steps and stood facing her daughter. She spoke with a quiet and steady voice. "For your information, young lady, it was your father's idea to leave Antoine. He convinced me to leave."

Michelle's open hand whipped through the air directly toward her mother's face.

Justine caught her hand and held it tight, returning Michelle's hard glare. The two momentarily locked in a clash of wills. Finally Michelle jerked her hand away and stalked into the cabin.

●　●　●　●　●

Thomas pulled the boat up to the small dock and idled the engine. He turned to Micah, who was now sitting in a chair behind him. "I'm going to go get your mom and sister. You okay by yourself for a minute?"

Micah appeared to think about it, then gave Thomas a weak grin and a thumbs-up.

"Great. I'll be right back." Thomas hopped onto the dock and tied the boat down.

Justine was already running toward the boat. Thomas met her at the end of the dock. "Is he . . . ?" Justine blurted out.

"He's okay."

Thomas looked down at the 9mm in Justine's hand. He raised his eyebrows.

"Water snake." She smiled

at Thomas and handed him the gun. Then she ran to Micah. Thomas rolled his eyes as he tucked the pistol into the waistband of his trousers and walked toward the cabin to find Michelle.

* * * * *

Justine stood at the throttle as Thomas and Michelle ran back down the dock, and Thomas barely had time to untie the boat and jump in before she began pulling away.

"Where do we go now?" he asked.

Justine shrugged, blinking back tears. "I don't know. This was the one place on Earth I actually felt safe. Now that Charles . . ." She paused a moment, swallowing a sob. "Now that Charles is gone, I just don't know."

"One thing's certain," Thomas said. "It's not safe around here anymore."

"But where do we go?" Justine asked.

"Anywhere. Just as long as it's away from here. We need time to sort things out, and we've got to go someplace they won't think to follow us." Thomas thought a moment. "I saw an old blue car behind Charles's trailer. Does it run?"

Justine nodded. "It was Charles's car."

"Then I vote that we take the car and head for New Orleans. No better place to get lost for a while than in The Big Easy."

"Doesn't look like we have any other choice," Justine remarked as she cast a final glance toward the cabin that had been her home for the past three years.

She pushed the throttles to full and headed back toward Richard's Landing.

Thomas made sure that Micah and Michelle were securely buckled into the backseat of Charles Richard's 1968 Plymouth Belvedere before leaving the tin-roofed carport in search of Justine.

The sound of the rear passenger-side door closing reminded Thomas of a bank vault. He rapped on the car's heavy steel fender. "Well, we should be safe in this old thing. It's built like a Bradley assault vehicle."

Micah nodded, grinning. Michelle wallowed in the brooding silence that had come over her since he'd left her with her mother. Something had gone on between the two of them, but Thomas wasn't sure exactly what.

"You two sit tight. I'll be right back."

Leaving the shelter of the tiny carport that stood behind Richard's Bayou Tours and Souvenirs, Thomas walked out into the quiet drizzle and saw Justine standing motionless near the front of the building. She was gazing toward the Range Rover that held the body of her benefactor, Charles

Richard. As Thomas approached, he saw quiet tears streaming down her cheeks.

Thomas put his arm around her shoulder. "I'm sorry," he said.

Justine took a shuddering breath. "We can't just leave him."

"What other choice do we have?"

She shook her head. Frustration colored her voice. "I don't know. But it's just not right."

"None of this is *right*, Justine. It's all *wrong*. But if we're to have any chance of surviving this, we have to get out of here *now*. If we take the time to call someone about Charles—even if we just call on our way out—we'll be held for questioning before we even have a chance to sort all this out.

"Look," he said, "as soon as we find somewhere we can lay low, I'll call the sheriff. But as soon as I do, even Charles's old car is going to be hot. If someone finds Charles sooner, we have even less time to use this car."

She looked up at him. "So, why can't we move Charles into the building and take the Rover? You told the kids that nobody's going to be looking for it, and you're right about that. The Fellowship will never report it missing."

"Oh, that would be great," he said. "Let's add tampering with evidence *and* a crime scene to the list of charges that'll be filed against us, not to mention the fact that we'll be driving a vehicle with a murdered man's blood staining the back carpet. We can't take the Rover *or* the Taurus that Rainart rented.

"If we touch anything here, we only dig a deeper hole for ourselves. If we leave things exactly as they are, there's a chance—however small—that someone may actually believe our story."

Thomas put his hands on her shoulders and turned her to face him. "Justine, please. We *have* to leave him."

She averted her gaze and nodded.

"Let's get to the car," he said.

● ● ● ● ●

Thomas drove Charles Richard's battered Plymouth along
the I-10 bridge toward New Orleans. They had barely
been on the road for ten minutes when they noticed that
both Micah and Michelle had fallen asleep.

"They've had a rough time of it. It's amazing they're
doing as well as they are," Thomas observed.

Justine gave him a wan smile. "They're tough all right.
Like their father."

Thomas paused for a second, then asked the question
that had bothered him ever since he had encountered a
brooding, angry Michelle at the cabin. "What happened
between you and Michelle while we were gone?"

Justine took a deep breath, as if pausing to collect
her thoughts. "She thinks her father is dead, and she's
blaming me for it."

"Justine, I think she may be right."

"Don't go there, Thomas. I cannot bring myself to
believe that they outsmarted Peter."

"What do you mean?"

"Peter knows their systems and plans better than they
do themselves. He would have planned for every possibility, figured every angle."

"So you're saying that he would have been able to
help the children escape without Sawyer Wynne or somebody else catching him?"

"Exactly."

"But how would Peter explain the children's absence?
Sooner or later someone would notice that they were
gone. I mean, you said that he had remained loyal, didn't
you? How would he explain himself?"

Thomas turned to glance at her and noticed the blank
expression on her face. "Justine?"

"Thomas, I—uh, I'm sorry. I haven't exactly been
straightforward with you."

"About what?"

"Peter never remained loyal to Antoine or Sawyer. I wasn't sure I could trust you earlier, and I couldn't take a chance on blowing his cover. Actually, it was Peter who persuaded *me* to leave."

"What brought that about?"

"You can blame my brother. *And* Peter."

"Michael Guidry convinced you to leave the Fellowship?"

"Not exactly. He convinced Peter."

"He convinced Peter. But *you* left?" Thomas chuckled. "I'm sorry, but you're losing me."

Justine smiled. "My brother and I were raised Catholic, but we never went to Mass. When we hit our teens, we both left the church. We took very different paths from there. I wanted to party. Michael got holy on me. He started going to a little home Bible study. Said he'd 'found the Lord.'"

Justine laughed and shook her head. "I turned him off. Told him the last thing I wanted in my life was religion. He kept telling me that he hadn't gotten religion, that he had found a *relationship* with Jesus. I just told him he was strange.

"I ended up going to Syracuse University on a women's basketball scholarship. That was where I became a follower of Antoine and where I met Peter."

Thomas interrupted. "How did you decide to follow Antoine?"

Justine shook her head. "I'd rather not go into that, if you don't mind. Too many bad memories."

"I'm sorry," Thomas said. "Go on."

A pained expression came over Justine's face. "Anyway, I got involved in the Fellowship in college. After I met Peter, I convinced him to join.

"By the time I joined the Fellowship, Michael was pastoring his first church. From the moment he heard I was following Antoine, my pastor-brother took it as his personal mission in life to deprogram me.

"I resented it. I resented *him*. But I couldn't get him to leave me alone. He wrote letters; I threw them out. He called; I hung up. Finally, he flew to Syracuse to confront me face-to-face.

"Michael and I met down by the lake. It was a beautiful day, but you'd never know it because of the storm that was raging between us. Peter was with me, but the hotter things got between my brother and me, the quieter Peter got.

"It ended up as a shouting match. Michael finally stormed away in frustration. But he turned around and fired one parting shot. For me, it went in one ear and out the other. But it hit Peter like a spear in his heart."

"What did your brother say?"

Justine smiled at the memory. "Michael's Cajun accent always got thicker when he was angry. He pointed a finger at me and said, 'You may not believe dis, Justine, but dere is such a thing as truth. And, whether you like it or not, truth matters.' He turned away, and I never saw him again until I left the Fellowship."

"But what about Peter?" Thomas asked. "You said that *he* convinced *you* to leave. What happened with him?"

A loud yawn broke through from the backseat. Thomas heard Michelle's drowsy voice from behind him. "Are we there yet?"

Justine looked over her shoulder at her daughter. "Almost."

They drove in silence the rest of the way to New Orleans.

33

Sawyer Wynne sat at his dining room table, the china and crystal place setting pushed aside, and an open notebook computer before him. Cold beads of perspiration trickled down his neck.

After accessing the Fellowship's network, Wynne entered a simple command: "Hiroshima." Instantly, another window opened on the screen: "Authorization Code?" Wynne responded by entering a password. The screen went blank for a few seconds; then a new window opened: "Enable?" Sawyer Wynne typed, "Yes."

The screen was replaced by a new prompt that read: "Hiroshima enabled. Type YES to engage immediately or type DELAY for countdown mode." Below the prompt, a digital readout displayed "48:00:00."

Wynne typed, "Delay."

With "Hiroshima Enabled" displayed in red letters at the top of the screen, the countdown clock began ticking off the seconds. By enabling Hiroshima, Wynne had just given himself a forty-eight-hour escape window. Anytime within the next two days, he could engage Hiroshima by computer or cell phone. If he didn't engage within forty-eight hours, the program would automatically disable. Wynne could also disable Hiroshima by reentering his password. If, on the other hand, he chose to engage Hiroshima, he would trigger a chain of events that would result in the total destruction of the Fellowship.

The Hiroshima Protocol was probably Justine Bishop's greatest contribution to the Fellowship, Wynne mused. Shortly after Justine escaped, Sawyer decided that the Fellowship needed a self-destruct system. Code-named "Hiroshima" because of the devastation it would cause, the protocol provided a means of self-preservation whereby Wynne and the other leaders could escape if the Fellowship ever came under serious scrutiny from state or federal authorities.

Although Peter Bishop had been his head programmer and Bishop had proclaimed his loyalty loudly and often, Wynne had considered him too great a security risk to be allowed to work on, or even know about, Hiroshima. For that assignment, Sawyer had Llewelen scout out some other recruits with advanced programming skills. Assembling a secret team of three programmers, Sawyer had ordered them to design the system and encrypt the code so that not even the best hacker could break in. Sawyer was not used to handing out praise, but the programmers did an outstanding job. It was so tragic that none of them survived to see their fail-safe system implemented. Hiroshima was, after all, a monumental achievement in programming.

Once engaged, Hiroshima would initiate a wire transfer of most of the Fellowship's funds to a secret account in the Cayman Islands. When the wire transfer was complete, the system would then send orders to the Fellowship's five major regional centers in Syracuse, New Orleans, Dallas,

Chicago, and Los Angeles. All novices and indoctrinates would be told that Father Antoine had left earth to enter a higher Sphere of reality, and that they should join him by enacting a Heaven's Gate–style suicide pact.

A different set of orders would be sent to those individuals who had already been osmosed into society. They would be instructed to remain in deep cover and wait for a call to Ingathering: a planned restoration of the Fellowship's activities. Of course, no call to Ingathering would ever come, but the faithful didn't know that. Sawyer and his cronies would long since have begun enjoying a quiet retirement in the Caymans.

Once Hiroshima sent orders to the five centers and the osmosed members, it would release a virus that would infect every computer on the Fellowship's network. All data relating to the Osmosis Project and any of the Fellowship's other murderous activities would be erased so efficiently that even the most skilled experts in computer forensics would not be able to retrieve them.

Enabling Hiroshima was a desperate measure, but as Sawyer saw it, he had no other choice. Derek Rainart had not checked in for nearly two days. As difficult as it was to believe, Wynne had to conclude that somehow Justine or Thomas Kent had managed to eliminate him. Now Wynne had to assume that Justine Bishop had the project files *and* the brats. Since threat of possible harm to her children was the trump card Sawyer Wynne had played to keep her relatively quiet over the last three years, there was nothing preventing her from taking her evidence to the authorities. That left Dana Shipp as Wynne's only remaining source of information, his last chance to track down Justine and retrieve the files. Unfortunately, Dana had not cracked yet, and if she didn't talk soon, it would be too late to stop Justine.

Sawyer Wynne had enabled Hiroshima. He would *not* allow Justine Bishop to bring him down. If he didn't get a solid lead on her whereabouts soon, he would have to engage Hiroshima and make his escape.

"Runnin' away? And from a woman *no less! Like I said, boy, you're just plain worthless."*

Sawyer slammed his fist on the table, rattling the laptop in front of him. "No!" he shouted, trying to drown out Silas Wynne's sadistic, unearthly taunts. Sawyer picked up the crystal goblet and hurled it at the fireplace mantel. It shattered, scattering hundreds of tiny pieces across the parquet floor.

"It was her!" he screamed into the air. "She's the one who ran away. *She's* the one who betrayed *me*."

Her eyes had flashed anger and contempt at him, the same kind of contempt that he had seen in Silas Wynne's face every day of his life.

"You're sick, Sawyer," Justine had said. "You think that manipulating all of these lives and lying to all of these people makes you something. Well, it doesn't. You're nothing, Sawyer, *nothing*!"

That was the last time he'd ever seen Justine. He had immediately sent out a conversion order, but Justine escaped before Rainart had the chance to implement it.

But from that day forward, Sawyer Wynne had never stopped trying to destroy Justine Bishop. Not simply because she had become a liability, a threat to the organization. No, Justine's great sin was that she'd said that he was *nothing*. She had shown contempt for him—the same contempt his grandfather had shown.

Silas Wynne had been reincarnated as Justine Bishop. Sawyer would never silence his grandfather until he silenced Justine.

But it was all slipping away now. Justine was out there with the files, with the children.

She couldn't win; he wouldn't let her.

If Sawyer Wynne had to go out, he'd go out with a bang.

34

D ana Shipp fought her way out of a troubled dream. She felt as if she had been stretched out on a slab of ice. The cold, stone floor on which she lay, clad only in the white robe she had been given two days earlier, sucked heat from her body as a leech draws blood from its host. A dull ache throbbed in her hips and knees. Numbness crept into her extremities. Her eyelids felt like lead weights. She forced them open.

With great effort she turned her head from side to side, not even trying to lift it from the floor. She lay in a cavernous, empty room. High ceilings and white plastered walls gave it all the charm of a tomb. One wall sported a beautifully crafted fireplace. It was of no use to Dana. Not a splinter of wood was in sight.

She didn't think ringing room service would help.

Rays of sunlight streamed through a high window. The slowly deepening gloom warned Dana that nightfall was coming. She didn't care. She knew she was going to die. It was just a matter of where, when—and how.

In just a few days, her entire life had collapsed. She had arrived at the Chateau Antoine expecting fun. Now she felt like she was marking time in a cell on death row.

Eventually they would realize she had nothing to tell them, that she really had no idea who Justine Bishop was and could offer no useful information. And when they figured that out, they would kill her. Resisting the strong temptation to lie there and die just to spite them, Dana rolled onto her side and pushed up to a sitting position.

Where am I? I can't still be in the hotel. Where did they bring me?

Dana stood, holding her arms out to steady herself. She looked up toward the window. But it was at least nine feet off the floor, practically a skylight. She heaved a sigh. Michael Jordan couldn't get a look out of that window.

She turned her attention to the eight-foot, carved ash door centered on the far wall. Hobbling over to it, she pulled down on the ornate brass handle.

Dana's eyes widened in surprise when she heard the latch click. She tugged at the heavy door and it swung open. She stepped into a gloomy hallway, lined on both sides with doors identical to the one she had just opened.

Not sure of what to do with her unexpected freedom, Dana looked down the passageway. Colored light trickled through a tall stained-glass window at one end. The other end opened into a broad space. She edged her way along in that direction.

Dana's stomach was one huge knot. She could feel gooseflesh appearing on her arms. It had little to do with the cold. The place gave her the creeps. Toward the end of the hall, the light increased. Dana kept moving. *Move toward the light. That's what they say, right? Except I'm not dead. At least I don't think so.*

The end of the hallway opened into a long staircase curling downward in a gentle, counterclockwise spiral. Dana looked over the railing. She guessed she must be four or five stories up. On the ground floor, colorful stones had been beautifully arranged to create a mosaic of the FWR logo.

Dana began a careful descent, resting her left hand on an oak banister so large her fingers curled only a third of the way around its bulk. As she passed each floor, she found herself gazing down long corridors identical to the one she had come from.

Cold as it was, the temperature plunged even further as she descended the cream-colored marble steps. Dana began to shiver uncontrollably. Her hand left the railing, and she wrapped her arms around herself, trying to stave off the deepening chill. When she approached the final flight, the steps broadened, making a grand entrance into a central hallway.

The wall to her right bore an immense oil portrait of Anthony MacAsland. She had seen pictures of MacAsland before, but never one like this. His eyes were green icebergs, colder than the room itself. They held Dana's gaze as if by some demonic magic. She averted her eyes, feeling as if MacAsland were gazing down on her in judgment.

The walls were constructed of huge mortared stones, masterfully pieced together and accented by handcrafted, stained-glass windows. Together they formed a structure rivaling that of any cathedral. Dana glanced upward, then quickly back down. The sheer immensity of the building dazzled her.

Dana stood dead center in the FWR logo, a speck in the middle of a grand entrance hall. She had no doubts now.

I finally made it. MacAsland's castle.

Another shudder shot through her body.

But where is everybody? Surely they didn't just leave me here?

At that thought, a sense of

unalloyed panic overwhelmed her. Dana swung around and sprinted to the gargantuan double doors at the castle's front entrance. Whimpering, she wrenched down on the latch, leaned backward, and pulled with all her strength.

An icy blast surged through the open door. Snowflakes hard as sand stung Dana's cheeks. She stood in denial, shaking her head at the sight. Wind gusts flapped her robe like a flag in the breeze. Her teeth began to chatter. The excruciating blast brought tears to Dana's eyes. So did the realization that she had been abandoned on Diamond Island, all alone in the midst of a frozen river.

Dana leaned against the colossal door and pushed it shut.

She shook her head. Quaking with fear and cold, Dana stumbled across the room to a bank of light switches. She flipped them all. No lights came on. "No. No. No." Her trembling voice echoed off the rock walls.

At the back of the grand entrance hall stood what looked like a hotel's front desk. Dana ran toward the desk, catching her foot on the mosaic as she ran. She lurched forward, scraping her knees on the abrasive pavement. Warm blood trickled down her shins.

Panting clouds of breath in the frigid air, Dana pushed herself up and dashed around to the back of the desk. A moan escaped her lips as she ran to the central telephone system and grabbed the receiver. Red LEDs lit up. The phone was receiving power. But the line was dead.

She punched zero.

Nothing.

Numb fingers trembling, she jammed the number nine. Dead.

"You can't do this!" Dana heard herself screaming. She slammed the receiver back into its cradle.

To the left of the front desk, Dana could see what

appeared to be a large sitting room. Tears streaming down her face, she trudged, zombielike, toward the room. A giant-screen TV rested against one wall. A sectional sofa faced the massive television, surrounded by padded, stackable chairs.

Dana leaned against the doorway, exhausted. Her head rested against the frame as her fingers ambled up the wall toward the light switch. She flipped the switch, and to her amazement, the crystal chandelier overhead came to life. A warm glow filled the room.

Relieved to find at least one place where something worked, Dana entered the sitting room.

A faint buzzing and the crackle of static electricity caught her attention. Seconds later, the giant television screen glowed blue. A series of beeps erupted from the machine. Then the hateful face of Sawyer Wynne filled the screen.

"Good day, Miss Shipp. I hope you're enjoying your private accommodations on Diamond Island. It's a privilege few people ever enjoy. Of course, no one goes there this time of year."

Dana moved farther into the room and sat down on the sofa.

"I thought perhaps you might need some time alone to think about whether or not you wanted to talk to me." Wynne's thin lips stretched across his face, his eyes narrowing in a sadistic grin. "I wouldn't take too long to decide. The room you're in right now is the only one with power. And in case you're wondering, it doesn't have heat."

Dana watched, incredulous, as the hateful man continued.

"You don't have much time. The last person we left up there didn't last two days." Wynne's voice grew colder as he spoke. "When we came for him, we found him hanging from the chandelier in this very room."

Dana's hand went to her throat.

BLIND
SIGHT

"You see, it's in your best interest to cooperate with us. Tell us what you know about Justine Bishop, and we'll let you go.

When you're ready to talk, punch the letters *FWR* on the central telephone. It will immediately connect you with my office."

The man paused. Then, as an afterthought, he added, "Don't even think of escape. The phones have been programmed to connect nowhere but this office. Escape on foot is impossible. You would freeze to death before you traveled a hundred yards. "I expect to hear from you soon."

The screen went dark.

Dana wrapped her arms around herself, pulled her knees up onto the sofa, and sobbed uncontrollably.

J ustine saw that the children were nestled in front of the
television set. "I'll be outside," she said, "talking to
Uncle Thomas." The children barely nodded. She stepped
out onto the second-floor balcony and, after closing the
door of their motel room, wrapped her arms around
herself.

Heavy overcast caused the New Orleans Econo
Lodge's sign to turn on, casting a cool light on Thomas
and Justine as they leaned against the cold metal rail.
Thomas held two foam coffee cups. He offered one to
Justine. She pulled the plastic top off. Steam billowed
from the tiny cup.

"Thanks," she said, holding the cup but not bringing
it to her lips.

Thomas stood by her side, looking out toward the
traffic as it moved briskly along Interstate 10. "How are
you holding up?"

Justine shook her head and
bit her lip. Her chin quivered

slightly as she spoke. "I hated leaving him like that." Tears welled in her eyes.

"We didn't have a choice." His voice was soft, reassuring.

She sighed. "I know. It doesn't make it any easier."

"How long had you known Charles?"

Justine blinked back the tears. "My brother introduced me to Charles not long after I left the Fellowship. Told him I was mixed up and needed a place to hide. Charles was a widower—no children. He practically adopted me. Even trained me and worked me into his business."

She took a sip of her coffee.

"Every year at Thanksgiving he would fry twenty or thirty turkeys and give them away to families who'd had a bad year, couldn't afford their own Thanksgiving dinner. He'd always choose one or two families to come share ours too." Her voice faltered and broke. Tears spilled down her cheeks.

"I'm sorry. Sounds like a good man."

Justine sniffed. "He was. I hate them. They've taken everything away from me." She glanced back toward the motel room. "Almost everything."

"They won't stop," Thomas said. "As soon as they find out Rainart is dead, they'll send someone else. Our only chance is to get out of here while we can. Get as far away from them as possible."

She shook her head. "It won't do any good. They'd find us. And if they didn't, the police would. Do you honestly believe all four of us could travel long without being noticed? Now that I have the children, Sawyer Wynne will have their pictures plastered on every milk carton in the country."

"What else can we do?" Thomas asked.

Justine's eyes met his. "We bring them down."

"What?"

"You heard me."

"Yeah, but you'll kindly excuse my skepticism. A few hours ago, you didn't think that was an advisable course of action. What changed your mind?"

Justine fired back. "A few hours ago, you thought I should take them on. What changed *your* mind?"

"Uh-uh. I asked first."

Justine's gaze hardened. "Seeing Charles in the back of that Range Rover changed my mind."

"Look, I'm sorry about Charles too. But that doesn't alter the facts. Or have you forgotten that Rainart destroyed the only evidence we've got? So what do we do?"

"We go after the proof we need."

Thomas drained his coffee cup. "Oh, that's great. I suppose we'll just fly to Syracuse, stroll up to their headquarters, and ask if they have any incriminating evidence they'd like to share?"

She raised her eyebrows, a grin spreading across her face. "It'd certainly be a novel approach."

Thomas snorted. "Yeah. Right."

Her voice became quiet. "I'm serious, Thomas. There are ways it can be done. Besides, once we get up there, we can track down Peter. Together, we'll be able to come up with something."

A deep heaviness settled on Thomas. "Justine, I know how desperately you want to cling to hope, but I just don't see how Peter could possibly be alive. I heard his voice on my answering machine—"

"Did you talk to him?" she interrupted.

"No, but—"

"Then you don't *know* anything." She looked at him and smiled. "Thomas, I know you mean well, but I know Peter. He understood what these people are capable of, and he knew how to fool them. He would have found a way to escape, even if they *had* caught up with him. Besides, even if something *has* happened to Peter, do you have a better idea?"

"Yes! *Run*. You hid from

them for three years. That proves it can be done."

"But we'd be on the run for the rest of our lives."

"I can live with that."

"But should *they* have to?" She pointed toward the motel room. "Thomas, what kind of lives will Micah and Michelle have?"

He didn't respond.

"If we run from the Fellowship now," Justine said, "those two children will never have a normal life."

"What kind of life will they have without a mother? You won't last five minutes inside the Fellowship's headquarters."

"I'm not stupid," she said. "I don't plan to get caught."

Thomas threw his hands up as if in surrender, then turned away and stormed down the stairs and into the parking lot. "Nobody ever does," he called back over his shoulder.

"Thomas, where are you going?"

"I need time to think."

"Thomas, it's never going to stop unless we stop it. Thomas!"

Thomas waved her off, crossing the parking lot. He heard her calling after him. He ignored her.

As Thomas increased the distance between himself and the motel, a disturbing thought came to him. He'd kept the promise. He had delivered the children safely to Justine. Maybe now was the right time to walk out of their lives. Thomas came to the edge of the four-lane road that passed by the motel. Houses decorated with Christmas lights lined the road. The wet pavement glistened with red, green, and white reflections from nearby decorations. He walked along the roadside, not knowing, not really caring where he was going at the moment.

I've still got enough cash to disappear somewhere.

A pickup truck roared through a puddle near Thomas,

sending a dirty spray in his direction. Cold water soaked his trouser legs and shoes.

He wiped his wet hands on his pants. The road became an overpass, crossing over the highway. Thomas followed it. The farther from the motel he walked, the darker the surroundings became. A large apartment complex off to his left loomed in the darkness. Sparkling white lights outlined each building.

When a police cruiser passed by, a wave of self-consciousness overcame Thomas. He watched the cruiser disappear up the street. The last thing he needed right now was to be picked up for prowling or loitering.

About a hundred feet ahead of him, Thomas saw a small nativity scene in the front yard of a church. Several benches sat around it in a semicircle. He sat down on a bench, not bothering to brush away the water drops left by the rainstorm. Thomas rested his head in his hands.

"It's never going to stop unless we stop it, Thomas."
She's crazy.

Thomas looked around. Sparkling red Christmas lights dotted the overcast landscape, and he found himself humming. *"This little light of mine. I'm gonna let it shine."*

In his mind the Christmas lights transformed into tail-lights. Steven and Sarah flashed before his eyes. The bridge appeared before him. He saw Jenny. Their cries filled his ears. "No no no no."

Thomas beat his fists on his knees, grinding his teeth. His fingernails dug into the palms of his hands as he fought off the memory. But the images became stronger, bolder, more realistic than ever before. Trembling all over, Thomas watched an endlessly looping video clip that carried him far, far away.

Long minutes later, Thomas came back to reality, gasping and spent. He looked into the gray sky and spoke tired, bitter words—words filled with frustration and anger. "God, why didn't You let me die with my family?" His voice was hoarse.

An answer came from behind him.

"Maybe He knew we needed you."

Thomas looked behind him to where Justine stood. He returned his gaze forward, to the darkness in front of him. "If God needs to use me, He must be pretty desperate."

Justine sat down beside him on the bench.

Thomas hesitated. "Justine, I think maybe you and the kids would be better off without me now. I'll split the last of the cash with you. It's not much, but it should keep you for a while. Where *are* the kids?"

"Are you kidding? It'd take a SWAT team to drag them away from Bugs and Daffy. I told them we were going to pick up some burgers and fries. They didn't argue."

"Anyway, I think I should go," Thomas said.

"Thomas, what are you running from?" Justine asked.

Thomas swallowed, choking back the grief he had buried for two years. His voice was husky when he spoke. "I see it happening over and over. There we all are, in the car crossing the bridge. It happened so fast. One second Jenny and the kids were singing; then everybody's screaming. It was my fault. I only took my eyes off the road for a second or two. Next thing I knew, we were all in the water. I'm the only one who got out."

"I'm truly sorry," Justine said, resting her hand on his shoulder.

"I still have no idea how I got out alive. They found me clinging to one of the pylons under the bridge." He closed his eyes and dropped his head. "I was found guilty of negligence in the accident. Not long after that, my congregation fired me. Guess they couldn't abide the idea of their pastor being a killer." He shrugged. "It's okay. I'd have quit anyway. I couldn't go on serving a God who'd let something like that happen."

Justine hesitated a moment. Then she said, "Pardon me for interrupting your pity party, but you're way out of line."

Thomas's head jerked up. "What?"

"You talk like you're the only person who has ever had something bad happen to him. What makes everything that happened to you God's fault?"

"He could have stopped it," Thomas hissed.

"But He chose not to," Justine shot back. "So now He's to blame?"

Irritation tinged Thomas's voice. "Now wait a minute."

Justine faced Thomas. "No," she said. "Let me finish."

Thomas glowered at her.

"When I left the Fellowship," she continued, "I lost everything. My husband. My children. Everything that I had considered important was gone in an instant. I'd just come to Christ, and my whole life fell apart. I was on the run, people were trying to kill me, and just when it seemed that circumstances couldn't get any worse, they'd get worse.

"I was hiding out at my brother's then, and I fell into a major depression. I was angry at everything and everyone. Most of all, I got angry at God. I had tried to do the right thing by standing up to Sawyer and Anthony, and it all blew up in my face. I felt like God had abandoned me and hung me out to dry. I remember saying to Michael, 'If this is how God treats His children, maybe I was better off without Him.' That was when Michael straightened me out, but quick."

Sarcasm tinged Thomas's voice. "And what pearls of wisdom did the Reverend Michael Guidry drop on you?"

Justine laughed. "My brother isn't known for his tact."

"He has *that* in common with his sister," Thomas added.

"It was Christmastime. Michael took me outside, and we walked next door to his church. They had a nativity scene on the front lawn—" Justine motioned toward the scene before them—"like that one. For the longest time he didn't say a word. We just stood and looked at the baby Jesus in the manger. Then Michael finally said, 'God has everything under control, Justine. We live in a fallen world and bad things happen, but don't you ever forget that He has everything under control.'"

Justine smiled. "I was pretty angry at the time, so I spouted off, 'And what am I supposed to do when everything seems out of control? Tell me that, Brother!'"

"What did he say?" Thomas asked.

"Michael looked me straight in the eye and said, 'You trust Him and keep on serving Him. That's what you do. A faith that only trusts God when things are going good isn't much of a faith.' Then he quoted a passage of Scripture, walked away, and left me standing there. I've never forgotten."

Thomas heaved a sigh. "And what verse did he dump on you? 'All things work together for good'? I've already heard that one—too many times."

"Nope. He quoted the song of Habakkuk." Justine fixed her gaze on the nativity scene and quoted: "'Though the fig tree does not bud and there are no grapes on the vines, though the olive crop fails and the fields produce no food, though there are no sheep in the pen and no cattle in the stalls, yet I will rejoice in the Lord, I will be joyful in God my Savior. The Sovereign Lord is my strength; he makes my feet like the feet of a deer, he enables me to go on the heights.'"

Justine stood up and walked around behind the bench. She put her hand on Thomas's shoulder. "Don't you see? We live in a fallen world, Thomas. God hasn't promised any of us an easy ride, and bad things happen. But He is sovereign, and He has promised that if we trust Him, He will bring us through those rough times. He'll enable *us* to walk on the heights. And in the end, He'll be glorified."

Justine gave Thomas's shoulder a little squeeze. "God loves you, Thomas. He hasn't abandoned you. He's walked beside you with every tear you've shed. He's as near as He ever was. Stop blaming God, and run to Him for shelter."

Thomas heard her footsteps moving away from him.

He sat motionless, gazing at the nativity scene. Then his eyes rested on the church. Three large crosses stood in the ground in front of the building. Red and green floodlights had been positioned so that the crosses' shadows were cast in the direction of the nativity scene. The shadow of the center cross fell across the manger.

The crosses began to blur and flicker as Thomas tried to hold back the tears that forced their way into his eyes. Justine had pierced his festering inner wound. Thomas could no more hold back the tears than he could stop a Texas flash flood.

Rain began to fall as Thomas stood and slowly made his way toward the nativity scene. He reached into his pocket and found Jenny's cross. Pulling it out, he fell to his knees in front of the tiny manger.

The tears now streamed down his face, mingling with the raindrops that splashed in front of him. Oblivious to the wetness soaking his knees, the increasingly heavy rain, and the rumble of thunder, Thomas reached down and laid the little cross at the feet of the baby Jesus.

As he did so, two years of suppressed grief and guilt flooded from Thomas with the force of a million gallons of water bursting through a shattered dam.

Anyone walking or driving by the scene would have noticed only a man kneeling at a manger in a church nativity scene. Drenching rain and rumbling thunder obscured the sound of Thomas's anguished sobs.

The only ones who heard were Thomas and God.

● ● ● ● ●

"What's happening now?" Micah asked.

Micah had very little trouble following the action of most of the cartoons as long as he listened carefully, but Road Runner cartoons required narration. Otherwise he only heard music and sound effects, not enough to figure out what was happening. Michelle usually cooperated, keeping him filled in on the coyote's exploits with a blow-by-blow description.

But something was wrong. She didn't answer.

"Michelle?" Micah hadn't felt her leave the bed. "Michelle, are you there?"

He sat up and swung his legs over the side of the bed. As he stood, he reached out with his right hand, trying to find a nearby wall. He called out again, louder this time, trying to hide the tremor in his voice, "Michelle?"

Still no answer.

He slid his hand along the wall as he moved forward. Something caught Micah's toe, and he lurched forward, scraping his palms on the carpet. He cried out in pain as he landed.

No response.

Lying prone, Micah screamed, not caring *who* heard him. "Michelle!"

Finally, his sister answered him. But her voice was not the comforting voice he was used to hearing. She sounded irritated. "It's *okay*, Micah. I'm in the bathroom."

Feeling a little foolish, Micah began to push himself to his knees. As his hands moved along the floor, he discovered what had tripped him. It felt like a cord of some kind. His fingers carefully traced their way around the cord and began to follow it.

The cord led into the bathroom.

Just then, Micah noticed something else. He could hear his sister's muffled voice coming from behind the bathroom door.

• • • • •

When he finally got to his feet, Thomas felt emptied of energy. It was only when he began to shiver that he realized his clothes were soaked through.

I'd better get back and dry off.

Thomas retraced his path back toward the motel, this time taking in the colored lights and Christmas decorations in the surrounding neighborhood. Houses awash with tiny icicle lights. Yards with decorated Christmas trees. Luminarias adorning walkways. Floodlit angels, reindeer, elves, and Santa Clauses populating yard after yard.

His mind wandered back to happier Christmases.

Every year they'd set aside one special evening, bundle up Steven and Sarah, and drive and look at Christmas lights. It was so much fun to listen to the kids squeal with each new discovery as they cruised through the neighborhoods.

"Daddy, look over there!" Steven cried out, pointing at a house and front yard completely decorated with red lights, all except for a giant state of Texas that read, "Merry Christmas, y'all."

"Oooooh! Look at that one, Daddy," Sarah chimed in.

Thomas felt tiny hands coming from behind, hugging his neck. Sarah's cheek rubbing against his ear.

"Thank you for taking us," Sarah said. "I love you, Daddy."

Thomas looked over at Jenny. He reached across the seat and clasped her hand.

"I love you, too, sweetie."

Thomas realized that tears had begun to trickle down his cheeks again. But they were good tears this time, tears of cleansing not of pain. He realized also that for the first time in two years he had been able to enjoy a memory of the happiest time of his life without horrific visions of the accident intruding.

He smiled to himself as he walked across the four-lane road, but his smile faded as he saw the lights. Red and blue lights this time. The flashing, piercing strobes of a police cruiser.

It was parked in the Econo Lodge's parking lot.

Thomas looked up toward Justine's room.

The door was open.

A police officer stood in front of it.

• • • • •

Llewelen burst through the front door of Sawyer Wynne's home without knocking. Wynne sat in a plush recliner, facing a dead fireplace. His hair was disheveled, and he appeared to be drinking wine from a cheap kitchen tumbler. "What's going on?" Llewelen demanded.

"Have a seat, Mr. Braddock," Wynne said. He held out a trembling hand and motioned toward another recliner.

"I'm not interested in sitting," Llewelen said. "You enabled Hiroshima. Now, what's the deal?"

"Have a *seat*, Mr. Braddock," Wynne repeated. His dark eyes flashed at Llewelen.

Reluctantly, Llewelen sat down, knowing it was the only way he'd get the information he wanted from Wynne. You played the game Sawyer Wynne's way, or you didn't play at all.

"Why did you enable Hiroshima?" Llewelen repeated. "Anthony's in Washington for the announcement of his nomination tomorrow, and you've got your finger on the self-destruct button?"

Wynne shrugged.

Llewelen scowled. "And naturally you didn't bother to tell any of the rest of us."

Wynne dismissed him with a wave of his hand. "Disable it yourself if you want to."

"I can't!" Llewelen snapped.

Wynne nodded, grinning. "Oh yes, I did keep that little detail to myself, didn't I?"

"So, are you going to disable Hiroshima or at least give me the code?"

Wynne took another swig from the tumbler. A stream of wine trickled down his chin. "It's no use. We've lost track of Justine. If the Shipp girl doesn't crack, we need to be prepared to get out while we can." Wynne finished the wine in his tumbler, closed his eyes, and pushed the chair back into a full recline.

"Don't be so sure," Llewelen said. "Justine and her brats have been spotted in New Orleans." Llewelen paused for effect. "And Dana Shipp just called. She's willing to talk and wants you to come to the island ASAP."

Wynne snapped the recliner to the upright position. "We have Justine?"

"We've *located* Justine. And if you're going to do anything about it, you'd better pull yourself together," Llewelen said, heading for the front door. "I'll notify the helicopter pilot to be ready at dawn. He'll take you to the island."

"Why should I go up there?" Wynne asked. "Have him bring her down."

Llewelen pulled open the front door. "She insisted that you come personally. Otherwise, no deal. So make sure you're ready to go before dawn. And disable Hiroshima!" Llewelen exited, slamming the door behind him.

36

Nightfall transformed Shelby Castle's majesty into mausoleum-like gloom. But Dana didn't care. She preferred darkness now. Gliding up and down the frigid, black hallways as if she were a ghost, she felt at peace. Shelby Castle would become her tomb.

Cold tranquility enveloped her the moment she'd made the phone call. It had been astonishingly simple. Wynne—the hateful man—said to dial *FWR*. As soon as she did, she was talking to someone at Chateau Antoine.

Her lips curled, baring her teeth as she thought of Sawyer Wynne. *Hateful man. Hateful.*

Foolish, too.

She said she was willing to talk, to tell them everything.

But she would talk only to him.

And only here.

Alone, on the island.

Her feet were numb from the cold as she moved down

the hallway, checking every door. Most were locked. Enough were not. She had found the things she needed. A bathrobe for keeping warm. A small flashlight, its dim beam barely illuminating a path ahead of her.

They had forgotten to lock the kitchen too. She'd found some canned food. Nothing gourmet. But enough to keep her alive until tomorrow. And there were other things in the kitchen. Things that had given her an idea.

The hateful man underestimated her.

She checked the last of the first-floor doors. Three rooms down she'd found a nice, soft bed. She would use it later. No need to open any more rooms. She had what she needed.

She ambled back to the one room with electric power. She heard the electronic click as she tripped the beam that turned on the giant TV set. Static electricity crackled. The screen glowed blue. Then his face appeared. She wanted to watch it again.

"Good day, Miss Shipp. I hope you're enjoying your private accommodations on Diamond Island. It's a privilege few people ever enjoy."

She despised his smugness.

"Of course, no one goes there this time of year."

A hoarse, guttural whisper escaped her cracked lips. "No one but me. And you."

She walked up to the television, standing inches from Wynne's face, which now appeared more as a maze of red, green, and blue dots.

"You don't have much time," the hateful man continued.

Her fingers traced the outline of the man's face. "Neither do you," she hissed.

He continued. "When we came for him, we found him hanging from the chandelier in this very room."

Her eyes went to the dark chandelier. Reflections from the television bounced off the leaded crystal, making it look like a mass of varicolored twinkling stars.

"Too good for you," she said, shaking her head. "They won't find you there."

"Don't even think of escape," the voice said.

"No," she said, swaying slightly. "No escape."

She walked away from the set and sat down on the sofa. Her eyes fixed on the vile man's face, burning its image into her consciousness.

"I expect to hear from you soon."

The screen returned to a uniform blue color.

She grinned, her eyes focusing now on the small coffee table between the sofa and the TV. The blue light reflected off the shiny treasures she'd found in the kitchen.

They should have locked the kitchen.

She looked back at the blank television screen.

"You will," she said, nodding and grinning.

37

Despite the rain, a small crowd of onlookers had assembled to watch the action in the upstairs motel room. Some poked their heads out of their doors. Others gathered at strategic points along the balcony, wherever they could find some shelter from the rain. A group of fifteen people huddled underneath the carport near the motel office. Thomas joined that group, straining to see what was going on, yet also trying his best to remain hidden.

It wasn't that Thomas was afraid or unwilling to stand with Justine and the children. In fact, part of him hoped that the arrival of law enforcement meant that their nightmare was about to end. He had felt for some time that they were in over their heads, and he still had trouble believing Justine's insistence that the only way out was to take on the Fellowship directly. On the other hand, by hanging back, if only for a few minutes, Thomas could keep all their options open.

"What's going on?" he whispered to a young woman standing in front of him.

She shrugged, cracking her chewing gum when she spoke. "Cops just showed up a few minutes ago. It's been pretty quiet. No yellin' or nothin' like that."

"I think she's a kidnapper," said a plump woman nearby. "She's got two kids with her. I saw 'em. I bet she ran off and left her husband and took those babies with her." The woman shook her head and pulled her scarf tight around her neck.

"Here they come," a teenage boy's voice called from the front of the group.

Thomas looked toward the door of Justine's room. A uniformed police officer led the way. Justine followed, her hands cuffed in front of her. Michelle came next, followed by Micah. A second officer brought up the rear, guiding Micah with his hand gripping the boy's upper right arm.

"I told you," the plump woman crowed, satisfaction in her voice. "She's a kidnapper. She was gonna hurt those babies."

The small party made its way along the balcony toward the stairwell. Micah stumbled as they descended the stairs, and the officer hauled him up by hooking his hand under Micah's arm.

That's when Thomas noticed.

The children were handcuffed too.

Thomas was no expert in police procedure, but he was fairly certain that only in extreme circumstances would police cuff a child. Everything seemed peaceful enough here, but both Micah's and Michelle's hands were bound. Whoever these men were, Thomas suspected that they were *not* officers of the New Orleans Police Department.

Thomas waited until the "officers" were occupied with loading Justine and the children into the cruiser. He edged around the crowd until he arrived at the walkway in front of the ground-floor rooms. Thankfully, the motel had been nearly full, and he had not been able to get a room on the same floor as Justine's. At his room he inserted his key card into the slot, withdrew it quickly when the green light came on, and slipped inside. If he was going to rescue them, he didn't have much time. Thomas grabbed the keys to Charles Richard's Plymouth. He tucked Justine's 9mm into his pants and pulled his shirt over it.

Thomas stepped back outside. As he looked toward the patrol car, he caught Michelle's attention. Her eyes widened, almost in fear. Thomas put his finger to his lips and began a casual stroll farther down the walkway, in the direction of the Plymouth. Out of the corner of his eye, he saw another police cruiser rolling past the motel. Noticing the emergency lights from the Econo Lodge parking lot, the second cruiser slowed, turned on its emergency lights, and swung into a U-turn.

A wave of nausea swept through Thomas. Now the *real* police were about to get in on the action.

● ● ● ● ●

Justine sat in the backseat of the police car. Micah entered from her left and scooted across the seat toward her. Michelle was climbing in on her brother's far side.

How could I have been so stupid? Justine wondered.

After she left Thomas, she had walked to a nearby McDonald's and gotten the burgers and fries she'd promised the children. Then she returned to their motel room. She had been back for only ten minutes when a knock came at the door. Assuming it to be Thomas, she had dropped her guard and pulled the door wide open.

"Come in and get warm," she started to say, when two men in police uniforms burst through, knocking her to the ground. She knew instantly that they were phonies, partially because of their generally greasy and unkempt appearance, but mostly by the silencer-equipped .45 that the first "officer" pointed at her. Not exactly a regulation service revolver.

Tall, thin, and sporting a mustache so shaggy Justine could barely see his mouth, the first officer was clearly the dominant personality. "Not a sound," he said. The second officer, a fragile-looking man with stringy blond hair and a pasty complexion, looked like the incarnation of the word *wimp*. He hovered in the background.

Michelle and Micah sat on the bed, rigid and mute.

The pseudo-officer motioned with the gun, ordering Justine to the other bed.

"I see Sawyer has more goons in his stable to replace Derek Rainart," Justine remarked as she got to her feet.

The two men looked at one another, doubt clouding their expressions. Then the first one said, "Shut up. You're coming with us." He motioned to his companion. "Get cuffs on them."

"*All* of them?" the wimp whined.

Mustache man was exasperated. "Yeah. All of them," he sneered. "Hurry."

The men's demeanor spoke volumes. They were undoubtedly from the Fellowship, but these men were not from one of Sawyer Wynne's conversion teams. Wynne's teams were efficient, well trained, and prepared. Everything about these two suggested that they were not experienced at the particular deception they were trying to engage in. The second man's uniform was not even complete. He didn't have a service belt, and Justine could see no weapon. If this had been one of Sawyer Wynne's hit teams, everything would have been authentic, down to the last button on the officers' uniforms.

These men were improvising.

Micah's voice jarred Justine out of her reflection. "What's happening to us? Where's Uncle Thomas?" Micah asked.

"It's okay, honey."

Actually, the question of Thomas's whereabouts—and whether or not he was coming back—was one that Justine desperately wished she could answer.

She pulled against the handcuffs, hoping that she might be able to free one of her hands. Nothing doing. Justine leaned forward and looked over the front seat. A quick glance confirmed her suspicions. They were in an ordinary sedan made up to look like a police car. The car's exterior had been painted to resemble a New Orleans Police Department cruiser, but inside it had almost none of the equipment a genuine cruiser would have. It wasn't uncommon for the Fellowship's regional centers and cells to keep dummy equipment for just such occasions. If you acted quickly and didn't draw too much attention to yourself, you could fool almost anybody.

The raised door-lock button on the car door momentarily lifted Justine's hopes for a possible escape. But even if she did reach the door latch and pop it open, it would only allow her to escape. The children would not be able to follow her. She would be abandoning them to the Fellowship.

She would not do that a second time. Either they all escaped, or they all faced Mustache, Wimp, and their cronies together.

Suddenly Michelle gasped.

"What's wrong?" Micah asked.

"Uncle Thomas," Michelle whispered.

"What is it, Michelle?" Justine asked.

Before Michelle could answer, Justine's attention was drawn by the sound of a car pulling alongside them. A second police cruiser, occupied by a single officer, had stopped to investigate.

● ● ● ● ●

Thomas stood about twenty-five feet from the two police

cars and held his breath as he watched the police officer step out of his cruiser. He was a large, beefy man who easily weighed in at over 250 pounds—most of it muscle. Thomas knew that the fake cops would have a tough time fooling this man, and when the deception collapsed, the situation could become lethal.

Glancing around to make certain that no one was watching him, Thomas gently lifted his shirt and pulled the 9mm from its hiding place. Tucking the handgun into his jacket pocket, he slowly approached the police officers. He watched as the real officer approached the two counterfeits cautiously. Thomas hung back, wanting desperately to intervene, but realizing that any distraction he created would probably work to the advantage of the phony cops, not the real one. For now, he had to stay out of it. And pray for some window of escape.

· · · · ·

Justine assessed the situation. Wimp remained on the far side of the car, obviously hoping that his uniform would remain unnoticed. Mustache stood by her door and took the lead as the New Orleans police officer approached.

While she didn't want to fall into the hands of the Fellowship, if she and the children were taken into police custody, their chances would not be much better. In the capable hands of the New Orleans Police Department, her whereabouts would become a matter of public record. It wouldn't take long for Sawyer Wynne to track her down and send in a team who could get the job done right. As for the children, they might be put into foster care temporarily, but in tracking down another parent or relative, the trail would inevitably lead the authorities back to New York—and the Fellowship. As Justine sat in the backseat of the phony squad car, she wished there was a way she and the children could somehow become invisible and sneak away unnoticed.

That was not going to happen.

"What have you got?" the genuine officer asked.

"Uhhh . . . not much. Drunk and disorderly."

"Why didn't you call in?" the officer asked as he bent down to peer into the backseat.

Justine noticed that the name on the officer's tag was Robicheaux. Knowing that her options were exhausted and preferring to fall into the hands of a genuine police officer rather than the Fellowship, Justine looked toward Officer Robicheaux and mouthed the word, "Help."

The officer gave a nearly imperceptible nod, then slowly straightened up. He said, "I see you've got some kids in there. You call in CPS yet?"

Mustache stammered, "I . . . uh . . . no. Not yet. I was just about to do that when you pulled up."

Officer Robicheaux waved his hand and began to back away, moving toward his own cruiser. "Don't worry about it," he said. "I'll call it in for you."

Mustache wasn't about to give the officer a chance to call in reinforcements. He whipped out his gun and fired.

● ● ● ● ●

Thomas's heart froze when he saw the fake cop gun down the real one. The New Orleans police officer's body flew backward as if a horse had kicked him. He rolled back to the pavement, his head slamming down hard. The fallen officer's arms were flung out to his sides, and his legs were splayed. He made no effort to move.

In the seconds that followed, Thomas reacted as if he were on autopilot. Had he taken time to consider the prudence of his actions, he probably wouldn't have done it. Instead, what flooded his mind was not rational thought but the instinctual reaction of a man protecting those he cares about, those he loves. He knew that Justine, Micah, and Michelle remained at the mercy of a maniac who had just gunned down an armed police officer. Thomas had no intention of allowing them to be his next victims.

Anger flashed through Thomas as he pointed the gun at the fake cop, fully intending to blow him away before he hurt anyone else. But Thomas also saw that the crowd in the carport was in his line of fire. If he missed, an innocent bystander could be hurt or killed.

Instantly, Thomas swung his arm skyward and fired a shot into the air. "Freeze, maggot," Thomas growled.

As he brought the gun down and pointed it toward his adversary, Thomas realized that all he had done was to give the man fair warning of his intentions. The phony cop pivoted in his direction and leveled his weapon at Thomas.

●　●　●　●　●　●

Justine heard the muffled *pffft* of the silenced handgun. She knew that if she didn't act this instant, she would forfeit their one chance of escape.

Out of the corner of her eye, she saw Mustache swing around to his right, preparing to fire a second time. Whom or what he intended to shoot, Justine did not know. And at that moment she did not care. Mustache's hand was now only about a foot or two from the door and directly parallel with it.

Justine reached her hands over and grabbed the door latch, pulling on it with all her strength. When she felt the latch pop, she threw her full weight against the door and burst it outward. The doorframe and window worked almost as efficiently as a baseball bat, clubbing Mustache's outstretched hand at the same instant he fired the gun.

Mustache bellowed in pain as Justine tumbled from the car. His gun clattered to the pavement only a few feet in front of her. Lying on her side, she brought her hands up, stretching out her fingers, trying to close the last few inches of space between her and the .45.

A black sneaker slapped down on the gun before she could touch it. Mustache glared down at her as he reached for the weapon.

"I wouldn't do that," a voice called out.

Justine relaxed. The voice was Thomas's.

"Get away from the gun," Thomas said. His voice was cool and more relaxed than Justine had ever heard before. "Put your hands on your head. Now!" Mustache backed away and did as Thomas said. Evidently he knew when someone was not in the mood to be messed with.

Thomas helped Justine up and handed her the gun. "Keep an eye on him while I check on the officer." Thomas bent down and called to Micah and Michelle. "Everything's okay. You two sit tight for a minute."

The children just nodded.

Thomas walked over to the officer.

Justine called after him, "His name is Robicheaux."

Thomas knelt down by the fallen officer. Despite the bullet hole in Officer Robicheaux's shirt, the first thing Thomas noticed was that there was no blood on him or the ground. Thomas felt for a carotid pulse.

"Pulse is strong," he said. "He's breathing." Thomas unbuttoned the officer's shirt and smiled. "The bullet didn't do any lasting harm. He's wearing a Kevlar vest. He cracked his head pretty hard when he went down, though. He might have a concussion. He's going to need medical attention." Thomas patted the unconscious officer's shoulder. "Hang in there. We're going to get you some help."

Thomas stood up and walked back to Justine. He nodded toward Mustache.

"Where'd his partner go?"

Before Justine could answer, two young black men in oversize New Orleans Saints shirts and baggy denim jeans sauntered up, shoving Wimp in front of them. "We got that under control, dude." Wimp already had the beginnings of a black eye, and a trickle of blood oozed from a scrape on his right cheek.

Thomas grinned. "Thanks, guys." Then he looked toward Justine. "Get the kids. We've got to get out of here."

Justine held up her wrists, still cuffed.

Thomas said to Mustache, "Where's the key?"

Mustache just gave Thomas a deadpan look.

"Okay," Thomas said. He turned to the two black youths. "Gentlemen, do you think you could persuade this phony cop to give us his handcuff key?"

"You got it," they said in unison, taking a step toward Mustache.

"No way," he blurted out. "Key's in my pocket."

"I knew you could be reasoned with." Thomas reached into Mustache's pocket and withdrew the key. After he released Justine, he handed both the guns to the young men. "Guys, we've got to make tracks. Can you handle things from here? Officer Robicheaux needs para-medics, and these two—" he motioned toward Mustache and Wimp—"need a first-class escort downtown."

One of the young men lowered his voice. "You dudes undercover?"

Thomas smiled. "You could say that."

"Go on. We got your back."

"Thanks." Thomas joined Justine. Michelle followed with Micah trailing as always, his hand on her shoulder.

The sound of sirens in the distance began to break through the other city sounds.

"Come on," Thomas said. "We've got to hustle."

Justine paused for a moment, her hand on his arm. "Where are we going?" she asked.

An angry glint came into Thomas's eyes. "New York," he replied. "We're going to bring these monsters down."

Thomas and Justine sat side by side in the waiting area for Gate D6 at New Orleans International Airport. Micah slept in an empty chair next to Justine; Michelle dozed beside Thomas. Exhausted by the day's events, the twins had fallen asleep only minutes after they arrived in the gate area. A ceiling-mounted TV displayed a feed of the day's news from CNN. Thomas ignored it. He didn't need to hear the news. He was just glad they weren't *on* it.

They had ditched Charles's car a few miles away from the motel and caught a cab to the airport. Fortunately, the terminal wasn't crowded, and their progress through the myriad of security procedures was relatively quick and uneventful.

They managed to purchase tickets for a late-afternoon flight to Syracuse, connecting through Atlanta. The six-hour travel time would make for a long day, but they should be ensconced in a motel in Syracuse by midnight. For one reason, at least, Thomas approved of the idea of going to Syracuse. It was probably the last place the Fellowship would look for them.

Thomas yawned. "I could use some coffee," he muttered.

"Me too," Justine said. "There's a coffee stand not far up the concourse. I'll get us some."

Thomas nodded, too tired to answer.

As Justine walked away, Thomas allowed his eyes to follow her. He admired her strength and resolve. For three years she had remained hidden, hoping against hope that her husband and children would one day join her. For three years she had looked over her shoulder, never knowing when someone might make an attempt on her life. If anyone had a reason to give up, she did. But Justine Bishop pressed on.

What an amazing woman!

Thomas was very familiar with the Bible passage that Justine had quoted to him outside the church in New Orleans. Indeed, he'd preached from Habakkuk several times during his years of ministry. Habakkuk's prophecy was easy to preach but tough to practice. As Habakkuk reflected on the judgment that was to befall the nation of Judah, he nevertheless proclaimed his willingness to trust God, no matter what happened.

It's easy to love God when everything's going your way. But the real test is when the devastation comes.

That was what most people missed in the passage. Judah's society was agriculturally based. No figs, olives, grapes, crops, or livestock translated into total devastation, the ancient equivalent of a nuclear holocaust. Yet Habakkuk said that in the midst of such devastation, he would rejoice in the Lord.

Thomas looked down at the sleeping children. He smoothed Michelle's curly blonde hair. Micah and Michelle reminded him so much of his own Steven and Sarah. His heart still ached when he thought of them, when he thought of Jenny. The pain would never totally go away. Thomas understood that. But he also knew that he could not continue withering. He had to press on too. And the only way he could do that was through God's strength.

"Sovereign Lord, You are my strength," Thomas murmured. "You make my feet like the feet of a deer; You enable me to walk upon the heights."

Justine returned. "They only had decaf. I got some anyway," she said, handing him a Styrofoam cup.

Thomas took the cup from her. "Thanks. At least it may make me *think* I'm awake." He smiled at Justine, but he noticed that her attention had shifted to the TV screen across the waiting area. A picture of her husband, Peter Bishop, was on the screen.

"Justine, what's—?"

She held up her hand. "Listen."

"Investigators are still stymied," the news anchor continued, "by the strange case of a man who died Friday afternoon in a terminal at John F. Kennedy International Airport. The man, identified as Peter Bishop, collapsed while talking on a pay phone, and all resuscitation attempts failed. An autopsy has revealed that death was not from natural causes. While authorities are not revealing the cause of death at this time, unnamed sources say that Peter Bishop was poisoned. Some are wondering if this is part of a new wave of terrorism that may be about to sweep the nation."

Thomas stood up. "Oh, Justine, I'm so sorry."

Justine appeared not to hear him. The coffee cup slipped from her hand and splashed to the floor. Tears filled her eyes as Thomas came to her side and helped her into a chair.

"I was so sure he'd make it," she said, shaking her head. "I was so sure."

Thomas felt completely helpless. "Is there *anything* I can do?" he asked.

Justine blinked back the

BLIND
SIGHT

tears. "No," she said, holding up her hands. "No, I'll be all right."

Thomas looked into her eyes. He wasn't so sure. He took her hands in his own. "We're going to stop them, Justine. Somehow, some way, we're going to put Sawyer Wynne and the Fellowship out of business. They won't do this to anyone else."

She gave him a weak grin. She mouthed the words, "I know," but no sound came out. And the tears came in a flood.

Thomas put his arm around her as she rested her head on his shoulder and sobbed. "Go ahead. Let it out."

Later, as her sobs subsided, Thomas quietly whispered in her ear, "'Though the fig tree does not bud and there are no grapes on the vines, though the olive crop fails and the fields produce no food, though there are no sheep in the pen and no cattle in the stalls, yet I will rejoice in the Lord. I will be joyful in God my Savior. The Sovereign Lord is my strength; he makes my feet like the feet of a deer, he enables me to go on the heights.'"

Justine squeezed his hand.

So what is it? Tanks or an air assault?" Thomas asked.

Justine turned her gaze from the window of the Delta 737 as it began its descent into Syracuse Hancock International Airport.

She looked at Thomas, puzzled. "What?" Her eyes were red from crying.

"Hey," Thomas joked, "just because I agreed to join this dog and pony show doesn't mean I have any higher estimate of our chances of survival. I was just wondering how you plan to get into the Fellowship's headquarters. Based on what I've seen so far, it's not going to be a picnic. I favor tanks. A quick frontal attack. Blow up the front wall. Get in, get the records, get out while they're picking up the pieces."

She laughed. "You're crazy."

"It's nice to see you smile again," he said.

Justine thought for a moment. "I could probably get into Chateau Antoine. I remember all the access codes, assuming they haven't changed them. But you're right. I'm so well known there, I wouldn't last five minutes."

"Uh-huh." A smug grin spread across Thomas's face.

"But I never told you I was planning on going into the Chateau Antoine, did I?"

Thomas raised an eyebrow.

"The Fellowship has another headquarters on the Saint Lawrence River. It's a castle on Diamond Island up in the Thousand Islands. During the summers it's where most of the Fellowship's recruitment retreats are held. They close it down during winter."

"A castle on an island? You've got to be kidding."

Justine shook her head. "MacAsland's father built it back in the fifties. He patterned it after another larger castle up there."

"There's more than one?"

"Boldt Castle—the original—was built around the turn of the century by George Boldt, the manager of the Waldorf Astoria. He wanted it to be an expression of his love for his wife. But she died before it was finished. He ordered construction stopped immediately and never visited the island again. It's quite a love story.

"MacAsland's father wanted to buy Boldt Castle but couldn't get it. So he built his own version, smaller and less grand, but impressive nonetheless."

"Whatever happened to Boldt Castle?"

"The Thousand Islands Bridge Authority bought and restored it. It's a beautiful place." Justine smiled.

"So," Thomas said, "assuming we can get out to a deserted island in the middle of a frozen river, what then?"

"We tap into their computer system, get the information we need, and get out of there."

Thomas looked skeptical. "After three years, you think you'll still be able to access their files? Surely they invalidated your password."

"I'm sure they did, but I know another way in."

"What's that?"

"When Peter designed all their systems, he created a back door, a special entry code that only he knew about."

"And he told you what the code was?"

Justine nodded.

"But what do we do with the files once we have them?"

"That's the hard part," she said. "We'll have to find someone in authority who is willing to listen to us."

"Good luck," Thomas said, pointing to the copy of the New Orleans *Times-Picayune* in his lap. "Did you see the latest on our Father Antoine?" He unfolded the newspaper and showed her the headline "MacAsland VP Nomination Expected."

Justine's face blanched when she saw the headline. Thomas read the article to Justine:

"Sources in Washington report that billionaire philanthropist Anthony MacAsland will be the president's nominee to become the new vice president, filling the post left vacant by the resignation of Vice President Sherman Houston. Houston resigned rather than face impeachment after he was implicated in a money-laundering scandal and his ties to organized crime were exposed.

"Anthony MacAsland, widely known for his efforts on behalf of the environment and the poor and indigent, says he will bring a fresh voice to Washington and plans to be a tireless advocate for the poor. MacAsland's lack of political experience is considered a plus by the president, who has committed himself to creating a government free of Washington insiders. Favored by leaders in both parties, MacAsland is expected to face an easy confirmation vote in the Senate."

Justine clucked her tongue.

"What?" Thomas replied.

"The vice president was framed."

"How do you know?"

"I know the Fellowship. And I know the Project. Don't you see? This has been going on for years. We're in the endgame now. The Fellowship has been doing the same thing across the country. They recruit people, brainwash them to their way of thinking; then they reeducate them to fit back into society.

"The Fellowship doesn't want a bunch of white-robed nuts dancing around and singing the praises of Father Antoine. They want people who blend in, who look and talk and act just like you and me. Then they place them wherever they can out in the world. Once they've established themselves as model employees, the Fellowship sets up their superiors for 'accidents.' Then their pawns move up a link in the chain of command.

"They're building a power base in society. The fact that they've moved Antoine into position to make a play for the vice presidency shows that Sawyer's project is proceeding exactly as planned. And it won't stop there," she added. "He won't stop short of the presidency itself."

Thomas looked skeptical. "Come on. You think they'd assassinate the president? Isn't that a bit of a reach?"

Justine shook her head. "After everything that's happened over the last few days, what do *you* think? Besides, they don't necessarily need to assassinate him. They were able to get Vice President Houston to resign with just a few well-placed scandals. Remember what happened with Nixon and Agnew?"

Thomas nodded. "Agnew resigned in disgrace, and Gerald Ford was nominated to replace him. Then, when Nixon resigned, Ford ascended to the presidency."

"An unelected president. It's happened before." Worry creases formed on Justine's face. "Thomas, we have to stop them."

"Which brings us back to my original question," Thomas said. "How? This guy's more popular than the pope. How are you going to get anyone to listen to anything negative about him?"

Justine looked into her lap for a moment, then glanced at the two seats across the aisle. Michelle's head lay on a pillow against the window. Micah had reclined his seat. Both appeared to be asleep.

Justine dropped her voice barely above a whisper. "Anthony MacAsland wasn't exactly a model son. When his father sent him off to college, he lived the life of a playboy. Goofing off. Wasting Daddy's money. You know the type."

Thomas nodded.

"When it was obvious that little Anthony had no interest in studying, his father sent him to Shelby Castle to supervise a renovation of the property. Anthony's mother had died of cancer, and MacAsland had lost interest in anything except business after that. But he thought it might be a good work project for his son. Anthony didn't tell his father he was bringing a friend. His best friend, Sawyer Wynne, accompanied him to the island. Sawyer came up with the idea of starting their own religion. Sawyer was serious about it from day one. For Anthony it was sort of a joke, until he saw how easily people were taken in. Then he became *very* serious.

"So he and Wynne began to develop what would later become the Fellowship. It was a fairly small group at first, just about thirty people. But he recruited faithfully during the week, promising eager young college students just about anything they wanted. In time, he had a fully functioning religious commune operating on the island.

"That's when Daddy made an unexpected visit. He was furious. He told Anthony he was going to cut him off completely." Justine paused and took a deep breath. "Daddy never left the island alive. Sawyer Wynne ordered him killed."

"How did he manage to cover that up?" Thomas asked.

"After they'd killed MacAsland and his helicopter pilot, Wynne had someone fly the chopper into the mountains in upstate New York. They ditched it and burned it. Made it look like a kidnapping."

"Yeah," Thomas said, "I remember reading something about that in the paper. The police speculated it was some kind of mob hit."

A grim expression clouded Justine's face. "They never even seriously considered Anthony a suspect. He put on a very convincing bereaved-son act. And Sawyer Wynne was the original spin doctor. By the time he was done helping Anthony craft his reaction to the whole thing, Anthony had the authorities eating out of his hand and the board of directors of MacAsland Oil ready to hand the reins of the company over to him on a platter."

Thomas leaned back in his seat and stroked his beard. "So you're saying there's some way you can prove he arranged his father's murder? That's how you're going to stop him?"

Justine nodded.

"Are you positive you can do it? If MacAsland was so squeaky clean that the police didn't even consider him a suspect, what makes you think you can?"

A hard bump jarred them out of their conversation as the 737 touched down. Thomas felt the power of the jet engines reversing their thrust as the pilot decelerated the giant aircraft.

Micah and Michelle awoke with the impact and noise of the landing. They sat up, stretching and yawning.

Thomas turned back to Justine, expecting an answer to his question. But she was staring out the window, her face somber and determined, her eyes glued to the horizon.

He decided to keep quiet.

40

Sawyer Wynne yawned and stretched out on the plush sofa that occupied one wall of his office. He had chosen the sofa precisely for situations like this: times when he really didn't want to waste time with the commute from his house. As soon as Llewelen had left, Sawyer cleaned up and had someone drive him here to Chateau Antoine. Early tomorrow a helicopter would fly him to Shelby Castle. He wanted to be ready as soon as possible.

Dana Shipp cracked much sooner than he'd expected, and he desperately needed the information she had. Justine Bishop was a loose end that needed tying up. Apparently he couldn't count on Rainart to do it. Then reports had come in from a cell group in New Orleans. A call had tipped them off to Justine's whereabouts, and they'd made an unauthorized attempt to take her. Justine, the children, and Thomas Kent had all escaped. Worse, two New Orleans members were in police custody. Wynne had already ordered them silenced. Other inmates would beat the two to death in an apparent gang-motivated attack.

Fools.

If they'd done things by the book and contacted his office, he'd have made sure that Justine and company were taken safely. Now, he had lost them—again.

Like it or not, Dana Shipp was his sole remaining link to Justine. And soon she would tell him everything she knew.

She was probably planning something. But Sawyer Wynne wasn't worried. There was nothing Dana Shipp could do that he wasn't fully prepared for.

She would tell him where to find Justine Bishop.

And then she would die.

Thomas pushed open the lobby door of the Holiday Inn Express motel and jogged back out to the Malibu they'd rented only minutes before. Wind gusts, bitter cold, ripped through his light clothing, making him wish they'd taken more time to prepare for New York's weather.

He shivered as he sat down in the passenger's seat, closing the door. "I'll never complain about north Texas winters again." He handed a key to Justine. "You and the kids are in 236. They didn't have anything next door. I'm two down. Room 240."

They parked the rental car and quickly moved the children inside the building.

Justine unlocked her room and stood by while Michelle, then Micah hugged Thomas. Micah held on tight, not letting go.

Thomas smoothed Micah's hair. "It's going to be okay."

"Come on, Micah,"

Michelle said, taking the boy's hand. "Let's go."

Micah reluctantly released his grip on Thomas and allowed his sister to lead him into the motel room.

"You two get settled," Justine called. "I'll be right in." She closed the door behind them, then took Thomas's hand and led him a short distance down the hallway. "I need to talk to you about something," she said. "But I don't want them to hear this."

Thomas looked at her expectantly.

Justine kept her eyes fixed on the floor. "I want you to stay with the children tomorrow."

"But, Justine, that's—"

"No. Let me finish. There's no need for all of us to go up there. And there's certainly no need to put the children at further risk."

"I thought you said the island would be deserted."

"It probably is, but there's always a chance . . ." Her voice trailed off.

"Then let me go," Thomas said. "Tell me what I need to find and I'll get it and get out of there. And if something goes wrong, then at least you three have a chance to escape. It doesn't matter what happens to me, but you have those kids to live for. They need you."

Justine looked up into his eyes. Her green eyes brimmed with tears. "That's sweet," she said. "But you don't understand. The Fellowship wants me, not you. I don't plan on getting caught. But if I do, I want you to escape with the children."

Thomas took Justine in his arms. "I can't let you go alone."

She smiled, then pulled gently from his embrace. "Take care of them," she said. She barely choked the words out.

"But, Justine . . . ," Thomas protested.

She turned from him and walked into her room.

Thomas sat in a soft chair, gazing out the motel window at a crisp layer of snow that had fallen in the last two hours. Red numbers from the digital clock by his bed showed 2:30 a.m. He had given up trying to sleep over an hour ago. Now he just sat in the dim light of a floor lamp by the chair. The round, wood-veneer table beside him was bare except for a gold-covered Gideon Bible placed in its center.

For the first time since they had left Richard's Landing, he was able to sit quietly and think. Now his mind swam upstream, fighting a torrent of conflicting thoughts, all demanding his attention. How had Rainart found them? And who tipped off the goons in New Orleans?

And Justine's behavior mystified him. At first she wanted to walk away from the Fellowship, to go into hiding. Then she wanted to take on the whole cult, chiding Thomas for his unwillingness to participate. Now she'd changed directions again, wanting him to take the children and escape without her.

Thomas rested his right arm on the table. His fingers played absentmindedly over the closed Bible. He pulled the book toward him and was about to open it when he heard a sound at the door.

Thomas held his breath, not sure of what he heard.

There it was again. Quiet, almost imperceptible. But he wasn't imagining it.

Someone was turning the doorknob to his room.

Thomas swallowed and eased himself out of the chair. He reached toward the light and switched it off. His room had no balcony, but he closed the curtain just in case.

A rattling sound broke the silence. The knob rotated again.

The hotel management had equipped the door with a

peephole. Thomas looked through it. The hallway was deserted.

Cold sweat beads formed on his forehead. The palms of his hands felt clammy. He knew Rainart was no longer a threat, but after New Orleans, all bets were off. Could someone else have found them?

Looking around for something to use as a weapon, Thomas quickly settled on the small bedside lamp. He unplugged it and held it in his right hand. Standing behind the door, he quietly flipped the locks open and eased the knob around. He grabbed the lamp and held it upside down, ready to strike.

Then he waited.

A few seconds later, he saw the knob rotate again. Thomas jerked the door open and raised the lamp, ready to smash it down on the intruder's skull.

Taken off guard, the intruder sprawled forward onto the floor. In the darkness, illuminated only by light flooding in from the hallway, Thomas's arm froze where it was. Then he heaved an exasperated sigh and tossed the lamp onto the bed.

"Micah! What are you doing out here?" Thomas stooped down and grasped the boy by his upper arms, lifting him back to his feet. "Do you know how close you came to having a permanent dent in your skull?"

"I–I'm sorry," Micah said. "I didn't want anyone else to hear me."

"It's okay," Thomas said. "I'm just glad you're not hurt."

Thomas took him by the hand and led the boy to his bed. "Here. Sit down on the bed for a minute." Thomas closed the door, then sat down beside Micah. "Now, what's so important that you had to come see me about it in the middle of the night."

"Don't let her go alone," Micah said.

"What?"

"She wants to go by herself, doesn't she?"

"How do you know that?"

A broad smile spread across Micah's face. "I can't see. But I can hear pretty well. I opened the door a crack and listened."

"Micah, what she said makes some sense. It could be dangerous for you and Michelle up there."

The boy shook his head furiously, flinging his uncombed hair in all directions. "No! We have to go with her."

"She's not an easy person to reason with, Micah."

"I don't care. Promise you won't let her go alone."

"Micah, I—"

The boy reached out, grabbing Thomas's wrist. "Promise."

Thomas chuckled and ran his fingers through Micah's disheveled locks. "You're harder to reason with than she is. Okay. I promise."

Satisfied, Micah stood up and made his way toward the door.

"Hey. Don't you need help?"

"Naw. Your room's just like ours."

"But how will you find your own room?"

Micah pulled the door open and ran his fingers across the Braille dots below the room number. "Like this." Grinning, he stepped out into the hall and pulled the door closed behind him.

Thomas walked back to the chair by the table. Turning the floor lamp back on, he sat down and pulled the Gideon Bible toward him. He opened it and flipped the pages until he found the book of Habakkuk. Carefully, he paged through the book until he found the third chapter. Moving his hand down the page, he stopped at the nineteenth verse. Thomas's voice was calm as he read: "'The Sovereign Lord is my strength; he makes my feet like the feet of a deer, he enables me to go on the heights.'"

BLiND
SiGHT

"God," he prayed, "I have been angry at You for two years. I've railed, I've complained, I've hurled every ounce of venom I could manage." Thomas turned off the lamp, then stood and pulled on the cord that opened the floor-length curtains. The sky had cleared, and in spite of the city lights, hundreds of stars dusted the night view. A warmth spread through Thomas as his eyes found the constellation Orion. He recalled God's challenge to Job, when Job had questioned God's dealings with him.

> Can you bind the beautiful Pleiades?
> Can you loose the cords of Orion?
> Will the one who contends with the Almighty correct him?
> Let him who accuses God answer him!

"I couldn't understand why You would take my family and leave me behind to struggle along without them. And I guess I still don't totally understand that part of it. But I *do* believe that You're sovereign; You're in control."

Justine's voice reverberated through his thoughts: *"Maybe God knew we needed you."*

"And I know that You've brought Justine and those children into my life. And they need me. Lord, You could have taken my life that day, but You spared it. And You've gone on sparing it. It doesn't matter what happens to me now, but if I can help them, please let me do it."

Thomas closed the drapes and stood alone in the dark room. For the first time in two years, he was at peace with God and with himself. He knew what he had to do. Justine and her children would be safe, even if he had to die to make sure of it.

Thomas walked over to the bed and flopped down on top of the bedspread. Almost at once he fell into a deep slumber.

Tuesday, December 10

As early morning light streamed through Shelby Castle's majestic windows, Dana Shipp was on her knees in the kitchen. Sunshine glittered off the polished stainless-steel refrigerator and table surfaces, giving the long, narrow room a metallic brightness.

Dana hummed as she worked. Scattered around her on the floor were items she had scavenged from various cabinets and drawers: duct tape, scissors, rubber bands, sandpaper, and matches.

She took a handful of matches and bound them together with rubber bands. Yanking off a long strip of duct tape, she rolled it around the bundle of matches, then secured them near the bottom of the kitchen door. Another few pieces of tape held the sandpaper to the doorjamb.

"Almost ready," she sang to herself.

Very gently she eased the large swinging door shut,

taking care not to allow the matches to brush along the sandpaper briskly enough to ignite.

As streams of bright sunlight trickled through the windows, Dana smiled. "Won't be long now. He said he'd be here soon after the sun came up. Have to be ready." She started humming again—a song from a movie she'd seen when she was a little girl.

As she moved toward the kitchen's back entrance, Dana stopped by the large black stove. She bent over and blew out the pilot lights. Then she turned on the gas to all four burners and the oven. The unpleasant odor of propane began to fill the room.

Dana wrinkled her nose.

Standing by the back entrance, she looked back over the kitchen. Dana grinned and started humming her song again. Then, as she walked out the door and locked it behind her, she sang, "Ding-dong, the hateful man is dead."

43

J ustine took one last look at her children. She didn't dare touch them for fear of waking them. Micah lay on one double bed, Michelle on the other.

Justine suppressed an urge to laugh as she looked at her son. Shirtless, half-covered by a heavy blanket, Micah lay sprawled on his back with one foot hanging off the side of the bed. He had tossed his arms back over his head. A slight snoring sound escaped from his open mouth. His hair, scruffy on its best days, stuck out in every direction. He looked like the perfect choice for a film biography titled *Young Einstein*.

He was so warm, so loving. Her mind went back to the evening Charles Richard had brought them to her. Micah had crashed through the restaurant's chairs and tables, scattering them in every direction as he tried to get to her. "Mom. Mom," he had called out, desperately trying to figure out where she was. She had run to him, partly to keep him from killing himself on one of the tables.

When they embraced, neither one wanted to be the first to let go.

"Mom. Mom." He just couldn't stop saying it as he held her.

Justine's eyes went to the other bed. Regal and serene, wearing an oversize T-shirt as a nightgown, Michelle almost looked like Sleeping Beauty in quiet repose. She had pulled the bedspread almost up to her shoulders, keeping it so smooth she could practically slip out and leave the bed already made. Her long blonde curls appeared perfectly arranged. She was a picture of quietness and peace. How different she was from her brother.

When Charles had brought them both into the souvenir shop, Michelle hung back as Micah rushed to greet his mother. When Justine walked over to her, there was no embrace, no calling out, "Mom, Mom." Michelle had offered her hand and said, "Hello, Justine."

The coolness of her daughter's greeting might have saddened her, but Justine understood. It could take years to win her daughter back, particularly since Michelle obviously felt that Justine had abandoned her three years earlier.

Justine stood, studying her daughter's quiet breathing.

My babies. I wish I could watch you grow up. But there's only one way to stop Sawyer. You'll be better off with Thomas. I'll always love you both.

Justine dropped a note on the table, telling the children to go to Thomas's room when they woke up.

● ● ● ● ●

The parking lot was quiet as she made her way through the four-inch layer of snow that had fallen during the night. A crusty white blanket covered the Malibu, obscuring the windshield and rear window.

Justine brushed the snow off with her hand, but a thin

layer of ice droplets remained. She would have to scrape them off before she'd even be able to see where she was going.

"I don't have time for this," she muttered as she opened the trunk and looked for something to remove the ice from the windshield. Finding nothing there, she unlocked the car, hoping the rental company had left a scraper in the glove compartment. She sat down in the driver's seat and leaned over toward the passenger side. Aside from a few booklets and papers from the rental company, the compartment was empty.

"Where is it?" she said out loud to herself.

"Are you looking for this?"

Justine swung around. There stood Thomas, holding a scraper.

"What are you doing here?" she asked.

"I was about to ask you the same question."

"Look," she protested, "we went over this last night. Now give me the scraper and get back to your room. The kids will be worried if they wake up and can't find one of us."

"The kids'll be fine."

Justine breathed an exasperated sigh and grabbed the scraper. She stood at the windshield and shoved the blade along the surface of the glass. A sandpapery sound accompanied the ice as it sprayed in every direction.

Thomas walked to the other side of the car, facing Justine across the windshield. "What are *you* running from, Justine?" he shouted, trying to be heard above the scraper's rasping.

She flashed an angry look at him. "Nothing."

"Then why are you trying to do this yourself? Not long ago it was *we* need to stop Antoine. Now all of a sudden you want to go out like the Lone Ranger. Why the change?"

Justine shoved the scraper toward Thomas, sending a

spray of ice crystals into his face and beard.
"I just want to, okay?"

"No! It's not okay. I want some answers,
and you're not leaving till I get them."

Justine raised her eyebrows and showered Thomas
with another spray of ice. "And how are you going to
stop me?"

"I'll call the police and turn us all in."

Justine hesitated, then continued pumping the scraper.
"You'd never do that."

"Are you willing to risk it? I don't have anything
to lose."

"I don't believe you."

"I'd do it in a heartbeat. I promise you."

Justine stopped scraping, her eyes searching Thomas's
face. She threw him the scraper. "Get the back window."

Thomas moved behind the car and brushed the snow
off. With broad strokes he sprayed ice into the air, quickly
clearing the window. When he finished, he tossed the
scraper into the car.

"Justine, why are you trying to go off on your own?
What do you hope to accomplish that we can't do
together?"

Justine averted her eyes, wrapping her arms around
herself. "It's cold out here. We ought to get back inside."

Thomas took hold of her arm. "Not until you do two
things. First, give me the car keys. Second, tell me the
whole truth."

Justine looked at him thoughtfully. She reached into
her jacket pocket and tossed him the keys. "One out of
two isn't bad," she said. She whirled away and left him
behind as she marched back to her motel room.

Thomas wheeled the Malibu into the parking lot of the small airfield. In addition to a house trailer that apparently served as an office, three small hangars stood off to the right. Thomas's eyes wandered from the hangars to the two helicopters on his left.

A beat-up Volkswagen Beetle sat parked in front of the small trailer. A sign outside read, "Earl Cutler, Airplane and Helicopter Charter."

"Let me do the talking," Justine said as Thomas brought the car to a stop.

"Gladly," he said, thankful that she had broken her stony silence. From the time they had gone back to the motel room for the children until that moment, Justine had not spoken a word. She sat beside him in the car, sullen, obviously displeased that she had been unable to escape.

"Stay here, kids," Thomas said to Michelle and Micah. "We'll be right back."

Justine had arrived at the

trailer door and was already knocking by the time Thomas caught up with her.

"You sure somebody's home?" he asked.

She pointed to the Volkswagen and continued knocking. Soon they heard footsteps thudding along the trailer's thin floors. A muffled voice called out, "Yeah, yeah, I'm comin'."

When the door opened, a man in his late twenties stood before them in a tattered velour bathrobe. His curly hair had been cropped short and dyed in a combination of platinum blond and what looked like fluorescent orange. The man's bright hair stood in stark contrast to his dark skin. He wore a diamond stud in his left ear and a gold ring through his left eyebrow. After a prolonged yawn, he asked, "What time is it?"

Thomas looked at his watch. "Six thirty."

The man's eyes widened. "In the *morning*? Awwwww, man, what in the world are you people doin' out here?"

Justine broke in. "We need to charter a helicopter."

"Fantastic," the man said. "Come back at ten and I'll talk to you. I'm goin' back to bed." He started to close the door, but Justine stepped forward and put her hand on it, pushing it back open. She put her foot against the jamb.

"We need it now," she said.

"Lady," he said, "I'm not open for business right now. Now either move that foot or lose it."

Thomas said, "Are you Earl Cutler?"

"You're pretty sharp. You a rocket scientist?" the man replied.

"Mr. Cutler, what do you charge for a charter?"

"Two-fifty an hour. Fuel's extra."

"I'll double it—provided we can get going within the next half hour."

"Where we going?"

"The Thousand Islands. Well, Diamond Island, to be exact," Justine said.

Earl Cutler broke into a wry grin. "You ain't from

around here, are you? That ain't no place to go this time o' year."

"Just consider us a couple of crazy tourists. Deal?"

Earl raised an eyebrow. "It's your money. I'll start on preflight right after I'm dressed."

"Thank you, Mr. Cutler," Thomas said.

"Call me E.C. With the money you're payin', we oughta at least share nicknames."

"Okay. I'm Thomas. This is Justine."

E.C. raised an eyebrow. "Not very creative in the nickname department, are we? Come on in," E.C. called behind him as he went into a bedroom at the far end of the trailer. "And how 'bout makin' some coffee—extra strong? I need caffeine. Stuff's in the kitchen."

"You got it," Thomas said, entering the trailer.

"Can you afford to double his fee?" Justine whispered.

"It'll use up the rest of my cash, but I can do it."

Justine nodded, but the expression on her face signaled her displeasure.

●　●　●　●　●

In less than the half hour Thomas had bargained for, Earl Cutler had the helicopter ready. He helped Micah and Michelle into the backseats, then assisted Justine and Thomas as they climbed aboard. As they put on their headphones, E.C. throttled up the engines and they lifted off.

"Where'd you learn to fly?" Justine asked.

"Army. 'Be all you can be.' 'Find your future.' All that junk. Well, I did." A broad grin spread across E.C.'s face as he looked back at Justine.

Thomas watched the snow-covered landscape sweep by.

"What're you folks plannin' to do up there, anyway?" E.C. asked.

"You don't want to know," Thomas said.

"Hey. You ain't doin' anything illegal, are you?

'Cause I'll turn this bird around and go right back home if you are. I'm not losin' my license just so you two can run drugs."

"We're on the level, E.C.," Thomas said.

Earl Cutler fixed his gaze on Micah and Michelle. "You kidnappin' those kids?"

"Nothing illegal, E.C.," Thomas replied. "I promise."

"Promises don't mean squat. I want to know what your plans are or we go home now!"

Thomas looked at Justine. She shrugged.

"We're going to solve a murder," Thomas said.

E.C. raised his eyebrows and turned his attention back to the flight controls. "Sorry I asked."

D ana had to stand on a chair to see, but the second-story window gave her a perfect view of the heliport. Her legs were getting tired. She'd been standing there for nearly an hour with a wool blanket wrapped around her shoulders.

Her left hand held the blanket; her right held a butcher knife she'd found in the kitchen. The hateful man said he would arrive early in the morning. She was waiting patiently. Everything was ready. The surprise was prepared.

Dana's eyes fluttered. She fought to keep them open. She'd had so little sleep the night before. Her fingers relaxed and the knife clattered to the floor. Dana shook her head. "Got to sleep. Just a little."

She was about to step down from the chair when she heard the muffled sound of a helicopter's rotors. Instantly alert, Dana strained to see what direction the noise was coming from. She saw the helicopter appearing like a dark blue dot against the uniform gray of the clouds.

Dana smiled. The hateful man was coming.

Her ordeal was almost over.

● ● ● ● ●

"Wow," Thomas said, as Diamond Island came into view.

Shelby Castle stood in the very center. The massive structure was at least six stories high in some places, with steep-pitched roofs, spires, watchtowers, and several wings. At the south end stood a two-story stone boathouse and dock, connected to the house by a stone passageway. On the east, Thomas could see the helipad, where E.C. would soon put his aircraft down. Another tunnel-like passage led from the heliport to the castle.

Thomas turned to Justine. "And this is the *smaller* castle?"

Smiling, she nodded.

"Incredible."

E.C. dropped the helicopter to a dead center landing on the pad. As he shut the engines down, he spoke. "Now what?"

"Justine and I are going inside." Thomas turned toward the back. "Micah and Michelle, you stay here. We won't be long."

"But, Uncle Thomas," Micah protested.

"No *but*s," Thomas replied. "This is the safest place for you." Thomas looked at the pilot. "E.C., if anybody else shows up or if something bad happens, get the kids out of here and call the state police. Don't worry about us. Understand?"

"You got it."

"Ready?" Thomas asked Justine.

"Ready."

"Let's go before we rethink this," Thomas said.

Dana's eyes narrowed as she saw the man and woman climb out of the helicopter. It wasn't the hateful man. Not even Llewelen. Dana had never seen these people before.

"No!" she screamed.

The hateful man had tricked her. He'd sent someone else. He *was* afraid to come to the island. Dana smiled. At least she'd made him afraid.

These people had come to take her back to him. Dana shook her head. She would never go back to him.

The surprise would proceed just as she'd planned.

Dana dropped her blanket, stepped off the chair, and picked up the butcher knife. Then she ambled down the hallway to her hiding place.

⦁ ⦁ ⦁ ⦁ ⦁ ⦁

Thomas breathed out a low whistle as he craned his neck, trying to take in the view of the majestic structure. "Any ideas on how to get inside this place?" Thomas asked as he and Justine navigated the icy walkway leading to the castle.

Justine pointed up ahead toward the mouth of a stone tunnel. "That tunnel leads to the east entrance. As for how to get in, your guess is as good as mine. This is a formidable structure. We could try breaking a window, but even that's not going to be easy."

Stopping at the tunnel's mouth, Thomas ran his hand along the stones that made up the walls and arched ceiling. A row of lightbulbs ran down the center of the ceiling. Thomas flipped a nearby switch.

"No power."

Gray light streamed in through rectangular skylights, allowing faint spots of daylight to punctuate the walkway's darkness.

Thomas and Justine moved through the tunnel quickly. The

BLINd
SiGHT

dry concrete floor was treacherous where snow had blown in through the windows. Otherwise, the corridor provided a welcome relief from the conditions outside.

"Now I know how the pharaohs must have felt on their last ride into the pyramids," Thomas said.

"Keep your eyes open for anything we could use to get in. A concrete block. Something to smash a window with."

But aside from some loose pebbles, the place was immaculate.

An imposing wooden door stood enveloped in shadow as Justine and Thomas neared the end of the tunnel. "That's the east entrance," she said.

"Looks like we've hit a dead end," Thomas said.

Justine shook her head. "Not quite. There's a small service door just ahead on our right. If it's unlocked, we can get out of the tunnel and go around the north side of the castle. I'm hoping we can find something there that will get us in."

She felt along the wall until her hand found the knob. "Here it is. Yes! It's unlocked." Justine turned the knob and pushed on the door. It gave only a few inches. "Snow's piled up against it. Give me a hand."

They both put their shoulders against the door and shoved. The door opened a few more inches, but not enough for either of them to get through it.

"One more should do it," Justine said.

"Justine, look," Thomas said, putting his hand on her shoulder.

When she turned and saw where Thomas was pointing, Justine inhaled sharply. A column of light seeping through the service door cast a thin beam toward the east entrance. The huge oak door stood ajar.

"That can't be," Justine said.

"I thought you said these people were security conscious."

"They are. Beyond belief," she said.

"Then why would they leave one of the castle's main entrances open?"

"They wouldn't."

Thomas and Justine walked toward the dimly lit door. Thomas pushed it open wide. A short hallway before them led to a granite staircase. Thomas could see a hint of light filtering down.

"What do you think?" Thomas asked. "Burglars? Vandals?"

"Possibly. Could have happened anytime after they closed the island down for the winter."

Thomas ran his hand along the solid oak door. "No damage to the door or the frame. I don't want to burst your bubble, but there's no way you break through a door like this without doing some damage. This door was opened from the inside."

"Somebody could have broken in somewhere else and just gone out this way. There are lots of ways to get into this place."

Thomas nodded. "Maybe."

"Probably nothing to worry about anyway," Justine said. "If anybody did break in, they're long gone by now."

"We can only hope," Thomas said. "Let's go."

At the top of the staircase, Justine and Thomas stood gazing down a nearly pitch-black hallway. They could see a faint glow at the end of the passageway.

"Well," Thomas said, "you know this place better than I do. Where do we go now?"

"That way," she responded, pointing toward the light ahead of them.

"What's up there?"

"That's the grand entrance hall. From that point you can go anywhere else in the castle."

"Sounds like the place to be," Thomas agreed.

Their eyes gradually adjusted to the darkness.

BLiND
SiGHT

Heavy doors appeared periodically on either side as they moved down the hallway.

"Where do all these doors lead?" Thomas asked.

"Mostly bedrooms on the upper floors. Down here is where the novices stay when they come up for recruitment weekends."

"What's the difference?"

"Well," she said, "the term *dungeon* more aptly describes those rooms."

"Really?"

Justine nodded. "No frills whatsoever. They're large, bare rooms. The novices sleep here, go to training sessions here, eat here. All in a cozy little group."

"Kind of like an exotic summer camp, huh?"

Justine snorted. "Summer camp from hell."

"What do you mean?"

"The novices are lucky if they get two or three hours of sleep the whole weekend. They eat a starvation diet, and the leaders control them like they would a group of preschoolers. They move from meeting to meeting, constantly being harangued, lectured, and verbally abused. By the time the Fellowship is done with them, their power of independent thought has been shattered."

"Then what happens?"

"The Fellowship pressures them into cutting all their earthly ties, which usually involves signing over all their assets. If the person agrees, they're shipped to one of the Fellowship's five training centers across the country for a six-month to two-year 'reeducation.'"

"And if they don't agree?"

Justine paused and looked at Thomas. "They disappear."

"Come on! You can't tell me that anyone who rejects the Fellowship's overtures is eliminated. Someone would have caught them by now."

"The Fellowship is a lot more selective in its recruitment process than most cults," Justine said. "They mostly recruit from two social groups: the dregs of society and the cream of the crop."

"I don't understand."

"They go after drug addicts, street people, hookers—people who wouldn't be missed if they disappeared. They take them in and clean them up. Then they use them sort of as worker bees in a hive. They take care of the lower level responsibilities."

"What about the cream of the crop?" Thomas asked.

"Most of that recruitment is done on college campuses through MacAsland's front group, the Fellowship for World Renewal. There, they tend to gravitate toward people who don't have strong family ties or any family at all. When they find someone who has been in the FWR group a while and they think the person may be of use to them, then and only then is that person invited to a retreat. Even then, not all accept the invitation. But once you do, there's no leaving. At least not alive."

Thomas spoke as they continued walking toward the grand entrance hall. "That's incredible. But I still don't see how they can just make people disappear. Don't families inquire?"

"Well, the people don't actually disappear. When the Fellowship eliminates someone, it's generally staged to look like an accident, an act of random violence, something like that. And like I said, since most of the recruits either have no family or are already alienated from their families, there's usually no one left behind to make inquiries."

"How long has this been going on?" Thomas asked.

"Practically since the beginning."

Thomas stopped walking.

Justine turned and looked at him. "What is it?"

"You've known about the killings from the beginning?"

Even in the dimly lit

hallway, Thomas could see the color drain from Justine's face. "Well, I . . ."

"But if they've been killing unwilling recruits from the beginning . . ."

"Thomas, wait."

"That means you had to know what the Fellowship was doing the whole time! The Project wasn't any surprise to you. You've known about it all along."

"This is crazy," Justine said, blushing. "We need to get moving."

Thomas grabbed her by the shoulders and forced her to face him. "Justine, why *did* you leave the Fellowship?"

Her green eyes flashed, and she wrenched away from his grasp. "I don't have to tell you anything!" She ran down the corridor toward the grand entrance hall.

"Wait a minute, lady!" Thomas called after her.

• • • • •

"Our legs are getting sore," Michelle whined. "Can we get out and walk around?"

"Not a good idea." Earl Cutler responded. "Your dad said I was to keep an eye on you."

"He's *not* my father." Her sharp response startled E.C.

"Are you sure they aren't kidnappin' you?"

"No," Micah said, "they're not."

"Pleeeeease?" Michelle pleaded. "Can we just get out for a few minutes? I promise we'll stay close."

E.C. heaved a sigh. "I guess it's okay. Just you be sure not to go very far away. We might need to bug out of here without much warning."

"Thanks," Michelle said, holding out her hand to him. E.C. helped Michelle climb down out of the helicopter. He looked back toward Micah. "You coming?"

Micah remained in his seat, staring straight ahead. "I'm okay."

E.C. climbed back into his seat, keeping an eye on Michelle as she strolled around the helipad. She made a snowball and threw it at the helicopter. It exploded in a rain of fluffy snowflakes as it hit the windscreen.

"Hey. Cut that out, now. This thing's not paid for yet," E.C. called.

"Mr. Cutler?" Micah's quiet voice came from behind.

E.C. turned around. "Yeah?"

"Do you hear anything?"

E.C. cocked his head, listening. "Like what?"

"Another helicopter."

The two sat silent for a few seconds. "I don't hear anything, son."

"I'm sure of it," Micah said.

"Your imagination's workin' overtime, boy," E.C. said. He turned back around to check on Michelle. The area around the helipad was deserted. "Where'd she go?" He looked all around.

"Who?" Micah asked.

"Your sister. She's gone."

E.C. clambered out of the cockpit and onto the pad. "Girl! Where are you?"

"Her name's Michelle," Micah called out.

"Michelle! Michelle!"

"Mr. Cutler!" Micah shouted.

E.C. swung around. "What, boy, what?"

"Listen."

E.C. stopped for a moment. This time he could hear it. From a distance, the rhythmic thumping of a helicopter's rotors cut through the frigid air.

"They're coming," Micah cried.

"Stay right where you are. I'm gonna go get your sister. Then we're outta here."

Earl Cutler jogged along the icy walkway toward the entrance tunnel, calling "Michelle!"

The sound of the coming helicopter grew louder as he ran.

● ● ● ● ●

Micah dropped from his seat onto the floor, feeling with his hands. He didn't know what he'd find. He could only hope he'd find something useful. His hands skittered over the carpeting, feeling dirt, bits of stone, other things left behind by people's shoes and boots. He reached behind him under the seat. When he felt a satiny fabric with metal rods inside, his hand clasped it.

He pulled it toward him, feeling the metal point at one end and the canelike handle at the other. He felt for the strap and made sure it was secure. He didn't want the crazy thing to open on him while he was trying to use it.

Staying on his knees, he felt his way toward the exit. When his fingers found the handle, he pulled it, opening the hatch. He swung his legs out, sitting in the opening. Then he scooted forward, feeling with his toes until he contacted the ground beneath him. He reached behind him and brought the umbrella with him.

Now, where's the walkway?

Micah tried to stay calm. He'd walked this path many times, even by himself a few times, though mostly with Michelle. He was confident he could do it again. He had to. That helicopter would land in just a few minutes.

Holding on to the umbrella's handle, he gently felt the concrete surface with the metal tip. If he knew which direction the copter was facing, it would help. But he had no idea. And with all the clouds, he couldn't even determine his direction by feeling the sun's warmth.

Micah edged straight ahead until he felt the tip of the umbrella go over the edge of the helipad.

Now, if the castle's on the right, the walkway should be about three o'clock from where I am right now.

Following the circular edge of the helipad, Micah felt his way until the umbrella's tip jammed against something hard. He felt the rough stone walkway, making a ninety-degree turn to his left.

Yes!

Micah followed the walkway toward the tunnel. Once he was in the tunnel, he wouldn't have any problems finding his way. After all, he'd lived here almost six months out of every year.

He just had to get inside before the helicopter came. Before anyone saw him.

* * * * *

"Do you see that?" Sawyer Wynne pointed toward the castle, his other hand resting on the pilot's shoulder.

The helicopter pilot nodded.

A small figure was making its way carefully along the walkway, using what appeared to be an umbrella for a cane.

"That's Micah Bishop." Wynne spat out the name. "What is he doing here?"

"Look," the pilot broke in, pointing to the heliport. "Another helicopter."

"She's here," Wynne said. "They're all here." Wynne cackled. "They have to be. I can't believe this! Where can you set down?"

"Other side of the island," the pilot replied.

"Is there enough room?"

"Plenty."

"Then do it. We'll see if the flight training we paid for was worth the money."

"Yes, sir."

Sawyer Wynne eased back into his seat, scarcely able to wait for the pilot to land the helicopter. He reached into a briefcase on the seat beside him and pulled out a pistol just like the one he'd issued to Derek Rainart. Wynne caressed the cold metal as he held it in the palm of his hand.

This was going to be easier than he ever could have hoped.

I said wait a minute!" Thomas stormed into the grand entrance hall a few steps behind Justine.

She swung around, defiance darkening her expression. "What!"

Thomas towered over her, glowering at her. "I want to know what's going on here, and I want to know now. My whole life's been flushed down the toilet for you and your kids. I gave up everything! Are you hearing me?"

"Loud and clear," she shouted. "Now get out of my face."

"Not till I know what you're not telling me."

"Forget it," she said, turning and walking toward the sitting room.

Thomas stood where he was, shaking his head. "That's great," he said. "That's just great. I destroyed my life—what was left of it—so I could rescue your kids from a killer. And what did I do? I brought them to you. And you're a killer too. You're no better than the rest of them."

Justine stopped just short of the entrance to the sitting room. She turned around and slowly walked back toward Thomas, her cold eyes never leaving his. Her open hand hit Thomas's face with a crack that echoed off the walls.

He recoiled at the pain, rubbing his cheek where she had slapped him.

"Don't ever compare me to them," she said, her voice trembling slightly. "I'm nothing like them."

"Then talk to me." Thomas fixed his eyes on her. "Please."

Justine turned away. She stood silent for several seconds. Then she brought her hands to her face, and her shoulders began to shake. Thomas put his arm around her shoulder and led her to the foot of the marble staircase. They sat down together on the bottom step.

Finally Justine looked up. She took in a shuddering breath and spoke. "When Sawyer Wynne decided to start his own religion, he invited two friends to help him. Anthony MacAsland was one." Justine paused, as if trying to find the right words. "I was the other."

Thomas showed no reaction outwardly, but the hair on the back of his neck prickled at her statement.

"It was all a big joke at first." Justine shook her head. "We were so arrogant. We wanted to prove we were smarter than anybody else. What better way than to convince a group of fools that one of us was a messiah. Sawyer's favorite statement was 'If you want people to follow you, tell them a lie. The bigger the lie, the more dedicated they'll be.'

"Sawyer was the one who saw the potential for money and power. Power mostly. Anthony had more money than we'd ever need. But Sawyer wanted power and influence. When he realized just how easy it was to manipulate people—how they almost *begged* to be manipulated— he saw the potential."

"That was the birth of the Osmosis Project?" Thomas asked.

Justine nodded.

"When did the killing start?"

She took a deep breath and blew it out. "That started with Sawyer too. Like I told you on the plane, it began with the murder of Antoine's father. When Sawyer got away with that one, he was like a monster—out of control. It just escalated from there."

"And you knew?"

She nodded again, releasing a shuddering breath.

"So why'd you leave?"

For the first time since they'd sat down, Justine smiled. "A man named Peter Bishop came into my life, and he led me to the *real* Messiah."

Thomas cocked an eyebrow. "I thought you said that you'd recruited Peter into the Fellowship."

Justine brushed a tear from her cheek. "I did. When Peter came to Syracuse to do his master's work, he'd taken some religion and philosophy courses and become thoroughly confused. He wasn't sure that *he* existed, let alone God. It didn't take much effort to turn him into a follower of Antoine. Then something unexpected happened. Peter and I fell in love and wanted to get married."

"I imagine Sawyer didn't like that," Thomas said.

"Sawyer opposed it at first. Anthony didn't care one way or another. You see, all Sawyer Wynne loves is power; Anthony loves himself. Neither one has time for anyone else in his life."

"So why did Sawyer oppose your relationship with Peter?"

"Security. Husbands and wives talk. He didn't want Peter to learn about things he shouldn't know about."

"But Peter *did* find out, didn't he?"

"Not right away—and not in the way you'd expect. I was so afraid of what Sawyer might do, I never said a word about the Project to Peter. We were married and began our lives together. The group was still fairly small back then. When the twins were born, I moved into the background and Peter took a more prominent role.

"It was when he designed the Fellowship's computer systems that he figured out the truth. He was never given any specific details about the Project, but as he developed the systems, it wasn't hard for him to put two and two together. He didn't mention it at first, but I knew something was wrong.

"After my brother, Michael, came to confront us, Peter changed drastically. He went out and bought a Bible." She chuckled. "It was a little $3.95 job, and he got it at a convenience store, of all places."

"Not exactly a Bible bookstore," Thomas said.

"He'd lock himself in the bathroom and study for hours sometimes. Finally, one night after Micah and Michelle were in bed, he came to me and said, 'Your brother's right, Justine. There is such a thing as truth. And it *does* matter.'"

Justine turned toward Thomas and smiled at him. Thomas thought her green eyes sparkled. "We stayed up all night. Peter read me John's Gospel, and we talked like we'd never talked before. By morning, I'd trusted in Jesus. That day Peter decided that we had to get out."

Thomas stood to his feet and helped Justine to hers. His arm around her shoulder, they walked toward the sitting room. "Why did you leave Peter and the children behind?"

"If I had listened to Peter, we could have all escaped safely and been well hidden before Sawyer even knew we were gone. But I felt that Sawyer should be confronted with the truth. I faced Sawyer down and told him how sick I thought he was. I never anticipated how quickly he would respond. Before I got back from Sawyer's office, he had put out a conversion order on the whole family. Peter accessed the program that monitors conversion attempts, and he knew the wheels had already been set in motion.

"We figured that the only way to salvage the situation was for Peter to immediately go to Sawyer and disown me. Peter was able to convince Sawyer that he was still loyal to Antoine and that he wanted nothing more to do with me. Of course, I had to leave the children behind to make Peter's story look legitimate.

"I left immediately, with only the clothes on my back." A tear streamed down Justine's face. "I didn't even say good-bye to Micah and Michelle." Justine brushed away the tear with the back of her hand. "By the way she's been acting, I don't think Michelle's forgiven me yet."

"How did you get away from Rainart?" Thomas asked.

"Same way I've been able to stay alive the past three years. Peter sent Rainart some phony information, ostensibly from Sawyer, which sent him off on a wild-goose chase long enough for me to get away.

"For appearance's sake, Peter remained loyal. But behind the scenes, he's been sabotaging all the Fellowship's attempts to locate me. His next plan was to expose the Osmosis Project. He wanted to find a way to prove to the world what a liar and deceiver Anthony MacAsland is. Then he was going to escape with the children and join me. We had prearranged for him to go to my brother's in Lake Charles. Michael would send him to Charles Richard."

"And Charles would have taken him to the island where you've been hiding for the last three years."

"Yes. Something must have gone terribly wrong," Justine said. "They must have discovered what Peter was doing. That's the only reason I can think of that he would have sent the children on alone."

"So Peter sent the children to me to protect them from Sawyer Wynne," Thomas said.

Justine bit her lip. "Wynne hates me for putting all his precious plans at risk. He also knows that I'm the only one alive who can testify against him."

"And that's what you were about to do, weren't you? That's why you wanted me to stay behind with the children. You never planned to come up here in the first place. You were going to go to the police and turn yourself in."

"I was going to turn myself in, but not to the authorities. I was going to Chateau Antoine to turn myself over to Sawyer."

Disbelief clouded Thomas's face. "You were going to give yourself up to Wynne? But why?"

"As long as I'm alive, Sawyer will never stop pursuing us. I hoped that if Sawyer had me, he'd lose interest in the children."

"But why not go with the original plan? Why not go to the authorities and take Sawyer Wynne down too?"

Justine gazed at the floor. "I don't want Micah and Michelle to know what I used to be."

Thomas saw the shame on her face. He understood completely. "Does that mean there's nothing to find up here?" he asked. "No proof?"

"Oh no," she said, "that part's true. We can still access their computer systems from here. And Robert MacAsland and his helicopter pilot are buried somewhere on the island. But finding their bodies will be next to impossible, short of taking the castle apart stone by stone."

Justine took his hands in hers. "Thomas, there's still time. We can fly back to Syracuse. Then you can take the children and let me go to Sawyer. It's the only way this nightmare will ever end."

Thomas's eyes filled; his voice was husky. "Justine, what does God want you to do when everything seems out of control?"

"Thomas, I—"

He put his hands on her shoulders. "What does He want you to do?"

"Trust Him and keep on serving Him."

"Then that's what we're going to do. And trusting Him means you do the right thing, no matter what the consequences are. I don't know much about all of this, but letting Sawyer Wynne and the rest of them go unpunished is definitely *not* the right thing."

"But what if the police don't believe me? What if Sawyer gets off? What if he comes after the children?"

"Is God in control or isn't He?" Thomas asked.

Justine looked at the floor.

"'The Sovereign Lord is my strength,'" Thomas quoted.

Justine paused, then looked up at him. "'He makes my feet like the feet of a deer.'"

They finished together. "'He enables me to go on the heights.'"

"Are you with me?" Thomas asked.

Justine nodded.

"Now," Thomas said, "where are the computers?"

"There's one behind the main desk," she said, leading him toward the far side of the grand entrance hall.

Justine powered up the computer. When it prompted for a user name and password, she typed in "ynohtna dnalsacam."

"What's that?" Thomas asked.

"It's Peter's back door, *Anthony MacAsland* spelled backward."

"Pretty simple," he said.

"According to Peter, the simpler the better."

Her fingers flew across the keyboard as she entered the database, then requested the project files. "Pull out that drawer to your right," she told Thomas. "There should be some floppies or recordable CDs."

"You're pretty familiar with the layout," Thomas observed.

"Spent a lot of time here," she said.

Thomas took out a recordable CD and handed it to Justine. She popped it in the computer's CD burner. A prompt on the screen read, "Record Files to CD?" Justine clicked *Yes*.

"It'll take a few minutes to burn the CD," she said.

"Now," Thomas said, "where do you propose we start to look for MacAsland's father?"

"I don't have a clue," Justine replied.

They walked from the grand entrance hall into the sitting room. He noticed for the first time that the giant-screen television in front of them was on, the blue screen radiating the only light in the room.

Thomas sniffed the air. "Justine, do you smell someth—"

A voice from the television interrupted him. "Good day, Miss Shipp," came the silken voice.

"Who's that?" Thomas asked, pointing to the face on the screen.

"Sawyer Wynne," Justine replied as if the name left a bad taste in her mouth.

They listened as Wynne's message played for them.

"Whoever this Shipp woman is, he thinks she knows me," Justine said.

"Ever heard of her?" Thomas asked.

"No," Justine said, shaking her head. "The poor woman. I haven't a clue who she is, but I know exactly what they're putting her through."

"Wait. Shh." Thomas put his hand on her arm.

"What is it?"

"A helicopter's circling the island," Thomas said.

"Wynne! She must have called him."

"Let's get out of here!"

"No, wait," Justine said. "We've got to get the disk." She ran back toward the main desk.

"Make it quick!"

"Come on, come on," Justine said, slapping the counter as she urged the machine to go faster.

The sound of the helicopter grew louder.

"Justine!"

"Just a few more seconds."

The helicopter's engine began winding down.

"Justine, it's landed. We've got to get out of here. Now!"

"Done," she shouted as she pushed the drive's Eject button.

Thomas grabbed Justine by the arm, and they raced back to the east hallway. They had just passed into the darkness when Thomas felt something brush by him.

Searing pain shot through his right arm and he felt a warm gush of blood. Instinctively he shoved Justine forward and swung his left arm around, striking at who-ever had hit him. The impact of his blow knocked his attacker to the floor a few feet behind them. Thomas saw a butcher knife skid along the floor, back toward the light. Grunting and whining, a white-robed figure clambered for the knife. Thomas was about to go on the attack when he heard Justine's voice.

"Thomas, no! Wait."

The woman scrambled to her feet. She had managed to retrieve the knife and now held it over her head, ready to stab whoever came near.

Justine and Thomas froze in horror at the figure standing before them. With the light at her back, she looked like a cross between a ghost and an escapee from a mental institution. Her matted hair stood out in all directions. Shadows accented her sunken eyes. Her gaze was faraway, haunted. Yet she moved with an almost supernatural energy and agility.

Justine held out her hands. "Look. We don't have any weapons." Her voice was soft. "We're not going to hurt you."

The woman looked like a

hunted animal. Her eyes darted between Justine and Thomas.

Thomas opened his hands. "I don't have anything either."

"We're on your side," Justine said. "We want to help you." She took a small step in the woman's direction.

Immediately the woman backed up. "The kitchen," she said, her voice dry and raspy. "What you want is in the kitchen."

Justine shook her head. "No. We're not going to the kitchen. We have to leave. Come with us."

The woman exploded in fury. She ran straight for Justine and swung the knife at her chest. Thomas leaped in front of Justine and threw his arms around the woman in a football tackle, driving her into the stone wall. Thomas shuddered in pain as he felt the knife being driven into his shoulder.

"Let go of the knife!" He heard Justine's voice through a blur of pain and felt her trying to wrest the knife from the woman's grip.

"Owwwww!" The woman let out a high, keening wail, then tried to bite Thomas's shoulder.

"Let go!" Justine ordered.

Thomas heard the knife crash to the floor. The woman slipped from his grasp as she collapsed, sobbing quietly, as if she had expended the last of her energy.

With pain shooting up and down his spine and into his neck, Thomas dropped to one knee.

"Are you all right?" Justine asked.

Thomas looked at his bleeding right arm and shoulder, and grimaced. "You're kidding, right?"

She knelt beside him, examining his injuries. "The arm will need some stitches, but it's not serious. And I stopped her before the knife penetrated far into your shoulder. You'll live. Come on, we've got to move."

Thomas grinned. "Justine, if you're ever looking for

a career change, don't go into medicine. You're bedside manner stinks."

The woman raised her head. "Justine? Justine Bishop?" she asked, her voice little more than a croak.

"Yes," Justine said.

"They're looking for you," the woman said, a demented smile playing across her face. "Oh yes," she said. "They want you." She dropped her voice to a whisper. "And they're coming."

"We know," Thomas said.

"Let's go," Justine said. "Come on, Miss Shipp. We've got to leave, and we're not leaving you here."

"But I'll miss the surprise," Dana said.

"You'll have to wait till Christmas," Thomas replied. They helped the woman to her feet.

"Let's head for the helicopter," Justine said.

"Let's not," came a voice from behind them.

Thomas swung around. In the center of the grand entrance hall stood two men. One, a very short man, was obviously Sawyer Wynne. Thomas recognized him from the video. The other, a muscular man standing well over six feet. Thomas supposed he was the helicopter pilot.

"We'd hate to have you leave just as our little party's getting started," Sawyer Wynne said.

Michelle quietly climbed the spiral stairs. She wondered if Justine knew about them. Probably not. She hadn't had as much time to explore the old castle.

Michelle, on the other hand, had had plenty of time. When you're one of only two children on the island *and* everyone wants you to stay out of the way, there's not much else to do. So Michelle had busied herself by learning the ins and outs of Shelby Castle. She found this staircase when she was exploring some of the rooms near where novices were trained. It wasn't really a secret staircase or anything as exciting as that. She'd found it in a small room near the back of the east wing. The room was filled with boxes and other junk. It was so dusty, she doubted anyone went in there very often.

She had gone in there to play one day. And there it was. Right out in the open in one corner of the room. Someone had built a neat, spiral staircase that went right through the ceiling. Of course she had to check it out, see where it would take her. In the end, it was kind of boring. Just went up to a bedroom. Maybe the staircase was meant to be someone's private way out. Michelle didn't know. Didn't really care.

As her head poked through the hole in the ceiling, she stopped and peeked, just to make sure nobody was in the bedroom. Of course nobody was using it right now.

She crept to the door and gently pulled down the cold metal handle. Michelle tried as hard as she could to open it without it squeaking. She peered into the dark hallway. She could barely hear Justine, Thomas, and somebody else.

This was fun. Kind of like a game of hide-and-seek. But the adults didn't know they were playing. Michelle covered her mouth to muffle her giggle.

When she reached the end of the hallway, she got down on her hands and knees. Didn't want them to see her head peeking over the railing.

Trying to be as quiet as a mouse, she scooted down the entrance hall's stairs until she came to the bend. Then she turned over, lay on her tummy, and poked her head around the corner. She wasn't worried about them seeing her now. They were too busy. Michelle muffled another giggle. She could see Mr. Wynne and another man. She hadn't expected them to be here. They were pointing guns at Thomas and Justine. Another lady was there. She didn't look good at all.

Michelle wasn't real sure what to do now. So she decided she'd just watch.

●　●　●　●　●

As E.C. made his way down the dark corridor, he had no idea what the people in the other helicopter were up to. All he knew was that he hadn't signed on for this kind of foolishness.

"Shoulda turned right around when they told me they

were going to solve a murder," he muttered under his breath. "They wanna do this kind o' stuff, they need to hire Walker, Texas Ranger. Not Earl Cutler."

Up ahead he saw three silhouetted figures and heard angry voices echoing down the hallway. Two of them looked like Thomas and Justine. He couldn't make out who the third one was, but she was way too big to be Michelle.

"Hey! Thomas. Justine," he called. "Come on, people. We gotta get out of here. Someone else is coming."

Strange. Not only didn't they acknowledge him. They moved out of sight.

"This is not the time to be playin' games!" Earl hollered as he started to jog down the long hallway toward them.

* * * * *

Micah stepped inside the large door he knew to be the east entrance to Shelby Castle. Finding his way to the grand entrance hall would be a piece of cake. All he had to do was stay close to the wall and follow the hallway. He'd be there in no time. Problem was, he didn't know what he would do when he got there.

I should have stayed in the helicopter.

He shook his head.

That wouldn't do any good. I promised Dad I would help. And I'm going to.

But Micah was scared. More frightened than he'd ever been in his life. He knew if things didn't go right, none of them would leave the island alive.

Gotta help!

Micah forced his tired, aching legs to go faster.

* * * * *

Thomas watched for a chance to overpower Wynne. But with

the other brute standing there, he knew it'd probably never happen.

He'd made a commitment the other night in the motel. Not in so many words. But deep inside, he knew he had promised himself—and God—that he would do whatever was necessary to rescue Justine and the children, even if it meant dying in the process.

Justine had been right after all. God had kept him alive for a purpose. Justine and the children needed him, at least for today. And he'd be here for them today. Because if he wasn't, there wouldn't be any tomorrow for any of them.

E.C.'s voice reverberated off the hallway walls. "Hey! Thomas. Justine! Come on, people. We gotta get out of here. Someone else is coming."

Sawyer Wynne hissed, "Move." He waved the pistol in the direction of the sitting room.

The pilot stepped backward and pressed against the wall by the hallway entrance.

Cutler's voice grew louder. "This is not the time to be playin' games!" He ran through the opening and stopped short when he saw Sawyer Wynne's gun trained on him.

"Get your hands in the air," Wynne ordered, then nodded toward the pilot. "Check him out."

The pilot moved quickly to Cutler's side and patted him down. "Clean," he said.

Wynne motioned with his pistol again. "Over with the others." He smirked. "I didn't know Dennis Rodman would be joining us. You're shorter than I thought you'd be."

Cutler muttered, "I'm puttin' in for combat pay on this job."

"You'll have a hard time collecting," Wynne said. He turned toward Justine. "Where are the children?"

Before Thomas could answer, he heard Michelle's voice calling out. "Here! Right here."

Wynne turned toward the marble staircase as Michelle

bounced into view. To Thomas's horror, she skipped down the stairs and stood by Sawyer Wynne. He brushed her long curls with his hand. "Well done, my dear," he said, smiling down at her.

Justine shook her head, a horrified expression on her face. "No!"

Michelle broke into a smug grin. "It's true."

Justine's voice broke. "But, honey, why?"

The little girl tossed her head, flinging her curls off her shoulder. "Antoine is lord. And you're a traitor."

The tears flowed silently and freely down Justine's cheeks.

"Now," Wynne said, "where's the blind one?"

"In the helicopter," Michelle said.

"No!" Thomas shouted. "He's not."

"Don't believe them," Michelle said. "He's still out in the helicopter."

E.C. took a step forward. "No he isn't. I—I mean I hid him before I came in here."

Without warning, the barrel of Sawyer Wynne's pistol exploded in light and sound. Cutler's body tensed in pain, and he leaned back against the wall. A large red spot formed in his lower abdomen as he slid to the ground. Blood trailed down the wall behind him.

"Don't lie to me." Wynne's voice burned as cold as dry ice. "I saw him come in before we landed. Now, where—is—the—boy?"

"He's hiding," Dana croaked.

"Hiding?" Wynne asked. "Where, Dana? Where is he hiding?"

Dana grinned and cast a sidelong glance at Thomas and Justine. "In the kitchen."

"Thank you, Dana," Sawyer Wynne said.

The instant she spoke the words, Thomas understood. He flashed an angry glare at her for effect.

Wynne looked at the pilot.

"Go get him."

The muscular man walked briskly through the sitting room toward the kitchen door. Thomas waited till he began to push on the kitchen door, then screamed, "Get down!"

He pushed Dana to the ground and tackled Justine as the whole world exploded around them in a giant fireball.

Thomas's head pounded as though it had been smashed by a baseball bat. All sound disappeared in the eardrum-shattering roar, instantly replaced by a high-pitched ringing in Thomas's ears. He lay stunned. Debris rained down around him. He could barely will his leaden arms to cover his head.

When the hail of stone and particles subsided, Thomas tried to push himself into a sitting position. He felt as if half the castle had fallen on his back as he lifted his torso off the cold floor. His head swam. Caustic fumes scorched his nostrils and throat. The heat from the fire in the kitchen felt oddly comforting compared to the castle's freezerlike temperature. Everything seemed to move in slow motion. Thomas blinked against the searing heat.

He felt himself drifting toward unconsciousness. Unconsciousness would be death. He knew it. He had waited for it. Now it could come, and no one could stop it. He had only to give in. Go to sleep.

Can't quit. They need me.

He looked around him. Everyone lay sprawled on the floor; no one moved. The explosion's impact had knocked Sawyer Wynne and Michelle off their feet. They lay on their backs near the front entrance. Wynne's gun had landed a good ten feet from his body. A small pool of blood formed underneath his head. Justine and Dana lay prone, side by side.

Thomas looked toward the kitchen. Pitch-black smoke was quickly filling the sitting room and beginning to spill into the grand entrance hall, drifting upward toward its majestic vaulted ceiling.

Thomas turned his attention to Justine. Her hands were moving. She was trying to push up. "Are you okay?" he shouted.

She looked at him through narrowed eyes, as if she had to think for a moment to understand his question. Then she nodded.

"We've got to get them all out of here! Let's take them down the hallway. Get them away from the smoke."

Justine shook her head. Then she pointed toward the front entrance.

Thomas smiled. "You got it, boss! Can you get Michelle?"

Justine whispered, "Yes."

Thomas helped her to her feet. "I've got Dana," he shouted.

Justine stumbled over to where Michelle lay. She bent over, picked up her daughter, and moved toward the castle's door.

Thomas lifted Dana and carried her toward where Justine stood with Michelle. As he moved past Sawyer Wynne's gun, he kicked it out of the way. The pistol slid along the floor and came to rest against the far wall.

Dana had opened her eyes as they reached the door. He put her down on her feet. Justine pulled her over toward her. "Stay on your feet. Lean on me if you need to," she said.

Thomas pressed down on the door latch and pulled the heavy doors toward them. Instantly, he felt a gush of frigid air as the hungry fire drew in a fresh supply of oxygen.

"This place is going to go fast now." Thomas said. He pointed to a small gazebo about twenty yards from the castle. "Let's take them over there," he said. Thomas carried Michelle as Justine helped Dana to the gazebo.

"Wait here," Thomas said. "I'll be right back."

"Where are you going?" Justine asked.

"To get E.C."

"He's dead!"

"I'm not leaving him!" Thomas rushed back through the castle doors. Crouching to stay under the acrid smoke, he headed toward the sitting room in the entrance hall.

Earl Cutler's body lay on its side in a pool of blood. The well-built man was going to be a challenge to move. Thomas grabbed E.C.'s arms to drag his body out of the building when he noticed his eyelids flutter. Thomas put his fingers on E.C.'s neck. He could feel a faint pulse.

"Come on, E.C.," Thomas said, "don't quit on me now."

Staying in a crouch, Thomas dragged E.C. toward the front doors. As he moved across the grand entrance hall, a sickening feeling rushed through Thomas's stomach.

Sawyer Wynne's body was gone. So was his gun.

Thomas dragged E.C. to the gazebo and laid him down on a bench. Dana and Michelle were sitting on the opposite bench.

"He's alive," Thomas said, out of breath. "But he won't be if we don't get him to a hospital soon. And we've got another problem," he added.

Justine looked at him expectantly.

"Wynne's alive too. And he's gone."

"Gone!" Justine exclaimed. "Where?"

"I don't know."

• • • • •

Micah sat on the cold floor of the stone hallway. He guessed he had made it a little more than halfway toward the grand entrance hall when he had heard a gunshot. A few seconds later a sound like a giant cannon made the ground rumble like an earthquake. He had fallen to the floor as if someone had punched him. Now all he heard was silence and the crackle of a fire somewhere. He detected the rotten sulfur smell of the smoke.

On his hands and knees, Micah ran his palms across the floor until he found his umbrella. Using it as a cane, he clambered back to his feet. Micah wasn't exactly sure which way he was pointing.

"Mom?" he called, his voice quavering. "Uncle Thomas?" He held his breath, straining to hear any kind of response.

Nothing.

He wanted to run, to hide, to cry. But he had no idea where to go.

"Uncle Thomas? Mom? Michelle?"

As he stood, still and quiet, he gently turned his face one way, then the other. Judging by the heat and the sound, Micah was pretty sure the grand entrance hall was to his left. But should he go on or go back? He knew it was foolish to head into the fire. But that's where everyone else was. He didn't think he'd be able to help them. But he had to try.

Micah moved in the direction of the heat. He edged his way along using his umbrella to feel the stone wall. The smoke burned his throat, made him cough.

Then Micah stopped. He heard footsteps coming toward him.

"Uncle Thomas?"

The footsteps were coming closer.

"Mom?"

He felt the person drawing near to him. Micah reached out with his hands, feeling for whoever it was.

"Mom?"

Someone grabbed his wrist so hard it hurt. "Not hardly," came the answer.

Micah recognized the voice. "Mr. Wynne!"

"Shut up and come with me. And don't give me any trouble."

Micah felt something cold against his neck. He knew it was the barrel of a gun.

• • • • •

"Thomas, where's Micah?" Justine asked.

"Wynne said he saw him heading toward the castle when they flew in."

Justine stood up and started off in the direction of the castle. "I've got to go get him."

Thomas stopped her. "No. You stay here. He's probably in the tunnel or the hallway. I'll go get him." Noting her anguished expression, Thomas put his hands on her shoulders. "He's a smart kid, Justine. He'll be okay."

Thomas turned toward the castle, but he stopped about halfway there, looking toward his right.

Sawyer Wynne was walking toward them, dragging Micah along with him. "That's far enough," Wynne said, motioning with his pistol for Thomas to move back to the gazebo.

"Aaaiii," Dana wailed when she saw Wynne. She ran from the gazebo and back toward the castle.

Wynne took little notice of Dana. "Let her run. I'll take care of her soon enough." He shoved Micah forward. The boy fell to his knees onto the snow-covered ground. Thomas helped him up, brushing the snow off his hands and face. Then he handed the umbrella back to him and guided him toward Justine. She embraced him and glared at Wynne.

"It takes a big man to push a little boy around, Wynne. Want to try that with me?" Thomas asked.

Sawyer Wynne sneered. "I don't need to." He trained the gun on Thomas. "So," Wynne continued, "here we are. A nice cozy group. Now what am I going to do with all of you? I can't have you all standing around when the authorities come."

"Give it up, Sawyer," Justine said. "There's no way you can weasel out of this."

"Perhaps. What if the authorities arrive to find a group of squatters who had broken into the castle? But, sadly, they were all incinerated in an explosion and fire, just as my pilot and I arrived to investigate."

"Thin," Thomas said. "Very thin."

"Don't be so sure," Wynne said. "In today's world, reality is all a matter of 'spin.' And this time of year, particularly, I have a lot of time to set up a convincing scenario. It will be quite a while before the fireboats can get out here. I think we can turn this to our advantage, especially if none of you are around to contradict me. Now into the castle. All of you."

"You'll have to shoot us here, Wynne. We're not moving."

Wynne nodded toward E.C. "I'm perfectly willing to do that," he said, still aiming the gun at Thomas.

A black smudge flashed across Thomas's line of vision as he saw Micah's umbrella come down in front of Wynne like the blade of a sword.

Momentarily distracted, Wynne swung the pistol toward Micah. Thomas lurched forward and hammered his fist down on Wynne's forearm, knocking the pistol from his hand into the snow.

"Get the gun!" Thomas shouted as he tackled Wynne.

Justine grabbed for the pistol, but Michelle reached it first. She stood, trembling, pointing the gun at her mother. Her hands shook as she curled her finger around the trigger.

"Michelle, put the gun down!" Thomas commanded.

The girl shook her head.

"Michelle, please," Justine pleaded.

"No! I want to go back to Antoine."

Sawyer Wynne managed to get to his feet. "Good girl. Give me the gun."

Micah's quiet voice broke in. "Michelle, don't. Please don't." The boy reached his hand out in the direction of his sister. "Don't listen to Mr. Wynne. He's lying. He won't take us back to Antoine. He wants to kill us."

"That's not true!" Her face reddened.

"Don't believe them, Michelle," Wynne said. "Antoine loves you and wants you to be his very own princess. Give me the gun."

Michelle walked over to Wynne, handed him the pistol, and stood beside him.

Wynne took a step backward. His voice turned cold. "Thank you, child. Now go stand with the others."

Michelle looked at him in disbelief.

"Your brother was right. I have no intention of taking you back to Antoine. Not after the way your parents betrayed me. You'll die here on the island with the rest of them."

"No!" Michelle screamed. She leaped at Wynne like an angry cat, beating on him with her fists.

Wynne shoved her to the ground and aimed the pistol at her, ready to fire.

Thomas took advantage of Wynne's momentary distraction and grabbed his wrist.

Wynne swung around, trying to point the pistol at Thomas's head.

Even though Sawyer Wynne was smaller, Thomas found him to be incredibly strong. As they wrestled for control of the gun, Wynne forced the barrel closer and closer toward Thomas's face. Wynne looked up and grinned at Thomas as his finger closed around the trigger.

Suddenly his satisfied grin dissolved instantly into a grimace of pain. Wynne's eyes filled with disbelief, then glazed over. His hand relaxed and fell away from the gun.

Thomas watched as Sawyer Wynne fell facedown on the ground, the handle of a butcher knife protruding from his back.

Behind him stood Dana Shipp, trembling, arms wrapped around herself. Tears streamed down her face.

"He was a hateful man," she said.

● ● ● ● ● ●

"I don't understand what you've got in mind," Thomas said as he loaded Earl Cutler into the Fellowship's helicopter.

"This one's bigger. It can hold all of us," Justine said.

Thomas looked at the burning castle in the background. "It's going to provide wonderful shelter. But it won't help E.C. If we don't get him to a hospital soon, he's had it."

"I know," Justine said. "Get in."

"What?"

Justine flashed him an exasperated look. "Just get in!"

Thomas climbed into the pilot's seat.

"Not there," she commanded.

"What does it matter?"

"Do you plan on flying this thing?" she asked.

"Of course not," Thomas said.

"Then move over."

Thomas's jaw dropped open.

"Put your teeth back in your mouth and move over! Now!"

Wordlessly, Thomas moved across to the other seat.

Justine powered up the engine and the helicopter's rotors came to life.

"Where did you learn how to fly a helicopter?" Thomas asked.

A wry grin spread across Justine's face. "Charles Richard. Who do you think flew the bayou helicopter tours?"

Justine looked over her shoulder at all her passengers. "Everybody set?"

From the back, Michelle, Micah, and Dana nodded. Justine looked down at E.C.'s still form on the floor behind Thomas. "Let's hope we're in time."

She pushed the engine to full throttle and lifted off.

Thomas watched as a column of smoke ascended from the castle.

• • • • • • •

The man moved quickly down the hallway toward Sawyer Wynne's office.

For the most part, it was business as usual at Chateau Antoine. But that was only because the news of the events on Diamond Island had not spread through the complex yet. He had only just heard it on CNN. Once the news spread, it would be pure chaos here at the Fellowship's main headquarters.

Time was of the essence.

He breezed through the outer office, ignoring Jeanette Marshall's protests. Once he was at Sawyer's desk, he checked the counter in the upper-right corner of the computer monitor's screen. The display now read, "24:12:08."

It was a shame. They had come so close. But now it was everyone for himself.

He entered his personal code: "JB4803."

The main screen for the Hiroshima Protocol came up.

Jerry Braddock typed, "Engage."

48

In Alexandria Bay's E.J. Noble Hospital, Thomas walked down the hall toward the ER waiting room. Micah lay curled up, asleep on a recliner. Justine sat on one end of a sofa, while Michelle slept at the other end.

Justine looked up as Thomas entered the room. "How is he?" she asked.

"They rushed him into emergency surgery. He's still alive. Beyond that, it's too soon to tell."

Justine shook her head. "Poor E.C. Have you checked on Dana?"

Thomas sat down, shaking his head. "They admitted her, but her problem's not physical. It's going to take a long time to undo the damage the Fellowship inflicted on her."

"What do you think happens now?" Justine asked.

"Investigating officers will be here soon. Before long, I imagine the state police, the FBI, and just about every other law enforce-ment agency in the continental

United States is going to want to talk to us."

"Thomas," Justine said, "what will happen to Micah and Michelle if I have to . . . I mean, if they send me to . . ."

"I don't know," Thomas replied. Then he added, "God doesn't guarantee us an easy ride, does He?"

"No," Justine agreed, "He doesn't."

"But we can trust Him, even when we don't understand what He's doing," Thomas reminded her.

Justine smiled. "Well, we do have the disk," she said.

"And perhaps we can persuade the police to search the island for MacAsland's father and helicopter pilot," Thomas said.

Justine shook her head. "That was a long shot at best. The bodies are well hidden, and the burial location was one secret I never learned."

"Meanwhile, Anthony MacAsland's nomination announcement is proceeding as we speak," Thomas added. "Soon, but for the confirmation vote, he'll be our new vice president."

"Mom?"

Justine turned to see Micah sitting up in his chair. "Honey, lie back down. You need to rest. I'm afraid things are going to get very busy soon."

Micah climbed out of the recliner and felt his way over to Justine. "Mom, I know."

"Good." Justine smoothed his hair. "Then get some sleep, sweetheart."

"No, Mom. I mean I know where they are."

"What?"

"The bodies. Dad found out just before he sent us away. He didn't want to take a chance on writing it down or putting it on the disk. So he told me and made me promise to keep it secret. They're under the big mosaic in the grand entrance hall, Mom." Micah looked hopeful. "Will it help?"

Justine embraced him. "Oh, honey, you bet it will help!"

"But why didn't you tell us sooner?" Thomas asked.

Micah shrugged. "Dad told me not to say anything in front of Michelle."

"Micah," Thomas said, "why didn't your dad escape with you?"

"Same reason I wanted to leave the children with you this morning," Justine said. "He knew it would be too dangerous. By staying behind, he probably meant to mislead the Fellowship long enough for the children to escape. His only hope was to send them away to someone the Fellowship had no knowledge of. You."

"But he was signing his own death warrant," Thomas said.

Justine nodded, then put her face in her hands. Her shoulders shook gently.

Micah sat down beside Justine and put his arm around her. "Dad really loved us, didn't he, Uncle Thomas?"

Thomas embraced both of them.

"He sure did, Micah. He sure did."

EPILOGUE

One Week Later

Thomas Kent yawned and folded his newspaper. He looked at his watch. Justine and the twins should be arriving soon. He got up and looked through the hospital's front windows to see if they were on their way in. The parking lot still appeared deserted. He sat down and scanned the front page of his paper again. How things could change in a few short days.

Whoever said that the wheels of justice turn slowly was wrong—at least in this case. Thomas Kent had been astounded by the Justice Department's quick action once they understood the enormity of the events on Diamond Island. Enlisting Justine's cooperation, the FBI had enough evidence to obtain a search warrant for the ruins of Shelby Castle. The excavation of the FWR mosaic yielded two skeletons. Dental records confirmed the identity of one as Robert MacAsland and the other as his helicopter pilot.

But there would be no

prosecution of Anthony MacAsland; there would be no vice presidential nomination, either. Shortly after news broke about Sawyer Wynne and Shelby Castle, MacAsland disappeared. DC police found him shot to death in a cheap motel room. The death was ruled a suicide.

Both Thomas and Justine had been interviewed, interrogated, and grilled all but constantly over the last week. Thankfully, because of Justine's willingness to come forward and help in the investigation, the U.S. attorney granted her immunity from prosecution for her activities as part of the Fellowship. It looked like state and local prosecutors were going to follow suit. Without her help, it could take years to sort out the Fellowship's criminal activities and osmosed members. Based on the interviews, the U.S. attorney had planned to obtain search warrants for the Fellowship's headquarters, but before they could implement them, the Fellowship seemed to vanish before their eyes.

The cult's bank accounts were cleared. The hard drives on all of their computers were wiped clean. Most horrific of all had been the discovery of hundreds of dead bodies in the Fellowship's five regional centers. A full count was still in progress.

Thomas saw a squad car pull up outside the hospital. Justine and Michelle got out of the backseat. Micah climbed out of the front passenger side. When Michelle caught sight of Thomas, she waved and whispered in Micah's ear. Micah broke into a broad grin.

As they came in the front door, Thomas met them. "What did you think of your first ride in a squad car, Micah?" he asked, tousling Micah's already shaggy hair.

"Cool," Micah replied.

"Yeah," Michelle added. "Really cool."

Thomas turned to Justine. She looked more than exhausted; she looked troubled. "I was afraid I'd miss you. I've got to be heading to the airport soon," he said. "Now that I've sorted things out with the Louisiana State Police, the Texas Rangers, and the Grant County sheriff, I need to get back home and try to pick up the pieces. How are you doing?"

"Okay, I guess." Justine's face reflected deep sadness.

"Can we go see E.C.?" Micah asked.

"They just moved him to a private room," Thomas answered. "We'll all drop by in a minute. Here," he said, handing Michelle two dollars. "In the meantime, why don't you go get a couple of pops and watch some TV in the waiting room? Your mom and I will catch up to you in a minute."

"Great," Michelle said. "Come on, Micah." She started down the hall and Micah followed close behind, with his hand on her shoulder.

Thomas led Justine over to a chair and sat down beside her. "Looks like a week in foster care hasn't hurt them."

Justine nodded. "I'm just glad I got them back."

"Have you seen the latest?" Thomas asked.

Justine took the paper and opened it. The headline on the front page read, "Cultist Death Toll Could Top 1400." She closed her eyes and breathed a silent prayer.

"In the name of truth, they destroy people," Thomas said.

Justine's eyes welled with tears.

Thomas pulled a tissue from a box on a nearby table and handed it to her. "Justine, what's wrong?"

"I feel so guilty. I was a part of destroying many of those lives. I feel like I should be punished."

"What? You *want* them to prosecute?"

"At least it might make me feel like some justice was done."

"Justine, look at me," Thomas said. He put his finger under her chin and tilted her face up toward his. "Justice *was* done—on the cross two thousand years ago, when Jesus died in your place."

Justine dabbed her eyes

BLIND SIGHT

with the tissue. "So that means I should escape the consequences of what I've done here and now?" she asked.

"Not necessarily," Thomas said. "If the U.S. attorney changes his mind and decides to prosecute, you'll have to suffer whatever consequences come your way and trust God in the midst of the circumstances." Thomas took her hands in his. "But if God gives you your freedom, then you need to recognize that it's a gift of His grace, just like the forgiveness He gave you. That means you're responsible for using whatever freedom you have to serve God, helping in whatever ways you can to repair the damage you caused."

Justine nodded.

"And," Thomas added, "I think I know just the place to start. Follow me."

●　●　●　●　●

Dana Shipp looked up as a handsome couple with two children entered her room. They looked vaguely familiar, but so much of the last few days was a blur that Dana wasn't sure where she knew them from.

"Hi, Dana," the man said. "My name's Thomas."

"And mine's Justine," the woman added. The little girl beside her gave her mother a nudge. The woman put her arms around the girl and boy. "Oh, and this is Michelle and Micah. May we visit for a while?"

"Do I know you?" Dana asked.

"Not well," Justine said, sitting down by Dana's bed and offering her hand. "But I've got a feeling we're going to become very close."

Dana smiled and put her hand in Justine's.

Dear Reader,

On December 7, 2008, I heard an amazing story of how God used my novel *Blind Sight* to turn someone's life around.

Before dawn on March 1, 2008, two young men broke into Terry Caffey's home in Emory, Texas. They shot Terry and killed his wife, Penny, and then went upstairs and murdered the Caffey's two young sons. They then set fire to the house and left the family for dead. Although he had been shot multiple times, Terry escaped through the bathroom window and crawled more than three hundred yards to a neighbor's. To make matters worse, Terry's daughter, Erin, was implicated in the crime. Overnight, Terry Caffey lost his entire family.

Six weeks later, Terry went back to his property. The remains of the house had been bulldozed and little was left. Torn with grief and unable to understand why God had taken his family and allowed him to survive, Terry cried out to God, "Why did You take my family? Why didn't You take me, too? I don't understand."

As he stood there, Terry noticed a scrap of paper stuck to the trunk of a nearby tree. He went over and picked it up. The paper was part of a page from my novel *Blind Sight*.

The edges of the page were scorched and it was difficult to read. But the words were like a direct message from God.

Here's the portion of text that Terry found from page 348:

> "I couldn't understand why You would take my family and leave me behind to struggle along without them. And I guess I still don't totally understand that part of it. But I *do* believe that You're sovereign; You're in control."
>
> Justine's voice reverberated through his thoughts: *"Maybe God knew we needed you."*
>
> "And I know that You've brought Justine and those children into my life. And they need me. Lord, You could have taken my life that day, but You spared it. And You've gone on sparing it. It doesn't matter what happens to me now, but if I can help them, please let me do it."
>
> Thomas closed the drapes and stood alone in the dark room. For the first time in two years, he was at peace with God and with himself. He knew what he had to do. Justine and her children would be safe, even if he had to die to make sure of it.

Those paragraphs turned Terry's life around. He found the strength to go on and is now sharing his testimony in churches around the country. When he speaks, he brings the page from my novel, now preserved in a frame, and shows it to the congregation.

Because the page was only partially preserved, Terry didn't know what book it had come from until he spoke at Greenville Bible Church, where my daughter was present in the congregation. She and the pastor's wife both recognized the quotation as having come from *Blind Sight*.

That same afternoon, Terry called and shared the story with me. Tears streamed down my face as I listened to a story that is nothing short of a miracle of God's providence. Not only had the house burned, but the site had been long since cleaned up and the debris bulldozed and hauled off. What little material was left had been exposed to the weather for weeks. And out of a four-hundred-page book, the only scrap that remained was a brief passage where a man who had lost a wife and two children came to grips with the sovereign goodness of God, submitted to His will, and decided to move forward.

That scrap of paper lay there against a tree trunk as if waiting for Terry Caffey: a man who had lost his wife and two sons, a man who was in deep despair and who had contemplated suicide, a man who desperately needed to come to grips with the sovereignty and mercy of God.

Needless to say, I am deeply humbled to have been the one who wrote the words that God chose to use.

What an incredible, awesome God we serve!

James H. Pence

have you visited tyndalefiction.com *lately?*

Only there can you find:

- → books hot off the press
- → first chapter excerpts
- → inside scoops on your favorite authors
- → author interviews
- → contests
- → fun facts
- → and much more!

Visit us today at: **tyndalefiction.com**

Sign up for your **free** newsletter!

Tyndale fiction does more than entertain.

- → *It touches the heart.*
- → *It stirs the soul.*
- → *It changes lives.*

That's why Tyndale is so committed to being first in fiction!

TYNDALE FICTION